Praise for

"A captivating exploration ... passionate love...An enter... ..., deeply felt story of giddy hopes straining against harsh realities."
—***Kirkus Reviews*** **(starred review)**

"*The Last Grand Tour* is an elegant and evocative novel about lives at crossroads. The indelible pair at the heart of this complicated and tender love story are surrounded by characters I will carry with me the rest of my reading life. Not to mention, the novel is a flat-out enlightenment on European culture. Michael N. McGregor is a writer at the height of his powers: creative and intellectual."
—**Mitchell S. Jackson,** Pulitzer Prize-winning author of *Survival Math* and *The Residue Years*

"Sweeping and vivid, *The Last Grand Tour* is a trip into the deepest corners of one man's emotional excavation as he grasps for meaning, connection, and love amid life's ever-changing tides. Michael N. McGregor has written a gripping, entertaining, and ultimately transporting novel that feels at once personal and universal."
—**Chelsea Bieker**, bestselling author of *Madwoman* and *Godshot*

"An unforgettable tale full of hope, love, and loss, with enough European flair to satisfy your wanderlust. I loved every minute of it!"
—**Kate Shelton**, author of *The Novel Killings*

"With *The Last Grand Tour*, Michael N. McGregor has delivered a thoroughly absorbing novel. His prose has a kind of hypnotic, cleansing melancholy, and his emotional intelligence is formidable. I suspect anyone who loves travel or travelers will encounter some version of themselves within these pages."
—**Tom Bissell**, bestselling author of *Extra Lives* and *The Disaster Artist*

"*The Last Grand Tour* is a haunting story about love and disillusion, the clash of history and modernity, the price of freedom and the impact of loneliness."
—**Devi S. Laskar**, bestselling author of *Circa* and *The Atlas of Reds and Blues*

"Filled with castles and mad kings and canals and composers—and a love affair that feels both wondrous and dangerous—this is a contemporary novel that uncovers an extraordinary timelessness. Fans of Jess Walter's *Beautiful Ruins* will love this."
—**Sharma Shields**, author of *The Cassandra* and *The Sasquatch Hunter's Almanac*

"*The Last Grand Tour* is a frequently funny, often melancholy, always deeply romantic voyage through the history-haunted landscapes of Western Europe, accompanied by a busload of unforgettable characters. In the hands of tour guide extraordinaire Michael N. McGregor, it becomes a journey of the heart, filled with longing and brio."
—**Jon Raymond**, author of *Denial* and award-winning screenwriter of "First Cow" and HBO's "Mildred Pierce"

"Joe Newhouse, the protagonist of Michael N. McGregor's brilliant first novel, *The Last Grand Tour,* has reached the end—of his marriage; of his European touring business; of an idea of himself he suspects is no longer true, if it ever was. *The Last Grand Tour* covers a lot of ground. It is a love story and a road narrative and a profound meditation on history—both public and private. It's about the stories we curate about ourselves and those we use to sell ourselves to others. Brutally honest, masterfully crafted, *The Last Grand Tour* is one hell of a read."
—**Pete Duval**, award-winning author of *Night Work*

# The Last Grand Tour

### A Novel by
## Michael N. McGregor

### Published by
### Korza Books

All rights reserved. This book or any portion thereof may not be reproduced or used in any manner whatsoever without the express written permission of the publisher.
Contact the publisher by writing to Korza Books at
1819 SW 5th Ave. #293, Portland, Oregon 97201

No generative artificial intelligence was used in the writing of this work. The author expressly forbids any entity from using this text for purposes of training AI technologies to generate text, including without limitation technologies that are capable of generating works in the same style or genre of this publication. The author reserves all rights to license uses of this work for generative AI training and development of machine learning language models.

All of the names, characters, businesses, places, events, and incidents in this book are the result of the author's imagination or used in a fictitious manner. Any similarities to actual occurrences or people, alive or dead, are unintentional.

Published by Korza Books
Copyright © 2025 Michael N. McGregor
Cover Design by Olivia M. Hammerman
Author Photo by Brian McDonnell
Original Map Illustration by Dave Hoerlein
Interior Layout by Michael Schepps

*First Edition January 2025*
ISBN: 9781957024103
Distributed and printed by Ingram 9781957024103
Korza Books name and logo are registered trademarks of Korza Books LLC
www.KorzaBooks.com

*For Sylvia*

*...semo perduti, e sol di tanto offesi
che sanza speme vivemo in disio.*

Dante, *Inferno*, Canto IV

*Whither is fled the visionary gleam?
Where is it now, the glory and the dream?*

William Wordsworth, *Ode: Intimations of Immortality*

# Chapter One

She walked alone, with long resolute strides, moving so surely the crowd on the concourse parted for her and people turned to look at her a second time. Men did this, of course, but women, too. They couldn't help it. Her confidence caught your eye—the way it lit her up, made you think she was someone famous. From her face your eyes fell to her legs, so white they were almost ghostly but long and lithe between a wisp of black skirt and sandals clicking across the floor. As she moved, her eyes ranged from side to side, fast and alert, and when she saw someone looking at her, she smiled—a smile that was cool. Detached.

I had already been watching her when she turned my way. But the smile she gave me was different than the one she gave to others. She looked at me as if she knew me, as if she had known me a long time. I didn't realize yet that she was my client, the woman I'd spoken with on the phone, but as soon as she smiled I felt I knew her, too, or at least had seen her somewhere. Something about watching a face like hers move coolly through a crowd then change the moment it saw me—the features shifting, the eyes more alive—made what seemed at first a superficial prettiness turn the corner toward beauty. Her hair grew lush as it sliced past her ears, her eyes melted to liquid brown, and her cheeks, which had seemed too white in the fluorescent light, blushed attractively at the ridges.

"Joe? Newhouse?"

She cut through the crowd, raising her hand, the movement lifting the hem of her blouse to reveal a stripe of white stomach. Her voice was richer, more resonant than it had been on the phone. It was a voice I'd heard somewhere, of an actress I couldn't name. I must have looked surprised or maybe unsure because her eyes lost their shine for a moment. They fell to something in her hand.

"Tonia Gluck?" she said, holding up one of my brochures. "Your tour?"

"Yes," I said and took her hand as I would have taken the hand of any client I was meeting for the first time. But when I saw people looking at us I held it a little longer. "I didn't expect —"

"I recognized you from your brochure," she said. "I thought you might have a hard time finding us."

As she spoke, I studied her hair—the raven depths of it, the threads of white, the way the light reflected from its surface, as if she'd washed it during the flight. She was about my age and almost as tall, almost six feet, but without that stoop tall women often have. The way she held her head, erect but not stiffly, suggested she'd been raised well.

"I didn't realize your plane had landed yet," I told her.

"I'm glad I found you then," she said.

Though I listened for it, I heard no sarcasm in her tone. No censure. She spoke without the condescension I'd come to expect from those who have certain advantages, who look down on a tour guide as someone who only provides a service. I was used to clients who saw me as little more than a shield protecting them from the dirtiness of travel. They'd wait for me at the arrival gate, their bags circled like frontier wagons, their arms drawn across their chests to protect themselves from the *foreignness* around them.

The walk to where the others were waiting took us through the departure hall where Cat had left me. Tonia walked much slower now than she had when looking for me, and I matched her pace, trying to pay attention to what she was saying. The departure board no longer listed a flight to Chicago. On the spot outside the passport line where Cat had waved goodbye, a man in a plastic raincoat was wiping the nose of a small girl. I could hear Tonia saying something about hers not being "your average tour group" and I tried to listen, to put my life with Cat behind me and enjoy just walking with someone as attractive as Tonia. Cat was pretty but not in the way Tonia was; people didn't look at her that way. And few ever noticed me at all, unless I was giving a talk somewhere, some sight they were interested in. My face was too round and too many years of too many tours—nights in bars, wine with meals, cognacs or grappas or ouzos after—had taken their toll.

"Right," I said to keep her talking, "what kind of tour group are they then?"

"That's what I mean...they're not a tour group at all. They were expecting something else."

Tonia was looking away from me toward a cluster of people fifty feet away. They looked like business people on their way to a meeting. One of them waved and started walking our direction. "Where the hell have you been?" she called as she neared. Like Tonia, she was in her mid-30s, but she had flat hair and pasty cheeks and her shoulders were hunched inside a blue blazer. "Is this him?" she asked when she reached us, looking at Tonia rather than me, as if her question had nothing to do with me. Tonia nodded. She seemed about to introduce me when the woman continued, "Did you find Gerhard?"

"He's not coming," Tonia said.

"Not coming?"

Tonia turned toward me. "That's what I was trying to tell you."

"What do you mean 'not coming'?" The woman in the blazer looked at me now as if asking me her question. There was a softness to her eyes, as if her harsh looks were only the disguise of a gentle woman trying to be tough.

"Not coming," said Tonia, "as in 'won't be here.'"

"You know this for sure?"

"I know this for sure."

"He told you?"

"He didn't have to, Sarah. I've come to know him quite well by now. If he isn't here, he isn't coming."

There was a shout from the group. A stocky, middle-aged man in a gray suit yelled, "What are you doing over there?" His voice had a nasal edge. An irritated tone.

"Rudy's going to love this," the woman in the blazer—Sarah—said.

"He'll just have to deal with it," Tonia told her. She started toward the group and Sarah and I fell in behind her. Ten days, I said to myself. Ten days can seem such a short time when you're making a booking. Then, when the tour begins, it can seem to stretch to the end of your life.

"He's not coming," Tonia told the man in the gray suit when he asked where her husband was. I could see now that he was more pudgy than stocky, his face chubby, a man not used to being out-of-doors.

"What do you mean he's not coming? He told me over the phone he'd meet us here." He was peering at her through the thick lenses of horn-rimmed glasses, one hand smoothing the strands of hair he had left on top, the other plunged to the bottom of his suit coat pocket. He was about 50, I guessed. Nervous type. One to keep an eye on.

"He told me the same thing, Rudy, but he's not here," Tonia answered calmly. The two others in the group were stepping closer now—an older man with thin white hair and a red-haired woman with a painted face, her eyebrows plucked into a scowl. This second man was taller than the first, less ill-at-ease. He was maybe 60 and he wore glasses, too, but his were more delicate, with a rainbow frame that made him look younger. His head was shaped like a turtle's, oval with a slender nose and almond eyes that seemed kind.

"Well where the hell is he?" the redhead said, her voice high and thin. She was wearing a bright yellow jacket over blue leather pants and the way she held her head, the way she pointed her chin and turned it slowly, you could tell she thought of herself as pretty, or had once thought of herself that way. I couldn't tell her age with all the makeup but she had to be nearing 60 at least.

Tonia was right, they weren't the average tour group, not even in the way they dressed. They didn't wear the casual clothes Americans usually wore to Europe—no Disneyland sweatshirts or Easy Spirit shoes, no quick-dry pants or Eddie Bauer safari hats. Not a one of them had a camera out or seemed to give a damn where they were.

"If he's not here, he's not coming," Tonia said—to no one in particular. "This is our guide, Joe."

"What, you didn't see him leave your house?" the man in the horn-rims persisted. "You didn't go with him to the airport?"

"No, he left several days ago. I told you on the plane I thought he was going to New York to see you and then to London for something else. I don't always know where he is."

"He doesn't call you?"

"This is a tour, Rudy," Tonia said, "and we have a guide. It doesn't matter to me if Gerhard shows up today or tomorrow. Or ever."

No one said anything more. The redhead sat back down and looked out the window. The man in the horn-rims—Rudy—looked off the other way, out toward the concourse. His eyes stopped on a payphone next to the restrooms and he started toward it. The older man touched my arm. "Listen, I'm sorry about this," he said, his voice low and comforting. "Obviously, we were anticipating...I'm Donald Downs, and you're—what was it, Joe?"

Rudy was still at the payphone and the redhead had slumped back in her seat when Tonia lifted her suitcase and a small travel bag. "Which way do we go, Joe?" she asked. I pointed to an exit at the end of the walkway, then picked up one of Sarah's bags.

"Ready?" I asked.

"Of course," Sarah replied. "*I'm* here for the tour."

She lifted her other suitcase and hurried to catch up with Tonia. I felt again the tiredness I'd felt before meeting them all, the loneliness, the impossibility of entertaining even a small group for ten more days. When I glanced back, Donald was hoisting a garment bag to his shoulder and the woman in the yellow jacket was staring at him, hands on her hips. Rudy had hung up the receiver and was crossing toward the two of them, saying something and gesturing toward the departure hall. Maybe it will just be the three of us, I thought, these two women—Tonia and Sarah—and me. I pictured the others walking in the opposite direction to find the first flight back to the States. But the picture wasn't even fully formed when I heard the redhead's high-pitched whine: "You're not expecting us to carry our own bags, are you?"

My bus was a twelve-seat Ford Transport I'd bought second-hand from an all-but-bankrupt British company with the unfortunate name of Bland Tours. The owner, Harry Bland, had rented me a bus for a trip through Scotland years before and knew I was looking to buy something. He offered what seemed a good deal and I thought I could save money by simply scraping off the "B" and "l", replacing them with "G" and "r" in the same cherry red. I suppose he sold the bus for such a good price because the market for buses in Britain had slumped and I was the only one willing to buy one with right-hand steering to drive on the Continent. Passing could be a problem, but I was lucky to afford any bus at all.

"This is it?" the redhead said when she saw it. "We're supposed to ride in this?" She had managed to avoid carrying her luggage after all; Donald was plodding along behind her like an over-packed burro, a bag across his back, another under his arm, and one more in each of his hands.

I had modified the bus slightly—putting a microphone beside the dashboard and adding a cooler for drinks—but the upholstery was original, faded now to pale gray, and the paint outside was bleaching. While Donald waited patiently for me to find a place for each of his bags in back, he watched the redhead raise a leg by the bus door, her arms out at her sides for balance. "Do you need help, Felicity?" he asked.

"No, I don't need help," she said, looking for all the world like a yellow flamingo, "unless you're willing to put your coat down on the seat so the dirt doesn't soil my jacket." Her fingers gripped the metal doorframe and she seemed to half-fall, half-propel herself onto a seat.

"She'll be okay," Donald said quietly. "Felicity doesn't sleep well on planes." He smoothed the front of his suit coat before moving to the door to climb in after her. I waited at the back of the bus for Rudy, who was just coming out of the terminal, a suit bag over his shoulder and a black satchel in his hand. "Goddamn Gerhard," he mumbled as I took the bags from him. "Tonia, where the hell is he? I tried your home, the office...."

"I told you I don't know," Tonia replied, sounding weary. She was sitting in the last row of seats beside Sarah, her head against the window. Rudy paused in the doorway before settling into a seat just ahead of them, looking as if he'd rather be anywhere than there.

"What's with this bus?" he asked as I started the engine. I could see him—see them all—in the wide rearview mirror. He was fingering a piece of vinyl that had pulled away from a ceiling seam. "Is this one of Gerhard's jokes?"

"I booked the tour," Tonia said.

"I see," said Felicity. She and Donald were sitting in the seats just ahead of Rudy, the ones just behind mine. She looked straight ahead as she spoke, her face expressionless. "Then I'm sure everything will be fine."

I always kept myself aloof when a tour began. Didn't react to anything my clients said. They didn't know me, and it would have been stupid to take anything personally. I kept my mouth shut and drove. With this group I was especially distant. Ten days, I told myself. Ten more days. It was late September, the end of the season, and all I had to do was survive one last tour. As I made my way onto the autobahn, I studied their faces in the mirror, more as a diversion than anything else, to keep that morning's thoughts from returning, the questions about what I would do when the tour was over. They looked like unhappy schoolchildren in the small bus. Only Tonia was talking, telling Sarah some private story in a voice that floated forward as faint, unintelligible sounds. As I listened to them, my mind drifted back to the way Cat had been on the drive to the airport for her flight home. The disgust she'd shown. The anger. I tried not to think of the words she'd said, but my clients' faces echoed them: *Your tour business is dead.*

# Chapter Two

The route for that tour was easy: a pass through the Alps with a half-dozen stops—Chiemsee, Berchtesgaden, Salzburg, Zell am See, Lake Misurina—and a last day in Venice. Three countries, two languages. Well-rehearsed talks. When I first started Grand Tours, I told myself I was providing knowledge that would enhance people's lives, but my facts had become as banal as anyone's, the kind you get in a high school history class: names, dates, statistics. Sometimes I'd make a joke, but only if I was sure it wouldn't offend anyone. We'd cross the Po River and I'd say, "This is where the Po folk live," or I'd tell my group how many people drowned in Paris each year before saying, "Life in France can drive you in-Seine." My jokes and even my facts were like snacks for children, something to keep them amused. But before I'd been with this group even an hour, things felt different. The words coming out of my mouth sounded as if they actually meant something. As we neared the center of Munich, I recited the usual facts—1.3 million population, Bavarian capital, home of the Wittelsbach dynasty, Oktoberfest, BMW, Jugendstil art—but then we came to the river. The Isar. I'd just explained how important it was as an early highway, the city's connection with other towns, when the Deutschesmuseum came up on our left. I knew how to make a smooth transition: talk about the city's growth from trading hub to university seat to technological center. "The Deutschesmuseum traces the history of science and technology from the beginning of time to the present day," I'd always say. But this time the lines came out wrong. My voice was too emotional. All I could think of was the story Cat had told me about meeting her Swiss man there. I tried to catch myself, but before I could, Tonia noticed.

    I'd been watching her in the mirror as I talked, remembering her march down the concourse, the resolute way she picked up her bags, intent on continuing the tour even if she had to go alone. Reciting my lines, I glanced only inadvertently toward the museum, but that was enough to bring it all crashing down, everything Cat had told me about her affair. The others were all looking out the windows, their faces blank, but Tonia was staring at me, watching my eyes in the mirror. Her face didn't change but I could tell she heard the feelings in my voice. She didn't say anything until we'd gone another block or two, and even then she only asked a question— whether a certain Kokoschka was in the art museum I was pointing out—but the sound of her voice told me certain things were emotional for her, too, and this painting was one of them. Before I could answer her, Rudy asked a question of his own, letting me know Tonia wasn't the only one listening. "Why don't you tell her?" he asked, sounding tired and annoyed.

"Tell her what?"

"About the museum there, the Haus der Kunst. What Hitler did with her beloved modern art. You talk at us for half an hour and you don't even mention him? You don't think we know what happened here? Or were you saving him for just the right moment? Waiting to spring him on us when the setting was right, like some goddamn horror movie?"

"Why do you want to do that, Rudy?" Sarah asked.

"What is it I'm doing, Sarah?" He turned to stare at her. "I'm not exactly pleased to be here, but as long as we are, we might as well deal with things openly. How do you think it feels for me to be in this place? I'm sure Gerhard's having a great laugh somewhere over all of this: telling me to meet him here of all places, imagining all of us together without him after what happened the last time—"

"That was between you and him," Felicity snapped.

"That was between all of us," Rudy said. "No one forced Donald to do what he did."

"Let's not bring that up," Sarah said, and for a while everyone was quiet. I shut off the microphone and drove away from the city center. The truth was I *had* been saving Hitler for just the right moment. I always did. I was going to idle on the Odeonsplatz where the Feldhernhalle is framed by buildings and describe his rantings from its portico stage: The dramatic gestures. The hateful words. The grotesque tableaus. It was all theater to Hitler. And it was theater to me. Despite all I'd studied, all I'd seen, I didn't yet know just how real the past could be to some people.

We'd been driving away from the center for several minutes when Donald asked about the tower he could see in the distance. He wanted, I thought, just to break the silence. To loosen the tension. I told him it was the communications tower from the 1972 Olympics. "You remember," I said, "the massacre of the Israeli athletes?"

"We remember," Rudy answered, not asking me to elaborate this time. In fact, his tone suggested he wanted me to shut up entirely. A short time later, the Olympic stadium appeared through the trees, with its elaborate supports and tent-like roof. The weather forecast had called for clear skies, so I had planned a picnic on the former Olympic grounds. The last thing Cat had done with me was shop for it at the Dallmayr delicatessen. She hadn't yet packed for her trip home but she insisted on going, knowing that otherwise I'd shop at the local supermarket instead. I hated the way the matrons behind the Dallmayr counters scowled at you if you didn't dress a certain way or order enough of the right foods. I wanted to tell them where to put their pretentiousness, but I knew if I opened my mouth my imperfect German would only prove my inferiority.

Cat, on the other hand, loved to play their game. She used the large amount of food a tour group required to show that she could buy in sufficient quantities to satisfy their definitions of wealth. She'd spend an hour before we left home picking out the right clothes, arranging her hair, applying the right makeup. Because she'd learned German as a child, she could speak it perfectly, and they respected her for it. Every other aspect of living in Munich she'd come to despise, but this one thing—visiting Dallmayr's, playing at being wealthy—she still liked.

As we skirted the park grounds, I stared at the stadium, remembering how it looked on television that summer I turned fourteen. I could picture Mark Spitz with his seven gold medals, Frank Shorter's final sprint in the marathon, and the end of the basketball final when the U.S. lost for the first time. I could picture, too, the man in his black ski mask peering from a rooftop as my mother sat beside me on the sofa, neither of us speaking. Sports had become another part of life I could never view innocently again.

"So where's this museum?" Rudy asked. He was standing in the shade of a small birch tree, his hands in his suit pants pockets. I had suggested they look around the park while I set up lunch: take the elevator up the tower or visit the BMW museum. Donald and Felicity had set off for the tower right away but the others had lingered. "Come on, Sarah," Rudy said when I showed him the way. "I'm going to call Gerhard one more time and then we'll find you a car." He sounded falsely cheerful, as if trying to make up for how he'd been in the bus.

"You go on, Rudy," Tonia said. She was kneeling beside Sarah on the grass, her legs even whiter in the sun than they'd been at the airport. "Sarah and I have catching up to do."

Rudy walked off with a shake of his head, then stopped and came back. "Listen, Tonia," he said, "I'm going to try that son of a bitch one more time and if I can't reach him, I'm going to join you on this tour of yours."

"You might as well," she said. "It's all paid for."

"That's what I don't trust," he told her. "When has Gerhard ever paid for anything without getting something in return?"

"Go with him if you want," Tonia said when Rudy had left.

"No," Sarah said. "Not when he's in a mood like this. He'll be alright when he comes back...if he does."

"So things aren't any better?" Tonia lifted a block of Munster cheese to her nose and I handed her a knife before spreading the tablecloth Cat had embroidered to use for picnics.

"They're clearer," Sarah said, "or I thought they were until Gerhard didn't show up. Rudy's been obsessed with this trip—with seeing Gerhard face-to-face—for the first time in...what has it been, nine months?"

"Just before Christmas."

"He thought it would be like Mexico last year, using the time away from the office to plan the coming year. He's been watching the sales figures. With the slump in California, he thought Gerhard would give it back to him. Bring him back to the center. Now I don't know what he'll do."

As they talked, they busied themselves with unwrapping meats and cheeses while I set out a bottle of wine. One good thing about being thought of as a servant is that people will say anything in front of you.

"Maybe this time together will be good for the two of you," Tonia said. "Maybe it's good Gerhard isn't here."

"Right...if Rudy stays...but listen, Tonia, I'm sorry about Gerhard."

"What about him?"

"I mean, where is he?"

"I don't know," Tonia said, "and I don't care. Honestly, I'm glad to be away from him. Glad to be out of that house."

"That must have been terrible, having to stay inside all that time. At least you started painting again. I loved the things you did when we were kids."

"I made a few sketches," Tonia said," but every time I did, he was after me. 'Why don't you put that creativity to use?' he'd say. 'Why don't you get on the computer again?'"

Sarah glanced up at me. "You know," she said, "Tonia used to be well known as a painter in Portland. When we were still in high school, she painted a poster they used for the Rose Festival. She's always been creative in that way. In every way."

"I'm sure," Tonia said, touching my arm, "Joe doesn't want to hear all that." When I looked at her hand, I noticed her fingernails were broken off. Bitten to the quick. "But what about you?" she said as she sliced through the heart of an apple. "Tell us about you."

"There's nothing to tell," I told her. "I lead tours."

"But you must do other things than that," she said. "You must have other interests." She paused her slicing and looked at me as if she truly wanted to know.

"History, I guess..."

"The history of people like us?" She smiled and leaned back against a tree behind her as if to study me. The picnic was laid out between us—wedges of Camembert and Brie, an assortment of cold cuts, blackberries, cucumbers, Roma tomatoes, and slabs of Bohemian rye. I sat in the sun and gazed back at her, happy to be with a woman I wasn't involved with. It felt as if I was only looking at a painting, noting details: the unpainted toenails, the silver bracelet, the razor-thin scar above one eye. The details didn't have to have stories behind them or meaning of any kind. They could just be what they were.

"I'm not one to pry," I said, and as she continued to stare at me, I remembered something Cat had said. After my angry reaction to the news of her affair, I'd grown quiet and she'd accused me of never truly engaging with people. "You have to deal with this," she said. "You can't run from what's happened to us the way you've run from everything else in your life. You're not a boy anymore." She was the one running away, I'd told her finally. She was the one who'd never been able to open up.

"It's a *long* story, Joe," Tonia said finally.

"I have time," I told her, smiling.

"Well, you know," she began slowly, "my husband sells video games." She told me, then, about her husband's company, Luckspur Games. He'd started it with a single game a few years before, operating out of their home until the game became so popular he rented a warehouse and hired Rudy as his marketer, Donald as his lawyer, and Sarah and Felicity, among others, to work in the office. Rudy's main job was to find new markets while overseeing those where the game was already selling well. He insisted from the start that they make plans for the company's growth so they could maximize potential. "But Gerhard hates plans," Tonia said, "at least the ones you write down, because people expect you to follow them. He's not very good at sharing control. A year ago, though, he decided to take the six of us to Mexico, to get away from the office and talk about what was happening with the company. Rudy had taken the game—our *one* game—national and sales had exploded. We weren't prepared for the volume. Rudy thought Gerhard had seen the need for planning at last."

"So this is another planning trip," I said when she paused. The booking had been a last-minute thing, and while she'd told me the general route they wanted to take, she'd been vague about what they wanted to do with their days.

"Not exactly," she said as she reached for wine. "Maybe we should drink something before I go on."

"Is that alright for you?" Sarah asked.

"We're on vacation, aren't we?" Tonia replied. When she had filled a glass for each of us, she went on with her story. "The company paid for everything, of course," she said. "The whole time we were down there, Gerhard, Rudy and Donald sat in a room hashing things out while Sarah and I lay in the sun and Felicity...well, she was Felicity."

They both laughed.

"Together, they mapped out the year ahead, even made a two-year plan," Tonia said. "The three of them seemed happier than ever to be working together. But almost as soon as we returned to the States, sales went flat." She sipped her wine and I thought for a moment she was going to stop there, but she went on. "Rudy had been spending more and more time on the East Coast, making contacts there, and Gerhard jumped to the conclusion he was neglecting the West Coast, which had always been our best market. By November, income was down a lot.

Rudy was doing a decent job in new areas but in the old ones we were losing ground. Then came Christmas."

"Ah, Christmas," Sarah said, shaking her head. "That wonderful Christmas."

"It was too ugly to talk about. Gerhard had decided that Rudy couldn't handle doing all of the marketing for Luckspur. That Rudy was the problem. He wanted to hire some marketers Donald knew in L.A. to cover the West Coast and send Rudy to New York where most of his new contacts were. But instead of telling Rudy directly, he had Donald do it—the day of our Christmas party. That night at the party, in the middle of everything, Rudy asked Gerhard if what Donald had told him was true. Gerhard was drunk and everyone was standing around, watching him. 'Yeah,' he told Rudy, 'it's true. Your *shtick* works better back east.' When Rudy asked what that was supposed to mean, Gerhard said, 'I just think you do better with East Coast types.' Rudy went crazy."

She let these last words sink in.

"You understand now?"

"So Rudy's Jewish," I said, the day's events clearer. "But I don't understand why he still works for your husband." Or why you're still married to a man like that, I wanted to add.

"Rudy hasn't found anything that will pay him the same kind of money," Sarah said. "And since that time they've only dealt with each other by phone."

"But they were going to be together on this trip."

"That's what Rudy thought." Sarah smiled and sipped her wine.

"And Donald?"

"That's a whole other story. Isn't it, Tonia?"

But Tonia didn't answer. She was looking toward the tower. Two figures, one in bright yellow, were moving across the lawn toward us.

"Listen, I'm going to look for Rudy," Sarah said when she saw them coming. She pushed herself to her feet and brushed off her skirt. "This way?" I pointed her in the right direction before turning to watch Donald and Felicity approach. Felicity was looking at the ground, stepping carefully, while Donald watched three male runners make their way across the park. His head seemed even more turtle-like in the sun, with the rubberiness of something that has been underwater too long.

"I was just thinking," Tonia said when Sarah was gone. "It must be tricky figuring out relationships in a group."

"Everything about this job is tricky," I said.

"But then life itself is tricky, isn't it?" she said. "At least that part that deals with people."

I wanted to agree with her, to tell her how Cat had tricked me and ask why her husband had done what he'd done to her, why he'd paid for a trip and not come. But I only smiled. I wasn't ready yet to say what was in my mind. "I suppose you just can't care too much about anything," I said.

"What is there then, if you don't care?" She stared at me as if she truly wanted an answer.

"Money, maybe?" I said as a joke.

"Now you sound like Gerhard."

So there it was again: an opening. As if she was daring me to ask a more personal question.

"But he has money and I don't, that's the difference," I said. "And he must have a generous side, to pay for a tour for everyone."

"Any check from Gerhard is a business check," she said. "He's making an investment and expects a return."

"What kind of return?"

"That'll be the fun, won't it?" she said. "Finding out."

Donald and Felicity were only a few yards away now.

"From you, too?" I asked.

"Of course," she said, "I'm his wife. I'm an investment, aren't I?"

As I stood to offer Donald and Felicity a glass of wine, her eyes stayed on me, and when I reached down to pick up the bottle, she leaned her head toward mine.

"So are you," she whispered softly—so softly only I could hear.

# Chapter Three

The first night of a tour I always took my group somewhere for dinner, keeping them out as long as I could so they'd feel they were getting their money's worth. In Munich, it was usually the Hofbrauhaus, where they could gawk at the giant steins and cover their ears when the band started up and the drunks started singing. The band itself was nothing to cheer about: a half-dozen bleary men in grimy lederhosen talking their way through oompah versions of "Waltzing Mathilda" and "I've Been Working on the Railroad." Worse still were the surly waitresses, their breasts popping out from worn-out dirndls, pretending they spoke only Bavarian while overcharging for beers. A genuine German experience.

    This group, though, wanted nothing to do with the Hofbrauhaus or anywhere else. When the picnic was over, they bee-lined to the bus and took their same seats. "Just show us our rooms," Rudy said when I asked about sightseeing. I checked the mirror to see if Tonia, at least, was interested in doing something more, but she was staring out the window. So I drove them straight to their hotel.

That night comes back to me now as a blur of images. When I reached my apartment, sun was streaming in through the courtyard window, lighting the dining table where Cat's ticket home had lain so recently. In the back bedroom, the desk she had used to organize tours was neat and empty. The bulletin board had only a picture of me at the top of the Cheops pyramid, one of us by the Roman gate in Trier, and the Gluck itinerary. Cat had always been obsessively tidy, leaving her desk at the end of each day with only a list of things to do tomorrow. There was no list there now.

The first time I saw Cat, she was sitting behind a metal desk in a neon-lit office, her fingernails drumming the edge of a blotter. The fingernails were purple and sparkled whenever she moved—I remember because they were the only vibrant things in the room. The walls were white, the ceiling acoustic tile. The only decorations were airline posters advertising American destinations like Disneyworld and Mt. Rushmore. The receptionist had told me Cat was the one who'd have to decide about my tours. She directed me to a plastic chair where I waited, watching the fingernails.

It was my first year offering my own tours and I was looking for someone to take a chance on me. I was on my first swing through the Midwest, my first visit to Minnesota, and the agency was small and independent, the kind I'd decided to target. Cat was the manager, and when she hung up the phone and swiveled toward me, the first thing I noticed were her ice-blue eyes. "Mr.–?" she said as she reached out her hand. Her hair was shorter then, permed and lightened. Her cheeks had that rosy Midwest glow and her dress was the Laura Ashley type, not really business-like but stylish in a down-home way. I remember every detail now: how she held my hand longer than necessary. How she offered a seat in a closer chair. How she listened without interrupting me as I told her my idea for small, educational tours. Thousands of people have more time than money, I said, and they want their few days away to give them something meaningful. I didn't tell her my concept hadn't been tested.

As she read my new brochure, I watched her nails. Why purple, I wondered. And why the sparkles? I didn't learn until later that the small act of painting her nails was Cat's one protest against the life she was living, her way of reminding herself to keep hoping for something better. As it turned out, Cat's idea of better was smaller than mine. But then she had less to leave behind. She didn't dislike life in the States, not the way I did. When she agreed to move to Munich with me, it was because she was trying to move backward, not forward. Her family had lived in a small German town when she was a child, her father a low-tier diplomat. She had never forgotten how gentle life was there, how much more time her family had for her: the morning walks with her mother to the bakery or butcher shop; the afternoons with her father studying German and strolling the hills. I learned all of this much later, of course, when I knew her better. That first time we met, she simply listened to me and said she would do what she could.

The next time I saw Cat, I was on my way to Berlin to begin my first tour—the first Grand Tour. Thanks to her and a handful of agents in Santa Fe, Cambridge, St. Louis, and Boulder, I'd managed to fill three tours with ten clients each. My stop in Minneapolis was only a layover, but I wanted to thank her for the work she'd done by taking her out to dinner.

    Our meal that night was a small, disappointing affair. She took me to an Italian restaurant on the edge of St. Paul, hurrying me through a drizzling rain past an outside patio. "It was supposed to be sunny," she told me. "This is my favorite place in summer." We sat in a corner chilled by the air from an ill-fitted door and seemed to have nothing to say to each other. Her fingernails were unpainted this time and I reminded her they'd once been purple. She seemed to like that I remembered something so specific about her. "I've made some concessions, I guess," she said. "I'm trying to be more professional now."

    The restaurant was called Benito's, and I joked that calling an Italian restaurant Benito's was like calling a German restaurant Adolf's but she didn't understand. Or maybe she just didn't think I was funny. When the pasta came, it was drowned in a heavy sauce and the Caprese salad was made from dried-out tomatoes and old mozzarella. Only the wine tasted truly Italian—drinkable, watery, slightly sour. When I drove her home in my rented car, I didn't expect to ever see her again.

    My tours went well that summer and I thought I was on my way. When the last one ended, I sent each of my agents a commission check and told them to let me know if they ever came to Seattle. By then I'd forgotten my evening with Cat. But one afternoon in late December she called. She was spending Christmas with her brother in Anchorage, she said, and she'd be stranded at SeaTac for thirteen hours on her way home.

Her flight was delayed by fog in Anchorage, making it late afternoon when she arrived, an hour or two before sunset. The day had been one of those unexpectedly clear winter days you sometimes get in Seattle, so I suggested we go to a restaurant down by the water where we could sit outside and watch the sun set behind the Olympic Mountains. She was thinner than I remembered. Prettier, too. The perm was gone from her hair. When I had seen her in Minnesota her face had been round, but now it was angular. It was the face she would wear from that time on. Even after our marriage she never gained weight. Never aged. Her hair grew longer, her taste in clothes matured, but the body and face beneath them stayed the same, as if she'd become immune to change.

It was that night or maybe the next morning I first thought about marrying Cat. She seemed much more interesting away from her home, her view of the world more like mine. I can't remember anything specific she said, anything different about that night than the one in Minnesota. Except her looks. And the way she changed when the alcohol hit her. I was telling her something about my mother—skirting the edges of memories my move back to Seattle had awakened—when she took my hand, weaving her fingers through mine. The warmth of her skin affected me strangely, making my eyes tear. I stopped what I was saying and looked at her.

"I've thought about you, about this moment," she said.
"So have I," I lied.

We sat holding hands, saying nothing else to each other, until she began to shiver. Our glasses were empty by then, the sun gone from the sky.

"Do you want to eat here or at my place," I asked.

"Your place maybe," she whispered.

It was that night she told me she'd lived in Germany as a young girl and hoped to return someday. I told her I'd lived in Munich my last year of college and hoped to move my business there. The Wall had recently come down and the thought of living full-time in a freer Europe excited me. There were new countries to visit and lead tours to, and the Germans were already talking about reunification. I could get in on the ground floor, growing my business as freedom spread.

We talked late into the night, until long after the buzz from the alcohol had faded. Lying beside her in bed, I wondered how I could have been so wrong about her the first time. We talked about plans for my tours, ways to market them better, the advantages of having a European base as country after country opened up. Everything I didn't know about the tour business, she seemed to know. Meeting her seemed more than coincidence; it seemed we had so much to tell each other we'd never run out of things to say.

As I stared at that picture of Cat and me in Trier, trying to accept that she was gone, really gone, my mind kept going back to that night in my small attic room in Seattle, those early morning hours when everything that would happen between us still lay ahead: the courtship by phone; the few brief visits I made to St. Paul when we would sleep in separate rooms in her parents' house; the marriage in her parents' Lutheran church with all of her relatives and none of mine; and those first few days in Munich when the whole Old World seemed ours. I tried not to think about the gaps that grew in our conversation, the different lives we began to live—she never leaving Munich, I more and more on the road—or the drying up of our dreams as we realized our business had reached a plateau, that no matter how hard I worked or how many calls she made, it would never be more than it was.

    I couldn't stay in the apartment that night, not alone. I hurried outside to where the sun was going down. With no destination in mind, I walked into the light, closing my eyes momentarily before turning toward Leopoldstrasse, where the students gathered that time of night. In the shadows below the buildings the air was cold and I wondered briefly where I would be when winter came. Without really thinking, I followed the path Cat and I always took when I was home between tours. I was hoping to clear my mind but it was filling with images of her, as if my brain had become a garbage dump and the trucks just kept coming, emptying their loads, making it hard to think. Think—that was what I had to do, think about what I was going to do with my life.

    I had reached the edge of the Englisher Garten before I realized where I was. As soon as I did, the images of Cat transformed, becoming specific memories of us in the *biergarten* there. It was Cat's favorite place to go in summer. She loved to sit with the Munich natives and think of herself as a local. I remembered one day in late August our first year in Europe. I had just finished my last tour and we had gone to the *biergarten* for lunch. While we ate, Cat talked to the people around us and I saw for the first time how good her German was. I saw, too, how the German people responded to her. My way of meeting people had always been to ask them questions about themselves and keep quiet, letting them reveal themselves to me. But Cat chose instead to let people get to know her. That day she told a family about her childhood in Germany and how it had felt to move back to the States. "I loved it at first," she said. "There were so many conveniences we didn't have here. And I liked having people from my own culture around me." It was the kind of thing I would never say; I always wanted the people in the countries I visited to think I would never want to be anywhere else. But what she said excited the family. The father began asking questions about Chicago and the Mississippi. The mother asked if it was true every house in America had a dryer and a dishwasher. From their questions and the way they were dressed—the father in a workman's coveralls, the mother with a scarf on her hair, the children in clothes they'd clearly outgrown—I guessed they had little money or education. Cat didn't care. She took the boy onto her lap and sang him a German song. The girl tucked herself under Cat's arm. When the family left, they gave her their address and insisted on kissing her goodbye.

  We lingered into the afternoon that day, the sun going down beyond the trees as we drank from the heavy liter glasses, the kind that left you drunk before you were even aware. People who had heard Cat chat with the family leaned in toward her, wanting to talk, or came to sit at our table. They had little to say to me but I didn't mind. I was content to feel the warm air as my mind went numb from the beer. Up on a stage in the wooden tower, an oompah band was playing traditional German music—"Ach du Lieber Augustin," "Schnitzelbank," "The Beer Barrel Polka"—and from time to time Cat would sing along. She seemed to know every tune, even the ones I'd never heard, and when they played the song she'd sung to the little boy, she asked me to dance. As we twirled slowly near the edge of the tables, my eyes fell on the faces of those she had talked to and then on the bright green summer leaves. The limbs hung close to the ground, sheltering that place from the rest of the world, and I was glad to be home, to have a new home, and to have Cat there to love me.

But now the air beneath the trees was cold. The leaves were turning. When I reached the *biergarten*, most of the tables had been packed away for winter. I bought a liter of beer and looked for some food but the kitchen was closed. Stray bits of sauerkraut and chicken bones lay in puddles around me. A young couple in leather jackets laughed loudly from a nearby bench, their faces going blank when I turned their way. The other benches and tables were empty. An old man with glassy eyes and unwashed hair stopped in front of me, saying something I couldn't understand. When I waved him away, he cursed at me, and for the first time since moving to Germany, I felt like someone the locals didn't want there, like one of those immigrants from the east or one of those Turks the neo-Nazis were always burning out of their homes. I wrapped my arms across my chest and stood to start back.

Where it had been dark below the trees before, it was black now, and I started to run, stopping only when I reached Leopoldstrasse. Joining a clump of students, I floated with them through the crowds until they disappeared inside a club. Hearing jazz somewhere, piano and sax, I followed the sound to a basement around the corner, one of the places Cat and I would go. Another older man with glassy eyes called me over to where he sat by a stained wall, a bottle in front of him. He insisted he knew me and poured me out a glass of schnapps, then another, while chattering in heavy Bavarian. I lay my head against the wall and watched three girls laughing. One of them looked at me, smiled, then looked away. Closing my eyes, I let the music stream into me, feeling it soothe my head, lift me up, carry me away—the hazy notes of the sax, the dancing piano.

When I opened my eyes again, the room was empty. I lifted my head from the table, holding a hand against it to stop the pounding. The girls were gone. The old man, too. The stale taste of the alcohol reminded me of that night in Berlin—morning really, one or two a.m., after a night of drinking with a group of schoolteachers from Indianapolis. I could remember the taste of the pear schnapps on the woman's tongue, the red hair pushed from her eyes, the name Sheila or Shirley. She'd stayed with me at a club on the Ku'damm while the others went back to their rooms, and when the bottle was empty, she'd slipped her hand past my knees. I could remember the tart taste of pear, the salt of peanuts, the restless swipe of her tongue across mine. She had come on the trip by herself, she reminded me, her voice with the sound of the bar in it, of people having a good time. On the way back to the hotel, we laughed as we passed the prostitutes in their hot pants leaning against signs for Swiss watches and I reminded her I was married. She was, too, she told me. I'd been away on tour for almost four months by then, with only a day here and there in Munich, a day Cat and I spent mostly arguing about how we were living and what it was doing to us. Back in the woman's room, as she and I fumbled with each other's clothing, I wiped my mind clean of everything but the pleasure of being touched and feeling free from responsibility.

Somewhere in the taste of the schnapps was the memory of calling Cat the next morning, the silences in our conversation, the feeling she knew what had happened even though I didn't tell her. It was only later that we talked about it, near the end when the distance between us was wide enough to speak with some measure of calm. By then Cat had stopped saying more than was necessary to me or anyone else, stopped doing anything besides watching her operas, going to museums, and dreaming of moving back home. She still clung to the hope that I would return to the States with her, that living our days together rather than apart might magically change the past.

I don't know how I got home from Leopoldstrasse that night. The next morning I woke early, hours before I had to meet Tonia's group, and stood in the kitchen sipping coffee, waiting for the aspirin to work. As I sipped, I gazed into the living room at the furniture Cat and I had picked out together over the years. On the end table by the sofa I saw what must have been the only portable possession she left behind: a copy of Fellini's *La Strada* I'd brought home from an Italy tour. She had taken all of the other tapes—the operas by Rossini, Puccini, Verdi she would watch for hours, holding the libretto in front of her and memorizing the words. As she studied the inflections the singers gave to their lines, learning Italian from arias, she developed a romantic vision of Italy. But when I suggested she go there with me, she said no. She wanted Italy to remain unsullied in her mind, something Germany could no longer be.

I don't know if she ever watched *La Strada*. By the time I gave it to her, she had stopped appreciating presents from me and she probably knew intuitively that Fellini's Italy wouldn't be hers.

    I slipped the tape into the VCR and sat down on the sofa, watching only the first few scenes—of the happy Giulietta Masina with her family before Anthony Quinn takes her on the road. My headache was dissipating but I felt suffocated, in need of air. I wanted to leave right then, get on the road myself, but I had two hours to kill before the group would be done with its walking tour. For a moment I considered going to meet them, following them from a distance, checking on the local guide, Georg, who liked to slip into a bar whenever he could, even in the morning, if he could talk a group into it. I imagined myself watching them from across a square. Watching Tonia in particular. But as soon as her image appeared in my mind, I tried to wipe it away. Scooping my coat from the hook, I rushed out the door.

    The skin on my cheeks felt raw, my lips chapped, as I strode past the student cafes, remembering our Saturdays at the museums. Cat would go to the Alte Pinakothek where she could examine her Raphaels, Memlings, and Rembrandts, I to the Neue Pinakothek where I could lose myself in the landscapes of Friedrich or Waldmüller. Cat studied art with the same diligence she studied Italian opera, mixing books on artists and artistic periods with her books on composers and famous divas. She took classes at the university, tried learning to draw, even copied the paintings in the museums, but she never seemed to really *feel* art. Maybe because she could understand the way Renaissance paintings worked—could explain the scientific principles behind perspective, foreshortening and rendering of volume—she preferred them to those of later eras, especially those periods when passion overwhelmed line and form.

The one time we went to the Alte Pinakothek together, I tried to convince her that Rembrandt's Descent from the Cross was a masterpiece because it made you *feel* the sorrow of Jesus's death. I pointed to the obvious heaviness of Jesus's body, the expressions on the faces of those who were taking it down from the cross, the coldness of the glare from the winding sheet. But what about the placement of the figures? she said. The refinement of colors? His use of chiaroscuro? I used to tell her that real painting only began with Turner, that art could not express what it had to express until artists gave up their preoccupation with craftsmanship and concentrated on feeling. Why can't they go together? she said.

My favorite room in the Neue Pinakothek was a cramped chamber off a back hallway where several poorly lit paintings by Caspar David Friedrich were like a series of Rorschach tests for the emotions. One depicted a lush Bavarian landscape in summer. Another a thicket of pines with a dusting of snow. A third showed high-masted ships at daybreak resting motionless on a yellow ocean. But the best was a scene of bare rolling hills with no signs of humanity or vegetation other than the dark trunks of stripped trees. The trees stood marooned beneath a gray sky in a sea of morning mist that reminded me of places I loved—the Scottish Highlands, valleys deep in the Pyrenees, Tyrolean foothills—places I had wandered alone early in the morning or late at night. I saw heroes hidden in the mists, castles rising beyond the next hill, maidens waiting to meet their princes in the clefts of secluded dales. It wasn't so much I saw these things as felt them, felt a limitless possibility in that painted world where colors were subtly muted and everything lay in a netherland between the extremes of black and white.

When I reached the museum that morning, I found that the paintings had all been moved. A sign near the entrance said that the Alte Pinakothek was being renovated and some of its major works were being displayed in the Neue Pinakothek rooms. In a museum already full of unexpected passages and walkways leading to hidden chambers, the rearrangement disoriented me. I found Dürers where there should have been Goyas, Lippis where there should have been Spitzwegs, and Rembrandts where there should have been Delacroixs or Courbets. The museum walls, so seemingly cool and modern with their beige stone and clean lighting, seemed to have aged along with the paintings, their decay putting a mustiness into the air.

When I saw the Rembrandts, I sat down on a bench in the middle of the room to rest. I remembered my conversation with Cat about him...remembered, too, what she had told me before she left: that the Rembrandt collection was the only place she had visited with both the Swiss man and me. He loves Rembrandt, she'd said, smiling slightly, betraying for the only time in our conversation the intimacy between them.

I closed my eyes and tried to control my breathing. When I opened them again, I searched the walls for Descent from the Cross. A man was standing in front of it, a short man with ears too big for his head and a brown suit that fit too tightly across the back. For some reason I imagined it was her Swiss man returning to this place where he and she had stood together. My heart began to beat faster as I remembered her smile when she spoke about him. The man and I were the only ones in the room, and before I knew what I was doing, I was moving toward him. My steps squeaked on the hardwood floor and he turned toward me, frowning. He was uglier than I had expected, with a deeply furrowed forehead and a wart-like lump on his cheek. I had almost reached him when a woman called to him in English, calling loudly as if to warn him. Howard, she called. *Howard*. The man wasn't Swiss at all.

# Chapter Four

When I arrived at the hotel to pick up the group, whatever lingering thoughts I had about Cat were quickly nudged aside by Tomislav, the hotel manager, who smiled broadly as soon as he saw me and waddled out from behind the reception desk to motion me into his breakfast room. "For the driving strength," he said over his shoulder without another greeting. The lights in the breakfast room had been turned off and there were no windows; a cool fluorescent glow came from the kitchen door, bringing with it the smell of soap and baking bread.

It always made me smile to walk into a small hotel like Die Frauenkirche and be greeted by someone like Tomislav as a friend more than a client. If a group insisted on staying in four-star hotels—in sterile rooms that looked so alike you could be anywhere, with desk clerks and bellhops trained to be bland—that's where I'd book them. But I always suggested the smaller places, the family-run pensions with their idiosyncratic decorating and garrulous owners, the little unknown hotels that were clean and safe but hadn't had the life pressed out of them. Tonia had told me over the phone to choose what I thought best.

Tomislav stopped just short of the light that came from the kitchen, at the only table not littered with breakfast plates and napkins. The bottle of Jägermeister he picked up looked like a small vial in his beefy hand as he poured out two glasses, saying, "You go far today." After pushing one of the glasses toward me, he settled his fleshy body onto a bench by the wall, threw back his drink and stared at me. A curl of graying hair fell across his eyes. "What? Is no good?" he asked, shifting his gaze to my still-full glass. I had known him three years, had used his hotel for every group I brought to Munich, and this had become our ritual. It had always seemed a lucky way to start a tour: with his enthusiasm behind me, his grinning face in my mind. But he wasn't grinning now. "Is German, very good. Everything German is good, *nicht wahr*?"

"It must be for you," I said, moving my hand toward the glass, "judging by what you charge me."

"What! What I charge you? Nothing! Fifty percent off, not enough to pay for breakfast."

"Forty," I said, downing the Jägermeister in one gulp.

"Only forty?" He made it sound as if he was discovering this fact for the first time. "You must bring more groups, bigger groups. Five, six people...for others no discount. No free drinks." He pushed himself to his feet to pour out two more shots. He had fattened and slowed in the three years I'd known him, worn himself out working from early morning to after midnight, day after day, pleasing people. He was younger than I was, barely thirty, but he came from the east, from Croatia, where for years, as he once lamented, everyone had been "rotting inside."

"*Nostrovia*," he said without enthusiasm, draining his glass with a quick flick of his wrist. As I watched him I thought that Cat had been wrong about my tour business: it wasn't dead, only hungry, insatiable, and I no longer had the will to feed it, to let it devour me as it was devouring Tomislav and everyone else I knew who had stayed in tourism too long. When I first met Tomislav he had been in the West for two years and he still thought there was nothing like being free. Now he was used to freedom, to what it meant to run a business without enough income, to be responsible to someone else. Freedom was looking less free.

"I have to drive," I told him.

"Yes, is good for driving." He picked up the glass and held it out toward me.

"I won't be able to see the road."

"Ah, road! Is German road, *good* road."

His face took on a morose look.

"You go to Venice?" he asked.

I nodded.

"Lucky man. You go down coast of Croatia?"

I shook my head.

"Stupid American. Is beautiful! *Alive*. No stupid Germans."

He thrust the glass toward me again and when I refused to take it, he drank it himself.

"There's a war going on down there," I said.

"Yes. Cheap prices, no crowds." He collapsed against the wall again, taking the bottle with him. "Is war here," he said, tapping the stained T-shirt stretched across his chest. "Good Germans...good goddamn German everything."

I had just begun loading the group's luggage into the bus when I saw Georg coming around the corner from the direction of St. Michael's Church. He wore what looked like a gray greatcoat and carried a black umbrella, holding it out in front of him like a drum major with a baton. He was high-stepping down the street, past the somber pre-war facades, and I knew right away that he had taken them somewhere, talked them into visiting "ah *rrreal* Cherman beer hall." My group came into view behind him, one by one. Sarah was dressed more casually than the day before, more like a tourist, in blue jeans, loafers and a peach sweatshirt, but Donald and Felicity still looked as if they were going to the office or out to dinner, he in a camel hair coat and she in a gold serge dress with matching jacket. When Georg reached the end of the traffic-free zone that stretched back to Kaufingerstrasse, he stopped and turned, marching in place for a moment, his heels on the curb. Despite his fifty-plus years, his still-blond hair was shaved on the sides, a few thin strands left to form a Mohawk above. He had always seemed odd to me but my groups loved his antics. He spoke with a heavy accent, which made them sure everything he said was true, and when he told them he taught English during the school year, they smiled at the thought of hundreds of children speaking English as strangely as he did.

Georg's smile looked lipless, frog-like, as he peered through his wire-rimmed glasses, down his sharp nose at the three tourists in front of him. I assumed he was waiting for Tonia and Rudy to catch up, but then he spoke. "*Ja*, ladies and gentlemen, last but least I show you your guide." His hand shot out to the side, the umbrella extending toward me. "We had good time I think and you will not forget I hope that you have been here in Munich. Ladies, be careful here"—he slapped his hand against his butt—"when you come in Italy."

"Georg!" I glanced to my right and saw Tomislav's huge form filling the hotel doorway, the bottle of Jägermeister still in his hand. "You have had breakfast?" he called out in German, winking.

"*Moment, ja?*" Georg slipped the umbrella under his arm and held out his hand, palm up, toward my clients. Sarah reached out to shake it then leaned up to kiss him. "You have enjoyed it, I think?" he said, wincing as Sarah's lips brushed his cheek, and moving away from her to thrust his hand toward the others. Donald shook the hand, too, without putting anything in it. Felicity ignored him altogether.

"Josef, my friend," Georg said in German as he moved past where I stood on the sidewalk, "these are not good people."

"And you even took them—where, the Hofbrauhaus?" I answered with mock sympathy, smelling the beer on his breath.

"*Ja*, an extra ten marks thirty."

I handed him two hundred marks and he disappeared through the hotel doorway without a thank you or a goodbye to the group. I didn't care. I leaned back against the hotel wall and watched the corner for Tonia.

"Do you want us to get in?" Donald asked from the door of the bus just behind me.

"You put our luggage in already?" Felicity said as she climbed inside. "What if we needed something out of it?"

"You can get in if you want," I said. "Where are the others?"

"Tonia said to tell you she'd meet us here," Sarah called from the hotel door. Tomislav and Georg were gone, drinking inside somewhere.

"Where is she?" I asked.

"I don't know. She left when the tour began. Do you have to know?"

Sarah's tone was sharp, a response, I knew, to my own annoyance. I stifled the impulse to tell her no, I didn't have to know, I didn't have to do anything but pass ten days with them.

"Is Rudy with her?"

"I don't know where Rudy is," Sarah said as she came up beside me, the sharpness gone from her voice. "He left the room early this morning. You heard him yesterday. He's probably at an airline office booking his return to New York."

I didn't know what to say so I said, "If you need to use the toilet, this would be a good time to go," saying it loudly enough for Felicity and Donald to hear. They would think I was being condescending, I knew, and an hour down the road they'd tell me they had to stop so one of them could piss out the beer.

"We went at the Hofbrauhaus," Donald called through the bus door. He and Felicity sat once again in the seat behind mine, sitting without moving like children told to keep still. Cat used to ask sometimes why I didn't want children. I've spent enough time with children, I'd say. We remained like that, the four of us, for maybe ten minutes, no one saying anything. Sarah was watching the corner for Tonia or Rudy, I was watching Donald and Felicity, wondering how they could sit without talking or moving, without wanting to get back out and stretch their legs.

"There she is," Sarah said at last.

"*Wie schön!*" someone shouted from the hotel doorway.

Tonia was running toward us from the pedestrian plaza, wearing a tight black sweater and black Lycra leggings. I glanced behind me and saw both Tomislav and Georg ogling her. "You have been keeping something from me, Josef," Georg said in German.

"Go to hell," I told him, hating him without knowing why. Because he was cheapening her? Because he was implying something I was thinking myself? Because I had just paid him four times what he was worth as a guide? I was glad to be heading south, to be leaving Munich and all of the north behind. The thought flickered through my head that once the tour was over I could stay in Italy or go on to Greece. With Cat gone, I could do anything. Live anywhere.

Tonia apologized for being late, said she had been looking at paintings in the Haus der Kunst and lost track of time. She could have said anything. I forgave her the moment I heard her voice.

"Did you find your Kokoschka?" I asked.

"I did," she said, holding up a plastic museum bag. "I bought a postcard for show and tell." As she dug through the bag for the card, I directed her to the seat beside mine.

"I need help passing," I explained. "They drive on the wrong side here, you know."

When Tonia unbuttoned her sweater, I saw that she wasn't wearing leggings but a black body suit that stretched up over her arms to cling to the outer part of her shoulders. A string of pearls hung in the valley between her breasts. As I stole a glance at her stomach, I heard Tomislav and Georg laughing outside. When I looked up, they had already turned away.

"Here it is," Tonia said, holding a postcard out toward me. "This is the one I wanted to see." It took only a glance to recognize Kokoschka's view of Venice as the one I liked best: coming in from the Lido by boat, nearing the Doge's Palace and the *piazzetta*, with San Giorgio on the left, the Arsenale on the right, and the Grand Canal entrance with its huge gold ball straight ahead. It was the first view of Venice everyone had who went there before 1866, when the Austrians built their bridge. As I studied the painting, I thought about staying in Venice after the tour, living like some character from a Henry James novel.

"There's Rudy," Sarah said, rapping on the rear window to get his attention. She was sitting as far back in the bus as she could, twisting around in her seat to face the hotel. Rudy was stepping out of a cab. He looked disheveled, his hair mussed by the wind, his shirt collar open and tieless. It took him a moment to see us.

"Where have you been?" Sarah asked when he reached the bus. He took an empty seat by himself without answering.

"Well, did you find him?" Felicity asked.

"Find who?" Rudy said as I started the bus. He kept his eyes toward the windshield as I accelerated onto the street.

"Gerhard, of course."

"There's a subway to the airport from the train station if you need it," I told him. "I can drop you there."

"I'm not going to the airport," Rudy answered, the words coming hard and tight. "Why don't you just drive?"

The bus remained quiet after that. I drove as Rudy had told me to do, maneuvering my way past the train station and out of the city center. Ten minutes earlier I might have told him to go to hell, too, but I felt calm and tolerant now. I was on the road again where I belonged, sitting beside a beautiful woman, looking forward to nothing more—wanting nothing more—than an afternoon drive through the foothills. When I was moving, traveling, nothing could bother me. Nothing could stick to me or weigh me down. As I gazed at the monotonous post-war facades, watching them pass and disappear, I felt better than I had in days. I was moving from city to country, finished with Munich, feeling more and more sure that the life I had lived for the last five years would soon be part of the past.

# Chapter Five

By the time I met Tonia's group for that trip down to Venice, I'd been leading tours through Europe for thirteen years, the last six with my own company. When I started—while on a study abroad program in Munich—I had the same prejudices other people have toward tour guides, the same image of them as loud-mouthed hucksters who spout inanities as fast as they can. I used to stand on the Marienplatz watching them try to outshout the music of the Glockenspiel, describing the movements of the dancing figures as if their clients had no eyes of their own, or pause to listen to them in the Staatsgalerie, pretending they knew something about art when all they were doing was translating the placard beside each painting.

    A history major with a focus on Germany's past, I'd gone to Munich both to gain first-hand knowledge of the country and to improve my language skills. Having sent applications to a dozen graduate schools, I was already envisioning myself in an endowed chair or on the lecture circuit touting my book about why Germany would never reunite, when my home university asked me to show a group of visiting American scholars around. Once I'd worked with that first group, I became the school's official guide for all English-speaking visitors. After months of leading only city tours, I took an American army group—a busload of mostly black soldiers and their families—to Nuremberg. They laughed and joked the whole way, until I walked them onto the rally grounds and told them what Hitler had said there. Soon, I was taking the families of soldiers from rural America on trips down the Rhine or up to Berlin where they'd stand by the Spree and gape at the still-intact Wall. I loved the chance to see where history had happened and the impetus to study art, culture, politics. That spring, rejection letters flowed in from graduate schools overfilled with students of German history, but I didn't care. I'd decided to become a guide.

    Before long, I was working for a large American tour company. For five years I'd been scraping by on financial aid, spending my summers working odd jobs. Now I could double an entire summer's earnings with just one trip. My salary was small but there were plenty of other ways to make money. The tour groups stayed at hotels outside of cities and paid a fee for "excursions" to nearby sights and restaurants. Most of that fee went directly to me. The more people I talked into taking each trip, the more I made. If the excursion was to a gift shop or factory somewhere, the take from kickbacks was even larger: twenty-five or thirty percent on every vase or beer stein sold. At night there was always folk dancing, flamenco, or cabaret—another thirty percent per ticket.

Like most tour guides, I thought my life was good. I was the star on the microphone, I spent every night in a comfortable room, and, if I worked from spring to fall, I could make far more than my former classmates made, with my room and board paid. For seven years I gave myself over to a cut-rate version of celebrity life: eating good food, sampling good wines, traveling through different countries. Then one day, on the drive to a chocolate factory in Switzerland, I looked in the mirror at the elderly people packed into every seat, their eyes heavy from eating and drinking too much at a mediocre lunch, and I asked myself what the hell I was doing. I remembered my desire to become a professor and what I'd liked about guiding at the beginning: the chance to visit sites where history had happened, the incentive to study, the opportunity to teach people important things about the world. Right then, while spouting useless facts about the Swiss and chocolate, I began to plan a different tour, one based not on making money but on actually educating people. The group would be small and full of travelers rather than tourists: people willing to invest their few vacation days in something meaningful.

I called my company Grand Tours because I wanted to remind my clients of the journeys English gentlemen took in the 18th and 19th centuries to round out their education. I wanted them to think of my tours the same way: as an opportunity to learn about the culture of Europe first-hand. This is *teaching* I'm doing, I told myself. This is important.

But finding people willing to pay for a tour focused on education proved difficult. I wasn't there in the States to talk to prospective clients or make sure my brochures made their way to schools and civic groups. Though I told my agents I only wanted people interested in learning, I ended up taking anyone they sent me, just to fill the tours. Even then, many of my trips left half-empty. I began to take any group that needed a guide, however large or small, no matter what they wanted to do or see. I worked from early spring to late fall, doling out memorized lines, keeping my opinions to myself...for nothing more than money.

Somewhere between Munich and Chiemsee—when we were outside the city and the factories had given way to broad green fields—I told Tonia's group the story of Ludwig II, mostly to keep myself awake. The Mad King had always been a favorite with those who went on my tours, primarily because he built castles and lived in a fairytale world. But there was something more to it, too, something about the innocent way he looked at life, as if he were able to see with the eyes of a child.

In the mid-19th century, shortly before Bismarck united the German lands, Ludwig was the eldest son and legal heir to the Bavarian throne. But his father, Maximillian II, never prepared him to rule. When Ludwig should have been learning about armies and finances in Munich, he was living in the countryside with his mother, dreaming of performing chivalrous deeds like his ancestors. Then his father died when Ludwig was just 18 and Ludwig had to move to the capital, where he was surrounded by ministers and councilors and hangers-on. At the time, Bavaria was still the independent country Ludwig's ancestors had ruled for eight hundred years.

By the time his tragic reign ended, however, it was free no more.

Although Ludwig wasn't classically handsome, he was tall and dark with a sensitive face. The first time the people of Munich saw him dressed as the king, they fell in love with him. Though young, he did all he could to learn how to rule, but over the years the realities of *realpolitik* took their toll. He lost a war, wasted funds, and finally, his hand forced by Bismarck, he signed the treaty that made his once-free land a part of greater Germany.

By the time he ascended the throne, Ludwig himself had fallen in love—with the works of Richard Wagner. It wasn't Wagner's music he loved so much as the world Wagner portrayed, a romantic world of heroes and heroines, gods and goddesses, fortunes and destinies cobbled together from German legends, Norse myths, and medieval tales. In this make-believe world Ludwig found the land he had always wanted to live in, the land of his ancestors. It was a purer land, more devoted to goodness, a place where everyone was heroic or evil. It was a land where Ludwig could be Lohengrin, loved by the woman he defends, or the innocent Parsifal, charged with the solemn task of protecting the Holy Grail. Ludwig believed that by being good he could bring goodness to the land he ruled. He believed in redemption through art, in the Romantic idea that artistic beauty—perfection in painting, music, drama, and architecture—could lead humanity to a higher realm. Wagner was his prophet and the world of Siegfried and Brünnhilde the heaven he wanted to enter. But in the end he found that a modern king couldn't live like one in a fairy tale.

Ludwig's response to the disappointments of politics was to dive more deeply into his fantasy world. Early in his reign he brought Wagner to Munich, gave him a generous allowance and paid to have his operas performed. Eventually, though, going to the theater and dreaming of a glorious future weren't enough. As his political fortunes soured, Ludwig turned more and more to building the kingdom of his imagination in stone. He had a theater designer sketch out plans for a fairytale castle with turrets and a gatehouse. It was to be called Neuschwanstein and be built on a promontory near his childhood home. While engineers and stone masons were working to make this first fantasy a reality, he started another castle, Linderhof, this one less externally grand but more palatial inside. Behind this second royal residence he had his workers construct a grotto with staging platforms for Wagner's operas and even a lake a mechanical swan could pull the hero's boat across in the final scene of *Lohengrin*. In almost all of the myths Ludwig cherished, the hero or king fell in love with a princess or a maiden in distress. His willingness to risk death for her meant he was allowed to marry her and find eternal happiness. Ludwig tried to follow this pattern by marrying his cousin, Sophie, but before the wedding took place he began to fear even the thought of marriage. After breaking off his engagement, he never entertained the idea of marriage again.

For twenty years Ludwig navigated a tempestuous confluence of inner and outer life, reality and fantasy, alternating between participating in and withdrawing from public life. But in the end, his inattention to state affairs, his increasing isolation, and his lavish spending on personal fantasies led many in the government and even his family to look for a way to depose him. Unfortunately for Ludwig, they found an easy weapon to use against him. For years, many in the government and even Ludwig himself had feared his mercurial character was a sign of madness. In 1878, his younger brother, his only friend as a child, had been declared insane by a court doctor. By the time Ludwig's family had the same doctor evaluate him, his behavior had become bizarre enough to make the case easy. He was taken to Berg Castle, a place he'd once loved on the shore of Lake Starnberg south of Munich. The castle had been converted into a prison, with bars on the windows and doors that could be opened only from the outside. On the evening of the day he arrived, Ludwig went for a walk with his doctor. No one knows what happened next. When they didn't return, a search began and their bodies were found floating in the lake. Ludwig and his dreams existed no more.

"Maybe that's the game you've been looking for," Sarah said when I finished my story. She was talking to Rudy. "Maybe that's the next *Fire Mountain*. You could even use Gerhard as the model for Ludwig—dark and rich and paying people to build a fantasy world."

"Are you designing the games now, too?" Felicity said, dabbing her lips with a polished nail.

Tonia had mentioned the game, *Fire Mountain*, when she told me about her husband's business. It had given Nintendo and Atari a run for their money a couple years back, she told me, making Gerhard a multi-millionaire and Luckspur Games one of the largest privately-held companies in the industry.

"No, I'm not designing the games, Felicity." Rudy glared at her with a pained look. "We're just trying to find a new story for Tonia, give her something to get her started again."

Tonia didn't seem to hear what they were saying. She was watching the passing fields with a smile on her face. We'd entered the Germany Cat loved most, the land beyond the cities spared the scars of history. It was a place of half-timbered houses with whitewashed walls and rows of flower boxes spilling over with red geraniums. A place where villagers still made daily visits to the baker and the butcher. Where you could still pass a village square on a Sunday and see men in Bavarian jackets and women in embroidered dirndls, not because tourists were passing through but because those were their Sunday clothes.

"Well I suggest you *don't* choose Gerhard, of all people, as a model for Parsifal," Felicity said.

The highway was empty, the sun filtering down through a gauze of clouds, and we were passing through woods where the leaves had all turned orange and red, their colors deepening as the sun gained in strength. I tried to keep my mind on the road, on the beauty, ignoring the drama building in back.

"Maybe you're on to something there, Sarah," Rudy said. I couldn't tell if he was teasing her or being serious. "But we'd need some atmosphere..." In the mirror I could see him furrow his brows as if deep in thought. "...*Sound of Music*-type scenery, maybe. A Cinderella castle. We could borrow a page from Disney but go farther, darker, out-Disneying Disney. Doing the European thing, but doing it right, making it more authentic...we'd need some decay, the Fantasia thing, the nightmare of reality. Maybe we could keep it current by playing the madness angle, Phantom of the Opera-type stuff. The object would be to stay alive, to stay sane—that'd be a modern game."

"Rudy—" Sarah began, but Felicity interrupted her.

"What are you going to call it, Donkey Kook?" she said, looking pleased with herself.

Rudy ignored them both. "Every choice you make is either rational or irrational," he said, "helping you keep your kingdom or lose it. One wrong step and it's harder to get back to the right place—choose the wrong side in a war, for example, or pick the wrong composer to be your friend. What do you think, Tonia, is that something you could get interested in?"

Tonia said nothing, but her smile was gone. I had the uncomfortable feeling I was the only one who didn't know how to take what he was saying. Whether he meant any of it.

"We could find a way to simulate madness," Rudy went on. "Maybe unexpected image shifts, built-in bugs, Joan of Arc voices coming out of the speakers—"

"That doesn't sound much like Disney." I couldn't tell if Felicity was mocking Rudy or playing along.

"I said out-Disney Disney, Felicity. If Disney had the guts to take a chance on something."

"You mean what Disney would be if you still worked there?"

Despite the sharpness in Felicity's voice, and in Rudy's, too, it still seemed possible they were only teasing each other.

Playing games. But Rudy's next comment—and Donald's reaction—made it clear the only game Rudy was playing was some kind of one-upmanship.

"You have to stay ahead in this game, don't you, Donald? You have to make sure you know the market, keep in front of the competition. You don't want to find yourself odd man out."

Donald turned in his seat to face him. "Rudy, for the last time, I gave Gerhard the names he asked me for. I didn't know why he wanted them." The two of them stared at each other without blinking, neither looking away. I wanted to watch them, to see what would happen, but we were nearing the town where we'd catch the boat to Ludwig's island and I had to make sure I didn't miss the road.

"I'm not blaming you for anything, Donald," Rudy said, enunciating carefully. "You were doing what Gerhard paid you to do. That's why he made his deal with you, isn't it? Why he promised you what he did?"

"That had nothing to do—" Donald began, but Felicity cut him off.

"Don't listen to him, Donald," she said. "Don't indulge him."

"But we're not talking about the past," Rudy went on. "We're exploring the future here. Gerhard needs something new, doesn't he? *Fire Mountain* is old news. The company's losing money. And Tonia needs something she can relate to, something that will pull her back into the business. I'm just saying as long as we're here away from the day-to-day, let's be creative. Let's use this time like we did in Mexico. There's something in this for all of us, isn't there?" He paused as if expecting Donald to answer. "I mean, Europe is popular now, right? With the fall of the Wall and the east opening up? Everyone's talking about Euro-this and Euro-that. Freedom of every kind as communists discover capitalism. It's a new day for the Old World. This might be the right move—emphasize the difference between Luckspur and Nintendo—common heritage, you know. Fear of the Asian Invasion. That kind of thing has worked before. If Disney taught me anything it's that everyone loves a good story. We'd be fusing the past with the future, Fantasyland with Tomorrowland. It's the kind of thing Gerhard loves to do, isn't it, mixing the past with the future?"

    We had reached the edge of the lake. The wind had picked up and there were whitecaps on the water. The clouds had thickened, too. And the sun was gone. I waited for one of them to say something more but no one did. They were all looking off toward the lake—the gray water, the pristine shore, the natural wildness Ludwig had sought to preserve when he chose that place for his palace. When the silence had gone on too long, I switched the sound system from microphone to cassette and slipped in a tape. It began with a tune I often played on the way to one of Ludwig's castles: *Ride of the Valkyries*.

# Chapter Six

"So he never married?" Tonia asked as the island boat began to move. We stood braced by the railing, facing the wind and the wisps of fog that split and floated past us. The rest of the group had scurried into the boat's covered section, out of the wind. Two months before, I'd stood on the same foredeck in a pack of tourists so tight I couldn't lift my arms. Now Tonia and I were the only ones there. We were on our way to Herreninsel, an island in a lake called Chiemsee where Ludwig built the third and last of his castles, a mini-Versailles where he dressed in Louis XIV clothes for sumptuous dinners he ate alone. He even had a dining table that could be lowered into the floor, filled with food, and raised into place by unseen servants so his solitude wouldn't be disturbed. On a sunny day, Chiemsee is one of the loveliest lakes in Germany, its royal waters reflecting the Alpine peaks in the distance. But that day the lake was a solid slate of white-edged stone.

It was hard to believe how quiet Tonia had been in the bus only minutes before. Now she wanted to know everything I could tell her about Ludwig, especially the end of his life—his habits, his solitude, the signs of his illness. I told her about his nighttime rides through the countryside—in a gilded coach with baroque carvings in summer or an ornate sleigh pulled by four white horses in winter. When the country people heard him coming, they'd rush to the window and wave or stare in wonder. Sometimes he'd stop to chat with a peasant family, warming himself by its fire and sending a thank-you bouquet afterward.

In the city, though, he wasn't so friendly. He'd hide behind screens in his carriage or behind a plant if forced to attend a state dinner. He saw conspiracies everywhere, and near the end he kicked or punched attendants, making one wear a mask in his presence for over a year because he didn't like his face. His only true friends, he said, were animals because they didn't lie. He once invited his favorite mare to dine with him on his best china. Another time he rode round and round a track at the Court Riding School, pretending he was taking a trip with only his horse as companion. He even stopped halfway to his imaginary destination to eat an imaginary picnic.

"No, he never married," I said, looking out at the marshy shore. "He lived alone." From the corner of my eye I could see Tonia push back her hair, revealing a stripe of red like a blush on the ridge of her ear. Her eyes shifted from me to a crane on a rock.

"And you?" she said into the wind.

"Me?" I watched the crane lift itself into the air as the boat approached, flapping its awkward wings.

"Have you been married, I mean." She turned back toward me and her black eyes seemed to say she was interested in more than a simple yes or no. Beyond her, the island dock was approaching. Once we landed, I'd have to turn my attention to the rest of the group. I could avoid her question if I wanted to or I could tell her what had happened with Cat, using my own revelations as justification to ask about her.

"I am," I said at last, just as the deckhand hefted the painter coiled beside me.

"No ring?" The boat lurched to the left as the man caught the cleat on the dock with a quick, clean cast.

"Was. She left me."

The deckhand cinched the rope tight, tying us fast. "Herreninsel!" the captain yelled, opening the door to the seating area as the deckhand slid a bridge between the boat and the dock.

"I'm sorry," Tonia said, pausing a moment before following the others onto the land. I knew from the tone of her voice and the way she looked at me that I'd made the right decision. Here is a woman who can understand, I thought. One who has felt her own pain. As we walked the long wooden dock that took us onto the island, I wanted to ask her a dozen questions, but I had to rush to the front of the group and direct them up the stairs through the gift shop, past the empty outdoor restaurant and onto the path that led through the trees. I told them I'd meet them by the largest fountain.

"Isn't there a bus?" Felicity asked, looking down at her high-heeled shoes.

"No bus," I told her. "You have to walk."

"But what if it rains?"

Every question Felicity asked was like a knife working its way through flesh and muscle to scrape against bone. The long summer had worn me out, that was clear—the endless tours, the problems with Cat. I tried to hold my tongue as I watched them milling around, glaring at me before starting down the gravel path. Tonia had stopped to look at something outside the gift shop, so I waited for her by the restaurant tables. As I gazed at them, I thought of Renoir's painting of the boating party, the sun dappling the faces and shoulders of friends who had stopped at a place like this. It occurred to me that I'd never had that kind of friends, people I saw every day. I'd never stayed in one place long enough.

"Is this the castle we're going to?" Tonia was pointing to a poster that showed Neuschwanstein from the air, its minaret towers white against the blue of the Alpsee, the evergreens on the hills around it flocked with snow.

"No, sorry," I told her. "That's the Gothic one, the one Disney copied for Sleeping Beauty. You're going to be disappointed, I'm afraid."

"Too bad," she said. "I'd like to draw it."

"For the game Rudy was talking about?"

"No," she said without a pause. "I don't work with that anymore." Taking a step back, she studied the poster. "It's what you think of, though, isn't it? When you think of a castle. Or a prince."

"It was designed by an artist," I said. "It's make-believe—the province of art."

"That isn't the province of art," she said.

"You don't think it's reality...."

"Of course it is. That's exactly what it is."

I remembered Cat saying something similar in one of our many disagreements, just before launching into her explanation of why the Renaissance was the only great artistic period.

"We should get going," I said. "They'll be waiting for us."

"You don't agree," Tonia said.

"No, I don't agree. I mean yes, this castle is more artifice than art, a set designer's idea of what art is, but you're saying art is reality?"

"Well, yes, the artist's reality. Cezanne painted oranges the way Cezanne saw oranges. It's a Cezanne orange. Or a Kokoschka Venice. Van Gogh said he studied nature not so his colors would look exactly like those in nature but so the things he painted would be as beautiful as those in nature."

"I see," I said.

"You don't agree?"

"No, I agree." I didn't know how to tell her I'd misread her, talking to her as if she were my wife.

"You don't have to agree with me," she said. And then she laughed—a loud, lovely laugh—and I wondered how long it had been since anything I'd said or done had amused Cat.

As we started down the path, the land around us was still, the only sounds the crunch of our steps and the whoop of a bird somewhere. Below the trees, the ground was bare and brown with only grass and leaves strewn across it. We walked for a long time without speaking, through a silence that felt like a gift after months of running around. When Tonia spoke again,

I had the feeling she'd been contemplating how much to tell me. What to hold back.

"My mother was an artist," she said without looking at me. "A real artist, with her own reality."

"Is that who taught you to paint?" I asked.

"Yes," she said. "She and my father. He was a painter, too, but more like what you were implying earlier, the kind who can only see in conventional ways, who can't really see the world."

"And you?"

"Me?"

"You're a painter, aren't you? Isn't that what Sarah said?"

"Now, yes, I guess...yes."

I didn't ask more questions. Our conversation had been light until then, having to do with other places or people, but it was thickening now, coming around. The bird had stopped singing and I was afraid the lack of sound would make the moment feel too intimate, asking her to reveal too much.

"My husband doesn't want me to paint," she said after several steps. "He thinks it's a waste of time."

"Do you?"

"No. Definitely not. It's the only thing sometimes that seems worthwhile."

"So?"

"So what?"

"Does it matter what he thinks?"

She hesitated.

"Not really, no...except I have to live with him." She let out an embarrassed laugh.

"Have to?"

I knew I was overstepping bounds, but it seemed she was talking more freely, inviting me to ask more.

"I suppose so," she said. "It's his house. His money."

"His life?"

"In a way, yes. He held me together when my father died." She paused, her steps slowing for a moment. "You have to understand about...my husband. He's a powerful man."

"Strong, you mean?"

"No, not physically. It's a long history. You'd have to know Portland, how small it was not so long ago."

I told her I knew Portland.

"It's more than knowing the city," she said. "It's knowing the society there. The history."

"You mean Gerhard's? You mean the company he owns?"

"His, yes...and mine."

I wasn't sure what it was about her words that bothered me, maybe just a feeling that she had pulled back, that she was trying to find reasons why I wouldn't understand. I let her retreat. We were almost to the palace anyway.

"Listen, I don't mean to be circumspect," she said. "It's a whole long history I don't think you want to hear."

"Okay," I said.

"Maybe later, when we know each other better." She smiled—a sweet, disingenuous smile.

"*If* we do," I said.

"Yes, of course." Her smile changed into one of resignation. Or maybe pity.

I expected to find the group sitting on separate benches, but as we crossed the palace lawn, I saw them clustered together beside the main fountain, Donald's head clearly visible above the others. The gardens at Herrenchiemsee are the unimaginative kind brought to the Continent from England in the 17th century, the sort that were standard for all great palaces during the next hundred years. They all had rectangular lawns with crisscrossing paths that made them look suspiciously like huge Union Jacks from the air. And at the center of each lawn was a fanciful fountain.

"It is like Versailles," Tonia said behind me. She was looking past the gardens and fountains at the palace facade, the monotonous repetition of windows and statues and orange stone.

"Exactly," I said, slowing down to let her catch up. "Listen, I didn't mean to pry...."

"Don't be silly. Why shouldn't you know? It's just the timing." Her eyes followed the line of the lawn down to where it ended in water. "Is it *exactly* the same?"

"To the inch. Have you seen Versailles?"

Sarah had noticed us and was waving as she had at the airport. I wondered what she and the others would think, seeing us like that, walking slowly, in conversation.

"I went once with my father, when he was in Paris for a conference."

"And you speak French."

"What makes you say that?"

"That's just what girls like you do, isn't it—study French and art...learn to play the piano?" I meant it as a joke, a humorous pointing out of the differences between us, but my tone was harsher than I intended.

"What does that mean, 'girls like you'?"

"Girls...." But I didn't know what I meant exactly. I knew only that it bothered me I could distinguish her background from tiny details—the crispness of her vowels and the way she enunciated the endings of words, the confidence in her eyes when she looked at me and her voice when she spoke.

"Go on."

"You're smart. Things don't get by you. Wellesley or Vassar, I suppose."

"Reed College. I went there because it was near my home. *Et oui, je parle francais...et tu, brute?*"

"*Non, je ne parle pas bien francais,*" I told her, "*mais oui, je suis vrai un brute. Pardonnez moi, je suis pauvre.*" They were words that seemed admissible only because they were in a foreign language. I would never have contrasted the poverty of my childhood to the richness of hers, never have put myself at that disadvantage, if I had been speaking my own language. But something about our earlier conversation had made me feel I had to explain myself, let her know that though I didn't have a history anyone would know about, I had plenty. I've earned whatever I have, I wanted to say. I know how to survive.

"Did people come here by boat?" she asked, still looking down toward the water.

"No. No one ever came here at all except Ludwig. He was happy being here alone. The view was for his own enjoyment, not to impress anyone."

"Not to impress himself?"

She walked on ahead of me toward the palace, waving to Sarah, but then she stopped and spun around. "There's no crime in being poor," she said, her eyes large, unblinking, "and there's no crime in having money, either."

"Yes," I said as she turned back toward the palace, "but wouldn't we all prefer the latter?"

I approached the rest of the group feeling wary and angry, ready to pounce on the first one who said something about having to wait for me. But they didn't seem bothered by my inattention at all.

"This is great, Joe," Sarah shouted as soon as I was close enough to hear. "It's like the Hearst Castle."

"The Hearst Castle?" Rudy scowled at her but his tone suggested a kind of fatherly indulgence. "Couldn't you compare it to something in Newport at least, or the Hollywood Hills?"

"So I haven't been to Newport or the Hollywood Hills," she said, "so sue me."

"Shall we go see about a tour?" I asked.

"We already did," Felicity said. "The next one's in half an hour." I would have expected her tone to be accusatory but it was almost soft. In fact, they all seemed much more relaxed than they had that morning. "We don't mind waiting," she said without irony. "The fountains are about to come on." Before she had even finished speaking, one of the stone frogs coughed and a jet of uncertain water arced from its mouth.

"The marble woman there is Latona," I shouted over the growl of the fountain turning on, "and the boy is her son Apollo, the god of the arts."

"And music!" Felicity shouted back at me, using her scarf to ward off the mist and looking pleased with herself. I didn't know what had happened to them, why a short walk through the woods and seeing a palace would make them suddenly human. But I didn't argue. It wasn't unusual for people to begin a tour full of pent-up emotions and touchy with anxiety. They came from their jobs, their relationships, their frustrating lives. Used to being in control of their environment, they found themselves suddenly dependent on someone they'd never met in a place they'd never seen. They couldn't speak the language. Didn't know the customs. Had trouble finding anything familiar. Some never settled down, but most did, seeing eventually that they had been set free—from responsibilities, habits, expectations.

Fountains nearer the palace crackled to life as I watched Felicity giggle like a girl. For a moment I could picture the grounds as they might have looked the only time Ludwig held a party there, to celebrate the marriage of his cousin to the Infanta of Spain. I could see the women in their silk gowns, the men in their uniforms, and in the middle, moving among them, Ludwig himself, huge and impressive in his velvet robes. For a moment I imagined I was Ludwig...but then, as abruptly as it had come on, the water stopped. The frogs spit out a last feeble dribble.

"That's it?" Felicity said, her face going sour.

"For a moment you could see it, though, couldn't you?" Tonia said.

"See what?" Felicity asked, the harshness back in her voice.

"Tourism," Rudy answered, shaking his head.

Our guide for the tour was a small man with rough features and brillo-like hair he wore long and combed to one side. The look on his face was dour, almost disdainful, as he motioned us and ten or twelve others through a set of baroque doors. We came first to a plain hallway, then a foyer, then a florid room crowded with columns and statues and stucco putti winging their way through the glow from a translucent skylight. Signaling for us to stop, he climbed a set of marble stairs, turned dramatically and pulled down on the flaps of his vest. "*Das Treppenhaus*," he announced.

"The entrance hall," I whispered to my group when he didn't translate into English.

"*Ruhe, bitte!*" the little man shouted. He searched the crowd and glared at me when his eyes found mine. Then he put his stubby legs to work on the next set of steps, marching us under a chandelier twenty feet wide, past walls gilded with gold leaf. Beyond the next set of doors lay a series of rooms that ran the length of the building, all of them modeled after those of Louis XIV at Versailles. When the guide spoke in German again without giving an English translation, my clients looked at me expectantly but I only smiled and pointed to whatever item he was talking about. Each room had more gold than the last: gold vertebrae framing the mirrors, golden tendrils and leaves filling the walls between gilded ceiling moldings, gold-leafed arches over the doorways. After two or three rooms it was all too much. The guide droned on and on and my group grew more and more agitated as the words they didn't understand piled higher and higher.

Then we came to the Parade Chamber, a replica of the room at Versailles where Louis XIV would *lever* and *coucher* to great ceremony every morning and evening. Here gold threatened from every direction, dripping from cornices, gathering in corners, giving birth to fantastic shapes: female heralds with long awakening trumpets, vines and shrubbery dense as a jungle, a jumble of patterns and features and images as disturbing as St. Anthony's visions. Seeking relief from the gaudy display, I looked at Tonia, but she was drinking it in. When the group moved on to the next room, she lingered behind and spun around, her eyes following golden lines. When she stopped to gaze at the ceiling painting of Louis as Apollo, I tried to imagine what she was seeing. I knew in that moment that her interest in Ludwig hadn't been idle. She could imagine herself a princess or a queen just as he could imagine himself the hero of a Wagnerian opera.

By the time Tonia rejoined the group, we had entered the Great Hall of Mirrors and the guide had stopped us on a patch of worn carpet next to a heavy rope, keeping us off the polished floor that stretched the length of the gallery. Twenty-foot windows alternated with candelabras on one side and a wall of mirrors ran down the other, while huge chandeliers hung from a painted ceiling, their light glinting off golden figures—a breast, an arm, the face of a pudgy cherub. Here was a room that outshone the most famous room at Versailles, a jewel box where Ludwig could march in his robes of St. George, reigning like the absolute king he wanted to be. Yet, the guide said, Ludwig never held a gala there, never used the room at all except as a candlelit chamber he strolled through at night.

    I was still picturing Ludwig walking alone in the wee hours after eating dinner by himself—pacing back and forth with his heels clicking, his mind remembering, passing the dying night in solitude—when I realized the guide was leading the group to the next room. As I started to follow, a hand touched mine. "Don't move," Tonia whispered from behind. My only contact with her as I watched the others file out were the fingers she slipped between mine. When everyone had disappeared, I turned and saw her eyes lit up. "Come on," she said, ducking under the velvet cord and pulling me along. When my feet moved to the naked floor I felt a sense of illicit joy. For the briefest of moments, I remembered the face of the woman in Berlin, her tug on my hand as she led me up to her room. Then I was moving over the polished wood, the windows and mirrors swirling past me, dancing clumsily to Tonia's lead.

    "Relax," she laughed. "Let yourself go."

    I tried but I stumbled over her feet.

    "Close your eyes," she said, and when I did, I saw swirls of stars behind my eyelids. I could feel the press of her fingers, the touch of her hip, and suddenly something inside me let loose. Suddenly we were dancing together. Dancing in time. When I opened my eyes again, I could see us spinning from panel to panel, mirror to mirror, as if we were passing through the stages of life, the frames of a movie, her sleek black legs blurring with mine, her head tucked into my shoulder. Our dress became evening dress—the fringe of a gown, the legs of a uniform, the gleam of a jeweled tiara....

"Halt!"

With one harsh syllable, the fantasy ended. I turned to see the guide marching toward us, his hands on his stumpy hips, his hair flopping into his eyes. He was saying something about the *Polizei*, threatening to have us arrested. The rest of the crowd had poured back into the room behind him, and as he ushered us off the floor, driving us forward in front of him, he repeated the words I had missed before: how much the room was worth, how much it cost to restore. Do you want to pay for the damage? he spit at me in ugly, guttural sounds.

My clients frowned at me and I thought, *To hell with you*. I felt strangely elated and righteous, as if some useless stricture inside me had broken, making me braver and surer in some inexplicable way.

The last room the guide showed us was a bare chamber with a skylight and stairway but no adornment. The walls were made of exposed brick and bare wood. This was supposed to be like the first room, *Das Treppenhaus*, with its gold and its stucco, the little man said, but it was never finished. He spoke the words with obvious relish, his eyes finding mine. Ludwig's family discovered a way to cut off his funds, he said as he stared at me. They had him locked up. Declared insane. And *that* put an end to his fantasy.

# Chapter Seven

I stayed away from Tonia on the trip back to the bus that afternoon. The guide stopped me on the way out of the palace, demanding to see my guiding license, but I slipped past him and found everyone but Rudy by the gift counter. Tonia already had her credit card out, with a book about Ludwig, a stack of postcards, and a copy of the Neuschwanstein poster on the counter in front of her. I told them when to meet at the ferry and hurried out before they could speak to me. Dancing down the palace stairs, I could still feel the rush of those moments before Tonia and I were stopped, the feeling of doing something I should have been doing for a long time, breaking free in some way. As I started up the path to the boat, I could smell the soil, the dying maples, the damp air rising up from the lake. I could hear the wind and the robins, the two-tone cry of a cuckoo. I was afraid of how alive I felt. I wanted to let myself go again, do whatever I felt like doing, as Tonia seemed so able to do. My feet began to skip and then run. I could feel my smile widening. The tiredness, the worry about what I'd do with my life, had vanished. I'm free to let go of the past, I thought. To do anything I want to.

Then I glanced up and saw Rudy.

He was sitting at the outdoor restaurant, looking directly at me. "Newhouse," he said. "Come over here." A half-empty glass sat on the table in front of him. Calling to a waitress near the restaurant door, he held up two fingers and she disappeared inside without so much as a nod. "Friendly folks here," he said as I sat down across from him. We were the only customers.

"How did you get here so fast?" I asked. He was damp with sweat, his dress shirt sticking to his belly and chest.

"I cut out early—that stuff's not for me. I don't understand why people want to see it. I know they wish it was theirs, but it isn't, so why are they impressed by it?" When I didn't answer, he went on, "You got a job to do, I understand. This is what people pay you for. I'm just not interested."

The waitress arrived with our beers and when I tried to pay her, Rudy pushed back my hand. "This is on me," he said. "This isn't a social visit. I want to ask you something." He handed the waitress a five-mark coin and thanked her in German.

"You speak German?" I tried to remember if I'd said anything around him I wouldn't have wanted him to hear.

"Yiddish. My grandfather spoke it when I was a kid. I can understand some. Like when that dwarf told you to get off the floor, he used the word *schmutzig*. My grandfather called me that so often I thought it was my goddamn name."

I felt myself blush at the mention of what had happened in the palace but if he noticed he didn't say anything. He kicked at the metal chair beside him and put his feet up on it. His wingtips were smudged with dirt from the path and his suit pants had lost their press, but he didn't seem to care. "Tell me this," he said, his voice suddenly serious, his eyes focused on mine, "why didn't you take us to Dachau?"

"Dachau?" I didn't know how to answer. No one on a tour had ever expressed interest in going to a concentration camp before. Suddenly his absence that morning and his sullenness on the bus ride afterward made sense. "Is that where you went?"

He sipped at his beer and looked toward the lake. "I don't understand why you don't take people there, why everyone wouldn't want to go."

"Did you have family there?" I tried to feel sympathy for him.

"No, just a friend. I knew someone who was there for a while."

"Most people don't want to go," I said. "That's not the kind of place they go on vacation."

"Yeah, I suppose that's right." He filled his mouth with beer and swallowed loudly. "But don't you sometimes want to say 'Fuck most people' and take them someplace anyway? Take them someplace they *have* to think?"

"I used to...but that approach never seemed to work out. *Making* people think doesn't seem to be good for business."

He shifted his feet from the chair to the ground and turned to look at me again, his eyes magnified by his glasses. "No, I suppose it wouldn't. And a businessman's got to think about his business all the time. I guess that's right. You can't let anything too personal or meaningful get in your way. That's how you get ahead, right?" I couldn't tell if he was mocking me. His gaze drifted back to the lake.

"But you've been to Dachau, haven't you?" he asked after a while. I told him I had. "Okay, I want you to tell me sometime what you know about it. You don't have to do it now. Just sometime." He sipped at his drink, then swirled what was left in his glass. "You know, I went out there this morning just to cool my heels. And because this friend of mine had been there. I'd already called Lufthansa and booked a flight back to New York for this afternoon. Eighteen hundred bucks it would have cost. I was going to enjoy wasting Gerhard's money. But then I got to looking at those pictures in the museum there. At Dachau. And I came to this one of these prisoners standing behind a barbed wire fence. Some were skinny, of course, but if you took away the pajamas and the wooden shoes, they wouldn't have looked so different from anybody. Any group. They were just staring, their faces blank. The caption said they were listening to Hitler. I studied their faces awhile and I noticed this one face. It was a boy but older, almost a man, and he looked so earnest, so serious, as if he believed what he was hearing. It made me sick to my stomach." He raised his eyes to mine and rubbed a hand across his chin. "As soon as I saw that picture, I knew I had to keep going—to Berchtesgaden at least. Maybe after that I'll leave you and go back to New York, but I want to see where the bastard lived. How he lived. I'm here, so I'm going to let myself think about this. And I want you to talk to me straight. No more bullshit."

Donald ended up sitting beside me on the ride to Berchtesgaden that afternoon. The drive was short but the road was narrow in places and the traffic slow. If we were to reach town before dark I had no choice but to pass the trucks that crawled over the hills like giant caterpillars. Donald proved adept at knowing when the length of available road matched the torque of the Transport's undersized engine and seemed pleased to test his ability. Each time we squeaked back into our lane just ahead of a Mercedes, he nodded almost solemnly then chuckled like a schoolboy. He'd honed his skills, he told me, in his own car on the San Jose hills near his home. This was a different Donald than I'd seen before—less controlled, freer. I pictured him behind the wheel of his own Mercedes convertible, a thin grin on his face as a bleating horn dopplered behind him. He was the kind of man, I thought, who wouldn't panic even if an oncoming car appeared suddenly; he would steer calmly out of the way, trusting his own assessment of the time and distance needed.

Seeing Tonia talking to Sarah in the back, I strained to hear what she was saying but heard only the gentle tone of her voice.

"So you work for Luckspur, too?" I asked Donald to pass the time and distract myself.

"Used to," he said. "I worked with Gerhard's father."

"His father started the company?"

"No. He was a lawyer. I worked in his firm and he...you might say he 'loaned' me to Gerhard."

"But you don't work for him now?"

"It was only a short time at the beginning, to help him get started. Then I joined him for a year or so later, after his father's death. We made an arrangement."

"And now?"

"Now I do *pro bono* work in the city...and I enjoy myself."

"And Felicity?"

"With Felicity, yes." His eyes flitted toward mine then darted away. Though his answers came hesitantly, I had the feeling Donald wanted to talk. He was calm and warm, but he was cautious, too. I decided to let him speak when he was ready, contenting myself in the meantime with gazing down into the valleys or out at the mist that had thickened during the afternoon. On the way into Berchtesgaden on a clear day you could see the brittle teeth of a half-dozen peaks nearby. Even with high clouds you could see the upper slopes of Mt. Watzmann, its saddle-like summits rising almost straight from the town. Late in the season, after the rains had begun, the firs on the hills would be bluish-green, the valley floors the color of rice paddies. But that day the clouds were low in the hollows, and I could glimpse no more than a single field through the fog before the clouds swallowed everything.

"Have you been to California?" Donald asked as I downshifted behind a foul-smelling truck. "You can go."

"L.A.," I said above the muffler, accelerating through a carbonic cloud.

"Not San Francisco?" His eyes met mine for a moment, then wandered out into the fog.

"Drove through once on the way to Disneyland," I said, remembering the look of the Golden Gate Bridge in the sun, the long drop to the water as we crossed and re-crossed it, my mother laughing as she steadied the car on the bridge deck. I pictured her sitting cross-legged on a creosote dock by the waterfront, sucking the juice from the pale leg of a crab while the wind fluttered the scarf that held her hair. Although our time there had been happy, the memory made me sad. For years, I'd tried not to think of my mother.

"My house is near San Francisco," Donald said. "In the hills on the way to San Jose. Half north, half south. If you ever get there you'll have to come stay with us. It's a big place near a golf course."

"I don't play golf," I told him. My thoughts were still on the trip with my mother, the long stretch of 101 near Santa Barbara we drove with the windows open, the smell of the ocean rushing in. That was the first real trip we'd ever taken together, the first time I'd been outside the Pacific Northwest. I was thirteen—too old, I thought, to be going to Disneyland for the first time, but I was excited anyway. We stayed with my mother's sister for a night in Eugene then with a distant cousin, an odd reclusive man, outside Sacramento. Both stops were short—late arrivals, early departures. My mother spent most of each visit apologizing for inconveniencing them. The third day out we reached LA and that night, on a busy boulevard lined with run-down restaurants and shabby office buildings, I slept in a hotel for the first time. It was a motel, actually, with a musty smell that made my mother sneeze and an empty pool furry with algae. I didn't care what it looked like or smelled like;

in movies and books when people went on vacation they stayed in hotels. I stood by the door staring at the faded industrial bedspreads on the two single beds, the nightstand with the battered lamp bolted to it, the orange shag carpet. I was Sam Spade. Richard Burton. Hemingway at the Ritz.

"Neither do I, actually," Donald said with a chuckle. It took me a moment to remember we'd been talking about golf.

"My father played," I told him.

"And he didn't drag you onto the course?"

"Once he did." It was the same summer, I remembered. My father was in the last year of his life. Maybe he knew it. He called me—the only time he ever did—and told me he wanted to teach me something about golf. My mother said it was the only thing he'd ever done halfway well and I should go just to see what he was like for myself, so I wouldn't blame her for never having had a father. "My parents divorced when I was a kid," I said. "I never really knew him."

Donald told me then that he'd grown up without a father, too, but he'd been lucky. His mother had known Gerhard's father somehow. "Mr. Gluck gave me a job when I turned sixteen," he said. "I worked after school and on weekends whenever he was preparing for trial. When I was old enough, he sent me to law school, paying for everything. He was really taking care of my mother, I think, but when she died he spent even more time with me, talking through trial strategies, reminiscing about coming across from Germany when he was four, the difficulty of learning English so late and going to school when the Germans were hated during the First World War. He seemed to like to confide in me."

Donald paused and turned his head awkwardly to look behind him. Tonia and Sarah were still talking in back, but Rudy and Felicity had their eyes closed.

"We used to sit in his study late at night," Donald said when he had turned back toward the windshield. "Just the two of us drinking cognac, talking law. It was what he really loved. 'Without law and lawyers, there would be no civilization,' he'd say, his 'w's sounding more and more like 'v's, the more he drank. Sometimes Gerhard would peek in at the door. '*Ja*, come, Gerdy,' he'd say and Gerhard would walk over to his chair. Gerhard was a big kid but he always looked small beside his father. He'd stand by the chair looking down until his father spoke to him. 'Who is the greatest man in America?' Mr. Gluck would ask—always the same question." Donald smiled. "Gerhard would pretend not to know. Then, after naming and dismissing men like Jefferson or Lincoln, he'd say, 'Perry Mason?' Just like that, as a question, and the two of them would laugh and laugh. '"Why?' Mr. Gluck would ask. And Gerhard would answer, 'Because he never lost.'"

Donald let his smile fade as his gaze shifted to the passing trees. "He was a good man, Mr. Gluck," he said absently. "I was quite devoted to him."

"So you've known Gerhard a long time," I said.

"A long time," he answered, still staring into the woods. "Too long maybe."

Listening to Donald's description of his relationship with Gerhard's father made me think of how differently my own life had gone. Shortly after that trip to Disneyland, my mother moved us to a new neighborhood in Seattle, where I spent my afternoons reading by the living room window, waiting for her to come home. She and I were especially close that year—too close maybe for a boy that age, but neither of us had anyone else. And we both had dreams we wanted to share. *One day*, she'd say, she'd meet a man who'd change her life forever. She would describe the way he'd dress, the things he'd say, the house he'd buy for her full of anything she could imagine. I'd tell her, in turn, about the places I'd go, the things I'd see—things I'd read about in my books, almost all of which were novels. Their pages took me into the jungles of Peru, up the mountains of central Nepal, sailing alone across the Pacific, bound for foreign lands.

    My mother worked for a company that processed fish brought down from Alaska. The fish came in late in the afternoon and were packed during the night so they could be put onto trucks early the next day. My mother's job was to keep track of the paperwork and make sure each driver received his proper allotment. Mornings when I was small, she'd wake me before she left for work and talk to me softly while she made our lunches by the light of the bulb on the stove. When she was done, she'd fill a small saucepan with milk, heat it and stir in chocolate, then pour it into a cup for me to drink with my toast. As I watched her, I'd ask where the fish were going that day. Sometimes she'd tell me the truth, but if they were only going as far as Portland or Boise, she'd make up exotic destinations: Kamchatka, Uppsala, Timbuktu. She had a mother's knack for choosing names that would make me laugh. When she'd kissed me on the cheek and hurried out to her car, I'd watch her back the Chevy into the street before pulling the atlas down from its shelf, repeating the names in my head so I wouldn't forget them. I'd try to find them all before I had to dress for school, and on the school bus I'd sit by myself, imagining what each was like.

By the time we moved to that new Seattle house, however, I'd stopped rising early. My mother would knock on my door to wake me before she left for work and I wouldn't see her till evening. One morning, though, she knocked later than usual, too late for her to still be home, and when she opened the door, I was standing in the middle of the room in my underwear. "Joseph," she said as she straightened my blankets, "sit here beside me. Here, on the bed." It didn't seem to bother her that I was almost naked, but at fourteen I was painfully aware of my body. When I sat down, I sat as far from her as I could and pulled the blankets over my legs.

"Your father..." she began without looking at me. Her eyelids fluttered and she put a hand to her cheek. Only then did I notice she was holding something in her other hand: a newspaper clipping with a picture of a man in a military uniform. "Your father's dead," she said, passing the clipping to me. At first I thought she was mistaken—the face in the picture was thinner than my father's face; my father had a beard. At the same time, it didn't really matter whether her news was true or not. I felt nothing. "I suppose it was the only photo good enough to give to the newspapers," she said, reading my thoughts.

"Local Man, Family, Die in Tragic Accident," the headline read. According to the article, my father was parked on the edge of a road near the coast eating a picnic lunch with his wife and their two infant sons when a logging truck rounded the corner too fast and lost its load. The logs crushed the car, killing my father and the boys. The wife was listed as his sole survivor. There was no mention of my mother. Or me.

When my mother asked if I wanted to talk about what had happened, I said no. She seemed hesitant to go to work. "You're sure you're alright," she said. "You'll call me if you're sad later." I assured her I would, but all I wanted was to be left alone. The truth was I already thought of my father as dead, even after he took me golfing. I'd been telling my classmates for years that he died in Vietnam. I couldn't really convince myself that he'd died a hero, but because I never heard from him, I could imagine the *possibility*. The only feeling I had when I saw his picture—a feeling accentuated by seeing him in a military uniform—was disappointment. Not only had he never been a hero but there was no chance anymore he'd ever be one.

My mother never mentioned my father after that. His new wife called a year later and asked if she could see me, hoping perhaps to find some piece of the man she'd loved. My mother left the decision to me and I said no. Did I want some reminder of my father? the woman asked. No, I said again, but a month later a package came in the mail. Inside was a pair of tartan golf club covers with the name "Newhouse" stitched onto them and a note. "Your father picked these up in Britain when we were there last year," his wife wrote. "A little piece of your heritage." They were just big enough to slip over my fists, and when I worked on my bicycle that spring, I used them to wipe off the grease.

In the months after my father died, my mother was especially attentive to me. She asked sometimes if I missed him; other times she asked if I wanted her to date more, if it would help to have a man around the house. I was fourteen, tall for my age but too awkward to use my height to advantage in sports and too shy to play anyway. I was full of that anxiety that comes with having everything changing all at once and feeling you'll never do anything well. The last thing I wanted was a man around to see how incompetent I was.

But one night that spring while preparing for a history test on the flight of the Nez Perce Indians, I made a discovery. I was studying the Nez Perce route from Montana through Idaho to eastern Washington when I saw an "X" in southern Montana that marked the Custer Battlefield. It was closer to Seattle, I realized, than Disneyland. The thought—so ordinary to me later but unique then—that I could *travel* to a place where history had been made excited me. I began to plead with my mother to drive me to the Little Big Horn.

The Little Big Horn had carved its way down into me since grade school, forming and widening the channel through which, eventually, my love of travel would flow. A passing classroom reference to Custer had sent me to the public library near my house where I found two children's books on him. When I'd read them both, I asked the librarian if there were more and she directed me to the adult section, which, of course, was not a section at all but the rest of the library. The way I felt that day as I gazed at all of the books I could read was similar to the way I would feel years later when I realized I could go anywhere in the world and see anything I'd ever read about.

I never knew what it was about Custer that caught my interest, but once I'd discovered him, I studied his life as if it were a blueprint for mine. I pestered my mother to buy maps of the United States so I could trace his route from West Point through the Civil War and into Indian Territory. I ran my fingers over the states, from New York to Georgia and up through the Black Hills to Wyoming and Montana, wondering what each of them was like yet never thinking I could visit them.

All through that spring I begged my mother to take me to Montana. The prairie grass and dry, rolling hills became my dream. I went back to the library and checked out the books I'd read on Custer to memorize the battlefield layout. My mother grew impatient with me, but I thought over time I could wear her down. "We drove to California," I argued when she said that eastern Montana was too far to go with a car.

"Joe," she explained to me, "the route to California is mostly flat, and besides, we knew people along the way. To get to Montana we'd have to cross the Rockies. And who do we know out there?"

What she was saying was not that we needed to know people in a place to make it our destination but that we needed somewhere to stay along the way, friends or relatives with whom we could spend the night for free.

It seemed my pleading would never move her, but I was not about to give up. Then, one Saturday in early April, I hit on a strategy that worked: I used my mother's guilt to persuade her, not realizing I was sacrificing the closeness between us that had always meant so much. She was cleaning the house that morning, moving from room to room, and I was following her, pestering her about the trip, when she stopped and glowered at me.

"I don't want to hear any more about this," she said.

"You don't care if I don't have anything," was my reply, "if I don't even have a father."

I let my words sink in, then turned and slouched to my room.

I didn't speak to my mother the rest of that weekend. Monday morning she shouted goodbye before she left for work, but I didn't answer. When she came home that evening, I was in my room. She knocked, but this time she waited until I invited her to enter. She didn't sit on the bed or ask me to sit beside her. Instead, she laid down a set of keys.

"Do you still want to go to Montana?" she asked.

I nodded.

"You're sure?"

"Yes, I'm sure," I said.

"I've bought a trailer," she said. "God knows how we'll get it over the Rockies, but I won't have you bringing up your father for the rest of my life."

The joy I felt at knowing I'd see the battlefield that summer—and my excitement later when I stood where Custer had stood—was always tempered by an understanding of what I'd done to get there.

# Chapter Eight

We arrived in Berchtesgaden at six that evening. Our hotel, on a slope west of town, was a German farmhouse with a small courtyard and rooms up under the eaves. On a clear day you could see Mt. Watzmann and, at night, the town lights flickering like stars. I'd stayed there only once before, on a ski vacation with Cat the previous winter. The owner was a former Hungarian hockey player with the improbable name of Tibor Schliemann, a large, friendly man I'd met through a Czech-born neighbor in Munich. Although our neighbor had fled Eastern Europe as soon as he could, he was proud to be from what he called "the more human Europe." Tibor, on the other hand, insisted he'd only been exiled there, a refugee from Germany. "Look, last name— Schleeeemann," he explained over schnapps one night, blurring the vowels to emphasize the German diphthong. "Most famous German name after Beethoven. You know, he find gold at Troja." I assured him I knew who Heinrich Schliemann the archaeologist was. "Maybe great-great grandfather," he said, tapping his chest. "Maybe someday I find gold, too, now that I'm free of communists."

As Tonia and the others headed to their rooms, I remembered sitting up late that night with Tibor, listening to the hush of the fire while the snow fell silently outside. As usual, Cat had gone to bed early. To her, there was nothing said at night that couldn't be said in the morning. But I knew from experience that when you travel the things people say at night are those they never utter in daylight. I don't know where Tibor learned English but he spoke it in his own inimitable way, with sounds and rhythms borrowed from his mother's Hungarian, his father's German, and the Russian he'd been forced to learn in school. Sometimes he sounded like Leonid Brezhnev or Peter Lorre, other times like Colonel Klink. His uncle had been the richest man in Berchtesgaden in the 1930s, he told me, a contractor who handled most of the local construction for the new Nazi regime. Berchtesgaden had grown from a village into a town in the 19th century but the biggest building boom came when Hitler chose the nearby Obersalzberg area for his mountain retreat. Tibor's uncle was told the major building projects would all be his if he could accomplish one task: ridding the town of his brother's wife. Tibor's mother was from a small farm near Debrecen in eastern Hungary and dressed in colorful Hungarian clothes. When his father brought her back from Vienna as his bride, the people of Berchtesgaden called her 'The Gypsy.' Her skin was too dark, they said, and her energy was of the wrong kind, impulsive rather than industrious. One night Tibor's uncle came to his father and told him to send his wife and his son away. The father argued at first, then agreed, thinking he could follow later. The next day Tibor and his mother left for her parent's farm in Debrecen, but before his father could join them there, he was pressed into service in the German military. He died, Tibor thought, somewhere near Stalingrad.

Throughout the war and the long communist period that followed, Tibor remembered his German father and the farm he'd known as a young boy. As a hockey star in the days just after the Soviets invaded Hungary, he was allowed to travel, but only as far as Leipzig or East Berlin. When his hockey career ended, he tried to go west, but it was impossible to get a visa. For several years he worked as a cowboy on the Pusta, the broad central Hungarian plain, hoping the borders would open. When they finally did six years ago, he and his mother were among the first to flee. They were able to reclaim the family farmhouse, though not the farm, and with help from people who remembered his father, they managed to turn their former home into a small hotel. It had just opened when Cat and I stayed there.

Tibor had converted the farmhouse basement into a grotto-like restaurant with stuccoed walls made to look like those of a French wine *cave*. Above the entrance he'd hung a sign that said, *Lasciate ogne speranza, voi ch'intrate*. It was his little joke, he said, a jab at the Germans who thought there was nothing worth reading outside their own language. The restaurant ceiling was black from the smoke of candles he set in clusters on the tables and thick with coins his guests had shoved into the softened plaster for good luck.

When I went down early that evening, the restaurant was empty, the candles unlit. The only light came from a shaft of sun through a gap in the clouds. I sat on the stairs in its glow, thinking about my dance with Tonia. It seemed my life had been running along in black-and-white until those moments spooled out in color. What was it, I wondered, about something so simple? So seemingly small? The passion and the joy in Tonia's face? The privilege implied by ducking past the barrier? The feeling that we were breaking free by breaking rules, as if the ordinary prohibitions didn't apply to us? The only thing I knew was true was that I'd *felt* something during that dance I hadn't felt in a long time, if ever.

When the sunlight vanished, I felt the melancholy I often felt at the end of a tour day, but instead of trying to drive it away, I let it deepen. Feeling deeply, it seemed, was the only way to understand the dance. To have a chance of bringing back the color.

"Ahhh, what is this! You sit alone in dark! Stupid girl!"

I turned to see Tibor's giant form filling the top of the stairs. With the light behind him, he looked like a huge bear falling toward me. The *girl*, I assumed was the pale waif with the halting German who'd checked us in.

"You sit here like Dante, eh?" he said, laughing and putting his arms around me. "Lost in il Purgatorio." With the flip of a switch, he lit a gallery of lights. "Presto, Paradiso!" he shouted, his eyes lost in a doughy grin. In the light I could see his black hair was streaked with white and he had gained at least thirty pounds in the months since we'd had that schnapps together.

"Eh..." he said when he saw me studying him. "Big changes, huh? Owning a business...and Mama, she not well." He shook his fat head. "But tonight, you are here, and we have the celebration. Tonight we serve mama's specialty, the *palatschinken*! You will like. Sit, sit!" He pointed me to a heavy table where tiny American flags bloomed from shot glasses filled with sand. "You drink the Spaten or the Bull's Blood?" he asked, pronouncing *bull* as if it rhymed with *ghoul* or *fool*.

"The Bull's Blood, of course," I said and he disappeared into the kitchen, returning a moment later with four black bottles and a half-dozen glasses. "Tonight, Bull's Blood—I," he said, pointing to himself before putting a glass in front of each place setting. I tried to tell him my clients could pay for their own wine, but he cut me off. "No. Small group. Bull's Blood very cheap." He opened a bottle and poured out two glasses.

"*Prosit!*" he said, draining his glass with one quick flick of his fingers then reaching down to light the first of the table candles. "Tonight, one more surprise. Mama, she feel better, we play. You learn songs of Hungaria."

When the candles were lit, he turned off the overhead lights, bathing the room in a primitive glow. The candlelight gleamed from the coins on the ceiling and objects affixed to the walls: the blade of a skate, the wheel of a spur, the metal ring on a dusty saddle. In a frame near the stairs, it lit a jersey with "Schliemann" stitched to its back. I was trying to imagine how Tibor could ever have fit into such a small shirt when a pair of black-stockinged legs appeared on the stairway. My heart jumped at first, but then I saw the bent hand, the knobby knuckles—it was Felicity, holding something out in front of her.

The skin of her neck looked jaundiced in the candlelight but her face had been rouged to life, her lips painted a cherry red.

"It's good you're alone," she said when she saw me. For a moment she looked much younger than she had before, less dour and almost pretty. "It's not my way to embarrass someone in front of others." Raising her hands, she moved them toward me, opening them at the same time. "I thought you'd want to know."

I couldn't tell at first what she was showing me. It looked like the inside of a jewelry case, the uneven gleam of the silky padding. Then I realized what it was: a condom, resting on toilet paper.

"I found this in the toilet," she said. "Here."

"What do you want me to do with it?" I asked her.

"Get rid of it, of course. And say something to the people who run this place. I realize this isn't a first-class hotel, but they can keep it clean."

She set her treasure down beside my hand, then gathered her dress carefully and sat at the table next to me. Using the napkin from under the bread, I picked up her little pile and, without saying anything more, walked to the restroom to flush it down. As the condom swirled its way to the sewer, I washed my hands at the sink and thought of insulting things to say to her until I heard her speak to someone. Donald, I thought, when a deep voice answered. Once the flush had stopped, I caught a word or two—something about Gerhard— but before I could put anything together a second woman interrupted them. When I opened the door, they were all at the table—all except Tonia. Donald was dressed in a jacket and tie and Sarah had put on a black dress, but Rudy was wearing a flannel shirt and a pair of jeans.

"How do you get a beer around here, Newhouse?" he asked when he saw me. The others had already poured themselves glasses of the Bull's Blood wine. I was about to head to the kitchen for Rudy's beer when Tonia came down the stairway. She was wearing a sleeveless blouse unbuttoned to the middle of her chest, and below her short green skirt, her legs were bare. For a second, I forgot what I'd intended to do and even what I'd been thinking just a moment before. Her freshly brushed hair fell like a veil over one temple, leaving the opposite ear and its diamond earing exposed. I thought I'd never seen anyone lovelier.

"Hello," she said to no one in particular as she sat between Sarah and Felicity at the table. The only other seat was the one across from her and I sat down there, forgetting entirely about Rudy's beer. Not that he noticed. He was talking across us, to Felicity and Donald about some man they all knew—someone, I gathered, who had left Luckspur to work for Nintendo.

"But he *did*," Rudy was saying. "That's just it. Six months later they had the exact same game on the market."

"So you're saying *The Cavern of Doom* was your idea," Felicity said.

"I said the marketing was my idea, the packaging, the campaign. Luc came up with the concept, yes, and he showed it to me—"

"And you're the genius behind the ten million dollars in sales?"

"I would have been."

"I suppose you're claiming responsibility for the success of *Fire Mountain*, too?" Felicity glanced at Tonia, then Donald. "You can develop all the ideas you want but success comes from marketing, from letting the right people know what you have to sell."

"Can we talk about something else?" Sarah said, rolling her eyes at me.

Rudy looked at her a moment, then turned to me as well. "Newhouse," he said, "where's that beer?" He seemed willing to let the contentious subject go, but Felicity was not.

"I guess you proved that," she said, "with all your success in California."

There was an awkward silence as Rudy pushed himself to his feet and leaned across the table, jabbing his finger in Felicity's direction. "You don't know what you're talking about so stay out of things that are none of your business."

"What things?" Felicity asked in a voice that was somehow more irritating than her usual one. "What are these things that are none of our business? You forget that Donald still has a stake in Luckspur—"

"For God's sake, Felicity, Donald doesn't have anything and you know it. This little trip is all you're ever going to get out of Gerhard." Rudy straightened his body and turned his head toward me. "Damn it, Newhouse...."

"It's coming," I said and headed toward the kitchen.

"Listen, Rudy," I heard Donald say behind me, his voice more tentative than it had been in the bus.

"Don't tell me again, Donald...all you seem to be able to say to me is that you had nothing to do with it. We're not talking about that, are we? Or maybe we are—maybe we're talking about the reward you expected to get for your loyalty."

"He asked me to contact Vic..." Donald's tone was weary now. I stopped and turned to see what Rudy would do.

"Who just happened to know a couple of L.A. marketers...yeah, I've heard it before, Donald."

Standing there with his hands on his hips, Rudy looked menacing to me, but Donald showed no sign of fear. "I know how you feel," he said.

"You don't know how I feel, Donald."

"You mean *if* you feel." Felicity pursed her lips as if she'd just swallowed something distasteful.

"Will you all shut up?" Sarah said. "None of you cares how anyone feels."

Just then, Tibor appeared in a black waiter's suit with a cummerbund and a starched white shirt, carrying a glass of beer. As he approached the table, I felt that embarrassment you feel when a new friend discovers something shameful in your past—the same embarrassment, perhaps, Tonia had been feeling all trip. "You like the Bull's Blood?" Tibor asked, setting the beer in front of Rudy. "Bull's Blood is pride of Hungaria."

"Bull's Blood?" Felicity said, pursing her lips again. "It sounds disgusting."

Tibor gave her a look of injured pride. "You know the story?" he asked.

She shook her head—impatient with him but maybe interested, too. The others didn't react at all. As Tibor began his tale, however, Rudy sat back down and Donald and Sarah turned to listen.

"In famous war with Turkeys..." he said, "when Turkeys take over all of Hungaria, one peoples say no. In 1552 in battle of Eger, Istvan Dobo—you know Dobos?"

"The torte?" offered Felicity.

"*Brava*! Yes. It come from Istvan Dobo. With only two thousand fighters he win over mighty Turkey army with one hundred and fifty thousand men. You know why, young lady?" He looked directly at Felicity, who shook her head. "Because he tell his men two things...one, we no fight with each other...two, you drink the Bull's Blood. The next day the Turkeys they see the red dripping down beards of Hungaria army and they think these men have eated bulls and drinked blood for strength. If men drink the blood of bulls, what do they to us? they think...and you know what? They run away!"

"Here's to Dobo," said Sarah, holding up her glass.

"Wait a minute," I said, having some fun with him to help lighten the mood. "Isn't there a minaret in Eger?"

"Of course!" Tibor looked offended again. "But Turkeys have to wait forty-four years until Dobo is dead. That is Hungaria fighter!" With that, he turned and marched straight back to the kitchen, swinging his arms.

"Now can we find *something* to talk about beside Luckspur and Gerhard?" Sarah pleaded.

"Why talk at all?" Felicity asked.

"Tell us about you, Joe," Sarah said, ignoring her. "Obviously we know each other too well."

"There's nothing to tell," I told her.

"Well, are you married?" Rudy asked with a smile. He was staring at me. They all were. All except Tonia.

"I have a wife," I said.

Before I could say anything more, Tibor returned from the kitchen with thick bowls of soup he set in front of each of us. His mother, a gnome-like woman with a hunched back, inched around the table behind him, reaching her gnarled fingers into a small ceramic container and sprinkling a pinch of paprika over each bowl. As I watched her I tried to picture the way she might have looked when Tibor's father sent her away. What had it been like for her to be separated from him after only a few years together, to be trapped in another country not knowing if he was alive?

"For the eyes," Tibor said as he watched his mother. "You must eat—live!—with everything. Eyes, ears, nose, everything!" His mother continued to move around the table, sprinkling carefully and seriously, as if to show she fully believed what he said. Her hair was tied back by a simple black scarf but the dress below it was a field of flowers: fuchsia, magenta, orange, pink. When she came to me, she smiled and patted my shoulder, then tottered back to the kitchen.

"Your wife doesn't like to travel?" Donald asked when Tibor and his mother were gone. The others had their heads down over their bowls but he was squinting at me through his glasses.

"Not with me," I told him. The soup was goulash soup with a thick dollop of sour cream spreading over the surface.

"I noticed you don't wear a ring," he continued, his eyebrow arching.

"It gets in the way of things on tour," I said, "lifting bags, driving...."

Okay." Rudy raised his head. "You have a wife and you must be, what, pushing forty? So this is it?"

"This is what?"

"Why don't you leave him alone, Rudy." Tonia was turning toward him with narrowed eyes. "Why do you care if he's married or if his wife travels with him?"

"Donald asked about the wife, not me."

"As for what he's doing with his life, what's wrong with it? What's so much better about sitting in an office trying to make more money? At least he sees things...is exposed to things. At least he isn't confined to some small space. Some limited range of experience. What could be better than living the way he lives? I'd do it if I could."

"You would?" Rudy chuckled. "You'd give up your house in the West Hills. Give up your business?"

"It's not my business."

"Well...." But Rudy didn't seem to know how to go on. How to answer her.

No one spoke again until Tibor came to pick up our bowls. "You like?" he asked. "Now a special plate from my mother—the *palatschinken*." He set down serving-size platters of thick potato pancakes smothered in steaming pork steeped in a heavy sauce.

"What is this?" Rudy asked. He was looking at his plate like a man who'd just been served a testicle. "What *is* this?"

"*Diszno*," Tibor said.

"Pork," I translated.

"I can't eat pork," he said.

"Since when?" Felicity asked.

"I'm not eating pork."

"No problem," said Tibor, taking the plate away. "I find something else."

Felicity began to laugh. "Being back in New York is having some effect, huh?" she said. "Back in your old home."

"At least I have a home to return to," said Rudy.

For a moment Felicity sat without moving. Then she slammed her napkin down and stalked off toward the stairway.

"You can be a real bastard," Donald said.

By the time Tibor cleared our plates away, it seemed there wasn't much to be salvaged from the evening. We had eaten his mother's specialty in silence while he stood in the kitchen doorway shaking his head. "Now you will be like Hungaria fighter," he proclaimed with as much enthusiasm as he could muster while setting a Dobos torte in front of each of us. He smiled gamely, waiting in vain for a thank you from someone other than me before returning to the kitchen. Moments later, he re-emerged with eight glasses and a bottle of amber liquid. Despite the group's lack of interest, he seemed determined to go on with his act.

"When you have drinked the Bull's Blood and eated the Dobos you are almost Hungarian," he said. "But to be true Hungarian you must drink the *palinka*." He set a glass on the table by Sarah and poured until the liquid formed a bubble above the rim. Then he did the same for everyone else, including himself. "In Hungaria is insult to not drink all," he said, indicating with his thumb that he meant everything in one's glass. "*Prosit!*" he shouted, holding up his drink.

"*Prosit!*" my clients responded, to my surprise—even Felicity, who had returned to her place at the end of the table looking wrathful beneath a fresh mask of makeup.

One of the mistakes a young tour guide makes is to think he can keep a group from having a bad time, change the course of an evening with a word or two. I'd learned from my years of guiding to do what I could when I was out in front of them, and then step back. Stay out of quarrels. Maybe Tibor can calm them, I thought, but I didn't really care. I'd learned to endure until an evening ended.

It was a Tuesday late in the season and we were the only ones in the dining room that night, so after two rounds of *palinka*, Tibor pulled two chairs up to our table and ushered his mother across the room. He filled the last empty glass with *palinka* and handed it to her, then poured another round for everyone else. The alcohol seemed to be mellowing them, and Tibor's presence gave them someone to focus on besides each other.

"*Prosit!*" he shouted.

"*Prosit!*" my clients answered, louder and less inhibited than before.

The old lady nodded slightly without smiling before tossing back her drink. Her face was elephant-like, fold upon fold of brownish-gray skin baked hard by the sun of the Pusta. Tibor brought a battered black case from the kitchen, laid it beside her and took out a worn violin. He set the instrument in her crooked hands and she nudged it against her chin, the hump of her back like a hill behind it. When he gave her the bow, she drew it across the strings, a single note rising like a wisp of smoke. Then she began to play. A love song, it seemed. Mournful. Passionate. She sat so close to me I could smell the onion on her, the odor of mothballs. Her playing was labored, her fingers slow to find the right notes, but her slowness seemed right for the song, a sad adagio. Her eyes were closed. Nothing moved but her hands and her arms.

"She thinks of my father," Tibor said to me in German as if wanting only me to know, or wanting his mother to understand that he was remembering his father, too. He had told me the winter before that his mother knew only one phrase in English: thank you.

Tibor waited until his mother had worked her way through several measures before quietly strapping on his accordion to join her. Some of the candles on some of the tables had gone out, leaving holes in the cosmos around us. The old lady's face reflected the light. These were the moments I loved on tour: when I was in touch with something meaningful. When who I was with didn't matter so much as the feel of the room. The look of the flames. The music.

The third time Tibor and his mother played the melody, he began to sing. Immediately, the old woman's eyes brimmed with tears. Tibor's voice sounded strangely distant and deep, as if coming from a cleft in the ground. At the end of each line his mother added an eerie, high-pitched keen. Their voices danced like spirits, one heavy, one light. I tried to imagine what the music meant to the woman, whether she was crying for the loss of her husband or her homeland, for friends or the days of her youth. Maybe, I thought, she's crying not because she misses her husband but because of the years she wasted with him, the pain he caused her in this house. It seemed as I gazed at her thickened fingers, the rice-paper skin by her eyes, that no matter how relaxed we become with each other, no matter what atmosphere we're in, we remain unknowable to one another, landscapes hiding the depths of the earth. I was half the old woman's age and already I'd left my own homeland, lost my wife...and who knew why? Who cared? I had tried to put off Donald's questions earlier, but I'd wanted to answer them, too. To tell someone my story.

The music went on, but I began to notice only the old woman's mistakes: the missed notes, the fingers pressed too long on the strings. The scene that had seemed charming moments before became more and more pathetic—the showiness of the candles, the phony Hungarian decorations, the overdone food, the folksy stage show. Tibor and his mother were Gypsy bears, performing for people who paid them money. What was this old woman doing but biding her time, filling the hours until her death? And Tibor? A man without a real country cursed with even more hours to fill. The loneliness they must have been feeling ate down through me, the strain of having to smile and serve to make a living while their minds were swimming in memories of other times, other lands. I begged them mutely to stop. But they played on.

They had played half a dozen songs when Tibor asked, "You like one more?" He was pouring another round of *palinka*, as he had after every song. Sarah had already gone to bed complaining of a headache. The rest of the group had kept up with him.

"God, yes," said Felicity.

"I like this lady here, Joe," said Tibor. "You have husband, lady?" He put his arm around her shoulder.

"Husband?" She glanced at Donald and laughed. "Of course not."

"Your name?"

"Felicity."

"Okay, we play this song for Felicity."

Tibor said something to his mother and filled her glass. She, too, had kept up with him. She was just picking up her bow when Rudy stopped her:

"No...no, no, no. I've had about all I can stand of that thing." He waved his hand vaguely toward the accordion.

"Go ahead and play," said Felicity. "He can leave if he doesn't want to listen."

"Why should I have to leave? We've heard enough."

"*I* haven't," said Felicity.

"It's okay, we no play no more," said Tibor. "Mama is very tired."

"No. Damn it, Rudy," said Felicity. "Get out of here if you don't want to listen."

"Why don't *you* leave," Rudy said. "You're good at that."

It was then that the evening ended. Tibor had already slipped off his instrument and was starting to pack away his mother's violin. The old lady had her hand on her back and was moving slowly toward the stairs. Tonia slid out to help her.

"*Danke schön, danke schön*...thank you," I heard the old woman mutter.

I followed Tibor out to the kitchen where he placed the instruments in a carved wooden chest. "Thank you, Tibor," I said. "That was beautiful."

He shook his head. "Is not right," he said.

I could hear Felicity and Rudy arguing in the next room.

"I'm sorry," I said.

"They should respect old woman. Yes, she not play good, but she play for them."

"I know." I didn't know what else to say. I tried to apologize again but he waved me away. Feeling drunk and sick to my stomach I left him and ran up the stairs. I needed desperately to get out of that basement. Away from those people. Out into the open air.

# Chapter Nine

The hotel courtyard was empty and dark, the cold air smelling of pine and maple. There was a sweet scent, too, the fragrance of perfume or maybe soap. The sky was a spread of stars undimmed by city lights—the Pleiades and Cassiopeia, the stark belt of Orion. The only sound was a persistent dripping I traced to a puddle under my bus. In the dark the liquid looked as black as oil. But when I touched my finger to it, it smelled of the fragrance in the air. Someone had washed my bus.

    A narrow gateway led through the courtyard wall to a strip of ground beyond which the hill tumbled toward Berchtesgaden. Just outside the gateway stood a long wooden bench I'd found Cat sitting on one morning, gazing at skiers across the valley. "I used to like to ski so much," she said without looking up. "Why don't I anymore? Why not here where the mountains are so much better than in Minnesota?" Not knowing what to say, I sat down beside her and put my arm around her. I might as well have rested it on a ledge. How long after that did she meet her Swiss man? I wonder. How much of being with him was just a desire to feel *something* again?

At the end of the courtyard I stopped to stare at the timbers woven into the whitewashed walls. Something about them relaxed me—maybe the knowledge that they had been there for centuries and would still be there long after I had passed on. I pictured the courtyard as it once was, with peasants in lederhosen shoveling shit to spread in the fields, a horse cart standing where my bus stood now. A simpler time, a simpler life. The kind of life I wanted.

"They look like diamonds, don't they?"

When I turned around, she was framed in the gateway arch, her eyes lifted to the stars. "Bright star, would I were steadfast as thou art," she recited, her words echoing from the farmhouse walls as she walked toward me. "Keats. His last poem. He was on his way to Italy, too."

"On a grand tour?" I asked.

Her skin looked moon-like in the dark, pale and luminescent. "To die," she said, moonlight glistening from her lips.

"Did you see the view from the walkway out there?" I asked, pointing back the way she'd come. My tongue felt thick in my mouth and my heart beat faster. The wine, I thought. The Bull's Blood.

"No, I didn't get that far," she said. "Shall we have a look?"

As I followed her back through the gateway, I gazed at the backs of her legs, trying not to think about what I was doing. The bedroom windows floated above us like squares of painted light hung high in a gallery. We followed the trail along the ridge into a stand of trees so dark her hair and skirt joined the night. All I could see was the ghost of her blouse and the faint wisps of her legs and arms. At the end of the woods she slowed and touched my arm. "It's dark," she said, as if to explain. And then her fingers closed around mine.

"Can you see anything?" I asked but she just led me along. Breaths of fog billowed up from the valley and where they thinned I saw a cluster of lights, a string of street lamps. The trail became a wooden walkway suspended above a fog-filled abyss, the weathered boards attached to a granite face. When we had cleared the trees, she dropped my hand and skipped ahead to stare down into the valley. Berchtesgaden looked like some miniature Bavarian Brigadoon emerging out of the mist.

"It's like a fairy tale," she said in a childlike voice as she leaned out over the railing.

"What fairy tale?" I asked as I peered over the edge beside her, my arm against hers, breathing in her perfume.

"Any fairy tale."

"*Any* fairy tale? Don't most fairy tales end badly?" The town below us was a labyrinth of lighted streets separated by dark rectangles. High on the mountain across the valley I could see a single light through the fog. Then it was gone.

"Not all fairy tales," she said. "And even if they did, you'd read them, wouldn't you? You'd think about what they'd be like to live."

Before I could answer, a church bell rang to our left, sounding the time in ten even tones. Another one echoed it to our right. We stood and listened until the ringing faded. "Ask not for whom the bell tolls," I said to fill the silence. "That's about all the poetry I know."

"I know enough for both of us," she said. "My father used to make me memorize it. It comes to me when I see certain things. Or feel certain things."

"Such as?"

"Such as what?"

"Such as when?"

I thought she was being playful, wanting me to draw her out. But she grew quiet.

"I don't know, when certain things happen."

Her voice was no longer a whisper but it was still hushed and slight.

"Like when?"

"Like when I'm scared."

"Like when we went through the woods? When you took my hand?"

"No, I had you with me." She smiled. "I had the guide."

"You're not afraid to be out here with me?" I said.

"Should I be?"

"Maybe."

"Why?" she asked, looking puzzled.

"Because we're alone. And you don't know me."

"Who ever knows anybody?" She lifted her hands to her arms and rubbed them.

"You don't know anyone? Not even your husband?"

"Did you know your wife?"

I could feel the wind picking up, see the fog shifting. The sky above us was still empty space but things around us were changing quickly. Already the moon was gone. She had been looking away from me, but now she turned, her face a gray mask. I didn't know how to answer or what my reply might mean. "Yes," I said finally, "I think I did. Too well."

"Lucky for you." She sounded disappointed as her eyes shifted back to the fog.

"Why would that be lucky?"

"You don't think it's lucky to know the person you're with? Know how they're going to react to things? How they're going to react to you?"

"No, I don't." For some reason it was important to me at that moment that she understand. "In fact I think it's unlucky. About as unlucky as you can get. What it means is that you know everything someone will do before they do it. There's no surprise. No adventure. No mystery."

"You need some things to stay the same," she countered. "Things to come back to. You have to have a reason to come back."

"Come back from where?"

"From anywhere."

"But don't you ever think about going somewhere you don't have to come back from?"

"All the time." Whatever had left her voice before was returning, making it stronger again. She shifted her weight to the leg next to mine. I looked at the skin below her throat, the white strip of bra above her blouse.

"So where would you go?" I asked, bending toward her.

"Tibet. It's the only place...." But then she paused, as if thinking twice about saying more. "Shall we walk?" she asked, folding her arms across her chest. She stepped back from the handrail but I caught her arm.

"No," I said. " Tell me about Tibet." The fog was starting to rise, all of it together, and for a moment we were wrapped in it. Then the lights of the town returned, clearer than before.

"I went there as a girl," she said slowly, as if she had to lift each word and carry it into the open. "My father took me."

"How old were you?"

"Thirteen," she said. Her hand moved on the sleeve of her blouse, and, without thinking, I covered it with mine. "It was just after my mother died. My father had always wanted to go there, and he thought a trip would be good for us."

"But wasn't Tibet a closed country then? How did you get in?"

"We were invited in. My parents knew an old Indian couple who lived in Lhasa, people who had been there for forty years. They had contacts in China who could get us through. The wife, Meena, had known my grandmother as a child and had met my mother somewhere along the line." Tonia sighed. "It gets complicated...you have to know that my great grandparents lived in India. My great grandfather was British and worked for the military there. Until my grandmother was fifteen she lived in Delhi, where she met Meena at the English school. At the end of the First World War my great grandfather moved his family to America and about the same time Meena married Raji and moved to Tibet. He had a job there helping set up the Tibetan mail service." Her hand shifted under mine, but she left it there. "Are you sorry you asked?"

"Of course not." But I did feel sorry in a way—sorry I knew so little about my own background. My own heritage. I didn't even know who my grandparents were or how they had lived. They all died before I was born, and my mother would never talk about them.

"We had to go through Beijing and travel by bus to some city in the north where we caught a small plane to Lhasa. I remember my father holding my head against his chest as we rode in the bus. I was already sick to my stomach and he was worried about me. If he hadn't wanted so badly to see Tibet—to be somewhere totally remote—I don't think he would have gone on. He kept his hand on my head, stroking my hair the whole way. Most of the ride I slept while he stared out the window, his eyes far away. He seemed oblivious to everything—the chickens, the smells, the faces."

"How did your mother die?" I asked. But as soon as the words were out of my mouth, I regretted my question. I could feel her stiffen. She pulled her hand out from underneath mine. We had been standing close to each other, almost cheek-to-cheek, but now she turned her face away. Several seconds passed before she spoke again.

"I never liked it while I was there," she said, speaking into the wind, her words drifting over her shoulder to me, "but once we had left and returned to the States, all I wanted to do was go back. I felt safe there somehow. Something about the starkness of the land. The simple life Meena and Raji lived in a house Raji had built himself. It looked like an old wooden mansion that was falling apart. All around the courtyard were sheds full of carvings—old doorways and window screens, railings, latticework. He'd been collecting them for thirty years, Meena told us. Some he had brought from China or India—anywhere the British had been. Others he'd bought in the local market or carved himself. Every day I'd hear him out in one of the sheds, see his shadow moving among the bits of wood. My father and I went out to the yard to talk to him once but Raji only stared at us and put his hands out to his sides as if to cover up as many of the carvings as he could. The whole time we were there he never talked to us. He's just old and suspicious, Meena would say. She told us he was trying to rebuild the home he'd lived in as a child. 'You know,' she said, 'we never had children of our own.' Raji had drawn up all the plans himself, sketched out the way each side would look. This was his dream—the thing he'd dedicated his life to—but in the three months we were there the house never changed."

She paused for a moment, remembering.

"I was afraid of Raji. Of his silence. But I liked Meena. I suppose she reminded me of my mother or was just there when my mother wasn't anymore. Every morning she'd take my hand and walk me down to the market where we'd buy eggs and whatever vegetables we could find. The market was only an empty dirt lot, with little stalls and tents set up. The old women would smile and stare at me. And the children would come up to touch my skin because it was white."

Tonia shivered and I rubbed her arm, afraid she'd want to go back. Her words had come faster and faster, as if she was trying to get them out as quickly as possible. I wanted to keep her talking, to hear everything, but the wind was rising and it was cold.

"I was afraid of everything at first," she continued, "sick from the dysentery and the altitude, sad every day. My father spent all of his time with me, taking care of me. Every night he would sit on my bed, his hand on my head, stroking my hair. 'Are you happy?' he'd ask—the same question every night. I didn't know it then but it was a question he had asked my mother over and over at the end. A question he could no longer ask himself. By the time we left I was feeling better. I'd forgotten my mother a little, what she had gone through. My father moved us into a new house when we got back to Portland and after a while that whole period seemed to belong to someone else."

Tonia shivered again and this time I put my arm around her.

"That feels nice," she said.

"You don't mind?" I could feel myself shivering, not from the cold but from what I was doing. She turned to look at me, her face shadowed again.

"Should I?" she asked. Her leg moved against mine and I slipped my hand down onto her arm. Her eyes closed and at the touch of my lips her mouth opened. Every part of me felt cold except where she touched me. She slipped her hand under my belt then pulled out the tails of my shirt, pressing her body against mine, warming me more and more as her hands moved over my stomach. There was a ferocity to the way she kissed me, a completeness, as if she were trying to squeeze herself through my skin. Trying to leave the cold behind. Let yourself go, I told myself. But I couldn't. Not entirely. Some part of me was wary of her.

When the kiss ended, I reached up to push back a strand of her hair.

"Were you ever here before?" she asked. "In Berchtesgaden, I mean."

"No," I lied.

"I was," she said. "With Gerhard."

I let my arm drop from her shoulder and edged away as her eyes studied my face.

"Strange, isn't it?" she said. "I thought that was why he wanted to come here this time, why he had told me to put Berchtesgaden on the itinerary. I thought he wanted to see if we could go back to those times."

Looking down the valley toward Salzburg, I tried to think of something else. Somewhere out there, I thought, is Obersalzberg where Hitler had his headquarters. I pictured the ruins and tried to reconstruct the buildings in my mind. To remember the date of the Allied bombing that all but obliterated them.

"Coming here together was part of a deal we made when we were having problems," she said. "He didn't understand why I wanted to return to Tibet, why I wanted a break from the business when things weren't going well. My father was too sick by then to go with me, but he wanted me to go. He said he would pay for the trip if I would think of him there, if I would write to him and bring back pictures. I saw it as a kind of pilgrimage, a return to that simpler time just after my mother died. When Gerhard realized he couldn't talk me out of going, he told me he would go, too. But I didn't want him to go. Tibet was mine, my kind of place, not his. He finally said angrily that he had to make a pilgrimage, too. He had to come here. But he wanted me to come with him. We worked out an arrangement to meet in Munich."

She was speaking fast again, as if the words were only flowing out of her, as if she had no control over them. It didn't seem to matter whether I was there or not, whether I wanted to hear what she had to say.

"We had only two days, one to get down here by train and one to get back. He couldn't miss any more work, he said, but this was his pilgrimage. He kept using the word, as if he wanted to prove to me that there was something meaningful in his past, too. Something I didn't know about." She leaned out over the railing and pointed straight ahead, toward the hill where I'd seen a light earlier. "We stood on a hill like this somewhere that night—over there somewhere, I think—and he told me about being here during Vietnam. He had lived in a private home and worked in an office. It was like having a regular job, he said, but better. The base had a swimming pool, tennis courts. It was like a resort. The army had sent him to Germany, he said, because he spoke German. It was near the end of the war when only a few were still being sent to Vietnam. His platoon was unlucky enough to be scheduled to go, but before they shipped out he was pulled. Reassigned. He had never told me this before. Never told me about his time here. Never told me anything about his past I didn't already know. 'They sent me here because I spoke German,' he said again. His voice was wavering and I thought he was going to cry. I'd never seen him cry. That wasn't the way he was with me, the way we were with each other. 'They sent me to Germany,' he kept saying....it took him a long time to tell me the rest."

In the silence before she continued, I could hear a river somewhere making its way to some distant sea. Otherwise there was nothing, no sound at all.

"He tried to keep in touch with the others in his platoon," she said, "but once they'd gone to the war he never heard from them. He followed the fighting, the peace talks in the papers. He wrote letters and sent them to Saigon, but he never heard anything back. Then one day he was out on the tennis court and saw an officer walking toward him." She paused and looked up as if searching for the now-absent stars. The clouds had thickened over us. "It was the only time he told me anything that seemed to mean anything to him," she said. "I don't think he would have told me even then if we hadn't come here together. If we hadn't left Portland behind. As soon as he saw the officer, he knew what had happened. His old platoon had been killed in an ambush. All of them. All of his friends. He should have been there with them, he said. He should have died, too. Twenty years had passed, but he still felt guilty. Still hated that he was alive."

For a long time we stood looking down at the town without speaking. The only sounds were the rush of the river and the sigh of a tree in the wind. Tonia stared off into the distance, off toward Tibet or some other past. The bell to our left rang out eleven, its peal timid and far away. A moment later the answer came from our right, the ringing closer, more resolute.

"You can't live like that," Tonia said when the chimes had stopped. "You've got to forget those things—the things you can't change. Or could have changed once but can't anymore." By then I'd almost forgotten what we'd been talking about. It was time to go back, I knew. I reached my hand out for hers but she didn't respond. Didn't move. I felt foolish touching her after what she had told me, but I left my hand there anyway, feeling the warmth of her skin.

"I thought he might be here," she said. "Maybe at the hotel when we arrived. I guess I'm just like the others, willing to believe in something I know will never come true."

After a while she turned and laid her head on my chest. "Put your arm around me again," she said. So I did. And with my free hand I stroked her hair. We stood like that for a long time. Long into the night. Doing nothing but listening. To the wind and each other's breathing. To the sigh of the trees. To the sound of a river down in the valley. Murmuring. Rushing on.

# Chapter Ten

We were scheduled to leave for Salzburg at nine the next morning. At nine-ten I went downstairs, expecting my group to be waiting, but the only one in the courtyard was Rudy. He was leaning against the side of the bus with his arms folded, his eyes hidden by sunglasses. "You might as well relax," he said when he saw me. "Sarah's going to be a while." When I glanced at my watch, he said, "What's your hurry? You don't have to give us your usual spiel. No one cares if we see your tourist sights."

"The sun—" I began. The morning was clear but the weather report called for clouds by afternoon.

"Forget about it," he said.

I wasn't in the mood to talk to him, so I went back inside and tried to eat some of the breakfast I'd skipped. It was the usual Continental fare—coffee, marmalade, *brötchen*. Only the coffee went down easily. As I was pouring a second cup from the pot, Tibor's mother pushed back the kitchen door and peeked out. "*Schon genug?*" she asked, her gnarled fingers gripping the jamb. I remembered the way they'd moved across the strings the evening before—slowly, imperfectly. I assured her I had enough and she went back to whatever she'd been doing as if I were just another customer. I thought back to a morning the spring before when she had taken Cat and me by the hand, insisting we follow her into a larder behind the kitchen. She used a candle to light the jars of jam she'd made—row after row on wooden shelves, each marked with a piece of tape on which she'd written the type and the date of the canning. She'd used the same word then—*genug*: enough. We have enough for all your groups, she'd joked. Something had made her think I'd be filling her hotel with tourists, making her son wealthy.

    I was back outside when Sarah finally appeared. She was wearing dark glasses herself. They made her eyes look like two large periods, the cheeks below them powdered and rouged.

    "There's Princess," Rudy said.

    "Give it a rest," she told him.

    "See?" Rudy glanced at me. "No problem missing a sight or two."

    "God, what was in that wine?" Sarah asked as I unlocked the bus.

    "Blood, honey," Rudy said in a deep voice. "*Boool's* blood."

    "I don't care what anyone says, I'm riding up here." She crawled into the front seat beside me. "God help us if this road isn't straight."

    The others came at the honk of the horn. Although I'd been anxious to see Tonia all morning, I felt oddly chilled when she appeared. She was wearing sunglasses, too, as round and opaque as Sarah's. I watched her climb into the rear of the bus and take the seat farthest back. She sat with her hand covering her mouth, her head turned toward the window, and I wondered if she wished the previous night hadn't happened.

Everyone was subdued that morning. Even me. I didn't have much to say about Salzburg so we rode in silence for a while. Most Americans know nothing about the city except that scenes from *The Sound of Music* were shot there and it has some connection to Mozart. Eventually, I told them about Mozart's childhood, but I didn't say he hated the city, thought it a two-bit provincial town, or tell them Salzburg never cared for him. Everyone in Salzburg loves Mozart now, just as every town loves its dead, especially if they earn it money. I told them about the Mozart Festival that draws people from around the world. And then I told them we'd be seeing one of his operas that night, a special performance of *Cosi Fan Tutte* to celebrate Salzburg's one-thousandth year.

"Tonight!" Felicity shrieked when she heard what we'd be doing. " Are you joking? You told us we were going to a 'concert.' I assumed it was some *tourist* affair. We can't go to an opera dressed like this!"

I assured her she could, that Salzburg was used to tourists going to the opera and didn't expect them to dress any particular way.

"You're unbelievable," she said.

Donald tried to calm her. "We'll do some shopping."

They were both dressed better than I'd ever dressed for any event, she in a knee-length dress with a matching coat, he in slacks and a sport jacket.

"Why should we have to spend our one day in Salzburg shopping?" Felicity said. "I've been waiting a long time to see this town and I'm not going to spend my time shopping. Why didn't you tell us?"

I should have said I was sorry then. What would it have cost me? I'd said it to people on tour a thousand times. I didn't have to mean it. But I was tired of saying things I didn't mean, of doing things for other people I didn't want to do. "You don't have to go," I said instead. In the mirror I saw Rudy smile.

"I don't have to go?" Felicity let out one of those mock laughs people use to let you know you've said something unbelievably stupid. "I would rather miss every one of your little sights—*including* Venice—than miss seeing the best thing Mozart ever wrote in the town where he lived."

Fortunately, the drive to Salzburg was short. We'd already crossed the Austrian border and were entering the outskirts of town. "Beyond the hill to our right," I said, hoping a change of subject would lull Felicity back into silence, "there's an arm of the Alps that stretches to Switzerland."

"Oh, no, here it comes," Sarah groaned beside me. "The Hills Are Alive...*da-da-da-da-daaa-da*..." Her voice was hoarse and deep. "My God, I used to love that show. I memorized every word. When Tonia and I were girls at St. Agatha's, I wanted to be a nun because of that movie." When I told her there was a *Sound of Music* tour that left from the center of town, she said, "Are you out of your mind? Give me a soft bench somewhere."

Her words gave me an idea.

"If you're all feeling you'd rather do your own thing today," I said, "I can give you a quick orientation and leave you—"

But Felicity wouldn't let me off the hook so easily. "You're going to just *leave* us?" she cried.

"I can show you something if you like," I said, "but I thought you might be happier—"

"Let Sarah and Rudy do something on *their* own if they want to."

"Do you *want* me to show you something?"

"That's what you're paid to do, isn't it?"

"Leave the poor sap alone," Rudy said.

"No, we're going to get *this* much out of Gerhard at least." In the mirror I could see Donald give Felicity a slight shake of his head. Rudy seemed about to say more but before he could, I had the bus parked. Salzburg was waiting across the river.

Not one of my clients smiled or said anything when they saw the line of picturesque buildings along the river—the pastel facades with their white-framed windows or the zigzag of rooflines pointing past domes and carillon towers up to the castle. Normally, I would have stopped on the footbridge for pictures and an overview, but this group didn't have cameras and I'd decided to see how quickly we could tour the town. Once we'd crossed the river, I hustled them through a passageway onto Getreidegasse, the street the guidebooks call a 'medieval lane.' It was thick with tourists despite the season. Most of them waddled aimlessly along—their arms full of woodcarvings, marzipan, cuckoo clocks—or peered at displays below wrought-iron signs for old-time shops: Gucci, Adidas, Benetton. I pushed through the crowd, and when we reached the house where Mozart was born, I told them the little I knew about it.

"What is this opera we're going to about?" Sarah asked.

"Love," I said.

"Infidelity," Felicity corrected me.

From the end of Getreidegasse it was a fast march up Judengasse to the statue of Mozart where I stopped to say a few words about the old and new bishop's residences, the cathedral, the carillon. I pointed the way to the castle and told them they could take a funicular up to it. "And the festival, where is it held?" Felicity asked. I explained how to get to the Festspielhaus. Sarah asked if that was where the von Trapp family had sung in the movie. No, I told her, that was the Felsenreitschule, carved out of rock, behind it. Donald asked what the dominant architectural style was. Baroque, I answered. And where's the best place to get a beer? Rudy asked. I suggested Die Fledermaus, the beer hall across the street where I would meet them in the cellar room at six that evening.

"Any more questions?" I looked at my watch: twenty-five minutes flat.

"That's it?" Felicity asked.

"What more would you like?"

"You could at least tell us where to go."

Holding my tongue, I looked past her to where Tonia was buying a book from a vendor, an Arab-looking boy in a Tyrolean hat.

"What is it you'd like to see, Felicity?" I asked as Tonia turned and walked away.

"Just something. Something to do with Mozart. I've waited most of my life to be here."

Her voice had turned softer and I could tell that what she was saying was true.

"Okay, I'll show you something," I said. I called to Tonia to see if she wanted to join us. She looked back long enough to understand my question, then shook her head. Rudy and Sarah had already headed off to find a café.

"Felicity's something of a Mozart aficionado," Donald said as I watched Tonia go.

"Oh, Donald," Felicity chided, "you don't use that word to describe someone who knows opera."

"If you can just show us a couple of places," he said. "Maybe where he walked or—"

"He walked everywhere, Donald," Felicity said. Donald's ignorance about Mozart and the world of opera seemed to embarrass her, or maybe she just needed to show me there were subjects *she* knew something about. The only place left to show them that had anything more than remotely to do with Mozart was a rebuilt house by the river where he and his family once lived. I took them back to the bridge and stopped halfway across to point it out.

"You know Felicity used to sing opera," said Donald. He leaned back against the railing and took out a cigarette case, offering me one. Though I hadn't smoked in years, I accepted. I was biding my time, trying to be pleasant until I'd been with them long enough to leave.

"I wanted to come here four years ago, on the two hundredth anniversary of his death," Felicity said as she stared across the water at the house. "I have always loved Mozart. From the time I was little. From the time my mother first took me to the Met."

Felicity began to talk about her childhood then, telling me—or simply reminiscing out loud—about traveling into New York with her mother for singing lessons when she was a girl, attending operas at the Metropolitan Opera House, dreaming of one day singing there. The breeze was gentle, the smoke warm, and the sudden softness in her voice made me feel lazy. There are worse ways to earn a living, I thought. I didn't have to listen to her, didn't have to do anything but wait while she said what she had to say. Then I could do whatever I wanted.

But the more Felicity spoke, the more I listened. It had never occurred to me that she might've been different in the past than she was now. Or that she might've known Rudy as a child. Her family lived in New Jersey, she said, not far from where Rudy grew up. The two of them went to the same grade school in Manhattan, a prep school somewhere on the Upper East Side. By the time they met, she'd been singing for several years and was already training for opera. Her mother's dream was to see her perform at the Met. Once a month the two of them would attend a performance there and her mother would take her backstage afterwards to meet the stars.

"My mother knew everyone in opera," she said when I asked how they got backstage. "She was a benefactor."

"I was good then," she added. "They all wanted me to sing something for them...even Maria Callas, the night she debuted at the Met." She looked down into the river, watching it flow. "I was like the young Mozart, my mother told me. As soon as I heard his name—just the sound of his name—I fell in love with him."

Her thin fingers gripped the railing and she turned back toward the Mozart house, gazing at it as if her own memories had taken place there.

"So what happened?" I asked when she'd been silent a while.

"I got married, what else? Isn't that always the ending to those kinds of stories?" The softness was seeping out of her voice, the harshness returning. She saw me glance toward Donald. "No, not to Donald," she said. "Things might have been different if I'd met him then."

Donald smiled, and as is often true when you don't know people as well as they know each other, it was clear her words meant more to him than they did to me.

"We can go there later on our own," Felicity said, nodding her head toward the Mozart house. "What else can you show us?" It seemed she wanted me to stay with them as much for the conversation as for my guiding. I'd seen the same response in other clients, especially those who were older: hearing the history of a famous person made them want to tell their own stories. They needed to say that their lives were important, that if this or that had gone differently I might be telling groups about them.

I spent the rest of the morning with Donald and Felicity, showing them the Salzburg music school, then walking them up to the castle. Along the way, Felicity told me more about herself. After high school she traveled with a European company for a while, singing *The Abduction from the Seraglio* in Istanbul and *Aida* on an open stage in Alexandria. "All the time my mother was begging me to come back. I'd tried out for the Met once already and been told I needed more training, but she thought she could arrange another audition."

"But you married instead?" I asked.

"No. I was smarter than that, at first. I just moved in with Pablo—Pablo Ortega was his name. He was the traveling company's director. He wanted to be my mentor, he said. He told me *he* would train my voice, *he* would make me great. For what? So I could get the audition my mother was already arranging? But you can't take it back...you can't change the things you've done."

Felicity said she had to rest for a moment, so we stopped at a viewpoint halfway up to the fortress. Our view was nothing but tile roofs and cupolas, all too perfect to seem real. "I was so young," she lamented as she gazed out over the buildings, "and there was so much I wanted to do. To see. The least he could have done was bring me here."

"So you never sang here?"

"I never sang anywhere I wanted to, not at the Met, not in Milan or Vienna, not even here. I learned too late that all Pablo really wanted was to live in Miami. I was his ticket to life in the good old U.S. of A." As she spoke, Felicity leaned forward onto a stone parapet. I wondered if she could hear the music she loved rising from the squares and the churches or if the death of her dream had left the city of Mozart mute.

"Well, enough of that," she said finally. "Let's go see this castle if we're going to."

We continued up the sloped road without speaking. At the castle gate I paid their entrances then led them past the outer walls to a terrace with tables that looked out over the valley to the south. "Maybe this is the best place to leave you," I said as the two of them sat down. I was beginning to feel gloomy, to think too much about my own past. My own mistakes. I wanted to find Tonia and talk to her about the evening before.

"Fine, thank you, Joe," Donald said, standing again. "But please let me buy you a beer." He pulled back a chair for me and, much as I wanted to go, I sat down. It was not yet noon, too early for me to start drinking, but I liked Donald, liked the tender way he looked at me through his rainbow-rimmed glasses, the generous way he dealt with Felicity. When we had ordered our drinks, I asked how he'd come to be so kind. He chuckled.

"I suppose my mother had something to do with it," he said, "with any kindness I have. She was always kind."

"Not always." Felicity frowned as she spoke, as if she thought his words had been meant to irritate her.

"Maybe not always, maybe not when you knew her." He took out another cigarette and looked beyond the railing toward the hills. "My mother didn't have it easy." They lived in a section of Portland, he told me—just he and his mother—where the neighborhood was always changing but always poor. She worked as a secretary when she could find work; other times she volunteered—with the Red Cross, the PTA, the Library

League. She was running a craft fair for some hospital when she met Gerhard's father. "Mr. Gluck believed in giving something back," he said. "He was different from Gerhard in that way. A different generation." Donald seemed to consider this for a moment before going on. Mostly they lived off a tiny pension his father had left them, he told me. He did what he could himself to help out—paperboy, bellhop, grocery clerk.

"Are you going to tell him about your father?" Felicity asked.

"What I told you before—in the bus yesterday—wasn't quite right," Donald said. "I had a father...but I never really knew him. Something like your situation."

"Your parents were divorced?" I asked.

"No, my parents stayed married until my father died. They were from the old school, where you stuck by each other no matter what. My mother moved us from Kansas to Portland to be near his hospital. I remember her driving around, looking for a house we could afford. I didn't even know my father. The first four years of my life he was off in Europe fighting the Germans. He went through the invasion of North Africa, Sicily, even Normandy. Maybe twenty percent of those who went through them all survived. My father made it to the Bulge. They got him there, in Belgium somewhere. A mortar took off his arm and ripped a hole in his chest."

Our drinks arrived and as Donald was paying, I looked out toward the hills to the south. On a clear day from where we were sitting, you could see the Untersberg—the towering central peak where they say Charlemagne lies sleeping, waiting to reclaim his continent—but that day the clouds had swallowed the peaks.

"Here's to enjoying Europe," Donald said as he raised his glass. While I waited for him to finish his story, I thought back to that day on the golf course with my own father, the one time he phoned me and asked me to do something with him. I could see him sitting in the gold Cadillac, honking instead of coming to the door. I could hear him saying, *No clubs?* as I slid in next to him, feeling the leather seat on my skin. I remembered watching him practice his putt through the clubhouse window while using the money my mother had given me to pay for a set of rented clubs. The rest of the afternoon was a passel of images, most of them views of him far down the fairway yelling back at me, "Keep your eye on the ball!"

"They kept him alive for thirteen months before he died," Donald said at last. "I didn't know all that had happened until years later when my mother thought I was old enough to understand. She would leave me with my father's sister when she went to see him each day. I begged to go, but she always said no. Then one day—the day the war ended—she took me with her. I remember seeing the people in the streets as we drove through downtown. There were flags everywhere. When we reached the hospital, everyone was smiling and hugging."

Donald was staring at the table, no longer talking to me. Felicity was looking away.

"They had pulled the blankets up high on his right side so I wouldn't see that his arm was missing. He was as thin as those people you see in the concentration camp films. I don't remember how I felt. I remember the smell was awful and my father's eyes looked dead already. He stared at me for several seconds before saying anything. Just stared. His skin was as white as the sheet. Then he spoke. 'We won, son,' was all he said. Then, with the hand he had left, he gave me the victory sign."

    I told him then that *my* father had died from a war injury, too. It was the same lie I'd told my classmates in grade school, that he was a hero, the first pilot shot down in Vietnam. I don't know why I told it again. Maybe I was trying to cheer Donald up in some way. Maybe it just seemed a better memory than an angry man yelling at me from a fairway.

# Chapter Eleven

When I left Felicity and Donald, I went looking for Tonia, but I had no idea where to find her. I knew little about her: her interests, her habits, how she'd spend free time. Sarah had mentioned a school they'd gone to together—St. Agatha's. Catholic, I supposed, so maybe the cathedral or the Nonnberg convent. The convent was on the same hill as the castle so I tried there first. When I arrived, the courtyard was empty but the church door was open. Inside, the trapped air was chilly and heavy with the smell of stale incense and old candle smoke. I held my breath and peered through the gloom, trying to remember the last time I'd entered a church. I usually avoided them on tours, describing them from the outside and letting my clients go in on their own. Churches depressed me, making me feel that change was impossible–that things would always be as they'd always been.

The church ceiling was a maze of late-Gothic ribbing—raised ridges of stone that crossed and intersected. Translucent windows let some light into the upper area and the stained glass threw a few colored stripes across the floor, but otherwise it was all shadows. Sitting down in a pew in the dark, I studied the church in silence. As my eyes moved from crucifix to crucifix, I remembered my first days as a student in Munich—and then I remembered the girl.

I'd gone to Munich to escape her as much as for my studies. She was a religious girl but that wasn't the problem, not at first anyway. Something happened to her—some kind of breakdown, it seemed. We'd only been seeing each other a few weeks but I thought she was the one I'd end up with. She was smarter than anyone I'd ever met and would stay up late with me talking history and politics or go for a midnight walk across the campus discussing Nietzsche or Thoreau. She could turn anything into a joke and had a particular love for puns. When she really got going, she could talk faster than anyone I knew and I loved to just listen to her. She wouldn't do more than hold hands, but that was all I needed with her.

Then she changed. Overnight, it seemed. She'd always had a good imagination, but now she thought the things she imagined were real, especially the ones that frightened her. Her puns, which had always seemed clever, stopped making sense. And her mind filled with religious imagery, her mouth with talk of *Jesus* and *Satan*. Normally, I could laugh about that kind of talk, but she seemed scared of them both and the things she said about them were truly chilling, making it seem they were stalking her. From one day to the next, she stopped walking with me, and then she stopped coming out of her room. One time, after she'd refused to open her door for me, I glanced back as I walked away and saw her holding a cross against the window while flipping me off. I didn't know her family or how to get in touch with them, and I was too scared to talk to anyone in my family or at the school. So I went to the chair of the history department and asked if I could still go to Germany the next term. I'd applied for the program the year before but given up my place in it when she and I got together. The chair told me they still had one spot free. A week later, I was on my way to Munich. One of the first things I noticed when I landed there was how many crosses there were. They all reminded me of her —of how she'd been, of how I'd left her. Eventually, my feelings of guilt dissipated and then disappeared. In Germany, guilt was a part of life. Everyone had something to hide, and the country's collective guilt was so great it dwarfed any personal sins.

The longer I gazed at the church—the delicate arches, the vertebrae of smooth stone, the trefoil pattern that ran down each wall—the less important it seemed to find Tonia. I couldn't remember ever being in a church alone before and I was surprised at how peaceful it felt. I closed my eyes and found myself back on that trip to Montana with my mother, back to those days before she changed, too.

We set out early on a late June day. The fir-clad slopes of the Cascade range were already familiar to me, but as we climbed Snoqualmie Pass, with the trailer laboring behind us, the trees seemed different somehow, like the garlands on a portal I was passing through. Beyond them lay the fruit fields around Yakima, then the desiccated grasslands that gathered into folds like padded cloth to form the hills of eastern

Washington. By the time we reached the end of the state, I'd fallen in love with the land.

In the late afternoon we veered off the interstate to drive through the town of Pullman. My uncle had spent two years there attending Washington State University before being called to war. It was the last place he'd lived before busing off to boot camp—the last place my mother had thought he'd been happy—and she had never seen it before. She told me a little about him as we turned off the highway, about the days before he left for school. They had been close then, closer than other times in their childhood. She was two years younger than he was and their plan was that she would follow him to college as soon as she graduated from high school. "But the war intervened," she said. "Nothing was ever the same after that." When her brother was killed, she gave up her plans to go to college and took a job making airplanes at the Boeing plant near her home.

"I never considered—never *imagined*—going to school without him," she said as the sun went down, just as we pulled into town. We had planned to spend the night in Pullman, but when she saw it, my mother dismissed it as nothing more than a forlorn farming town. It depressed her, she told me, to think of her brother spending his last two years there. "Let's get across the border," she said, taking us on to Idaho.

We spent that night in the town of Moscow, another college town but one without the sad associations of Pullman. My mother was quiet as she parked the trailer then cooked our dinner, but by the time we had finished eating she'd regained her humor. We talked excitedly about the mountains we'd see the next day and the prairies beyond. Later, as I climbed up into the bed that pulled down over the trailer table, with the odor of the mildewed mat beneath my sleeping bag in my nose, I felt at home in a way I never had before. Perhaps the feeling came from how my mother had been earlier that day—nervous at first but then calmer as we came down the back side of the Cascades. She'd talked about her dreams that afternoon, her childhood, and how she'd thought her life would turn out when she was young. For dinner she'd toasted bread and cooked scrambled eggs on the trailer's gas stove. The smell of the toast mingled with the scent of pine that came in through the small vent by my head and, as I closed my eyes, I thought I'd like to stay in that trailer with my mother forever, having passed through empty watercolored fields, with the promise of the mountains ahead.

    The next morning my mother woke me early. "You can sleep in the car," she said, "but we have to move if we're going to make it over the mountains today." The mountains she meant were the Bitterroot range. We'd be following a small road over them, taking the most direct route to Missoula. The road ran through the Nez Perce reservation and as we passed it I looked for the descendants of the people I'd read about in my history book, those who had traveled with Chief Joseph on his quest to find land where the U.S. army would leave him in peace. I saw nothing but dilapidated houses with rusting cars or disemboweled couches outside. "Have you seen enough?" my mother asked as we neared the town of Kamiah. She had been driving slowly so I could take a good look. "It's not what you imagined, is it?" she said. I shook my head but I didn't answer. I was thinking ahead to the battlefield—would it be run-down, too, I wondered, the places where Custer and his men fell overgrown, all signs of the battle obliterated? Montana suddenly seemed a long way to go for something so trivial. I couldn't understand why my mother had agreed to take me when she knew nothing about Custer or the Little Big Horn. She had known that the Nez Perce reservation would disillusion me; did she want me to see, I wondered, that what I imagined from reading books had little to do with reality?

    My mother was not as talkative that day. Her face was a grim mask of concentration as we sliced through thickening forests, the towns becoming infrequent then ending, the road beginning to rise. She stopped once on the side of the highway and told me to adjust the mirrors for her. They were extra mirrors we had positioned above each of the front fenders so she could see the back of the trailer as she drove. The right one had a loose swivel joint and the wind rushing past the car pushed it out of alignment, which meant my mother couldn't see the shoulder. This time she wanted me to adjust the left one, too. "Be careful," she said. "Stay next to the car." The wind from each vehicle shoved me hard as it passed and I thought of deer I'd seen on the side of the road killed by cars going 60 or 70 miles an hour.

    When the grade grew steep, the trailer bucked and hesitated like a horse whipped into movement against its will. My mother stopped talking entirely, her eyes flitting nervously from mirror to mirror. "Watch the side of the road there," she said once. "Tell me if I get too close." Our car was an aging Impala. My mother had never had any trouble with it, but now the transmission began to act up. Instead of downshifting to accommodate the drag caused by the weight of the trailer, it stubbornly stayed in a higher gear, slowing the engine by robbing it of power until the car almost stopped. It would eventually find the right gear, causing the car to leap forward, but as soon as the speed picked up, it would shift to a higher gear again.

Each time the car slowed, my mother gripped the wheel harder and faced straight ahead, as if trying to will us up the hill. I understood then what she had feared from the beginning: that we would end up stranded somewhere, a boy and a woman who knew nothing about cars in country where we knew no one.

By the time we reached the pass, the strain showed clearly on my mother's face. I'd never thought of her as old but she looked old at that moment. I could see that the lines on her forehead had been there for years and a thick patch of hair was already dead behind her ear. Though I wanted to stop at the turnout to gaze out over the Bitterroot Range, I said nothing. She'd told me that morning that downhill is always worse than up because the weight of the trailer is rushing you forward, increasing your speed, rather than holding you back. We passed a sign for the summit—Lolo Pass. I remembered the name because I thought it was funny—a summit called Lolo. I wanted to make a joke about it, but I didn't think my mother would laugh. "Are the mirrors okay?" I asked instead, just to break the silence. I wanted to hear her speak, to be assured by the sound of her voice she didn't blame me for what she was having to do.

"The right one is useless," she said, but I couldn't read her tone. When I looked behind, the trailer filled the back window. There was nothing to do but go on, I knew, but I wanted to ask if she thought we should turn back.

"The hitch—can you see if it's okay?"

I climbed over the seat and tried to see the hitch through the back window.

"I think so," I said.

"I think we're almost there," she told me. "When the road levels out, we'll stop for some lunch."

She could have said anything; I knew by the sound of her voice that we had come through it, though I didn't know if she would forgive me for what I'd made her do.

It was late in the afternoon when we stopped to eat. We had reached Missoula and my mother looked tired and sad somehow, as if she'd received news of a death. The restaurant was one of those interchangeable places you always end up eating when you travel in America, a plastic-and-vinyl room with nothing to make it distinguishable from hundreds of places like it.

"I'm glad that's over," I said, hoping conversation would improve her mood.

"There's always another mountain ahead, though, Joe," she said. "Sometimes I get so sick of it."

We found a trailer park on the outskirts of town, just off the interstate to the east. The sun was close to the horizon but the clouds that had gathered during our mountain descent had dissipated, leaving the sky clear and wide—the Big Sky our map of Montana promised. The trailer space cost five dollars with hookups. I remember because my mother tried to negotiate a cheaper price.

"We don't need the water," she said. "It's just me and my son."

"Five bucks," the man said. "That's the only rate we got."

When my mother had paid him, he directed us to a spot at the end of the last row. Beside it slouched a dirty Airstream. The hitch was rusted and a thin carpet of moss crept down the aluminum sides from the roof. While my mother was backing the trailer in next to it, two men drove up in a square, beige Fairlane—windows open, Creedence Clearwater's "Someday Never Comes" streaming out into the park. They sat in their car watching my mother try to remember which way to turn the steering wheel to maneuver the trailer while backing up. I don't think they saw me at the back end of the space until my mother yelled, "Okay?" and I started directing her as best I could. One of them, a leather-faced man with a drooping mustache and shoulder-length blond hair, got out of the car and, squinting his eyes into the smoke of his cigarette, began to wave my mother back. But my mother couldn't see him in the broken right mirror and would have run over him if he hadn't whistled her to a stop.

"Lady," he said, walking up to her window. "Why don't you let me do it." I was standing on the edge of the park, my feet in the high prairie grass that stretched out across a field beyond. The man had his back to me but I could see my mother's face clearly. The western sun suffused it with yellow light and as she looked up at the man I saw that the age was gone. She smiled and bobbed her head to the side to indicate her assent. In the moment before she opened her door, her eyes caught the light and I wondered why I had never noticed how pretty she was.

The man knew exactly how to maneuver the car to place the trailer precisely. His friend watched with his arms folded across the roof of the Fairlane. "Why don't you invite 'em over—the boy, too?" he called to the first man. He wore a crew cut like my father's, but what I noticed first was that his face and arms were unnaturally white and his eyes had the beety redness of those I'd seen on a possum that had crawled out in front of me in daylight. His movements, too, had the possum's slowness as he walked to the Airstream and disappeared.

We left the car hitched to the trailer. We were only staying the one night. My mother fixed us dinner, then combed and arranged her hair. The trailer filled with the smell of hamburger grease and hairspray. Through the open window I could still hear a Creedence song with the words "gonna be tonight" spilling from the car next door. One of the men was singing along to it.

"You're so quiet," my mother said. "Don't you want to go over?" I realized then that she had been humming to the music, too.

I assured her I did. She was happy again, the day's difficulties forgotten, and I wanted her to stay that way.

"Can you believe we're in Montana?" she asked excitedly.

We had left the curtains drawn during dinner except over the window that faced east across the grasslands, which had become a tangling of yellow light and shadow. I stared at them, trying to imprint them on my mind, knowing that at any moment the sun would go down behind the mountains and the interplay between day and night would end.

"Are you ready?" my mother said. She had left her traveling clothes on but put a white cotton sweater over her shoulders and painted her lips red. I thought she looked less pretty than she had in the sun with her uncombed hair rising slightly with the wind.

I went to bed early that night, the sour taste of beer in my mouth. The longhaired man had given me a can of Budweiser to drink and my mother had said okay. It seemed she would have said okay to anything that night.

The man had introduced himself as Chit. "No, not Chet," he said when my mother misunderstood him. "Chit. 'Chitterling.' It's a nickname. 'Cause my mama come up from the South and served 'em to these hicks here who didn't know what they were."

The other man's name was Darden. I never found out if it was a first name, last name, or another nickname. It sounded to me like "garden," which I thought perfectly matched his possum-like looks.

For most of the night I sat in a folding beach chair and watched Chit inch closer to my mother. Whenever she finished a beer, Darden would reach into a cooler and hand her another one. Most of the conversation was about music and Montana. They left the doors to their car open and every hour or so reached in to change the tape and turn up the volume.

"No, don't. You'll disturb the other people," my mother said once when Chit turned up a song she had said she liked.

"What other people?" he asked. He laughed and she tried to laugh, too. He was right; we were the only ones on that end of the park.

"You know what they call this freak?" Chit asked me just before I went to bed.

"No," I answered.

"Come and look at him," he said. He was quite drunk by then and grabbed my shirt to pull me close to the Coleman lamp where Darden sat. "Darden, hold up your arm," he said. "Now put your hand on that arm there." He pushed my fingers down onto Darden's skin. "See how much whiter than you he is?" Darden's skin felt scaly and I was afraid it would come off in my hand. "You know what we call him? Mayonnaise Man. The Whitest Man on the Planet. That's something to be proud of there." He and Darden laughed, for several minutes it seemed, until Chit began to choke. My mother laughed, too, but she had sunk down in her chair and I didn't think she knew what he had said. When Chit stopped coughing, I excused myself.

"I'll be there in a minute," my mother said.

When I reached the trailer, I laid out her bedding on the cushions beside the table and climbed up into the bed that pulled down over it. For a while, I lay awake listening to their voices and staring at the trapezoid patches made on the wall by the lantern light through the window. The dinner smells had gone stale and I could feel the quiet of the land, the emptiness of the vacant prairies rushing to the east. I thought my mother had been right not to want to come to a place where everything lay exposed.

I'd already fallen asleep when I heard her come in. At first I thought she was alone but then I heard Chit with her. He was humming a Creedence song, but I didn't figure out until the next day—until we were racing east through the hot morning sun—which one it was. She shushed him then called my name, not loud enough to wake me but just enough to make sure I was asleep. The smell of stale smoke and beer rose from them to where I lay on my back and watched the ceiling, my head so close I could see the grain in the plastic wood. All I heard was the fumbling of clothes and then the wet slap of skin before Chit grunted several times. My mother never made a sound.

In the morning I looked down at her, one bare leg poking out from the sheets, her face puffy from alcohol. She didn't move until the sun was well up in the sky and the trailer, even with the windows open, was stifling.

"Don't say anything," she warned when she finally stirred. "Turn your back."

I looked at the wall while she sponged herself clean, then we ate a silent breakfast and locked up the trailer. When I asked if she wanted me to adjust the mirror, she shook her head. "We'll do it on the highway," she said quietly. Pausing only for one quick look at herself in the rearview mirror, she shifted the car into "drive" and guided the trailer onto the highway, leaving the moldering Airstream behind.

That morning we drove the saddle of land between the Bitterroot and the Rocky Mountains, stopping at a Deer Lodge drive-in for lunch. Even while we were eating, my mother said nothing. She hid behind her dark glasses and stared off into the distance as she had in Missoula at dinner the day before. After

Deer Lodge, the road began to rise toward Butte. The transmission responded much as it had the day before, letting the car slow dangerously before shifting to a lower gear. Cars honked angrily as they swerved around us. My mother rested her forearms on the wheel each time and put her chin on the tops of her hands. I began to long for the flat country I knew lay beyond, the prairie land we had sampled back in Missoula. The fir trees lost their beauty in harsh sun that gave their boughs a bleached-out look. There were patches of bare rock and in the distance we sometimes saw a naked spire of stone jutting up from the forest.

When we had crossed the last pass, my mother began to cry. She pulled the trailer into a turnout for trucks and sat looking over the highway away from me, her body shaking as it pumped the tears to the surface from some deep well of sadness or guilt or fear.

"I'm sorry, Joe," she said when she could speak. "So sorry..." The tears submerged her words. When she had cried herself out, she turned and looked at me, still wearing her sunglasses, her lips clenched tightly.

"It's okay, Mom," I said. But even as I said it, I was remembering the pale look of her naked leg that morning, the skin below her eyes that had the puffiness of a bruised boxer's. In my mind I could hear Chit's grunts and his laugh. It was then I recognized the Creedence tune he had been humming and remembered the words—a warning to a boy whose father has left him that the "someday" he hopes for will never come.

For miles I couldn't sweep the words or the tune from my head. We didn't speak again that afternoon and my mother didn't stop driving until long after dark, by which time we'd put a broad stretch of prairie behind us. Once, just as dusk was settling, she had to brake suddenly to avoid a buck that had ventured onto the highway. The trailer pushed hard against the hitch and I thought it was going to smash through the back of the car. The car swerved and slid toward the deer, the brakes and the tires smoking. But we didn't hit it.

"Good job, Mom," I said.

"Are you okay?"

I assured her I was.

She drove slower after that, but despite the coming of night she never removed her dark glasses.

Twelve years went by before my mother died but after that night in Missoula we were never close again. Chit was the first of a succession of men who passed through her life while I did my best to avoid them.

It was on that drive to Montana I first understood how life can change suddenly, how you can think you're winning the fight one day and end up massacred the next. It was on that trip, too, that I first felt the lure of travel—as I stood on a low hill, the tall grass around me already brown, and studied the names on a handful of tombstones. They were names I knew by heart from my years of reading about the Little Big Horn. The battlefield was nothing more than empty grassland and long, unkempt ridges that remained mute unless you knew what had happened there. I tried to picture the fight that day—where each man had stood and fallen—but each time I did, the face I saw on the man in the middle, the man whose life I had studied so long, was that of Chit with his long blond hair and his beer-soaked mustache. I knew then that I'd never be able to think of Custer again without thinking of him. Over time, I hoped, I'd forget what he looked like. But I never did.

It was almost dark when I left the Nonnberg convent. I didn't know how long I'd been sitting there or standing at the back of the nave peering through the murky air at the frescoes. They seemed like shades gathered there in the gloom, souls pausing to speak on their way to the underworld. Their faces were somber, their mouths severe. Each had a saucer of light behind his head and a book opened in front of him. The eyes of several were gone, erased through the fading of paint or the furious scratchings of people who didn't want their deeds to be seen—invaders, perhaps, wary of being observed while they raped the nuns. I stood there for a long time staring at those figures as if I were a penitent who actually believed in their power. They made me think not of religion or prayer but of the ability some people had to transcend life, to reach a level of understanding that had eluded me.

While I studied the eyeless faces, I remembered how Tonia had looked in her dark glasses that morning, the emptiness of her face without eyes. I thought again that I knew almost nothing about her. Was that what intrigued me? It seemed my life had always been a struggle between wanting to know—someone or something—and not knowing. Between wanting to be known and running away.

The only person I ever felt sure I knew was my mother, before—and then, in a different way, after—that trip to Montana. But at the end of her life I realized I'd never known her at all. It was her stroke that brought me home from my first time in Europe, from those months in Munich I spent putting life in the States behind me. Though my mother was young—only 54—she didn't last long. Some days she was lucid and smiling; other days she thrashed around in a fog, spitting angry words at everyone. I didn't want her to die, but I was relieved when she did. The way she was at the end was not the way I wanted to remember her. Even before the stroke, she'd become bitter, angry that her life hadn't turned out the way she'd hoped, regretful that she hadn't done more, that her marriage hadn't survived. She was angry at me, too, I knew, for having left her and never come back. Since moving to Idaho for college I'd returned to Seattle for only a week at a time, preferring instead to spend my summers in the Rockies, my Christmas vacations alone at school. The longest we'd spent together in almost four years had been the two weeks I'd stayed with her just before leaving for Munich. It wasn't enough time to become comfortable with each other again or with the life each had chosen. I could never forgive her for what she'd done in Montana or how she'd lived since then—drinking more and more, running through a succession of men. It was as if abasing herself with Chit had taken her into a land from which she couldn't return. At first it was men she met at work, then men from bars. The only good thing I could say was that they never stayed long. I would clean up after them, after her, in the morning before school—the bottles, the take-out boxes. If she was home alone in the evening, I'd fix her dinner. But we never spoke anymore. I spent as much time away from home as I could, and as soon as I graduated I was gone—to Idaho, to

Moscow, to the town where I first dreamed of living a life on the land.

My mother, on her side, couldn't see my leaving for college and, later, for Europe as anything other than abandoning her. In a letter she sent later, she tried to explain how she felt about that brief time I spent with her before moving to Munich. "I only had you for a moment and then you were gone again," she wrote. "Don't be angry with me. All I've ever had is you."

The day the letter arrived was a cold day, late in November, and I was almost done with my first term of classes. I had decided to stay in Europe through summer instead of going back home to look for a graduate school. The words I read made me more determined than ever to stay far away from the neediness that had so clearly come to characterize her. As I read the letter a second time, I pictured her face the way it had looked the day I left for Munich. She had driven me to the airport and dropped me off at the curb, refusing to go to the gate. "You go do what you think you have to do," she said as I took my bags from the trunk. I tried to kiss her goodbye but she turned away and I stood there a moment to look at her face, studying it so I could remember it. Her skin was smooth except for the lines beside the eyes. Her hair was lightened by only wisps of gray. I wanted to tell her how lovely she looked and that I would miss her, but she wouldn't look at me, so in the end I said nothing. Before I'd shouldered my bags, she'd put the car into gear and was driving off, without a wave or a wish of good luck. The last I saw of her were the lights on the back of her aging Chevy, blinking then going dark, as she braked for the corner then sped away.

    The streets I passed on my way down from the convent that evening were empty except for the doorway lights of cafes and restaurants. The sky had cleared and the air was cool, almost cold. It was only at that time of evening—that violet hour when the sun had gone down, before the lamplight had sharpened—that I ever felt like a stranger in Europe. It was only then that I really needed to be with people, that I came down from my room to join my clients in the bar or started a chat with someone I didn't know in a restaurant. Once the night had completely come, I could be on my own again.

# Chapter Twelve

When I lifted my head, the room was dark, lit only by candles. For a moment I thought I was back at Tibor's. Then I remembered coming in from the street, the two quick shots of schnapps at the bar, taking a beer to the cellar.

Sarah was standing beside the table. "I wasn't sure it was you," she said, sitting down. The candles were all behind her, their shadows blurring her face. The cellar was empty except for us, the only sounds coming down from the bar above. "Are you alright?"

I tried to focus on her face. To find the line of her nose. Her eyes. It was hard to form words, but somehow I told her I was and watched a smudged line cross her face. I remembered the cold of the streets upstairs, being jostled in the bar, a waiter apologizing for how chilly it was in the cellar. How long had I slept? My fingers were numb and my wrist had indentations from the press of my hair.

"Do you want another drink?" Sarah asked, laughing at her own question. "I didn't think I'd even want to *smell* alcohol after last night." When she turned toward the stairway, the candlelight lit her face and I thought she looked almost pretty with the hard edges softened, her cheeks a buttery color. She started to get up from the table but I took her hand.

"Someone will come," I said, leaving my hand on hers for a moment, feeling the warmth of her skin. "Is it cold in here? Are you cold?"

"I never get cold," she said. "I move too much. I always have."

I tried to think of questions to keep her talking, but my mind was empty and my head throbbed. The light was stinging my eyes and when I opened my mouth, the air made the back of my throat feel raw. "Where's Rudy?" was all I came up with.

She laughed again. "You won't believe it...*he* went on the Sound of Music tour. Salzburg gave him the creeps, he said, even *being* in Austria, and he could walk around a city at home. He wanted to see the countryside."

I asked what she had done and she told me she'd run into Tonia in one of the squares. As she described what they'd done together, I tried not to think that Tonia might have been waiting for me, choosing a public place so I could find her.

"Where is she now?" I asked, trying to keep from sounding anxious.

"Don't worry." Sarah looked back toward the stairs where the legs of a waiter had come into view. "She went up to the castle to watch the sunset. She'll be here soon." When the waiter paused on the bottom step, gazing into the room, she added, "She told me about last night."

"Listen," I began, but the waiter interrupted.

"*Zum essen?*" he asked. As I translated for Sarah I tried to imagine how Tonia would have described what had happened. The way we'd touched. The kiss.

"Wiener schnitzel—do they have that?" Sarah asked. "I'd like to have something authentic." I ordered the same, hoping the breading would help my stomach, and Sarah added two shots of schnapps.

"Relax," Sarah said when the waiter had left. "I think it's great for her. These past months haven't been easy for Tonia. Gerhard has been a bastard—as if she needed that with what she was going through. What she needs is someone to be gentle with her."

"What was she going through?" I asked. But Sarah didn't answer. I was about to ask again when the waiter returned with the glasses of schnapps. Sarah pushed one toward me.

"Here," she said, "loosen up. You're too worried about what we're all thinking. You don't have to impress anyone." She touched her glass to mine and emptied it in one gulp.

"So how long have you known Tonia?" I asked, staring into my still-full glass.

"We met in junior high," she said, "We'd gone to the same school for years, but I was a grade behind her and she was the most popular girl in the school. She didn't know I existed." As she spoke, she looked around for the waiter, who was placing napkins on a distant table.

"Here, take this one," I said, pushing my glass toward her.

"No, you need that." When the waiter looked up, she signaled for two more drinks and I knocked mine back.

"Tonia could have done anything she wanted back then," Sarah said. "The nuns at the school all loved her. Everyone did. But that all stopped when her mother died."

"She told me about her mother," I said as the schnapps burned my throat.

"She did?"

"Well, she told me she died when Tonia was young."

"Did she tell you she dropped out of school?"

"No, only that her father took her to Tibet."

Sarah nodded but didn't say more. The second set of drinks arrived and again she pushed one toward me. "Drink it," she said. "You're going to need it to get through an opera."

We touched glasses and she drank the second as she had the first, with one quick flick of her wrist. She looked for the waiter again but he had disappeared.

"Tonia told me your wife just left you," she said. "So what are you going to do now?"

"I don't know." I was feeling the first schnapps already, knowing I didn't need a second. "What are you going to do?"

"I don't know either. Tonia told me she might stay in Europe for a while. Maybe I'll stay with her."

"Stay where?"

"I don't know. She said something about staying in Venice maybe. To paint."

"And Gerhard?"

"You don't really want to talk about him, do you?"

The waiter returned with our meal and Sarah ordered a third schnapps. She tried to get me to join her but I said no. When the shot arrived and she had taken it the same way as the others, she leaned forward and stared at me. "Tonia is a good friend of mine," she said, "remember that. Whatever you do, remember that." She went back to her meal but I couldn't eat anymore. For several minutes, until the others arrived, I sat watching her, wondering—but afraid to ask—what exactly she meant.

"*So this* is it."

The words came from the stairs behind me. I turned to see Felicity peering down at us through the dim cellar light. She was dressed in what looked like a new maroon gown. In her hand she carried a white shopping bag with tiny rope handles and *Christian Dior* on the side.

"It's so *dark*." She made a show of looking around at the stone walls.

"That's atmosphere," Sarah said.

"*At*mosphere." Felicity waved dismissively and picked her way down the rest of the stairs.

"Where's your darling?" Sarah asked.

"Getting us some decent wine." Felicity stepped down from the last stair and stared at us a moment before sitting at a table across from ours. "We didn't know if there'd be anything *down* here." She picked up one of the napkins and, using only the tips of her fingers, pushed it across the table in front of her, section by section, like a janitor sweeping a floor. "We met someone you should know today, Joe." She continued to focus on her cleaning, reaching farther and farther across the table. "He was the most amazing man, a Swiss man—wasn't he Swiss, dear?"

Donald had entered a few steps behind her carrying a bottle of French wine and two glasses. He was wearing a new black suit. Something about the way he looked at me made me think for one absurd moment they had met the same Swiss man Cat had slept with.

"Swiss, I'm sure he was Swiss," Felicity went on. "But he's lived here since the war. He *knew* the von Trapps, Sarah."

"Thanks, Felicity," Sarah said, "but I don't want to be Julie Andrews anymore."

"He told us this performance tonight is a *very* big event. The mayor of Salzburg is going to be there. We were *very* lucky to get tickets. Here—" She thrust a business card toward me. "Next time you should use him. *He* knows everything about this town."

I only glanced at the card before slipping it into my pocket. "Guide," it read, in four languages. I thought about the bored local guides I'd seen in museums or leading groups across squares, giving the same information in three or four languages, each with the same intonation. When the waiter appeared again, Sarah and I both ordered another round. Felicity continued to chatter on about what they'd done that day but by the end of the next drink I could no longer hear her. My mind was finally shutting down, emptying of everything except a harmless muddle of sounds.

"Joe, are you alright?" Tonia was tapping my shoulder. I tried to keep my eyes closed, keep the world from spinning. "Shouldn't we be going? It's six-thirty."

I could hear what sounded like drums beating louder and louder, my head pounding worse than before. When I finally looked up, I saw them all on the stairs leaving the cellar, all except Tonia. "We have to pay—" I said, my words swimming through beer and schnapps.

"We already did," she assured me. She took my arm to help me up. "We got yours, too. Don't worry." As I tried to navigate the stairs, she slipped her hand into mine.

Outside, the others were already moving across the square, Felicity leading, telling them something about the opera. That morning, I'd shown Felicity where the performance would be and I was glad now that I didn't have to lead, that I could pretend to be the tourist. Tonia continued to hold my hand as we walked, falling farther and farther behind the others. "No one can see us in the dark," she whispered when I tried to let go of her. When the others rounded a corner, I stopped and tried to kiss her. Her skin smelled of soap and beer and I could see a double moon in the blackness. "Later," she said, her voice soft, as she pulled away.

"Are you two coming?" Sarah shouted from somewhere.

"Come on," Tonia said, squeezing my hand. "Let's go see what Mozart thought about infidelity."

By the time the opera ended, it was eleven o'clock. Tonia had taken the tickets from me and passed them out, sitting me on the end where I could fall asleep without the others knowing.

"Are you feeling better now?" she asked when the applause woke me up.

My head was splitting. "Who's missing?" I asked when I saw an empty seat.

"Rudy. You don't remember he never showed up?"

I didn't remember anything, not even what building we were in. Our seats were on the orchestra level ten rows back from a huge stage where a spotlight lit a faded curtain. Down the row, Felicity was still clapping, her face flushed and beaming. Donald sat beside her looking stoic, Sarah next to him looking bored.

"It's over?" I asked.

"It's over."

"Was it good?"

"Oh, yes, it was. It made me think about all kinds of things."

"Like what?"

"*Cosi fan tutte.*"

"You know what that means?"

"Of course," she said, her eyes teasing me.

An elderly man in what looked like livery stepped onto the stage to renewed applause. He was followed by a short woman in a judge's robes, two men in Arabian costumes and two women in lace-trimmed dresses. Shouts of "*Bravi!*" rang from the walls as bouquets of flowers somersaulted onto the stage. "Are you ready to go?" I shouted to my clients. The noise was making my headache worse.

"Oh, are you awake?" Felicity said without looking at me.

"Do you know where Rudy is?" I asked Sarah.

159

"No, but don't worry about him. He's probably at the hotel. He hates opera."

"But how would he get back?"

"Taxi, I'm sure. Don't worry. Rudy was born in a cab."

But I did worry, all the way back to Tibor's. On the way to the bus I checked the beer hall cellar and every bar we passed. No one else seemed concerned, except Tonia. "He's a lone wolf," Donald said, as if he thought that would console me.

When we reached the hotel, Tibor was sitting in a plastic chair by the door, wearing a soiled apron and holding a half-full glass in his hand. He waved to us without enthusiasm.

"Joe," he said when I stepped out of the bus. "There was phone call."

"That was a fine show," Donald called over his shoulder as he and Felicity moved past us. Felicity said nothing.

"From Rudy?" I said.

"Rud-ee? No. A Herr Gluck."

"Was there a message?" Tonia asked him.

"Come," he said and led her into the hotel.

"Can you handle another drink?" Sarah was still standing by the bus, looking at me. "I'm going to sit up a while, maybe wait for Rudy."

"You think he'll still come?" I had almost forgotten Rudy already. I was thinking only about staying near the hotel door, hoping to hear what Tonia said.

"Maybe. Then again maybe he got too drunk and checked into some hotel in Salzburg. I don't know. But I feel like a drink."

"Bull's Blood?"

"God, no. Doesn't he have anything else? Schnapps?"

I told her I'd go in and see. Tonia was standing by the front desk with her back toward me, the phone to her ear. I descended the stairs as quietly as I could, listening for the start of her conversation. I found Tibor in the kitchen putting dishes away.

"Joe," he said when he saw me, "why these people?"

"I don't know, Tibor." Tonia was saying something but I couldn't make it out. "They got my name from somewhere."

"No good," said Tibor. Tonia was talking louder but still too softly for me to understand. It was strange to hear her speaking in a familiar voice to another man. I tried to picture the house they lived in: something old and stately, a brick Tudor maybe, surrounded by a vast lawn, with a tennis court, a swimming pool.

"I know, Tibor," I said. "I'm sorry. We'll be gone tomorrow." I promised him the next group would be better and asked him to sell me a bottle of schnapps.

"Why can't I just call *you*?" Tonia was saying as I passed through the reception area. "And if they ask me...?" I walked as slowly as I could but she didn't say any more.

"Don't worry about that," Sarah said when she saw me look back over my shoulder. She was sitting in the seat Tibor had vacated, drumming her fingers on a table. "He probably just forgot where he put a disk or a tie or some damn thing."

"You don't want to know where he is?"

"No. I'm glad he's not here."

I poured out two glasses of schnapps and sat beside her, trying to think of something besides Tonia. The night was still and muggy and I was pondering what we'd do if the weather was bad the next day when a burst of angry words streamed out from the lobby. As abruptly as it had started, it stopped, and Tonia appeared at the door. She motioned for Sarah and the two of them spoke quietly for several seconds—Tonia gesturing, Sarah nodding—before coming over to me.

"You'll stay up with her, won't you, while she waits for a phone call?" Sarah asked me. "I'm suddenly very tired." She seemed to have forgotten Rudy entirely.

"Schnapps?" I said when Sarah was gone, but Tonia didn't answer. She sat looking away from me, her face toward the path we had walked the night before. I thought about touching her, the feel of her lips on my mouth, her leg moving up against mine. We sat like that for half an hour or more, without speaking. And all that time I stared at her, wanting to take her hand but lacking the courage to do it. From time to time she picked up her glass, sipping the schnapps, but she never looked at me. I left her alone with whatever thoughts she had, content to be sitting beside her.

By the time Tonia spoke, it had been quiet so long her voice startled me. "Give me one more," she said, turning and focusing her eyes on mine. When I'd filled her glass, she dipped her finger into the schnapps and touched it to her lips. It was all I could do to breathe. Her hand fell to her blouse as she spoke again, her words so soft I had to lean in to hear them.

"I'm not expecting a phone call," she said. "I want you to take me to bed."

# Chapter Thirteen

I woke to a knock or a shout with my heart racing and my head pounding. Sitting up quickly, I listened for more, but the only sound was the tick of a radiator coming on. A dusky blue had returned to the carpet and the room was hot with the smell of bodies. Then it came again, clearly a shout this time.

"Yes," I said softly, trying not to wake Tonia.

"You need to come out here," the voice said. Tonia shifted in her sleep and the sheet covering her back fell away. All I wanted was to slide up behind her and burrow back into the bedding.

"Joe, are you in there?"

Slipping my pants on without answering, I saw Tonia's ring on the nightstand, its diamond twice the size of Cat's, and my eyes returned to her pale skin. Just the thought of touching it made my pulse race. When I pulled back the door, Sarah was standing in the hallway in a peach nightshirt, her feet bare.

"What time is it?" I asked.

"Never mind," she said, "look at him." When I poked my head past the jamb, I saw Rudy leaning against the wall without a shirt on. "Show him," she said, but he turned away, eerily quiet. "He came home like this," she told me. "Just now." Then Rudy moved and the morning light fell on the swollen skin around his left eye.

"Jesus," I said. "What happened to you?"

The eye itself was the color of sun through tomato juice, the flesh around it puffy and distended.

"Look at the rest of him." Sarah said. She jabbed her finger at nebulae of red and purple skin on his chest.

"Would you stop that?" he said, pulling back into the shadows. What bothered me more than his battered flesh was how pliable he seemed. How oddly vulnerable.

"Tell him what happened," Sarah demanded.

"I don't know what happened."

"Tell him what you told me."

"It's no big deal. I had some drinks. I fell down somewhere. I just want to shower and get some sleep." He shifted his body again and the light fell once more on the bruised socket, the bloodied cornea.

"What the hell happened to you?" I asked. I thought of my half-hearted search through the bars the evening before, the feeling I'd had that I should have done more.

"I woke up in a hospital," Rudy said. "And I didn't know where I was or how I got there. I didn't even know about this." He touched his finger to a cut above his brow. "All I knew was my head hurt like a son-of-a-bitch and I had to get out of there. So I ripped out the IV and ran."

"You ripped out an IV?" Sarah said. "Were you drunk?"

"How did you get back here?" I asked.

"I don't know. I ducked behind a dumpster to piss and put my pants on. Then I started walking. Listen, I'm going to bed. Don't expect me at breakfast." As he walked away, Sarah opened her mouth as if to say more. Then she turned and padded after him.

"You heard that?" I asked Tonia when Sarah had cleared the corner. The room was cooler than before, almost cold, and Tonia was lying on her side facing me. She had the comforter draped casually under her breasts, as if she was used to waking up beside me.

"I heard it," she said. "Come here."

When I knelt down on the bed, she put her hands on the back of my head, easing my mouth down to her nipple as she had the night before. At the touch of my tongue she slid out from under the bedding and widened her legs, arching into me. As her tongue burrowed into my ear and her hands guided my chest toward hers, I forgot all about Rudy.

When I woke up again, my head was deep in a mound of pillows. "What time do you think it is?" I asked, but Tonia just murmured into my stomach and ran her hand up my ribs. "He looked horrible," I said, finding my watch. "Do you think he got into a fight?"

"Rudy will be okay," she cooed before lowering her lips to kiss my stomach. "Rudy's always okay."

Are you sure *we're* okay? I wanted to ask, but I kept the question to myself. I didn't want to talk about what was happening, or even think about it. "We can't be late for breakfast," I said.

"Why not? I'm paying you...." She breathed a laugh into my skin. "I'm paying for you to show *me* a good time." Her playfulness cut against the memory of Rudy's bruises, the sense I had that I should have tried harder to find him the night before.

"You aren't still worrying about Rudy?" she said when I didn't respond to her joke.

"What the hell was he doing?"

"Maybe he was fighting." She pulled herself up to a sitting position. "I told you he went after Gerhard once." Lifting her left thumb, she slipped it into her mouth and began to bite the nail.

"Don't do that," I said and took her hand in mine. "Let them grow."

"I have to do that," she said. Then she laughed again, a second too late, as if she had just remembered a joke about fingernails. "Gerhard used to get mad because I let my nails grow. He hated anything too feminine. He wanted people to think his wife was smart. Pretty and smart. But not too pretty and not too smart."

"What do you mean?" I asked.

She smiled wistfully. "Gerhard doesn't like the people around him to seem too intelligent. It threatens his picture of himself. He wants to believe he made all that money without any help. He wants to believe he built Luckspur by himself." The smile slipped from her face and she looked at me with eyes that seemed to sadden as she spoke. "That's what started the trouble with Rudy, really. Even after he hired Rudy and Rudy took the game national, Gerhard thought he had done everything himself. That was fine with Rudy—he was making money and the game was taking off. But when sales slowed, Gerhard panicked. Rudy had been telling him to do things differently than he was, but Gerhard didn't want anyone telling him what to do. Instead of listening, he shipped Rudy off to New York. Rudy was too smart. Too capable."

"Then why did he hire him in the first place?"

She lifted her knees to her chin and wrapped her arms around her legs. "He met Rudy at a computer fair in LA, just after *Fire Mountain* came out. Gerhard had read some article about Disney's approach to marketing a product nationwide and he wanted to do the same thing with *Fire Mountain*. When Rudy told him he'd worked for Disney, Gerhard hired him on the spot. Right from the start, though, Rudy made him nervous. Gerhard was used to thinking of himself as uncommonly clever, but Rudy was from New York and had lived in Hollywood. He made Gerhard see how provincial his thinking was, and he hated that. He couldn't argue while things were going well, but once things turned bad—"

"Rudy was the fall guy."

"I think Gerhard took a certain pleasure in sending Rudy to New York, suggesting that Rudy was just as parochial in his way as he was."

She lapsed into silence and for several moments we sat on the bed without touching or looking at each other. It seemed for those moments that we were only strangers sitting on a bench somewhere talking about the weather. Then she turned and put her hand on my chest. "Rudy's mistake," she said as her eyes found mine, "was liking his job too much—wanting too much to work for Luckspur." Her hand moved to my chin and she held it still, inches from hers. "You can't be like that with Gerhard. You can't seem needy. Not ever."

I realized then that I had no mental picture of Gerhard. I didn't know how tall he was, whether he was fat or thin, even the color of his hair. I didn't know if that made what I was doing with Tonia seem better or worse. When she returned to her room to dress, I lay with my eyes on the slopes of Mt. Watzmann. Between the mountain and the eave the sky was a deeper blue than I'd ever seen it in Europe. It reminded me of college days skiing at Sun Valley, and suddenly I felt both spent and alive.

There are no mandatory sights in Berchtesgaden, unless you're a student of World War II or fascinated with Hitler. After the war the Allies bombed the Nazi headquarters there, leaving little more than a half-dozen damaged foundations and odd bits of stone. The town itself is a resort town, as it was before the war. My plan for that day was to take the group to the Eagle's Nest, a teahouse-cum-lookout Martin Bormann had built for Hitler's 50th birthday. Below it on every side are fertile valleys and lakes, and in every direction but north the mountains seem to multiply as you watch, line after line stretching to the horizons. We'd have breakfast there, wander across the ridge, and then I'd turn them loose, letting them choose how to spend the rest of the morning. They could dress up in miner clothing and go down into the old salt mine, gliding down a miners' slide and crossing an underground lake. Or they could shop in the town, buying a music box or a woodcarving. I had other plans for Tonia and me: we would drive to the Königsee and take a boat to the end of the lake where the shores had been left untouched, where there would be nothing but birds and trees and the sheltering walls of Mt. Watzmann.

"So we're on our own today," Rudy said when I'd given the schedule. His eye was blacker than it'd been before, but with the other bruises hidden beneath his shirt, it didn't look as bad. I wondered what Felicity had said when she'd seen it.

I nodded.

"Then show me how to get to this Obersalzberg place."

"Hitler's place?" I told him we'd pass right by it on the way to the teahouse. "But there's nothing to see there."

"Don't worry," he said, his hand reaching up toward his eye, "I have a good imagination."

The road to the Eagle's Nest angled up through a series of wooded hillsides before spilling out across a flat plain. The area looked harmless enough, little more than a souvenir kiosk and a parking lot where visitors like us climbed into square orange buses with local drivers that took us up to the elevator. Only a sharp eye would have noticed the odd edge of wall or concrete foundation that jutted through the trees or lay toppled and forgotten in the undergrowth. Called the Obersalzberg, this was where Hitler and his minions built a small village for themselves, a Valhalla of sorts, complete with industrial kitchens, a sports hall, a greenhouse, a post office, a grid of guard houses and even a children's nursery. Beneath the main buildings, miles of tunnels led to underground bunkers, safe rooms and storage caches, each tunnel corner or stairway protected by machine gun emplacements. The tunnels were still there but the buildings were gone, destroyed at the end of the war by the Royal Air Force.

I showed Rudy where the Berghof had been, the huge stone-and-timber house Hitler loved so dearly. All you could see from the road was the fringe of the forest. I knew from a previous trip that inside the woods he'd find no more than a foundation wall. Here and there on the stones would be bits of graffiti praising Hitler—*Der Führer lebt* or *Deutschland über Alles*—while all around he'd see swastikas, as if the woods had become infested by tiny, crook-legged insects.

When we reached the Eagle's Nest, the bus driver motioned us dully toward a doorway beyond which a long stone hallway led to an elevator. The hallway was bare, as dreary as everything else from the Nazi era. The elevator itself was a square of shiny brass that gave distorted reflections. It opened at the top to an empty foyer where a waiter ushered us into a small, pine-paneled room, seating us by a window. I didn't know how high we were but I could tell by the white on the mountains that we were above the snow line. It seemed too early in the year for the snow to be there and I wondered if we'd have trouble crossing the pass the next day.

"Where did I get the idea you were going to make us *hike* up here?" Felicity asked, lifting what looked like a new hiking boot onto the seat next to mine. She was seated across from me with Donald to her right. The others sat at a second table. "I've got blisters," she said, "just from the parking lot."

"In Italy we'll hike," I told her, not really paying attention. I was seated with my back to the doorway, my face toward the window and Tonia's table. For some reason, looking out at the snow reminded me of what Sarah had said the night before: that Tonia might stay in Europe after the tour, finding a place to paint. I thought ahead to where we would be in a couple of days, a small lake called Misurina, near Cortina d'Ampezzo. I'd been there once when the first snow fell. It was a heavy snow and the road in and out was covered. It seemed that day that the lake was detached from the rest of the world, a real Shangri La with mountains on every side. I thought as I waited out the snow that Misurina would be the place to go if you ever wanted to lose yourself. Never be found.

"Tell us something about Venice, Joe."

When I realized what Donald had said, I thought he was making a joke. It was an odd place to talk—or even think—about Venice: thousands of feet up a German mountain. But when I looked at him, I could tell he was serious. He had his hands folded in front of him like an attorney taking a deposition. Intent but emotionless.

"What do you want to know?" I asked.

"Felicity and I were just talking about what we'll be doing there." He glanced at her and I remembered the look that had passed between them in Salzburg, the feeling I'd had that the words being spoken were more significant to them than to me. "You may have noticed we're not mountain people." I'd become so used to seeing him in a sport coat and slacks I hadn't stopped to think how out of place he'd look on a mountain. He had one leg crossed over the other; the dress shoe I could see beyond the table was scuff-less, as if it had just been shined.

"We've seen mountains," Felicity said, as if that explained everything. As if one view of anything was enough.

"We're going to be seeing quite a few mountains in the next few days," I told them.

"That's just it."

I stared at her and she stared back, and I thought that somewhere along the line this was how she had learned to deal with life: stare at it, set your jaw, and never ever flinch.

"Just what?"

"We're not sure what we'd be doing at this lake," Donald began.

"Misurina."

"Yes, Misurina." He blinked his eyes several times and gazed up toward the pinewood ceiling as if unsure how to continue.

"Just tell him, Donald," Felicity said.

My eyes drifted over to where Tonia was sitting.

"We were wondering if there was a train or something...maybe a bus...from this lake."

"A bus?" I said, not really comprehending.

"Yes, from this...from...Misurina, was it?"

"Yes."

"From Misurina to Venice," Felicity said. She clicked her fingernails on the table and looked through the window. Donald sat with his hands in the same place, the same look on his face. I couldn't tell if what she'd said had made him angry or left him relieved she'd bailed him out.

"You want to leave the tour?"

"Not leave it really."

"Donald. Yes, we want to leave the tour. For a while. For a few days."

"It's not you, Joe."

"No, it's not you."

Cortina d'Ampezzo was only half an hour from the lake. There had to be a bus, at least, from there. Fortune, it seemed, was flowing my way. Without Donald and Felicity, our time at Misurina wouldn't be a tour at all. Just two couples staying by a lake.

"It's just the mountains?" I said, turning my eyes toward Rudy.

"Yes. That's right," Donald said. "Just the mountains."

I told them I'd see what I could do.

As soon as I stopped, I saw him coming. After a quick cup of coffee with Donald and Felicity, I'd left the teahouse and climbed up the ridge to see how far I could see. I wanted time alone, time just to look out over the valley and feel good. I didn't want to *think* about what was developing between Tonia and me; I wanted to *feel* my life changing, the luck coming toward me for once, my past bleeding away. I was just leaning back against a spire of stone—just closing my eyes to feel the wind, hear the birds—when I saw him climbing toward me. He took the path where it went straight and veered from it to crawl up the rock when it curved. He moved more nimbly than I'd have expected, his silver parka like a huge pinball rolling toward me.

I hadn't thought much about Rudy till then. If forced to describe him, I would have said he was sharp, with all the characteristics that term implied: quick wit, tart tongue, keen perception. There was something impetuous about him, too, suddenly forceful, even violent. Or maybe I thought that only because of the bruises I'd seen on his body that morning.

"Newhouse," he said when he reached me, pulling his jacket open to let in air. The bald front of his head was wet with sweat and he was having trouble catching his breath. When he took off his sunglasses to wipe the mist from the lenses, his eyes squinted at the sky. "Jesus, I'd forgotten what it's like to get exercise."

I had nothing to say to him so I stood quietly watching him. The left side of his face was toward me, the side without bruises. He looked more vulnerable with his glasses off, his face softer and rounder, the face of Mr. Magoo. The huge coat made his legs look spindly in their jeans; his shoes were broken-down loafers with rubber soles—I didn't know how he'd climbed over rocks in those.

"Listen, Newhouse," he said when the lenses were clean, "I didn't come up here to bother you." He traded his sunglasses for a pair of regular glasses, taking them from a case in his pocket, then fished out a box of Gauloises. "But sit down here a minute with me, would you? I want to tell you something." He lowered himself onto a rock and took out a cigarette. Before it was lit, he was turning to stare at the mountains.

"I forgot how great it was to look out and see mountains," he said through a puff of smoke. "In Portland I had a place with a view of Mt. Hood from several rooms.

Everywhere I went I could see it, even the bathroom. All you see in Manhattan are other people's windows, or maybe a square of river between two walls. I miss seeing something like that." He motioned vaguely toward the nearest peak.

For a long time Rudy continued to gaze at the mountains, putting his cigarette to his mouth occasionally, holding it there while he sucked in smoke and blew it out.

"I came up here to thank you," he said at last, without turning toward me.

"Thank me for what?" I didn't mind his being there, even his talking, but I didn't want to have to talk myself.

"For this morning. For not saying anything. Or asking too many questions." He held the last of his cigarette to his lips, pinching it with his fingers and inhaling quickly. "It's not something I'm proud of—what happened. And Sarah doesn't need to know anything about it. I guess you could tell I didn't want her to know."

"I'd think she could have guessed," I said.

"No, not Sarah. Yeah, she knows somebody hit me with something, beat me up. But that's about all. She thinks it was somebody wanting my wallet or my passport."

"It wasn't?"

Instead of answering, he took out another cigarette. "You remember I told you I went out to Dachau?" he said. "And I said I wanted to see where Hitler lived?" I nodded. "What I didn't tell you was it scared the shit out of me." He lit the new cigarette and took several puffs. "Dachau, I mean. I'm not sure why I'm telling you this. I don't talk about that kind of thing.

That's one thing I like about Sarah, she doesn't ask too many questions."

A group of schoolchildren had crawled up onto the rocks behind us and were talking noisily, jabbing each other and pulling hair as they lined up for a photograph. Rudy waited until they had left to continue.

"I guess what I want you to know is...you've got to understand I've been running from this stuff my whole life. Not running from it, really. Just avoiding it. And now here I am—it's right in front of me—and instead of getting away as fast as I can I'm finding this morbid fascination. It keeps hitting me that this is *it*. This is where these things happened. It's frightening as hell, but it's real. You look at those ovens out at Dachau and you can't help thinking about the bodies that were burned there...I know I'm not telling you anything you don't know. You just don't know it the way I do...the way I do now, I mean." He shifted on the rock and glanced at me through his glasses. "Newhouse—what's that? English?"

"My father was, yes," I said. "On my mother's side I don't know what I am. She never talked about it."

"Maybe you're lucky there. My mother talked about it all the time. Talked about being Jewish, I mean. She was good, my mother. She came from France with her parents just when the war was starting and she knew what it was like for people, her people, back there, the way they tried to hide who they were. She swore she would never do that. She met my father in New Jersey while the war was still going on. My father's people came from Salonika, in Greece. But they were originally from Portugal. They had been in America for a couple generations already and they didn't want to talk about where they'd come from." He looked at me fully. "You understand what I mean?"

"About being Jewish."

"About being anything but American. They wouldn't even go to a Greek coffee shop. I mean, Vasco—what kind of a name is that? They took it from somewhere. Maybe Vasco da Gama, I don't know. My mother's name was Levi. It was a sacred name, she always told me, a holy name. She wanted me to remember that. She used to encourage me to think about becoming a rabbi. The Levites were priests, you know. But you know that." He paused.

"Listen," he began after a while, "I didn't come up here to tell you all this—"

"No, it's interesting," I said. "Where I grew up—in Seattle—there weren't any Jews."

"Sure there were," he said. "Somewhere. You just didn't know about them. That's why I went to the West Coast in the first place—to avoid being Jewish, or being obviously Jewish. Don't think I wasn't proud of being Jewish, but I wasn't like my mother, I didn't like *just* being Jewish. That's why I stayed there after school, after college. I could get away with being anything I wanted to be. On the West Coast you could be Jewish and not Jewish at the same time. That's the way it is when you're young, isn't it? My father never went to temple or wore a yarmulke, but my mother made me...so I end up at Berkeley, of all places. And the first thing I do is put it all away. In a little box I kept in the closet. I never got rid of anything, just never took it out. I had a small Torah my grandfather carried with him in World War I, a Hebrew copy I couldn't read. Some old yarmulkes, too, and an old black-and-white of my grandparents, taken in Portugal somewhere. I kept them all, hidden away." He was looking at the mountains again, off toward Italy. "But you can't escape it. Who you are. I don't know why I tried to. Maybe it was going to Hollywood, being smarter and quicker than everyone else. At Disney I worked my way up faster than anyone. It didn't matter who you were there...it was the same when I left for computers. You get to believing all that—all the nice things people say to you, the phone calls asking for favors, the power you feel when someone asks, 'How can we make a deal?'" He laughed suddenly. "The funny thing is—the craziest part—I never would have seen through it all if it hadn't been for Gerhard."

"Tonia told me what happened," I said.

He looked at me as if he'd forgotten I was there. "She did? She told you...what?"

"Just what happened at Christmas. What he said. What you did."

He looked away from me again. "Yeah, what happened at Christmas...I should have seen it then. Maybe I did. Maybe that's why I reacted the way I did. But it wasn't really until I got to New York...or maybe till I came here...that I began to see things for what they are. It's a fucked world, Newhouse. You spend your time trying to get somewhere, and one day you wake up knowing something you realize you suspected all along: that *somewhere* is nowhere at all."

"So what do you do then?" I asked him.

"You start looking more closely at what does exist. You start remembering what people said to you who figured it out before you did. And maybe you start hating people who don't want to wake up. Hating yourself for not waking up sooner."

I looked at my watch. I had told the group I'd meet them at the elevator in an hour. "It's just about time to go back," I said.

"Let me tell you then," he said, "what happened last night. You're the only one who's going to know this. I'm trusting you, Newhouse. I've been watching you. You know how to keep your mouth shut. When I first came here, I didn't want anything to do with this place—with Germany, I mean. I told you I was going back home that first day. I didn't want to leave the airport. I was angry at Gerhard, first for making me meet him here, then for not showing up. That anger never went away...it just changed. I've been trying to get rid of it, get it out of me, but I can't. Yesterday I tried being on my own, staying away from all of you and thinking that maybe being here could clean me out, clean all the hatred out of me. Last night I took a bus back to Berchtesgaden because I couldn't stand to see Felicity—that's another story, one for another day. I spent the evening walking around town. I was walking by a bookstore when I saw an orange book with the word "Obersalzberg" on the cover. It was in English, a guidebook to the place. I remembered you saying something about that being Hitler's place on the way in, so I bought the book and I took it down into a little restaurant—some place with a sign that said Ratskeller or Bratskeller or something like that—to read it. It was nothing fancy. A wooden bar, a few tables. I took a table in the corner and ordered a beer.

"The writing in the book was lousy, almost unintelligible, but there were pictures—Hitler accepting flowers from children, greeting crowds, that kind of thing." He reached up under his glasses and rubbed his eyes. "You know when I left New York to come on this trip some people there asked why the hell I'd come here. Of course I never planned to come here, to stay with this group more than a few hours, but I didn't tell them that. I told them you've got to know your enemy. It's a basic principle of marketing, I said: know your competition. If I go to Japan, I visit Nintendo. If I go to Germany....anyway, I'm in this bar, reading this book, and these men come in. They're polite and all, they ask if they can take a chair from my table. In German, but I understood. There were four of them—three old guys, two in lederhosen—crusty types, their pants old and shiny, in scuffed boots. You could see that their faces were hard from years of smoking and drinking. But then there's this one young guy, this kid with a baby face, one of those people who look like they haven't worked a day in their lives. Fat and loud, he's talking from the time they come in. Seems to think he's a real entertainer. I couldn't make out how the others saw him— as a kind of mascot or someone they admired for some reason— but he was definitely the focus.

"So they sit there a while—at the table by mine. They order a round of beers, then another. They don't really pay attention to me until I decide to order dinner. When the waitress brings it out, the young guy starts talking to her. They're obviously friendly with her—they've been giving her shit since they came in—but now this young guy says something she doesn't seem to want to hear. She smiles, but she doesn't say anything, doesn't give it back to him like she did before. He gets up to say something more. She's standing beside my table, setting my dinner down, and he's got his mouth by her ear...and then he sees my book.

"'You go to Hitler's?' he asks—in English—forgetting about the waitress it seems. He turns to the others and says something to them in German. The only word I can make out is Hitler again. 'You know,' he says, his eyes back on me, 'dose vhere gut times in Berchtesgaden.' I can see the old guys watching me behind him, smiles on their faces. 'Yeah, why's that?' I say, like some tough guy from an old movie." Rudy turned away from me and shook his head. "I don't know why the hell I did it. I just did it, without thinking. The guy didn't speak English well. It took him a while to focus on what I'd said—but then he says, 'Dere vhere *keine Juden*....' He turns to look back at the old guys—looking for the English word—and when he turns toward me again—pow!" Rudy's fist shot out in front of him. "I let him have it...I punched him with every fucking bit of anger I had. I could see him spitting blood right away, so I let him have it again." He jabbed the air once more. "He couldn't seem to get his hands up, so I hit him a third time, then a fourth...and he went down."

Rudy was leaning forward toward the mountains now, pantomiming every punch. I could see bruises and cuts on his knuckles. "As soon as he's on the floor, someone grabs my arms from behind. When I turn, someone else—one of the old guys—hits me in the ear. I get hit from the other side, too, and all I can see are lights and faces and the edge of a table. That's the last thing I remember—that table coming toward me." He fingered his eye. "The next thing I know I'm waking up in a hospital."

I didn't know what to say, so I kept my eyes on the mountains.

"So that's what happened." He stamped his cigarette out and started to push himself to his feet, pausing only to put his sunglasses on. "I didn't get a shot at any of them," he said. "Except the asshole. I got him."

He zipped up his coat and put his hands in his pockets before taking a step and hopping over a split in the rocks. "I'm going to stay here a while," he said, "go up there a little farther. I know how to get back on my own. I'll see you at the hotel at two." Turning his back to me, he scrambled onto the path. I watched him climb for a while then started back toward the others. When I looked for him again, I could barely see him. He was standing by himself far out on a pinnacle—a tiny silver figure, alone and motionless, peering down from the ridge. The image reminded me of a story I'd heard about the Mauthausen concentration camp, which lay less than a hundred miles from where Rudy was standing. There was a quarry there and a stairway with 186 steps. They called it the Stairway of Death because the prisoners had to climb it again and again, carrying heavy stones, until the burden of all that weight overcame them.

# Chapter Fourteen

"You're sure you know the way back to the hotel?" I asked Felicity and Donald as I closed the bus door behind them.

"We're not stupid," Felicity said.

I left the bus idling in the parking lot and walked them to the salt mine entrance to buy their tickets. The next tour was in ten minutes. "You go into a changing room first," I told them, "where they dress you in old miners' clothes."

Felicity hesitated. "Why, is it dirty down there?" Above the hiking boots, she was wearing a silk blouse and a wool blazer. Her slacks looked like silk, too.

"It's just for fun," I assured her.

She made a wry face. "Fun."

"You go on," Donald said, straightening his tie. "We'll be fine. The hotel is just up there, right?" He pointed to a walkway that ran up the hill toward the center of town.

"Two o'clock," I reminded them. "We're leaving at two."

Along the entrance wall were faded illustrations advertising the mine's interior: etchings of medieval miners working a vein; close-ups of salt fissures running white through seams of rock; photographs of visitors dressed in dark miners' tunics and pantaloons, looking like members of some Satanic cult.

Tonia was quiet as I settled back into the driver's seat. When I had pulled out onto the road, she opened her window and leaned into the breeze. The air was cold but warmer than it had been at the teahouse where we had left Sarah to wait for Rudy.

"I'm glad to be rid of those two," she said, "at least for a while." She breathed in the scent of pine from the woods along the river. She had worn a sweater and pants on the mountain but was dressed in a sleeveless blouse and shorts now. It was ten o'clock; we'd have four hours alone together.

"Aren't you cold?" I asked.

"No, I feel perfect," she said. "Alive. God, I haven't felt this good in months."

I tried to imagine how I'd be feeling if she hadn't been on the tour—the irritability that always came at the end of the season, the tiredness from drinking, the sense of despair each night when I turned off the light.

"You know you're the reason," Tonia said after a while. She leaned and put her hand on my leg. "You are."

"I have a feeling you'd be waking up no matter who you were with," I said. "I don't think you were ever asleep."

"You don't know."

"Don't know what?"

"How good it is for me to be here, to be away from home."

"That's what I meant," I said. "You don't need me. You just needed a change of scenery."

"I needed a change of life," she said.

When I glanced at her, she was looking away and I studied the smoothness of her cheek, the newness of her blouse and shorts. It seemed as if she'd been clipped from a different photograph and glued to the surface of mine.

"You seem perfectly capable of changing things on your own," I told her. "You have a feeling for things."

"A *feeling*?" She laughed. "Feelings are what get me in trouble." She continued to gaze out the window where the houses were giving way to forest, a line of larch trees already turned a Halloween orange. "I look out here—at what you see every day, what you're living—and I can't imagine a better life. If I open my ears and my mouth and my nose it all flows into me...all of it, everything I want."

"This is what you want?" I laughed in turn. "Riding along in a broken-down bus?"

"But you're free. You can do whatever you want. You don't seem to see how wonderful that is."

"I suppose it would seem more wonderful," I said, "if I didn't have to worry about what I would eat—do you know how many tours I've done this year?"

"But you don't have to lead tours, Joe. You can do anything. There's no one telling you what you have to do or watching you. There's nothing holding you back."

You don't understand, I was ready to say, but there was something true about her words. Hadn't I been thinking the same thing already? Without Cat to worry about, I *was* free, and there were plenty of places in the world where you could live for next to nothing. The grape harvest in France was almost over but soon the orange harvest in Greece would begin. Then came the skiing season in Switzerland. I let myself think about all I might do, even of doing it with Tonia, until we arrived at the Königsee parking lot. The lake itself was still three hundred yards away, hidden behind trees and a gauntlet of tourist shops. How many parking lots have I seen in my life, I wondered as I parked the bus. How many roads have I traveled? How would it feel to live differently?

"You get tired of running, Tonia," I said as we started walking, "of skimming over the surface of things." Her fingers had found mine and I tried to imagine the life inside them, the past that had given her the confidence to take my hand like that, the sense of freedom—a freedom different from mine—that allowed her to be with me without feeling guilty or hesitant at all. A memory, no more than a snapshot, flashed through my mind: my mother's fingers buttering toast in the morning to take back to someone—some stranger—still asleep in her bed. "And everybody has something holding them back."

"Better to run," she said, "as fast as you can—try everything, see the world as it is—than try to *buy* life or build it somehow."

Her words reminded me of when I first traveled—the things I said to justify leading tours instead of settling into other work somewhere. I tried to remember what it felt like to travel back in those days, to believe in the value of travel. Of movement.

"So what do you see here?" I asked. We were passing an empty bratwurst stand, a half-dozen outdoor tables smeared with mustard and grease, a trash can overflowing with garbage. Across the path an old man was waving toward us from a folding chair outside a tourist shop.

"Here?" she said, slipping her hand from mine to finger a machine that made souvenirs out of ten-pfennig coins. "Junk."

Another old man, this one in lederhosen, made a half-hearted attempt to interest us in a bin of stuffed bears. She waved him away with just the right combination of friendliness and firmness. "*Nächstes Mal*," he called out after her, smiling, standing a little straighter.

"Look at these people," she said. "All around them are mountains and lakes and palaces. Italy is only hours away. Switzerland. France. And they spend their lives in little boxes, chained to these businesses."

"But you've never had to live like that," I said, remembering my mother again, the early departures for work, the late returns in the evening. "You don't know what it's like for them."

"I have," she said. "I was like that. My husband still is."

"But there's a difference."

"No. No difference," she said. "I was as foolish as they are. I reached a point where I never left the house."

"But there is a difference," I insisted. "You, your husband—you can make *money*. Real money. These people make nothing. They live in little houses. If they're lucky they can afford to go to the Black Forest for a few weeks in summer."

"So?"

"So there's a difference."

We had reached the edge of the lake. The tourist shops had given way to wooden docks, a boathouse, a stretch of untouched shoreline. Beyond the water, the hills were bright with fall colors, their ridges rising to meet the mountains.

"You're right in a way," Tonia said, watching an overweight woman in a white smock washing a restaurant window. "But the money never mattered to me. Or to Gerhard. Neither of us needed money. But we did it anyway—we worked just as hard as these people do. Even harder."

"Why, then?"

"That's the question, isn't it?" she said. Her eyes looked across the lake at the hills. "Because you need something to do, maybe. Something that tells you you're worthwhile. Because you get into habits and patterns...and you're afraid to change." She reached up to brush back a wisp of hair, leaving her hand on her neck for a moment, then moving it forward to her cheek. "Maybe because all of the things truly worth doing seem so much harder to do."

I stared at the fingers that rested so lightly beside her mouth, the bitten-down nails beside her lips. "So is that how Gerhard feels, too?"

"No, for him it's something else. It's having power, maybe. Having control. Succeeding at some kind of challenge. The money he makes is like the score in a video game. He used to tell me—before we were married—that *I* was a challenge...but

I'm not much of a match anymore." She stood with her arms at her sides now, her shoulders stooped slightly as if she'd just noticed the heaviness, the seriousness, I'd sensed in her before. "But you didn't bring me here to talk about Gerhard, did you?"

"No," I answered, "but I wasn't sure we could leave him behind."

"*Jetzt, gleich*," the young woman in the kiosk said, leaning down until her chin touched the hand pushing our tickets toward me. She pointed through the glass to a man in suspenders and corduroy knickers, a Bavarian hat on his head. He was leaning against a wooden railing, sucking lazily on a cigarette. A wooden walkway stretched past him to a single tour boat, an unwieldy rectangular enclosure of shellacked pine above a shallow white hull.

"There's no wait," I told Tonia, taking her hand. "We're the only ones."

The man ignored us at first, finishing his cigarette, then took our tickets reluctantly, motioning us into the empty boat.

"*Sie haben Glück*," he said as he untethered the craft and cast off. "*In zwei Wochen nichts mehr.*"

"In two weeks...." Tonia repeated when I had translated his words for her. "Where will you and I be in two weeks?"

There were no outside seats so we sat by an open window, looking out at the forests and the sky through a pinewood frame. The bow was swinging around, leaving the tourist shops behind, when Tonia leaned back into me. "I'd like to be here then," she said, "when the boats don't run, when everything is closed and it's just the lake and the mountains and the sky."

The boat purred along, moving faster. I tried not to think of anything but her and me and where we were as I watched the autumn trees drift by.

"*Glück*," she said after a while. "Funny he used that word, isn't it? 'Luck.'" She shifted her head slightly, resting it against the window frame. "Did I tell you that's how Luckspur got its name?"

"No," I said. I hadn't thought about Gerhard's last name and what it meant; so much for leaving him behind.

"When we were kids, we used to put on plays sometimes. My father always wanted us to do Shakespeare because he thought Shakespeare 'knew life.' Those were his words. Of course he thought the Romantic poets 'knew life,' too...and painters like Delacroix. It was a phrase he used all the time—anyone he liked 'knew life.'"

We were entering a narrower part of the lake, a bottleneck that would lead to the broader, deeper water beyond. The dock had already slipped out of sight behind a ledge to our left. There were no houses or restaurants, nothing but trees and hillsides. I could feel the boat gaining speed.

"In the years after my mother's death, when we started talking about her again," Tonia continued, her mind seeming to drift through memories, "he would often say that she 'knew life.'"

I waited for her to say more about her mother, but she fell silent. Ahead I could see the lake widening again, the deep green of the narrow shadows giving way to the bleached reflection of open sky. I lifted my hand to point out an especially beautiful tree on the shore nearest us, its leaves a brilliant orange, but when I looked at Tonia her eyes were closed. I slipped my arm around her and watched the tree near and pass.

"Of course I always wanted to do *Romeo and Juliet* or *A Midsummer Night's Dream*," she said, her eyes still closed, "or maybe *All's Well that Ends Well*." A smile crossed her lips. "But Gerhard insisted we do the histories. Always histories. He always wanted to wear a sword he got from somewhere and this old German uniform his grandfather had given him—very formal and militaristic looking—Prussian blue with gold buttons he always kept polished. He was older than I was—by five years—so we did what he wanted...histories, one after another, until one time he hit upon *Richard the Second*—do you know that one?"

She opened one eye to see my answer. I nodded just to keep her talking. I was only half-listening, letting her voice blend with the color in the trees, the white of the mountains against the sky. I had never done tours of England, so I had never read much Shakespeare, and all her talk of Gerhard was starting to bother me. It wasn't just that she had known him for so long, that so many of her memories were tied up with him; it was the life they had lived—a life so different from mine. I envisioned long, manicured lawns and stately Victorian homes. At the edge of the yard a neatly groomed father took time to indulge his children while in the house somewhere his well-dressed wife was being attended by maids.

"You remember Hotspur? As soon as Gerhard found this character—one he thought was a *real* soldier, a man of 'bravery and action'—of course he had to be him. We had to do the same damn plays over and over—*Richard the Second, Henry the Fourth, Part One*—

"I had rather be a kitten and cry mew
Than one of these same metre ballet-mongers.
I had rather hear a brazen canstick turn'd,
Or a dry wheel grate on the axle-tree,
And that would set my teeth nothing on edge,
Nothing so much as mincing poetry."

She recited as if she were performing again, her hand moving to the rhythm of the lines, the accent exaggerated, as if she were a child playing. "That was Gerhard's favorite passage, his answer to any line of poetry I ever made the mistake of saying out loud."

"Luck*spur*—I get it," I said. She must have heard the agitation in my voice because her face became serious then and she turned her head to look at me.

"I'm sorry," she said. "I don't know what you want to know."

We were clearing a ridge to our right, the scored flanks of Mt. Watzmann gliding into place in front of us like the image on a giant color slide.

"I know," I said. My arm on her shoulder felt awkward and I was aware of how silly, how temporary, what we were doing was. Every time I let my mind drift at all beyond the moment, the scenery itself threatened to come crashing down, as if the lake and the woods and the hills were only make-believe.

For a while, the only sound was the dampered burp of the inboard engine. I could feel her heartbeat where my hand rested against her chest, could smell the perfume in her hair. The air from the lake rushed past us, coming down from the hills. It was cold, but there was a warmer breath beneath it, a murmur from the warmer lands to the south. We sat that way for several minutes, without talking or moving, breathing together, watching the mountains come into view and disappear, the trees glide by, the morning light flash in the roll of the waves off the bow.

"Tell me more about your father," I said when the silence had gone on too long.

Instead of answering me, she began to recite a verse I thought I'd heard somewhere or maybe read while studying for one of my tours:

"Are not the mountains, waves, and skies, a part
Of me and of my soul..."

She paused and glanced back at me, looking up from under her lashes as a child might, as she must have looked at her father when she recited for him. "Go on," I said, kissing her forehead.

"Is not love of these deep in my heart
With a pure passion? should I not contemn
All objects, if compared with these? and stem
A tide of suffering, rather than forego
Such feelings for the hard and worldly phlegm
Of those whose eyes are only turn'd below

Gazing upon the ground,
with thoughts which dare not glow?"

She recited slowly, as if each word had some specific memory attached to it. "That was my father's favorite." Her voice was low, almost a whisper. "He told me once that he moved to Oregon because of those lines. He wanted to be near the mountains and the waves."

"I want to pretend I know who that was," I said, "but I don't."

"Byron. My father loved Byron...and Keats. And Shelley. He had three big leather-bound books on his desk—*The Poetical Works of Lord Byron*, *The Poems of Percy Bysshe Shelley*, and *The Complete John Keats*—each with the title in gold. If I close my eyes I can see them as clearly as I did then. The spines were worn from his fingers, some of the lettering rubbed off. Instead of bedtime stories, he'd bring one of them to my room and read me a poem, still wearing his tie, smelling of cigarettes and cognac. Sometimes, I think of his voice and wish I could hear it again. I can't remember anymore what it sounded like, except when I recite one of those poems. Then I hear it once more, just for a moment."

She spoke as if the world of her childhood was one I would naturally understand.

"His office was just across the hall from my bedroom," she continued, "and when I had closed my eyes he would go back into it to work on his book. I remember night after night falling asleep to the click of his typewriter, the faint light from his desk lamp coming into my room from the hall."

"So your father was a writer?"

"No." She sat up a little and shook her head. "He wasn't a writer. Or a painter. Or any of the other things he tried. I don't know what he was—a romantic, maybe."

"Tough to get a job as a romantic, isn't it?"

She smiled. "Oh, he had a job. He was a psychiatrist. He told me once—I don't know, maybe he was kidding—he told me he started studying psychoanalysis in school because he liked the way Freud wrote. Can you imagine, picking what you're going to do that way?"

"The way a romantic might."

"I suppose. But it was the right profession for him. He loved to be with people, to think about what made them do what they did." She fell into silence, leaning back and closing her eyes. "You can't imagine how good this is for me," she said after a while. "I haven't thought about my father's poems for years. I'd forgotten how formal and grand they were, how impossibly overwritten. They remind me of that castle, the one I keep thinking about."

I thought at first she meant the Chiemsee palace, the one we had visited, the one where she and I had danced. "The palace, you mean—the Hall of Mirrors?"

She looked confused. "No, the other one—the one with the turrets and the gate and all those gabled roofs. I keep thinking about that king—Ludwig—and what he built out of his imagination. I can see now why I loved that poster so much, why I had to have a copy—it's like the poetry in a way...all these things that don't need to be there, things a practical mind would take away."

The pilot had altered the boat's course slightly, turning the bow toward the shore. The sun was falling directly on us now, warming our skin and the air. I tried to relax, to just let her talk. "Who determines that?" she went on. "Who says you can't write like Shelley or Keats today? Or paint like Van Gogh? Who decides that?"

"I don't know. Times change. Things change."

"Do you know who came up with the game," Tonia asked after a while, "the one that gave Rudy his job—and Donald and Felicity. The one that brought in all of that money and let Gerhard think he had finally done something for himself?"

"No," I said lazily, looking out at the mountain. "Gerhard, I suppose."

"Do you know the game?"

"No. I've been living in Europe, remember. I'd never heard of Luckspur before you called."

"I did."

It took me a moment to realize what she was saying.

"*You* did?" I said.

"I did," she said again, leaning more heavily into me, as if to reassure me, "although Gerhard has so completely taken credit for it I almost believe him myself."

The boat pilot interrupted her. He was pointing to a narrow defile where the ridges gave way to a thicket of trees. Just at the edge of the trees, on a skirt of land between the woods and the lake, stood three white cylinders with two higher towers behind them. They looked like three short grain silos pasted together, topped by onion domes. A farmhouse and boathouse rested beside them, the only signs of habitation we'd seen on the lake. "*Sankt Bartholomä*," the pilot announced. "*Sehr historisch.*" He asked if we wanted to stop.

"No," Tonia said when I translated for her, "let's just ride on. Let's just ride until we have to be back."

I shook my head at the pilot and he looked away from me, his lips clenched tighter than before. He tooted the boat's horn three times and leaned back against the doorway to light a cigarette. On the dock by the onion-domed buildings a woman about his same age waved once and turned away. For several minutes the boat continued to motor along, leaving the church and the farmhouse behind. In front of us was nothing but cliffs and trees. I tried to focus on them, ignoring the line of shadows ahead, where the lake doglegged left. I imagined we were explorers heading into unknown waters.

"Have you ever been to Tibet?" Tonia asked. She lifted herself away from me and thrust her head beyond the window. I followed her gaze to a rounded summit rising from a distant ridge.

"No, I got stuck in Europe," I said, glad to have moved to a different subject.

"You have to imagine a mountain like that one," she said, pulling her head inside and leaning against my shoulder. "Only bigger."

The pilot had reached the twilight edge of the shadows and was slowly turning the boat.

"What about the waterfall?" I asked him.

"*Nein, nicht heute,*" he said, as if it would be possible to visit it again tomorrow but today it was under repair. "*Keine Zeit,*" he added, tapping his watch without looking at me. He steered far out into the water and, once he had brought the bow around, increased his speed, plowing a furrow down the middle of the lake.

"So we have a mountain," I said to Tonia, putting my arm around her. She closed her eyes once again, and when she spoke, her voice was louder than before, the voice of someone reading a story to children:

"And on the top of this mountain, surrounded by snow, there's a huge monastery, the biggest monastery you've ever seen. It spills down the sides of the mountain, layer after layer of buildings, all with windows and patios, a cascade of rooms all linked together. You're climbing this mountain, starting from a city where people dress in traditional clothes—belted robes that reach to the ground with sleeves that come down over their knuckles, colored strips woven through the hair of the women, silver jewelry inset with coral or turquoise. You have to dodge people prostrate in prayer, herds of sheep, long rows of hawkers as you try to collect what you'll need for your trip—a variety of food and clothing, some climbing gear, a weapon maybe, a *sherpa* if you're lucky. You want to avoid the yaks. They can make traveling easier at first by carrying supplies, but once you reach the mountain they'll slow you down. When you leave the town, you have to cross a stretch of open ground. Your footsteps stir up dust. Unless you've saddled yourself with a yak, you're running for whatever you can find—a shrub, a hut, an outcropping. If you're not careful you'll run across a soldier who will try to stop you. It's better if you can slip beyond them or pay them off, but if you have to, you use your weapon— maybe a knife, maybe a gun, maybe a bit of rope. If you make it safely past the soldiers, you begin to climb, using the climbing gear you picked up in the village, following your *sherpa* if you have one. You have to be careful because there are snakes on some of the ledges, leopards that come out of caves, maybe a wild goat that will knock you back to the bottom. If you make it past the animals and your hands don't slip from the rocks so you fall, breaking your arm or your leg, you come to the first of the monastery buildings. You have to find the door that hides the way in, the tunnel that gives you access to the monastery itself, to its labyrinth of rooms. Once inside, you have to make your way through the rooms—some are empty, some have doors you have to open and hope there's no one inside who will try to stop you. Monks in purple robes are everywhere, their shaved heads waiting to sneer at you or grin as they try to grab you. They hide behind the closed doors, in unseen closets, on ladders that drop from the ceiling. You have to be quick and clever to get past them. If you do, though, you can pick up items to help as you penetrate deeper—more food, disguises, a book of maps that will show you the way through some of the passages. All this time you're moving uphill, rising through layers, until you reach the main building. Here the walls are covered with rich fabrics and the candles lighting your way rest in candlesticks of gold. You're looking for the central courtyard where there's a kind of sacred fire. You have to make it to this to warm yourself before you freeze to death because the walls behind the fabrics are made of ice and the wind is coming in, threatening to blow out the candles and plunge you into a darkness from which you can't escape without being captured by the monks or eaten by one of the tigers that roam the corridors. If you find the sacred fire, you burn the book of maps, taking a torch from the fire instead. This is a special torch that gives off a heartbeat sound as it lights your way–a sound that grows louder when you are going the right way. You climb a narrow staircase into the uppermost part of the monastery where monks in blue robes, their faces expressionless, try to bar your way, offering bags of gold, tables laden with food, beautiful women. One of them carries a key, hidden in his robes somewhere. You have to find it to open the door to the room at the monastery's highest point. This room has no walls, only windows on every side and a skylight above. The sky you can see from it is the bluest you've ever seen and when you sit down on the single cushioned chair in the room, your legs pull up under you, your hands stretch out, the fingers coming together, and you begin to smile because you've won— you've found your way to that place that offers perfect peace."

"That's the game?" I asked as she opened her eyes.

"That's the game."

"*Fire Mountain?*"

She nodded. "I wanted to call it *Peace Mountain*. Gerhard wanted *Power Mountain*. That was the last time he compromised."

"And this is what made all the money."

"Eventually, yes." We were approaching the narrow part of the lake again. Another three or four hundred yards and we'd begin to see buildings. "At first we didn't make anything. It was too new. Too different. Gerhard was angry because he'd put so much money into it. It wasn't violent enough, he said. It wasn't cute enough. He'd trusted us and we'd let him down. Of course it wasn't his money in the first place. It was his father's. He never had money of his own—he never had anything of his own."

"'Us'?"

"What?"

"You said he had trusted 'us.'"

She grew quiet. "Yes, us," she said softly. "There was a young man who helped me—a kid, really—Brent Sirkov." She gazed at the empty bench across from us, its blond wood lit by the sun. "He was just out of M.I.T. The smartest kid I ever met. He was working there for the summer because he didn't have a job yet and he wanted to work on something where he wasn't just being told what to do. Gerhard had met him somewhere—at one of his computer fairs or a coffee shop. He worked almost for free, just to get the experience, just to be using his mind, he said. Of course Gerhard promised him better things, painted this whole bright future. But I don't think Brent ever cared about any of that.

"The game he came up with is almost outdated now. Everybody is doing what we did—but they weren't then. The graphics then were still jerky. Brent worked on smoothing everything, making it not ten times but a hundred times more realistic than anything else on the market. He was in there all the time—in this little garage we had behind our house, staring into his computer. Gerhard would try to laugh about him, but he made Gerhard nervous. 'It's spooky,' he'd say about how focused Brent was. He'd leave for the weekend and when he got back Sunday night Brent would still be working. Sometimes I'd be there, too, working with him, explaining things to him. He used my pictures of Tibet to make the landscape, the buildings, even the people more real—the kind of thing everyone's doing now. He was always asking me about details: the necklace a woman was wearing, what the huts were made of, what a prayer wheel was. He was way ahead of them all. He gave the game possibilities, options—more than one way to win. He was opening the whole industry up, giving the player more control. But nobody recognized it at first."

She lifted her hand to her head to comb her fingers through her hair, letting them rest on the nape of her neck. "You can't imagine," she said, her gaze rising to the window, "how disappointed he was—how devastated—when the game didn't sell." Her voice was thick with sadness, and I felt a twinge of jealousy. It seemed to me she'd loved him. Maybe loved him still.

"And what's he doing now?" I asked. "Does he still work there?"

She shook her head. Through the window I could see that we were coming to the end of the narrow channel, the open water far behind. The boat had returned quicker than it had gone out, like a horse heading home to the barn. Just ahead of us the lakeshore was thinning to its narrowest point. Beyond the trees on the promontory to our right I could see the roof of the first building, its lines too angular, too determined, after the unplanned wilds of the lake.

"No," she said, "he left. Just before Rudy came. Just before people in Tokyo discovered his game, before Rudy took it to California and the East Coast and sales picked up. He never saw what happened—the way production increased. The buildings we bought. The people we hired. The hundreds of thousands we sold, and the millions of dollars we made."

"Didn't he ask for a part of it?" I said, thinking of being so close to all of that money and missing out. We were nearing the dock by then, the tourist shops, the bratwurst stands. The pilot sounded his horn—three quick blasts, like a train signal warning people out of the way. "*Absteigen*," he mumbled, positioning the short metal landing ramp by the door.

"I think sometimes of all he didn't see," Tonia said as she stood, freeing her hand from mine to steady herself. I followed her to the ramp, putting my hand on her elbow as I ducked to avoid the overhead beams.

"I wonder what he would have thought about all we'd done," she continued when we had stepped out onto the wooden dock. "He was the one who always kept after me, telling me how much my imagination was worth. He couldn't see the mountain, he said, and neither could Gerhard. 'Forget about him,' he'd say when Gerhard wasn't around. 'You think it up and I'll do the rest.' He could convert whatever I imagined, he said, make it into something someone could sell. He thought he'd done exactly that, made a bestselling product—right up until it didn't sell. Even then he wouldn't blame me, or Gerhard. He was to blame, he thought. There was something—there had to be something, he said—he hadn't done right." She crossed her arms over her chest, rubbing the skin below her sleeves as she walked, as we threaded the alley of pilings leading us back to the land.

"What happened to him?" I asked from behind her.

She paused at the end of the walkway to gaze out over the water. "One day he didn't show up for work," she said. "He never came back. It was only later we heard what he'd done." Turning her back to the lake, she took my hand and led me up the street toward the bus. We walked for several minutes in silence. The shops had closed, the old man in lederhosen was gone. When we reached the parking lot, she stopped. "How could he know," she said, looking at me, "someone as young as that, that life has a way of turning around?" She leaned up to kiss me, tightening her grip on my fingers. "How could you know that something was about to make a million overnight? Or that one day even a hundred million wouldn't mean a thing?"

# Chapter Fifteen

We could see her from the end of the road, wearing a hat of some kind, her hands on her hips, her legs in those harem pants spread far apart. "Oh, God," Tonia said, hiding her face. We laughed as Felicity began to wave, flagging us down like a city bus she was afraid would skip her stop.

"Well, you'll have to wait now," she said when I pulled into the courtyard. She bent over to slide one of her suitcases toward me. "Donald has gone for the water." The hat she wore was a broad-brimmed Panama with a red band saying, "Salzburg."

"Water?" I asked.

"Yes, of course." She scowled at me as if tiring of my thick-headedness. She remembered, she said, that the water in Italy was bad. I told her Italian water was fine and we wouldn't be in Italy until late the next day anyway. "Well, it's too late now," she proclaimed. When I asked where Rudy and Sarah were, she said, "How would I know? You're the guide, aren't you?" I lifted her luggage into the bus without another word and went inside to pay Tibor.

"You remember, next time," he said. "Good people." He followed me outside and said an abrupt goodbye to Felicity. When Donald arrived with five liter-size bottles of water, I did my best to find room for them as he hunched through the side door. But Felicity didn't follow him.

"I *have* to sit in front," she said. "I get *violently* ill if I sit in the back on winding roads."

"Lady," Tibor was saying to Tonia behind me, "you visit me anytime." As he kissed her on both cheeks, I imagined the two of us returning after the tour—lying in the same bed in the corner room every night and taking the path to the wooden walkway every morning. Tonia could paint the view of the town from the hill and I could sit nearby, watching her or staring off at the mountains, recovering from half a decade of too much running.

While Tonia and Tibor were talking, Rudy appeared, wearing a Bavarian hat and carrying a cheap alpenstock with "Berchtesgaden" stamped on a shield on the handle. Sarah was right behind him. "He was showing me where he climbed up the hill this morning," she explained.

"Ja, vee go now und vee put our backsides to zis country," said Rudy. He gave the Nazi salute with his middle finger extended, then slapped his butt as Georg our guide had done back in Munich. "You know zee vay, Herr Guide?" He tapped me with his stick as he passed as if to knight me.

When everyone was on board, I shouted to Tibor, "Next time!" He waved his hand briefly then fluttered it back and forth as if shooing us away.

Even with Felicity beside me, I was glad to be moving again, leaving Germany and all of its associations behind. The quaint farmhouses with their whitewashed walls, the roadside markers hung morbidly with crucifixes, the obsessively neat fields and gardens and rebuilt churches were not for me, not any longer. I longed for the easier life of the south.

It took us an hour to make our way down from the mountains and over the border to Austria. Clouds rolled in briefly outside Berchtesgaden then continued past. Most of the drive was through narrow valleys between limestone hills. The valleys were full of shadows, only occasionally widening enough to let in light or give a view of the mountains ahead. When we came at last to an open plain, an amber sun was lighting the tops of the distant peaks and I imagined that everything in Italy would be lit like that.

For much of the ride the bus was quiet. When I could, I glanced in the mirror and met Tonia's eyes but we never spoke. Felicity stared straight ahead in the seat beside me, her hands in her lap, her face pale. Now and then she swallowed loudly as if to keep from vomiting. Eventually, Donald and Rudy fell into conversation and I realized they were talking for the first time about something they'd done on the trip rather than things at home.

"...but it's a real lake," Donald was saying when I began to follow their conversation, "like a huge mirror, absolutely still. And the salt cave is like a giant canopy above you. To get there you ride a—how can I describe it?" The road was narrow and windy at this point so I couldn't see what he was doing but he must have acted something out because Rudy and Sarah started laughing. "It's like a pommel horse...on a narrow-gauge track...and you ride like this, with a leg on either side and your hips against the waist of the person in front of you." Tonia was laughing now, too, and I glanced in the mirror to see what was happening. All I could see was the side of Donald's face, his eye closed behind his glasses. I pictured the little train that carries visitors down into the mine, the leather bench like a long saddle that runs down the middle. "Felicity was behind me," Donald said, "and she kept scooting me forward until I was almost in this man's back pocket...Not that I minded."

"I don't know why you feel you have to say something like that," Felicity said without turning around. Her face had changed from pale to red.

"Let him talk, for Christ's sake," Rudy said. "It's not like he has any secrets from us."

I drove on, waiting for Donald to respond to Felicity, but when he spoke he was talking to Rudy again. "It's just that you wouldn't expect it there," he said, "this broad lake. You go down a small slide the miners used a hundred years ago and there it is. They put you on a kind of wooden raft and it's almost entirely dark, with only a few lights off in the distance. Then they pull you across the lake with a rope—the whole group—and for some reason no one says anything. Everyone's standing together, gliding along, and you can't help smiling, it's so peaceful. I haven't had much time for that kind of thing this past year." Donald's voice was pensive, wistful, and I was surprised to hear him express so much emotion. Maybe he's feeling freer, too, I thought.

The bus remained quiet after that, as we made our way through the last of the valleys. Colored hills crowded in, then moved away. Felicity leaned toward the windshield as if to distance herself from everyone else. I'd put on music and focused on the road, thinking we'd make Zell am See by dusk. Then Sarah spoke. Maybe she couldn't abide the silence, I don't know. She seemed to be talking to no one, or everyone. She seemed to need to fill the void. It took me a while to realize what she was talking about. She described picking her way over stones, pushing past branches, following Rudy on his "quest."

"What's wrong with you?" Rudy said, his words loud and sudden. He was wearing the sunglasses he'd worn that morning, his face looking almost normal with the damaged eye covered up. But his mouth was twisted into a sneer. "Huh? What is wrong with you?"

"What? I'm making conversation. I'm telling them what *we* did."

"You're making it sound like some misguided adventure, as if we were off to find some lost kingdom."

"I'm just telling them what we did," Sarah countered. "I'm not making it sound like anything."

"Talking about my *quest* like I was King Arthur."

"You tell them what we did then. If you think I can't tell it right."

"It's not that you can't, Sarah. You won't. You don't want to think about all of this. I don't have that luxury."

"You have that luxury, Rudy, if that's what you want to call it. It's not like no one knows about all of this. Just because we're here doesn't mean we have to dwell on it."

"Am I dwelling on it?" Rudy asked. "Am I really dwelling on it, because I don't think watching *Schindler's List* is enough when you're standing in middle of the goddamn place?"

"It's not the middle of anything anymore," Sarah said. "It's just a bunch of stones."

"You think they bombed the place, the war ended, and suddenly everyone forgot what had happened? You didn't see the swastikas scratched on the rocks?"

"You don't think those are just kids?"

"No, I don't."

The thing for Rudy to do then, to make her see what he meant, to make them all see, was tell what had happened to him the night before. But for some reason he didn't.

"Aren't you being just a little paranoid?" Felicity said. "That was fifty years ago."

"I'm sure you're right, Felicity." Rudy's voice was heavy with sarcasm. "It was a long time ago, wasn't it? Nothing you'd want to think about. Nothing with any connection to any of us." He waited for her to answer but she only lifted her chin and stared straight ahead.

"So what was it like?" Tonia asked, breaking the silence. "What did you find?" She was sitting in the very back of the bus, away from the others, and had kept to herself until then.

"We didn't find anything," Sarah said.

"Sarah didn't find anything." In the mirror I could see Rudy looking not at Tonia but forward toward Felicity and me.

"Sarah didn't find anything because she didn't want to find anything. She didn't want to think about it. You understand that, don't you, Felicity, not wanting to think about something? Sarah just wanted to buy postcards. She saw a building with a gift shop in it and she dragged me over there."

"You didn't have to go," said Sarah.

"But while she's looking at postcards, I'm noticing there's a turnstile in the corner of the building. When I ask somebody about it, he tells me it leads down to the bunkers. You didn't tell me there were bunkers there, Newhouse. You didn't tell me there were underground tunnels you could go down into."

My first impulse was to defend myself, but I kept my mouth shut. He wasn't interested in a reply anyway.

"No, you didn't tell me some of it was still there, just the way it was. I go down this stairway and there it is—the old whitewash on the walls, the concrete floor. I can feel the hair standing up on my arms. I want to get the hell out of there...but I keep going. Sarah, I keep going. I can't stay away from it like you can. It's there. It happened. And I'm thinking that all I have to do is walk to the other end of the building. Then I can go out. Then I can think I've experienced it as much as someone can today. So I get to the bottom of this first set of stairs and I turn the corner and there's this corridor—or what looks like a corridor—with a gate across it barring entry. And there on the wall beside it, what do you think I see?"

"We don't care what you saw," said Felicity.

Rudy hesitated. You could almost hear him debating in his head whether he should answer her. But he went on instead,

"Someone had written a word beside it, with an indelible marker. Two-inch letters. '*Hunde-something.*' *Hunde*, I think. What the hell does that mean? It took me a while to figure it out. It's taken me a while to figure a lot of things out, it seems. I finally remembered that '*hunde*' was dogs. It wasn't a corridor, it was a dog pen."

"So what? So they had dogs." Felicity glanced at me, perhaps to remind me again that I was the guide, that I should be stopping this.

"So nothing. So you're right—they had dogs, big deal. So I go on down the next set of stairs and this time there are big squares cut in the walls. I can guess what those are—gun emplacements. Machine guns protecting the entry. But I'm still not at the bottom. There's another flight of stairs. And now it's getting darker. The only light comes from these bulbs with grills over them to keep them from being broken. I go down these stairs and I'm right back there, wondering if the moisture on the walls has been there as long as the walls have. There's nobody around and it smells as if nobody has been there for years. This lighting is throwing shadows across the walls, scaring the hell out of me. But I keep going. I can see the other end, see a wall and what looks like a set of stairs going up. Leading out. It's all I can do to keep from running. But I don't. That's what's important, Felicity, I don't. Instead I look at the walls. I try to fix them in my mind. My memory. I run my hand through the moisture and my fingers leave a trail of dark lines. All this time I'm walking toward the other end. Walking slowly. Trying to breathe. There are these doors in the wall with rooms behind them. At first, I think they're just bunkers, somewhere to hide from an air raid. Then I look more closely. They're only about five by five and there's no light in them at all. They're cells, I realize. It seems I see blood on the concrete floor, under the dirty prints of shoes and jackboots. The smell in the air, the wet on the wall come, I think, from the piss of prisoners. It's all I can do to keep from gagging. I slip past the door of one of the cells without touching it, and when I'm inside I feel nothing at all except hatred. The only thing that keeps me sane is thinking he died in a place like this. In a bunker. At least he spent his final days underground. Knowing he was going to die."

Rudy stopped and waited. Seconds passed, then minutes. I imagined he was waiting for Felicity to say something flippant to that, or Sarah to suggest again there was nothing there. The mirror was filled by his glasses, the black oversized eyes looking at me as if I should have been telling the story, as if I should have been forthcoming with what was there.

"I was standing there," he said finally, "just standing there...and I didn't think I could do anything more. I'd been trying to imagine what it was like to be there, but I couldn't. My mind was blank. I couldn't imagine anything, couldn't think. And I felt guilty—not because I was alive and whoever had been there wasn't. Not because I hadn't done anything to prevent the same kind of thing from happening somewhere else. No shit like that. I felt guilty because I'd never thought much about it before. And I never would have, even now, if some arrogant son of a bitch hadn't fooled me into coming over here. That's what pisses me off, Sarah. That's why you piss me off."

I saw her nod and put her hand on his shoulder, carefully, still unsure. "I understand," she said.

"No, you don't. I don't either. I was down there standing like that..." His voice broke and he stopped to wet his mouth, shrugging off her arm as he did. "I'm down there standing like that and I hear this sound, this jingling, this sound that I think is keys, as if someone is coming to lock me in...and I fly through that door. I *fly*. I'd have done anything to get out of there." He wet his mouth again, audibly, then swallowed. "But once I'm out in the hallway again, I feel ashamed. There's no one out there, no one with keys. The sound is coming from another cell further along. When I lean down to look inside, I see an old man sitting against the wall. I have to step back to let enough light in to see him clearly, and when I do I see he has a dog. A German Shepherd. And this dog is looking right at me, its ears straight up.

"At first, I wonder if this is some sick-fuck German idea, some reenactment, but then I see the man's eyes. I'm easing the door open by now, scared as shit of that dog, but he isn't moving, hasn't barked or growled. I don't know why I'm going in there—maybe I thought the guy was hurt. He was an old man, wearing old clothes. He looks up at me as if he's heard something but he doesn't say anything. He doesn't seem to know I'm there. I've never seen anything like it—this dog and this guy sitting there in the shadows and these eyes...shriveled up, pulled back into his head. And here's the crux of it all—what I'm telling you...it takes me a while to realize the guy is trying to get up. The dog isn't concerned about me at all because he's standing still so the man can get the right grip on the leather, can balance himself with the handle to push off the wall. His cheeks are wet and he keeps wiping them instead of pushing at the right time, when the dog leans forward."

Rudy stopped again.

"So what happened?" Tonia asked. "Did you help him?"

Rudy shook his head. "No," he said. "I turned around and slipped back out."

"Why?" Sarah asked. "Why didn't you help him?"

"I couldn't stand the sight of him. I couldn't stand the smell of his dog. He spoke to it in German, and I thought fine, you German fuck, you rot there."

"Well, that's compassionate," Felicity said.

"I would have been okay," he said, "if I hadn't seen him. Hadn't seen the irony. Even if I hadn't seen his eyes. If he had bothered to cover them up."

"Maybe you should have given him your sunglasses." There was a slight smile on Felicity's lips as she said it and I wondered how anyone could be so spiteful.

"You know, Felicity," Rudy said, speaking slowly, measuring his words, "I don't give a damn what you say. You messed up your life and now you think nothing can matter anymore, nothing can mean anything to anyone else."

"It's just that I didn't know anything ever meant anything to you, Rudy," she said. "And as for my life, it was you who ruined it."

"What's that supposed to mean?"

"Felicity, don't bring that up," Donald said.

"You don't even have the sense to know when someone's helping you, Felicity." Rudy was leaning forward, jabbing his finger in her direction. "Gerhard and I gave you a chance. All you had to do was work for him for a while."

"Like a slave?"

"Well, isn't that what you'd been already?"

"Just follow orders, is that right?" she said.

"It was his money that got you out." Rudy said.

"Isn't that all these people were doing?" Felicity asked.

"What people?"

"The Germans."

I could see Rudy's face color. "I would have thought a comment like that was too low even for you, Felicity. Even for wanting to get back at me somehow."

Felicity dabbed at her lips with a finger. "You were the one who wanted to talk about something meaningful."

We had reached the outskirts of Zell am See. A few clouds had drifted down from the mountains and out over the valley, sprinkling rain across the windshield. Cooling the air. I kept my eyes on the road, not wanting to look at any of them, not wanting to hear anything more. I forced myself to think about something else, about the drive over the pass we'd make the next day: the steep grade, the hairpin turns, the narrow roadway that would take us over eight thousand feet. I hoped the morning's sun would return, the air would be warm, and the mountain snow would be higher up than it looked to be.

# Chapter Sixteen

Evening was already coming on when we reached our hotel, a new place by the lake with gingerbread carvings below the eaves and huge murals of mountain men marching across the walls. Inside, it smelled of fresh wood and carpet. The owner, a tall man with narrow shoulders and a large gut, greeted us formally and gave us our rooms without further pleasantries. My room was clean but featureless, with a deck that looked out over the lake and a trail that followed the shore into town. The storm had moved on, so I took a cognac from the mini-bar and settled into a patio chair to watch the sun set across the water. Birds were chattering from the wet limbs of trees that gleamed in the evening light. Putting my feet on the pinewood railing, I sipped the cognac slowly, waiting for the muscles in my arms and legs to relax. There was a freshness to the evening that almost made me forget what had happened in the bus, forget everything but being on the Königsee with Tonia that morning.

My eyes drifted from the sun to a sailboat tacking near shore, then to two figures walking the trail toward town. They were moving slowly, arm-in-arm. The taller one looked like Donald but the woman moved too naturally to be Felicity. It wasn't until they had turned and started back that I realized it was Tonia. What startled me about seeing her there was how comfortable the two of them seemed together. They hadn't talked much on the tour, but I could see by the way they leaned in that they knew each other well. I felt envious of him—of the things he knew about her, the past they shared. I thought of all I'd once known about Cat—her moods, her dislikes, the way she'd react to a joke or movie. I tried to imagine what she was doing or who she was with, but I couldn't picture her at all.

I was late going down to dinner that night, reluctant to see them all again. When Donald and Tonia had gone inside, I watched the band of sky between clouds and mountains darken. When I'd finished the two cognacs in the mini-bar, I mixed the two Smirnoffs with ginger ale, then toasted the night with Glenfiddich. By the time I descended the stairs, my legs were unsteady but my mood had improved. I found Sarah leaning against the dining room doorway with her hands behind her back. "I was just watching Rudy," she said when she saw me, "trying for the thousandth time to figure him out." I followed her gaze to where the others were sitting at a single table near the far wall. Only Rudy and Donald faced us. Tonia had her back to us and Felicity was at the end to our right, looking away from the others. Rudy was leaning toward her, pointing his finger and saying something that was making all of them—even Felicity—laugh.

"I thought you and he were together," I said.

"Mostly we just keep each other company," she told me. "I don't think Rudy needs anybody. I mean, look at him. Who could ever really be with him? Two hours ago he was ready to kill Felicity. Or be killed by her. Now he has her laughing as if they're best friends. You can't figure him out."

"How long have you been together?" I asked.

"Not so long." I heard a sadness in her voice, as if she meant they wouldn't be together much longer, or maybe it was my own sadness I was hearing. "Sometimes I think he asked me to go back to New York just because he needed a secretary. Or he didn't want to be alone."

Just then, Rudy glanced over and saw us standing together in the doorway.

"Well, Sarah," he said. "I was wondering where you went to. Damn it, Newhouse, I've got to hand it to you."

"For what?" I said as we started toward the table. Tonia turned halfway around in her seat and motioned for me to sit by her.

"First this one, then that one."

No one laughed. I tried to edge around the end of the table, but the room was spinning slowly and I had to wait until it stopped. My head hurt, and the moment went on and on. Sarah had taken her seat next to Rudy and was whispering something to him. "Come on, sit down, Newhouse," he said. "Don't worry so much." He laughed and passed the carafe my way. "We're way ahead of you. Way, way ahead." He laughed again, and some of the others joined in. "You have no idea how far ahead of you we are, how damn much we already know about each other."

I had just reached the seat when a girl with reedy arms and unwashed hair appeared with a tray in the doorway. She set a deep bowl of milky broth in front of each person and a fresh carafe of wine on the table.

"You know how far back we go?" Rudy said when the soup had been served. "How long Felicity and I have known each other?"

I shook my head and concentrated on eating. Tonia had slipped her hand onto my leg.

"You don't need to go into all that," Felicity said, but there was an odd tone to her voice, an encouraging tone, as if she'd like nothing better than to have him go into all that, have him recount the happier times of their childhood.

"You know I knew her when she was a skinny little—"
"Rudy...."
"No, it's okay, Sarah," Felicity said. "It would be interesting to hear how Rudy remembers those times. We've never really talked about them."

"There are a lot of things we've never talked about, Felicity." He had a sour smile on his face, one Felicity couldn't have helped noticing, but she continued to encourage him anyway.

"Tell him how I was," she said. "Tell him about the time I sang at the governor's reception."

"What I remember," Rudy said, the smile still there, "was all your yammering about the Met and how you were going to sing there one day."

"I wasn't 'yammering,'" Felicity said, "I *was* going to sing there. I told you, Joe, about my mother."

"You told him about your mother?" Rudy asked. "Did you tell him about the time she tried to visit you in Florida?"

"You don't need to bring that up," Donald said.

"No, let him." Felicity had put her spoon on the table and was leaning forward with her hands in her lap, her eyes on Rudy. "It would be interesting to hear what he says about that time, too. We've never really talked about that either, have we, Rudy? What you did."

"Donald's right, Felicity, you don't want to go into all that." His words made it seem he was backing down, but he had his elbows on the table and was staring back at Felicity. "I was just talking about your mother. I saw her the other day, you know. When I was back in Livingston."

"Go ahead, Rudy," Felicity said. "You might as well tell it—you brought it up. What were you thinking? Back then."

Rudy looked down at the table.

"Well," Felicity prodded him, reaching across Donald to nudge his arm, "we're waiting...."

"Why don't you tell it?" Rudy said.

"Because it was your little adventure."

The girl returned for our soup bowls. "*Fünf minuten*," she said apologetically.

"Five minutes should be just enough time to get yourself in trouble," Felicity said when I'd translated.

"You know we did it for you, Felicity."

"For me. How very kind."

"Would you rather be back there still?"

221

"Yes, Rudy, I would." She let her words sink in. "I wish you'd never messed with my life."

Rudy rubbed his chin then turned his eyes from Felicity to me. As he started to speak, I felt Tonia's foot brush my ankle.

"Okay." He paused to take a sip of water then reached to refill his wineglass. I tried to concentrate on Tonia's foot, on being alone with her again after dinner.

"How much did you tell him?" Rudy asked when his glass was full. "Did you tell him about Europe, about meeting Paco or Pepe or whatever the hell his name was?"

"You remember damn well what his name was," Felicity said.

"Well, you see, Newhouse," Rudy began, "I used to get these postcards from 'Felicity and Pablo.' This was when I was at Berkeley, my first year, just after high school. They seemed to come from everywhere—Rome, Berlin, Cairo, Istanbul. I thought Felicity had gone over there just for the summer like everyone else—you know, doing the *Grand Tour*. But the next thing you know there is no Felicity, there's only 'FelicityandPablo,' these damn postcards coming from everywhere."

"Would you stop saying that name? Please?" Felicity dabbed at her lips then picked up her wineglass. It was empty but she lifted it to her mouth anyway.

"So 'this man'..." Rudy hesitated, gazing at Felicity from the corner of his eye. It was obvious now that he was having fun with her. But she let him go on, as if she was hoping to trip him up somehow, catch him in some error. "...this man promises Felicity he's the ticket to her future. He's going to make her the next Maria Callas, he tells her. And he gets her to marry him. That's right, isn't it, Felicity?"

"I'm seeing now that this was a bad idea." Felicity seemed determined to stay calm but the rigid way she sat told me he was getting to her. "You don't have an ounce of sympathy. It's all a joke to you. You're just trying to embarrass me." She studied the table for a moment before getting up and leaving the room, her heels clicking against the bare floor.

"Why don't you just forget it, Rudy," Donald said.

"No," Rudy insisted. "She wanted me to tell it. I'm not going to stop in the middle."

The young waitress came back just then, followed by a gaunt, older Turk in a white kitchen smock carrying a tray. He smiled at Tonia from under a thick mustache as the waitress set a plate-size slice of Wiener schnitzel in front of each of us. "*Guten apetit*," she said. A moment later the Turk returned with a new carafe of wine.

"Okay, now finish it," Donald said, getting up from the table.

"Yes, sir." Rudy watched him until he disappeared through the doorway. "Isn't this fun?" he said to me.

"Rudy...."

"Alright, Sarah." He tried to pat her hand but she pulled it away. "The short version, Newhouse, is this Pablo guy was from Spain and thought of himself as some kind of grand impresario. He ran a broken-down opera company and let Felicity sing the lead in small productions. He had her convinced he was going to make her a star. She lived over there for five or six years, traveling all over with him, and eventually she married the guy. About then, the postcards stopped coming. I didn't hear anything about her for years. Then one time on a trip home I ran into her mother. It seemed old Pablo wasn't interested in furthering Felicity's career so much as moving to the States. He told her he had a job offer with some opera company in Florida. He'd make her the star of the company there, he said, and then she could move on to the Met. That's what her mother told me. I don't know how much of it is true. I don't know how she could have been that naïve."

He paused to cut off a cube of veal and fork it into his mouth.

"So somewhere along the line Felicity gets pregnant. I don't know if it was in Europe or after they got back to the States—her mother didn't say. Anyway, she has this boy. By this time, I haven't seen Felicity since high school. Her mother tells me she's in bad shape. Somewhere along the line—maybe when she had the kid—she stopped singing. Her mother has seen the boy only a couple times and both times he seemed cold toward Felicity, even contemptuous of her. The last time was only months before and Felicity looked terrible—skinnier than she'd ever been, with black circles under her eyes. Her mother wanted to know if there was something I could do. 'Like what?' I say to her. 'Like get her out of there,' she says."

We could hear Felicity and Donald out in the reception room now, arguing about something.

"Hurry up, for God's sake," Sarah said.

"So I do some asking around, and it turns out a couple of people I know have talked to Felicity. She called them, out of the blue, and told them part of the story. This Pablo, it turned out, didn't have a job with an opera company when they moved to Miami. He didn't have a job at all. He just wanted to live in the U.S.–and Felicity was his ticket. Before long, he was involved with moving drugs up from Latin America. And he'd turned Felicity into his best client."

Rudy looked past me toward the doorway. Donald was coming back, leading Felicity by the hand. "I'm just about done," Rudy said, but Felicity ignored him. "So I tell Gerhard all this. I check it out first, as well as I can. It turns out other people have heard from Felicity, too. They give me her number and I get her on the phone. She adds a few details, but she won't say much. She's fine, she says, but I can tell by her voice she isn't. So I talk to Gerhard about how we can get her out—"

"Stop it!" Felicity was lifting a trembling finger toward him. "Goddamn you, Rudy, stop it. You are not going to make Gerhard into some kind of hero—not at my expense."

His answer was measured, each word drawn out: "What the hell is wrong with you?" Without waiting for a reply, he stood and threw his napkin down on the table. "You have no appreciation for anything, do you? No gratitude. I can't stand the sight of you anymore."

Felicity waited until he had left to answer him. "And how do you think I feel about you?" she said to her plate. Donald put his hand on hers but she moved it away.

We ate the rest of the meal in an awkward silence. Tonia took her foot from mine and I avoided looking at her. Before dessert came she excused herself and I followed her out, stopping only to call the Italian couple who ran our hotel at Misurina. When the wife, Katerina, answered, I rushed through the expected greetings as fast as I could. I need you to do me a favor, I told her: book two tickets for the day after next on the earliest bus to Venice.

I found Tonia down by the lake, not far from where Donald and she had been earlier. Clouds had moved in overhead and it had started to rain. She was sitting on the wet grass, her legs stretched out toward the water, her damp hair already flat against her head. She sat absolutely still, the rain soaking into her clothes. I stopped a few feet away and called her name. Instead of turning around, she shifted her arms and lay back against the wet grass. The light from the windows tinted her cheeks a faint rose, like the wash on an old black-and-white. From the other side of the building came the hushed whoosh of tires on the wet highway. The only other sound was the faint purr of a motorboat out on the lake. I sat down beside her and ran my hand slowly down her hair. The cold pinpricks of rain raised goosebumps on my arms and the moisture from the grass seeped through the seat of my pants. "Should we go in?" I said.

She didn't look at me, but her fingers moved across the grass to my waist and traveled past my hip to my thigh. "No," she said, her voice soft, far away. I wondered if she'd taken something, a Valium maybe, something to flush Rudy and Felicity out of her head. "It's peaceful here," she went on. "The black of the trees and the lights reflecting off the clouds. Is there a city near here?"

"No, not really." The rain had completely soaked her clothes. Her thin blouse clung to her skin like the gown on the Victory of Samothrace.

"The lights of the universe then." She laughed a drugged sort of laugh. "The lights of the cosmos...the celestial lights...the sounds of heaven in the wind...."

I started to ask the poet's name but she put her hand to my mouth. "Sshhh," she whispered, "just listen. Feel. Forget everything else. Just lie here with me." Her hand moved above my belt to the last button on my shirt, unfastening it before sliding in, cold against my skin. I tried to relax, lying back on the grass beside her, but the damp was uncomfortable and the cold made me want to take her inside, into a bed.

"I saw my father and mother lying like this once, in the rain," she began, her voice thick and low. "Look!" She pointed straight up to a break in the clouds, a jagged tear where a single star was bright enough to be visible. "'Would I were steadfast as thou art,'" she recited,

"'not in lone splendor hung aloft the night
and watching, with eternal lids apart....'"

For the first time since I had come outside, she looked at me then. Her eyes had an intensity I hadn't seen before. "This is how they were, barely touching," she said, "as wet as this...but it was summer and the rain was a summer rain, and there was thunder...." She cocked her head, lifting it slightly from the damp grass as if to hear the sound again. "...and they watched the lightning flash without moving. Without moving at all, even when it came close. They were so in love...it seemed they wanted the lightning to pass right over them—to kill them together...or maybe they wanted to believe that it couldn't strike them, that they were immune somehow."

The boat I had heard before was far down the lake now, its light still visible but the sound of its engine gone.

"I watched them from the deck of the cabin...the water beyond them like this, with a light from somewhere, and they just lay there, without moving, for hours—until I fell asleep." She closed her eyes and laid her head against the grass, her hand still on my stomach. I studied her eyelids, the line of her nose, the curve of her lips where they parted. Then I ran my fingers over her breast, down to her belly, feeling the way the fabric stuck to the skin, the warmth that radiated from her. I couldn't remember wanting a woman more than I wanted her then.

"Tell me more about your childhood," I said when she fell silent. I needed her voice to keep me from feeling the cold, the throatiness that crept into it when she spoke in soft tones, the soothing notes that worked like a counterpoint to the flow of her fingers across my stomach. Let go of the cold, I told myself. Let go. And I thought of the mountain she had described in Tibet, the room at the roof of the world with the sky above, the light flooding in. I closed my eyes and tried to imagine the earth as she might see it, as something warm beneath us, magma heating the roots of the moistened grass. My hand burrowed into the gap between her legs, but somewhere at the edge of my consciousness I was afraid if I thought too much about what I was doing I'd wake up alone.

For several minutes, we lay like that, with my skin growing numb, the wet highway breathing rhythmically, endlessly, car after car. I could taste the wine on my tongue, the last of the meal. I could smell the leaves moldering, their parchment spans breaking down, the loamy soil drinking the rain.

"My father," she murmured at last, the words almost indistinguishable. "My father...." It seemed she was praying. "...he was the one...." It was spooky the way the words came from her motionless mouth. Only her hand moved, stroking my stomach. "...he was the one you should have met...." I lifted myself to my elbows and leaned toward her to hear her better. Her breasts rose and fell with her breathing. The pink that had lit her before was gone, replaced by a yellow light. Her eyes were closed and for the moment before she spoke again I pictured her dead, trying to imagine how I would feel. The wind was coming off the lake, blowing the rain at my face, my eyes tearing. "Are you alright out here?" I asked as I leaned to kiss her mouth.

"I'm from Portland, remember," she said, smiling as her eyes opened, fixing on me. "I used to sit for hours in the rain. My father would come and get me when he came home, always knowing where I'd be."

"And your mother?"

"And my mother, too...he'd find her...when he could. Come down here with me." Her hand tugged at my shirt.

"Aren't you cold?" I asked from the ground beside her. "Shouldn't we go in?" She shook her head.

"You wanted to know about my childhood, what it was like," she whispered. She pushed me into the ground and rolled over on top of me. Her face was still yellow but different now. Lit and alive. "My father wrote a book once," she said as her hands moved up my shirt, freeing the buttons one by one. "And when it came out, everyone knew him. The whole city of Portland knew him. Knew us. They thought they knew us, anyway." When the halves of my shirt were free, she wrenched them aside and lowered her mouth to my chest. The cold tips of her hair fell against my skin like brushes painting my flesh as she inched upward. "Then the book became a bestseller..." Her tongue flicked at my chin as her hands tugged at my jeans. "...and the whole country thought they knew us." My fingers moved to the waist of her pants. Turning her over onto the earth, I put my hands on her shoulders, my mouth on her breast. "It was his book..." Her breathing was coming faster now, making it hard for her to speak. "...about my mother...." The wind was rushing up my back, the rain falling from my face to hers. The mud and the grass were smearing the skin by her breast, her stomach, her throat, and I thought I understood what she'd been saying: about her parents and how they'd loved —the way they'd watched the lightning approach and hoped it would kill them together.

# Chapter Seventeen

From the deck, I could see the patch of flattened grass where I'd been with Tonia the night before. In the dark it had seemed we were rolling naked across the entire lawn, but the patch was small, hard to find. Above it the fog had thickened enough to obscure not only the lake's far shore but anything farther than twenty yards in any direction. The success of the next three days depended almost entirely on good weather—there were no museums or shops where we were going, only mountains and vistas that would take your breath away if you had the weather to see them. But my concern was more immediate than that: unless the fog lifted soon, we'd be driving up into it and I'd have to concentrate more than I wanted to. I'd taken six aspirin already that morning, swallowing them with glass after glass of water, but my head continued to pound, my hands to shake.

My room was heavy with the smell of drying clothes and shellac from the new wood walls. But Tonia's scent was still on my skin. While I dressed I forgot the drive ahead and thought about being with her again that coming evening, lying together in a hotel I knew by a lake I loved. Normally, I kept tours away from places I loved. Once you've heard someone complain about the taste of the food somewhere or the stain in a toilet, you always remember them there. I was taking this group to Lake Misurina only because I hadn't had time to find a different hotel. It was a small group, I'd rationalized, and the many pleasant days I'd spent at the lake would overshadow anything that might happen.

I first saw Misurina on a travel poster in a tourist office in Milan. It showed a grand hotel rising from the edge of a glass-like lake with nothing behind it but a sky-filling mass of mountain. It seemed to be at the very top and end of the world, like one of those Nepalese villages you see on television, a place lost in time with Annapurna towering over it. I imagined that to get to it you had to be helicoptered in or climb to the top of an Alpine ridge. For years, I remembered it without ever going there. It was the place I called to mind whenever something unpleasant happened. I can always go there, I'd tell myself.

But as is often true when you fantasize too much about a place without having been there, my first visit to Misurina disappointed me. I hadn't expected the highway that ran along the edge of the lake or the charmless hotels and tourist shops. I hadn't pictured the water stagnant, with bits of debris—a Coke can, a plastic bag—mired in the algae. And I hadn't imagined that what looked like a grand hotel in a travel poster might be something else entirely. Still, the first time I went I stayed several days—far off the road in a smaller hotel—and slowly the enchantment returned. From my room I could see only those things I'd seen in the poster: the trees, the mountains, the grand hotel. I spent my days hiking alone and went down to the lake only in the early morning or late at night when the tourists were gone, when a soothing calmness prevailed. In subsequent years, Misurina became a place I visited often, a peaceful place where I could think without anyone bothering me.

"Don't you look like hell," Rudy said when I entered the dining room. He was sitting with Sarah next to the window. The tables had all been separated and moved from the wall. Shakers of salt and pepper and little containers for waste stood where the carafes of wine had been the evening before. Sunglasses covered the welt by Rudy's eye, but the bruising had spread beyond the frame, covering half of his forehead.

"And you," I said, trying to smile.

Sarah glanced up without greeting me. "Felicity and Donald *were* here," she said.

"I seem to have driven them out," Rudy added.

"And Tonia?"

"Not down yet that I know." Sarah raised her eyebrows questioningly. "Coffee?"

The thought of putting anything into my stomach nauseated me. I shook my head and went outside to load the luggage into the bus. The air was colder than I had expected but it felt good on my head, like an ice pack put to a bruise. I'd just opened the back of the bus when Donald came around the side.

"Are you still planning to take the pass?" he asked.

I assured him I was.

"The man here told me there could be snow up there." He leaned against the rear fender and I noticed that he was wearing a parka instead of a sport coat. The collar below it was loose and tieless, and he wore walking shoes rather than wingtips.

"We're going over," I said. There was a way around the pass but it would take twice as long. We'd be hard-pressed as it was to reach Misurina by dark.

"You have chains?" Donald glanced inside the rear door where the jack and the spare were.

"We'll make it," I said, sliding in the final suitcase. Donald brushed the arm of his parka where it had touched the bus, then walked back toward the hotel as I climbed in and started the engine. It had been running rough the day before and I wanted to give it time to warm up. I wanted to give myself time, too—time alone before I had to listen to Rudy or Felicity again, time to clear my mind so I could concentrate on the drive ahead. When I cranked the key, the engine turned over several times before catching. A cloud of black smoke shot out the back, giving way to a series of pops that increased in tempo until the motor was running smoothly. Almost immediately, Felicity appeared at the hotel door and, one by one, the others came out behind her—all except Tonia.

"I'll go get her," Sarah said when everyone else was in the bus. It seemed Felicity had forgotten her fear that the curves of the road would sicken her. She sat in the very back, away from Rudy, who sat behind me, while Donald sat in the middle row between them. They looked like children told to line up single file and keep their mouths shut. I was glad to have them quiet, glad to be free of their bickering. Katerina, who ran the Misurina hotel with her husband Luca, had told me the bus to Venice would leave Cortina at eight the next morning. That meant in twenty-four hours Felicity and Donald would be gone. Twenty-four hours. That was how long I had to fill with something other than Tonia. That was how long I had to forget the way she'd moved under me. That was how long I had to avoid dreaming of being with her alone.

    The hotel door opened and Sarah's back appeared, her body hunched slightly. She was moving something heavy, sliding it onto the porch. She paused to speak to someone inside, then Tonia appeared and I didn't see Sarah again until she was standing beside my door. "Can you open the back for me," she was saying, but my eyes were on Tonia. She was wearing the short black skirt she had worn before and both her feet and her legs were bare, the skin reddening as she moved out into the cold. Above the skirt she was wearing a thin leather jacket, the V at the neck revealing nothing but flesh below. In her hand she carried a pair of running shoes, and as she neared I could see that she was wearing more makeup than usual. I might have thought she was trying to cover her lack of sleep but she didn't look tired at all. In fact, her skin seemed to radiate energy. There was something else, too, something that gave her eyes and her mouth an almost frightening openness. What Rudy had said about Felicity's husband the night before was still in my mind and I wondered again if Tonia might be taking something. I wanted to believe her look came from our night together, but it seemed to come from some part of her I had nothing to do with.

"Can you open it?" Sarah asked again, less patiently than before. When I stepped out to help her I saw that the bag she held was Tonia's. While I stored it in back, I watched Tonia settle herself on the seat beside mine, then turn and smile at the others.

"Where have you been?" Felicity said from the back.

"I'm sorry," Tonia purred, her voice lush and low. "I overslept." Her eyes sparkled as she glanced out the window toward the mountains. The fog had lightened just enough to expose the trees on the lower hills. "It's going to be beautiful up there." Her words had a spark to them as well. They were ordinary words but they made the air around them seem bright.

"You're awfully cheery," Felicity said. "You must have had quite a night."

Before climbing into the cab I checked the tires and ran my eyes over the fenders, the windows, the side panels. The paint on the driver's side had started peeling. "Grand  ours," it read now, the "T" having freed itself somewhere between Munich and Zell am See. The whole bus looked embarrassing. Broken down.

Tonia was still looking back at the others when I slid in behind the wheel. Her bare knee jutted across the seat and I grazed it with my fingers before putting the bus in gear. I didn't look at her or anyone else; it would take all my attention—all the concentration I had—to get us over the pass. The bus lurched into motion and for a moment, as I inched up the hill beside the hotel, I thought about that ride to Montana twenty years before—how my mother's old Chevy had sputtered and balked at the prospect of pulling a trailer over the Bitterroot Range.

    We'd been on the road only twenty minutes, passing mostly through empty woods, when the first soft flakes appeared. Tonia's knee had moved gradually closer and was resting against my thigh. The bus had been running well and the fog had been lifting, and I had begun to think the day might actually turn out fine. My headache had even retreated, remaining as only a pressure at the base of my skull. Tonia had been more talkative than usual, as if she thought she had to charm the others to make up for being late. She'd already told them about sitting in the rain by the lake: the chill of the raindrops on her skin, the gauze-like fog, the impulse she'd had to strip off her clothes and plunge into the water naked. When the snow began, she was trying to describe the smell of the bread coming up from the kitchen below her room that morning, the pleasure of lying in bed in a dark room with that smell in the air. She didn't mention that I was there.

    There were only a few small flakes at first and no one seemed to notice. I thought they might be an aberration, a preview of what would come to the mountain in another month or two. Only when they had thickened enough to require the wipers did I remember how low the snow had been on Mt. Watzmann the day before. By then we had reached the toll station below the pass. I asked the man in the booth about the snow and he assured me it was only a passing flurry. It wasn't until I had paid him and driven another mile that the flakes began to fall in earnest.

"Do you know how to drive in this stuff?" Rudy asked as the road began to climb. I assured him I did. Though there was no snow on the roadway yet, I slowed to a crawl as I took the curve, afraid the wet pavement wouldn't hold the tires if I had to brake suddenly. My bus's odd right-hand steering was an advantage now because it allowed me to see exactly how much room I had on the shoulder.

"Would it be better to turn back?" Tonia asked. I gave an almost imperceptible shake of my head, hoping she'd understand. I needed her to talk about something else, get the group thinking about something else. There was no way I was going back. We had just the one mountain pass to cross and we'd be in Italy. "It reminds me of going skiing when I was young," she said without taking her eyes off me. "That first snow. I used to love when it snowed in Portland." When she paused, the bus was quiet. Too quiet. She tried again, "This kind of weather makes me think about Christmas—about the Christmas parties we used to have."

This time Rudy responded. "Yeah," he said, "there's nothing like those Christmas parties you used to throw." I didn't understand what he meant at first. Then I remembered that his fight with Gerhard had come at a Christmas party.

"I meant the parties my parents used to have when I was a girl," Tonia said. She shifted her weight, pressing her knee more firmly against my leg. "This whole area makes me think of those Christmases. My mother made these little gingerbread houses like the houses here, with little eaves out of frosting, and put them in every room. Then she dragged out the woodcarvings she and my father had bought on their trips over here—nutcrackers, music boxes, manger scenes. Even the trees remind me of how our house looked—the evergreens. My mother had Christmas trees everywhere, all of them flocked...she loved Christmas. Do you remember, Sarah? The way our house looked? The parties we used to have?" When Sarah didn't answer, Tonia continued her description, adding details: the red satin ribbons strung along the staircase railing, the holly sprigs tucked behind picture frames, the assortment of angels lined up across the fireplace mantle. "Sarah, you *must* remember some of that," she said finally.

"I didn't know your mother," Sarah said then. The effect of her words on Tonia was startling. She didn't say anything more. Lowering her eyes, she turned back toward the front of the bus, folding her arms over her chest. Her leg pulled away from mine and she crossed it over the other as if trying to cover as much of herself as she could. Her shoulders slumped and she stared off through the window away from me, out into the worsening weather.

"Tonia, I'm sorry," Sarah said. The words hung in the air, in that silence snow always seems to bring. I kept my eyes on the road. The flakes weren't sticking to the pavement yet but the ground on either side of the highway was speckled with white. Through the fog I could see waterfalls rushing down toward the valley, their sources lost in the clouds above. The trees were all firs now, the few clusters of orange larches like discolored patches of mildew.

"Isn't it wonderful to think about the past?" The words were Rudy's. He said them loudly, in a lighthearted tone that let you know right away he wasn't planning on stopping there. The thing to do, I knew, was to cut him off. To break in with some historical anecdote or a few facts about the area. That had always been my way of keeping a group from noticing when something went wrong or defusing tension between tour members. But I didn't say anything. "Isn't it, Felicity? To think about the old days. To look out here at the snow and think about those days when we used to go skiing in Vermont."

"Rudy, leave her alone," Donald said. "Haven't you said enough already?"

In the mirror I could see Rudy smile. I didn't know where he was going with this but it was obviously somewhere darker than his smile suggested. When I glanced at Tonia, she had her fingers up to her mouth. I waited—we all did—to see if Felicity would answer.

"You were the one who chose to go there, to look at all that," she said finally, sounding as if she had carefully assembled the words before speaking. "You could have left it alone. Left everything alone. The past is the past."

"A couple of days ago," Rudy said, "I would have said you were right. The past is the past. Pay attention to now. Do what you came here for and go home. Then I was standing there in Munich, wasting the morning...standing there wanting only to get home...and I remembered about Dachau. Remembered it wasn't far away."

"You didn't have to go there."

"No, Felicity, I didn't have to go. But when I got to thinking about it, how could I be that close and not go? That wouldn't have been right, would it?...No, that wouldn't have been right."

Felicity said nothing. I could see patches of snow forming on the roadway now. Between curves I was driving as fast as I could to save time. If the snow continued, we wouldn't make it to Misurina until dark.

"I wouldn't even have mentioned it now," Rudy continued, "if I hadn't seen the snow, if I hadn't felt the tires give as we came around the corner."

"Rudy," Sarah said, "what are you doing?"

"Just remembering. Just thinking back to those pleasant days when Felicity and I were young. Carefree."

"It wasn't my fault," Felicity said defiantly.

"The past," Rudy said, "sometimes you need to think about the past, don't you, Felicity? To remember what it was like to leave New Jersey and the City behind, to pack the ski gear into the car and drive north, up into all that beautiful, wonderful nature? Didn't you used to love the snow—the way it piled up on the roads in Vermont before the snow plows came along?"

"I was seventeen," Felicity said.

"I don't know what you're doing, Rudy, but stop it," said Sarah.

"No. Felicity will want to remember this. It would be hard not to, wouldn't it, Felicity? With where we've been and now the snow? You remember that ski trip, don't you—up to Stowe with you and me and Henry and Abe?"

The snow was eating away at the highway now, moving across it in broadening swaths—a white presence consuming the black. The weather, or maybe what Rudy was saying, was making Tonia anxious. She squirmed in her seat and hummed to herself like a child who doesn't want to hear what she's being told.

"You remember how nice it was that afternoon, the way the trees looked as the sun was going down? You remember, right? Henry and Abe asleep in the back and you and me in the front. Everything peaceful."

"I wasn't thinking," Felicity insisted, her voice weaker than before. "I was seventeen years old!"

"It's true. She was young." Rudy sounded eerily calm. "It's a terrible thing to live with all these years."

"For god's sake, leave her alone," Donald said, but there was no movement in back; he would defend Felicity with words but nothing more.

"Poor Abe. After all he'd gone through. He wasn't even awake."

"You're going to say that was my fault?" Felicity asked.

"Wasn't it?"

No one said anything for several seconds.

"Are we okay?" Tonia asked when the engine hesitated coming out of a turn. Outside the window I could see nothing but white. The road was completely gone.

"Wasn't it, Felicity?"

"Leave her alone," Donald said. But nobody in the bus thought Rudy would, not even Donald. You could hear it in his voice.

"It's rich, isn't it," Rudy continued, "talking about Abe here, with the weather like this? He would have loved it here." When he paused, the whole world seemed silent except for the engine's laboring. I was following the tracks of a car that had passed us a moment before, trying to steer away from the shoulder. The car had already disappeared above us, swallowed by the maw of the hills. We had come to that perilous moment when the snow is thick enough to make the road slick but not to give the tires traction. I had slowed the bus as much as I could, afraid if I slowed too much it would stop and I wouldn't get it started again.

"Neither of us considered what being here might bring to mind, did we, Felicity? We never imagined that after a few days together we might start thinking about the past."

"You have your own past," Felicity spat from the back of the bus. "You want me to get into that?"

"It's different now, Felicity. I couldn't leave it alone if I wanted to. I can't forget what happened to Abe. I keep seeing his face."

"You mean you're not going to let me forget. You disgust me."

I couldn't see Felicity in the mirror, but I could see the others. They were all looking out the right-side window, watching the narrow shoulder fill with snow.

"No, Felicity, it's not about you. You were just stupid. I'm not talking about him dying on a highway. Can't you think for once in your life about someone else?"

"I do think about him. Don't you think I remembered him when we were so close to that place? Don't you think I still see him the way he was?"

"Then say something. Tell these people about him. Show that you understand what your stupidity took away."

"I'm not going to talk about it. Isn't it enough that I have to think about him? That I have to remember what happened?"

"So who was he?" Tonia asked before Rudy could say anything more. Her tone was impatient. I couldn't tell if she had tired of their childish bickering or she simply wanted to know. "What does he have to do with Dachau?"

Go ahead, tell it, I thought. I was glad for the diversion, glad they had something to take their minds off the weather. It seemed Felicity deserved it, too, for all her unpleasantness.

"Abe came over from France," Rudy said. He paused momentarily, perhaps waiting for Felicity or Donald or Sarah to try to stop him. "He was my mother's cousin. He was older than me by fourteen or fifteen years. He came over after the war, sometime around 1949 or 1950. I was only five or six but I remember driving out to Idlewild to pick him up." He paused again as I watched the snow fall steadily, my hands cramping on the wheel. There seemed to be nothing else in the world but the snow and the sounds of our bus: the engine, the wipers, Rudy's voice. "I was scared of him. He was the skinniest person I'd ever seen. Skinnier than you can imagine. And when he looked at me, he didn't seem to see me. As if I wasn't there. My father wanted me to sit in the back with him but I refused, so my mother sat beside him, trying to talk to him in the little bit of French she knew. When we got home, I wouldn't let them leave me alone with him. He seemed as old as my grandfather, older even, and he smelled different—the smell of misery, of squalor. It was the smell of European Jews in those days, the life they'd been forced to live. My parents hadn't told me he was going to live with us. They fixed up the storeroom in the basement and he lived down there—in the dark mostly, reading books my mother got for him at the library, coming up only to get his meals. He never went anywhere. He never ate with us. Sometimes my father would go down into the basement to talk to him. I'd hear their voices coming up the stairwell, but I was too afraid to go close enough to hear what they were saying. It wasn't until I was older that I started talking to Abe myself, until my father told me what had happened to him. He was from the eastern part of France. Chamonix. Because he lived near the mountains and Switzerland, he was able to evade the Nazis for most of the war, but they caught him near the end, on a trip back home. We never learned the whole story—my father thought he was helping the resistance somehow, maybe smuggling people across the border. When they arrested him, they shipped him to Germany and put him in a concentration camp. That was the first time I ever heard the name Dachau.

"In high school I started hanging around with Abe, going down into the basement and sitting near his door until he came out. I never asked about his past but we would talk about books and sometimes he'd tell me about things he'd once done—or once liked. He'd been some kind of skiing prodigy as a child, when he was six or seven, before the war. He couldn't have been more than ten or eleven, I guess, when the Germans invaded. He spoke about most things as if they were part of another world, one he didn't live in anymore. But skiing was something else for him, something he thought he'd like to do again, the one thing that seemed to have remained pure in his mind.

"We'd never gone anywhere together, but this one weekend Felicity and I were going on a ski trip with one of our friends. I was a lousy skier—I'd only skied a handful of times—and after what Abe had told me, I felt guilty going without asking him along. I didn't expect him to say yes, but he did. Felicity and Henry had never met him and I didn't know how to explain that he'd been living in our basement for ten years, so I told them he was an exchange student, that he had just arrived from France."

"I didn't know any of this," Felicity interrupted. "I didn't know he wasn't what you told me he was."

"But you did later, long before we came over here."

"I was seventeen!"

"So you've said."

"So what happened to him?" Tonia asked. Just as she said it, we passed a sign that said *2,000 meters*. The roadway was still white and slick but the snow had thinned. I tried to remember at what altitude the road straightened out. The clouds ahead seemed lighter but I thought I was only imagining they were, wanting them to be.

"We'd been driving all day," Rudy said. "*I* had been driving all day. We were two or three hours past the Vermont border, getting close to Stowe. Abe and Henry were asleep in back and Felicity was nodding off in the seat next to me. The road was like this, but there were mounds of snow on the sides and it was icy. We were going downhill, rounding a corner, when the car began to slide. I was turning the wheels into the slide and we were just about out of it when Felicity panicked—"

"I was seventeen," Felicity said, but she was talking to the window now, explaining herself to someone somewhere beyond it.

"She grabbed the wheel," Rudy said. "Next thing I know we're spinning across the highway. And there's nothing I can do. Nothing. There isn't any traffic, but the edge is narrow there and the car jumps a ditch, smashing into a tree. I couldn't even see it coming—we were sliding backwards and sideways. The tree struck us just behind Felicity, busting in the back door. When I looked back, there was blood everywhere...and Abe was dead. He'd been sleeping with his head against the window. I don't think he even woke up."

Rudy went quiet then. Just ahead, I could see a sign with a large blue "P" on it—we would be able to park at least. I tried to concentrate on my driving, on keeping the bus on the road, but I kept seeing it all—the blood, the pale face, the scrawny neck below a mouth that would never smile. Another sign emerged: *2,300 meters*. We came to a curve and the tires gave slightly, but the snow had almost completely stopped and the roadway seemed to be leveling. The silence in the bus was too much for me. My headache was back and I wanted nothing more than to get away from them all. How far can it be? I thought, pounding my hand on the wheel. Then, without warning, a patch of sky sliced through the haze around us. It widened rapidly until suddenly we were rising above the weather, the sun spilling out across the highway. All around us, mountains appeared, rising from mist in capes of snow. The ground was rocky, empty of trees, and everything everywhere was bare, including the highway ahead.

# Chapter Eighteen

On the way down from the pass I stopped in the small town of Heiligenblut and set the group free to find lunch. Heiligenblut was once a quaint village, but the ski crowds had turned it into an upscale shopping mall: Cartier watches, Hermès scarves, Ferragamo shoes. "Maybe we'll finally get a decent meal," Felicity said as she and Donald ambled away. Tonia waited for me. The sun was out, so I suggested we buy a picnic and find a place where we could look out at the mountains across the valley. The last thing she did before leaving the bus was take off the jacket she'd worn all morning, exposing a tank top stretched over bare skin. Then she marched down the street as if the cold air was summer warm while the codgers waiting for wives outside jewelry stores watched her pass. I remembered my first view of her at the Munich airport, the way the people followed her with their eyes, drawn by her confidence and looks. The draw this time was far more sensual and arresting and I wasn't sure I liked it. When I saw the men's eyes, the looks on their faces, I wanted to cover her up.

We found a delicatessen with cold cuts and rounds of cheese, shelves of bread and liters of Chianti. Tonia asked the old woman behind the counter if she spoke Italian and soon they were conversing rapidly. Tonia's Italian was flawless and passionate. She seemed to enjoy the way it rolled off her tongue. She joked with the woman, making puns from the names of the products on the shelves, and insisted on paying for everything, telling the woman to keep the change. Then she skipped out the door with a loaf of bread in one arm and a bottle of wine in the other, leading me beyond the shops and restaurants to a bench with a view. Before we laid out our picnic, I opened the wine and she drank it straight from the bottle, wiping her mouth with the back of her hand and looking elegant even then. When she started talking again, she spoke in Italian, speaking more rapidly than she had before, and I wondered if the language alone had loosened her up. She'd learned it, she said, from an old Venetian her father had hired to teach her to paint. "My father wanted me to learn color," she said, slipping back into English while still using her hands. "And he thought only Venetians knew anything about it. Venetians, Venetians, Venetians—he was always talking about Venetians. Of course the Venetians he meant were 17th century Venetians, not Venetians like this old man who knew nothing about color and little about painting."

She seemed so intent on what she was saying, I let her talk and sipped the wine. I wondered if Gerhard had ever really listened to her. Her father had turned to art late in his life, she said, becoming a teacher of painting although he knew little about it. "It was mostly because he couldn't let go," she said, "couldn't forget the way things looked in the world around him. He'd draw perspective lines on his canvas and copy photographs of the things he wanted to capture instead of trusting his vision. His heart. The truth is he never had the vision my mother did. She was the one who gave me that, who taught me to *see*, whether I wanted to or not." Her lips began to tremble then and I noticed her fingers were shaking. I tried to put my arm around her but she looked away. "That was long ago," she said. "Long, long ago."

"Do you want to talk about something else?" I asked. I was worried I'd probed too much, drawn her out on too many things that disturbed her. Instead of responding, she took a swig from the bottle and gazed out over the valley. "What about last night," I said, "what Rudy said about rescuing Felicity. Was that all true? Did your husband really pay for it?"

For a moment she didn't say anything and I thought I'd brought up another bad subject, but then she started talking as fast as before, telling me Rudy was new to Luckspur and Gerhard didn't want to lose him. "He was always that way at the beginning," she said, "promising whatever you wanted, promising to help in any way, and then keeping score, using it to get something out of you some other time." She set the bottle down and took in a long, deep breath. "She was bad, Joe—bad, bad, bad. Her apartment was full of dirty clothes and take-out boxes, and it smelled terrible. She was strung out, Rudy said. Hooked on some kind of pills her husband had given her. I don't know if he'd left her there to die or what, but he and the kid were nowhere around. Somehow Rudy managed to get her on a plane to Portland and check her into a facility, but it took a long time for her to recover, and before she did, Pablo had gained sole custody of their child. Gerhard agreed to cover the costs for a while, but then he said she'd have to work them off somehow, and she did, she worked in the office, but it was a bad time for her. She still had to go to outpatient counseling and sometimes she ended up back inside—in that facility." Tonia shivered. "Then one day," she said, "Felicity met Donald and her luck changed. Gerhard wouldn't give her medical coverage and she was already swimming in bills, so Donald married her." As she said this, she let out a laugh that seemed odd in the midst of such an awful story. "Gerhard was angry, of course. He'd given Donald the health plan to cover his first wife, but they divorced and Donald, you know, is a helper. That was the only reason he ever worked for Luckspur, because Gerhard's father asked him to. You'll never see Donald get angry, but once he saw how Gerhard reacted, he started making plans to leave. He and Felicity were already living in San Francisco when Gerhard invited everyone to Mexico last year. While we were down there, he promised Donald part of the company if he agreed to work through spring. Like a fool, Donald did. Once he realized Gerhard would never make good on his promise, though, he sent a letter threatening to sue. I was there when Gerhard opened it. All he did was laugh and throw it away. He knew Donald would never get anything out of him because he never put anything on paper."

"So why did Donald and Felicity come on this trip?" I asked.

"I'm sure that was Donald," she said. "He has such a good heart. He probably thought Gerhard had changed his mind."

"So this trip is Gerhard's big 'fuck you' to everyone?" I asked.

"I don't know," she said, putting a hand to her head. "I don't know. It seems that way."

It was hard to say what exactly was different about Tonia that afternoon. What I noticed most was how fast she spoke, as if doors in her mind were opening up, allowing connections she hadn't made before. I was still absorbing all she'd told me about Felicity and Donald when she started talking about her father having grown up in Italy, near Como somewhere, and thinking of going there after the tour, staying somewhere for a long time. This was hardly out of her mouth before she began describing how her parents met in Paris. Her father told her the story, she said, more than once. "Every time he told it, my mother was lovelier, the weather was better, the city more magical. At first it was only a few minutes in the Jeu de Paume, where he saw her copying a painting by some master and loved the vision he saw on her canvas, the figures so full of life. Over the years, the story grew until they were spending days wandering the city together, planning their future, making love. I never knew what to believe. To my father, my mother was always alive, always beautiful, always changing, and so his story about her changed, too. All he ever wanted himself, he said, was to make her happy."

It was then that Tonia said something strange. "You remind me of him," she told me. "Of my father. You would have liked her, I know. You would have *loved* her. She was married already when they met but on her own, away from home. Not really married, you might say, in any way that mattered, except to Kandinsky, Modigliani, and especially Chagall. She loved Chagall's colors, so different from my father's Venetian ones. They were softer colors to her, colors that floated into the air around her, deepening as she looked at them, the greens turning to deeper greens, the reds bleeding out from the canvas. It was the passion she wanted to capture herself, the feeling that came from those figures floating upside down, but she couldn't paint like Chagall, not without adding edges, fragments, abstractions, more like Kandinsky, or Miro. She wanted to get at the *life* she thought she found in someone like Modigliani, some middle ground between what was real and what was imaginary, some place she could physically go. She wrote to him, you know, for over a year—my father—and all the time he was writing back to a post office box in Portland. He always pronounced it Port-e-land, like an Italian would, although he didn't have an accent. By reading his books at night, he became a specialist in Venetian art, in the post-Renaissance, in the grand canvas—the spectacle of Veronese, the reds of Titian, Tintoretto's gloomy darkness. He had a name for everything: the 'grand canvas,' the 'dark agony,' the 'life mystery' of a Giorgione. Oh, my God, *Gior-gi-on-e*—he loved that name, loved the very sound of it, the pure Italian feel of it—Giorgione...Giorgione...Giorgione...I'll show you, I promise, when we come to Venice—*Tempest*, it's called. I know it's there. He told me about it thousands of times. He went to Venice without me, you know, after Tibet—he went there alone to study that picture, to look for my mother in how it was painted, to see if he could see what she had seen. The 'life mystery' he called it, the 'life mystery,' but it wasn't my mother's mystery he saw in the painting. The lines he could see were too controlled, too expected, and the images were all familiar. There wasn't a single color that didn't come straight from the world, nothing that came from inside the artist's own head."

Tonia picked up the wine bottle and held it to her lips before noticing it was empty.

"There was a time," she said after a while, "when all I wanted was to see exactly like she did. Then for a long, long time I wanted to forget her—everything about her—and how she saw the world. My father did, too, at first. When she died, he burned all her paintings, then her clothes. After Tibet we moved into a new house and he wouldn't let me mention her. Nothing in the house could be hers. He hired a decorator and bought new furniture and made the walls all white. He wanted to get rid of that part of her that scared him. He wanted her to be the beautiful painter he'd seen in the Jeu de Paume, sitting there in her smock with her easel set up by *La classe de danse*, her own canvas a mass of figures and colors that didn't correspond in any way he could see to those of Degas. He would tell me about that moment over and over, after he started talking about her again. After he started writing his book. He would stroke my hair as I lay in bed, calming me by telling me how my mother looked surrounded by paintings she loved. He described her smile, how she stared at him when he stopped next to her, as if she'd been waiting for him, knowing the man she was married to in Portland was only a waystation."

Moving the picnic food aside, she slid across the bench toward me, laid her head on my shoulder, and closed her eyes. "It was only after my mother died that my father felt he knew her," she said, her voice softer and lower now. "When he started thinking about her again, writing his book, he'd close the door to his office at night and read her poems. I'd fall asleep to the clicks of his typewriter, imagining they were the heels of my mother's shoes clicking across the cobblestones in Paris. Those were the happiest moments for me, before everything happened. Before my father published his book and everyone read it, thinking they all knew who she was and why she did what she did."

Tonia didn't tell me what her mother had done and I didn't ask, but I could imagine. Her face had reddened and there were tears in her eyes. I hugged her closer to me and tried not to think of what we were doing. What might happen when the tour was over.

"From that time on," she began again, "wherever we went, someone always wanted to talk to my father, taking him here for a dinner or there for a conference, and he went everywhere he was invited because it filled his life. Because it distracted him. Making him think he had a purpose again. Sometimes he'd try to take me along, but I hated the very thing he loved. I hated people thinking they knew me because they'd read a book. For a while I hated him, too, hated what he'd done to me, taking himself away and bringing these strangers into our world."

Pulling away from me, she drew her legs up onto the bench and hugged her knees to her chest, resting her chin on them, her eyes on the ground.

"They'd follow me everywhere," she said, "follow me with their eyes, even though *I* hadn't done a thing. After a while, all I wanted was to be alone...and then my father ran for mayor."

Tonia began to cry, shaking her head at the same time. I wanted to comfort her but I knew by the way she sat she didn't want to be touched.

"I went to college at Reed," she said, "because it was near my house and after classes I could go straight home. Evenings, I stayed by myself and read or painted, waiting for my father to come home. Sometimes he'd make me go to political events and stand in receiving lines. It was sheer torture. Shaking hand after hand. Letting them look at me. I escaped by imagining they were Picassos, moving their features around at will."

She took a deep breath and stretched her legs, glancing at me but not really looking. She was still full of energy but the energy was different. I could see by the way she squirmed on the bench she was ready to move. But as soon as we started walking back, taking our picnic with us, she started talking again. After his single term as mayor, her father wasn't happy at home, she said. So he led a drive to build a new wing for the art museum. "He raised millions," she told me, "and all he asked was to have the wing named after my mother. But half of the money to build the wing came from one billionaire who wanted it named for his daughter. So my father retreated from the public he loved and started to teach painting. All he wanted, he told me once, was to think about art. He thought he had learned the important things from my mother and thought he could teach them to children. He thought he had finally learned to see."

"Had he?" I asked.

Tonia shook her head. "Not a chance. He had no idea. Even after writing his book, he could never understand what it took for her to see what she saw. The agony she went through."

We walked for a while in silence—past shops, past tourists, past restaurants—and I wondered how much of her mother's pain was lodged in her.

"Gerhard was part of those times," she said when we had almost reached the bus. "He was the only one I thought had any idea what I was going through. His father had been a community leader and our fathers were friends. I thought he understood the pressure I felt, the reasons I hated it all. I married him because I had no one else. I wanted him to protect me the way my father had when I was younger. He pretended to for a while—for a long time, in fact—but one day he said, 'All of this pain you have—it's your pain, not mine. It has nothing to do with me. Or with your father.' It was all inside me, he said. All my own. I had always been that way...and always would be."

"When was this?" I asked, wondering why she had stayed with him instead of running away. We had reached the edge of the parking lot. The others were waiting. Watching.

"That was in August," she said. "The day we booked this tour."

It took me several curves and kilometers of roadway to figure out what bothered me about what Tonia had said. She was asleep by then. The others, too. After Heiligenblut there were no towns for a while. No cars on the road. I was alone with the trees and the fields and the memory of our conversation: her words, her gestures, her tone. It was the tone that disturbed me. Most of what she had said had been sad, but much of the time she'd spoken breathlessly, almost excitedly, as if what she said was stimulating rather than depressing. For a moment I wondered if I had been fooled—if she had been planning to leave her husband before she even met me. And then it occurred to me that the opposite might be true: her husband was using the trip somehow to rid himself of her.

# Chapter Nineteen

It was early evening when we passed into Italy. The sky was still bright but the air had turned hazy and the light in the valleys was dim. It was that time of night that usually depressed me, but as I looked out at the thickening shadows I felt happy. The worst of the driving was over and in an hour or so we'd be at my favorite lake.

The road into Misurina bisects a valley trimmed with scrub brush and pine. Most of the way the mountains shoulder in close, but at one point a cleft gives a view of the Tre Cime peaks, the three chimney-like spires we'd hike around the next day. I pointed them out to the group, but only Tonia seemed to care. When we reached the lake a few minutes later, the sky was deep blue and the clouds in the west were turning pink. There wasn't another person in sight, and the water was as placid as ever. I was smiling at the peacefulness of the place when Felicity woke up. "My God, are we finally there?" she said. "I'm feeling nauseous."

The others were stirring, too, wiping their eyes and gazing blankly out through the windows. I pointed ahead to our hotel—a small two-story chalet tucked back into the woods. From the end of the lane that led down to it, it looked neglected. Uninviting. But it had an excellent view. "We can't stay there?" Tonia said. She was pointing across the lake at the building on the opposite shore that had once been a grand hotel. It was six stories high and a hundred feet wide, with a gray pitched roof and dozens of latticed windows. The walls were yellow, the balconies green, and lights gleamed softly from its upper rooms. Perfectly sited where the ground fell away, with mountains as its only backdrop, it seemed to be perched by a yawning abyss, as if the world ended there. More than once, I'd sat by the shore and imagined it in those turn-of-the-century days when the gentry came to stay: Carriages stopping at the gold-trimmed door. Sumptuous meals in the glassed-in dining room. Mahogany furniture on hand-woven carpets and window shades of the finest silk. It was never a stop on the grand tour, but it exemplified everything I imagined the grand tour to be. So I hated to ruin whatever vision Tonia had in her head.

"That's an asthma center now," I said, "for children who can't breathe at home." Instead of acknowledging that she'd heard me, Tonia kneeled on her seat and stared at the building as I drove down the lane to our little hotel. When I glanced at it, I could see the windows below the eaves and imagine the children leaning out in the twilight air, not to marvel at the evening but simply to try to catch their breath.

"We don't want to do this," Felicity said, "but we feel we have to." Her arms were crossed above the table where the last of our dinner dishes lay. She had changed into a dark blue dress for the evening and wore a strand of perfect pearls. Donald sat beside her in his gray flannel suit, his hand on the back of her chair. I'd done my best all meal to answer their questions about Venice and try to look interested, but my eyes were on Tonia now, on the table she shared with Rudy and Sarah across the room. She still wore the tank top and skirt she'd worn all day and I remembered the feeling of lying with her on the wet grass. "You can imagine how I felt last night," Felicity continued. "And today in the bus."

"I understand," I said as I watched Felicity finger her pearls. If I'd been honest, I would have told her I couldn't imagine how she felt about anything—how she could pick a condom out of a toilet just to make a point or complain about a drive along an Alpine lake with the last of the sun on the mountains. I couldn't wait to take her down to Cortina at daybreak and be rid of her for good. But I would miss Donald.

"It's nothing you've done," Donald assured me.

"Though there were times," Felicity said. As she spoke, she looked directly at me and I noticed for the first time that her eyes had a rusty color, as if they'd tarnished over the years. "Tell him what we expect him to do, Donald. What I told you to tell him earlier."

"You don't have to do this," Donald began, "but—"

"Just tell him," Felicity snapped.

"Why don't you leave me alone," Donald shot back, his mouth twisted with irritation. "I'll say this my way, if I say it at all."

"Okay, do it your way," Felicity said and pushed herself up from her chair. "I'm going to bed." Before Donald could even open his mouth, I knew what he was going to say. I knew by the finality of her tone, the note of triumph in her voice.

"I'm sorry," he said as he watched her leave. "It's about Venice, the extra nights...."

"You want me to pay for them."

"Well, Felicity was thinking...in exchange for the nights we're not here."

"No problem," I said. "I'll pay when I get there. Just tell them at the desk." I explained to him how to get to the hotel, just to change the subject. Then I suggested things to do before the rest of us arrived. "I assume you'll be joining us again there."

"We'll see," he said as he pulled a cigarette case from inside his jacket. "Do you mind? It's the one thing Felicity doesn't like."

The *one* thing? I realized then that he didn't see Felicity as I saw her and I felt sad I hadn't come to know him better in our time together. He seemed innately kind, the sort of man I would have liked to have had as a father. Or a friend. The way he held the cigarette to his mouth, with a kind of easy grace, made me wonder what his life was like before Felicity. Normally, I wouldn't have asked—I was used to getting only glimpses of people on tour, a handful of words and actions to figure them out—but this was our last time together on what I suspected might be my last tour. When he seemed about to leave, I asked him to stay for one more glass.

"I would've thought you'd want to get on with your evening," he replied, but he made no move to go, so I signaled for the waiter to bring us another carafe.

"It's just that I don't know much about you," I said.

"It's a little late to exchange intimacies, isn't it?" he said. He was looking directly at me, his eyes enlarged by his glasses. The waiter had blown out the candles on the empty tables and the room behind him was dark.

"That may be true," I said, "but I'm curious. Tonia told me you had another wife, before Felicity. Do you have children?"

Away from Felicity, relaxed by wine, Donald seemed quite different. Even an hour before when Felicity had prodded him to tell me why they were leaving the tour, he'd seemed hesitant, but now he seemed confident, in control. When the carafe arrived and I'd filled our glasses, he held his out toward me. "Here's to intimacies," he said. Then he added, "You don't think much of Felicity, do you?"

"I don't know her," I told him.

"You know enough." He gave me a droll smile. "I don't like Felicity much myself at times," he said, "But she hasn't had it easy and I understand her in a way. Understand what she's gone through. She understands me, too. Yes, she's obnoxious at times, but she's consistent. And loyal. I know what to expect from her." He paused to sip his wine and suck in smoke. "The truth is I'm with Felicity for a lot of reasons, most of which you wouldn't understand. One of them is simple—I'm lonely. And she's a person who lets me be lonely with her. I think you know what I mean. When you keep to yourself too much, you can find yourself drifting...gently at first, and then more severely. You can wind up judging yourself all the time. Or never looking at yourself at all. Never knowing you're dangerously close to not caring about anything or anyone."

He crushed out his cigarette and looked at me again. "I had no use for Felicity when I first met her," he said. "It was Rudy who told me to give her a chance. Give her time. She was just exhausted, he said."

"Rudy?" I asked.

"I know he can be awful," he said. "And I hate the way he rides Felicity. But Rudy's as straight-up and dependable as any man you'll ever meet. He gives everything his all. If it takes an 8 to get something done, Rudy gives it a 12. That's why he's the best marketer I've ever seen. The problem is he gets in his own way. And his passion can morph into meanness. In any case, he was right about Felicity. After a while, I saw what he saw before me: that she and I were alike. To answer your question, no, I don't have children. I never thought I was the sort of man to be raising them. It was the reason we divorced, my wife and I—that and the men."

It seemed unfair to listen to such intimate things without revealing something of my own, so I told him then about my mother and her men.

"The men weren't my wife's," he said, pausing to let this sink in. "The first few days on tour, I wondered about you. Then I realized your interests lay elsewhere." He glanced behind him to where the others were just getting up from their table. Tonia seemed about to come over, then turned away. "You should go," he said, and I stared at him for a long time before I responded.

"Do you think I'm wrong?" I asked at last.

He sniffed and rubbed his chin. "How should I know? Do you think you can make her happy?"

"Is that what you wanted to do for Felicity?" I asked.

"For Felicity? No." He took out another cigarette but it fell from his hand before he could light it. "I did what I did for me," he said. "I did it to help *me*. To make *me* happy."

There was so much I wanted to ask Donald—about Tonia and what she'd been like when he first met her, about Gerhard and the whole Gluck family—but his words had begun to slur and his head fell forward onto his chest. *For me*, I heard him say again. *To make* me *happy.* His words and what he'd told me before reminded me of another man I'd had on tour once, a choir director from the South—Alabama maybe or Mississippi. I couldn't remember his name but I remembered the sound of his voice—the same sad undertone, the same tinge of longing or maybe regret. I'd been hired to take his choir from a concert in Rome to one in Zurich and then to Paris. It was a small group. Baptist. When I took them to the Vatican, he was the only one who didn't cluck his tongue or make snide remarks. In fact, he was quiet most of the trip, keeping his thoughts to himself until the last night in Paris. After dinner that night he knocked on my door and asked if I'd go for a drink with him. It was the end of the tour, the end of the work, so I said yes. We bought a bottle of wine at a bar and wandered down through the Latin Quarter, coming out on the banks of the Seine. Along the way, after several aborted attempts, he managed to tell me he was attracted to me. I felt awkward at first, but when I told him I didn't feel the same, he seemed to understand. "It was worth a shot," he said.

"You know," he went on, "I love my life, love how I am, but it's killing me. The pastors preach sermons against me without even knowing it." He quoted a Bible passage he'd heard so many times he'd memorized it: *And the men gave up natural relations with women, consumed with passion for one another.* "Then my choir gets up in front of them," he said with a sad smile, "and people cry when they hear the music. The pastors tell me the choir has never sung with so much emotion. That's pain, I want to yell, *my* pain. The pain *I've* drawn out of them."

He was a big man, overweight and bald, with glasses, maybe fifty. He couldn't tell them he was gay, of course, and he wouldn't quit. He had nowhere to go, but more than that, he loved the church—the children, the hymns, the feeling that he belonged there.

When we had gazed at the Notre Dame in the floodlights—the awkwardly elegant buttresses, the slender spire, the delicate stone of the huge rose window now gone dark—we continued along the quay, mindlessly following the sounds of a saxophone playing somewhere. Eventually, we came to a young man standing below a bridge, using the stone as an amplifier. As soon as he saw the man, the director rushed forward. As he moved, he began to sway and then dance, gliding across the quay on his toes. His movements were surprisingly graceful, and after a time of dancing alone, he motioned to me. The quay was empty, the moon almost orange and almost full, and when he put his hand to my waist I *felt* the emotion flow into me. His eyes closed and he smiled and I closed mine as well, trying to let myself go as I would later with Tonia. As we danced across the stones I watched his face. His smile. It took me a while to realize he wasn't smiling because of me or even the night. He was smiling because the man with the sax had segued into the blues.

As I sat there drinking the last of the wine, I tried again to remember the man's name. I kept picturing his body moving. The joy on his face. Something more than mere dancing connected that moment to the one with Tonia in Ludwig's palace and even the nights we'd spent together. The first time we made love, she started to cry, and then, to explain her tears, she quoted a poem: "Oft rack'd by hopes that frenzy and expire, in the long Sabbath of subdued desire."

An hour had passed before I tapped at Tonia's room, not wanting to wake her if she was asleep. She opened the door right away, as if she'd been waiting beside it. The room was dark but I could see her silhouetted against the window and smell her perfume. At first I thought she was naked, but when I put my hand to her waist I felt a sheer gown with nothing beneath it. Her hands went to my neck and her mouth found mine, but when I eased her head back to study her face, her eyes were black and unreadable.

"What's wrong?" she said, her words too loud for the time of night.

"Shhhhh, nothing," I told her as I shut the door. Taking her into my arms, I inched her toward the bed, feeling her hands move across my back, her fingers press down into me.,

"Why didn't you come before?" she breathed as I lay her down, her breath hot against my skin. Her mouth moved to the edge of my hair and filled my ear with the crawl of her tongue. I wished I had come right away. Wished I hadn't drunk so much. Wished I had never been with anyone else or felt anything else in my life. I wanted to feel it all for the first time with her. Wanted it all to be new.

"Were you asking him about me?" she said, alternating her words with kisses. She moved her hand to my stomach. My shirt.

"No," I whispered, kissing her neck. "I know all I need to know about you." As I slid the nightgown strap from her shoulder, she buried her face in my stomach, her tongue tasting my skin.

"You don't need to know anything," she said between kisses. Her hands moved into my pants, the band of my underwear, touching me, stroking me, bringing me to the brink of a climax then backing down. Each time I touched her she flinched then pushed her body hard against mine. When I fumbled with the nightgown buttons between her breasts, she tore at the fabric, ripping the buttons away and slipping out like a snake shedding the last of its skin. Clawing at my clothes, she tore off my shirt, groped for my zipper, and tugged my pants from my legs. As soon as I was as naked as she was, she stretched herself over me, pressing down. "I want to be in you, Joe," she whispered. The best I could do was let her take me into her, let her control the way we touched. She moaned and broke into smiles as her body moved over me, her hands on my stomach, up in my hair. I could feel her juices wash over me, the flood of wet warmth, and still she rode me hard until a series of tremors seemed to lift her up and onto her side. When I rolled over to hold her, she pushed me away, her nails biting the backs of my hands until the spasms subsided. Something beyond the physical—some kind of spiritual elation—filled me as I watched her shiver, grow still. We lay with an inch of air between us but I felt as if we were still pressed together. I couldn't remember ever feeling so close to anyone, so aware of another person. Another body. I lay on my back with my eyes on the ceiling as the air cooled the sweat on my skin and she moved in the bed beside me, rolling from side to side. When she wouldn't lie still, I felt afraid of what I had touched inside her and how much I wanted to touch it again.

After she quieted down, I turned and saw her lying on her back, as I had been, her arms at her sides where her fingers dug at the skin of her legs. Reaching toward her, I took the hand nearest me and held it tight. Then I laid my other hand on her stomach, letting it rise and fall with her breath. For a long time we lay like that, the silence of the lake and the mountains flowing into the room as her fingers relaxed and clutched mine.

"I'm still awake, Joe," she said when I tried to roll over to go to sleep. She spoke softly but her words echoed off the walls. "I can't help smiling," she said, "wanting to laugh. This is the way it should be, feeling like this, the way life should always be." I could feel an energy enter me through her fingers, but I was too tired to respond, too worn out from alcohol and nights in a row of little sleep. I could feel her heart beating fast in my hand, the damp of the sheets, my eyes burning after they closed. A scent of fir trees or maybe pine had entered the room and it seemed with my eyes closed that we were lying out in the open. Out in nature. The world had never seemed so peaceful, my life so right. I emptied my mind of thought and let it drift away...until she spoke again.

"Do you remember the way everything moves in *Starry Night*," she said. "The trees, the stars, the *air?* I feel that now. If I looked out the window I know there'd be a halo around the moon, a pulsing glow, with all of the trees bending toward it. The world would be a field of wheat swaying together. Rising together. I want to stay here, Joe. I want to keep feeling like this. I want to paint this place and be with you and live like this...you and me alone together, with no one else around."

It took me a long time to say what I said next. The silence returned to the bedroom while inside my mind so many voices rushed together I couldn't separate them. My mother's was there. Cat's, too. They were telling me not to do what I was about to do, not to say what I was about to say. I shut them out and whispered, my voice dampened by fear, "Why don't we?"

Oh, but I was awake then...more awake than I'd ever been. Or ever hoped I could be. I'd never admitted the fear I'd lived with. Never seen it for what it was. But lying there like that with Tonia—listening to her, feeling her—made me see it all so clearly, giving me courage to leave it behind. It wasn't a fear of consequences, merely a fear of letting go.

Tonia didn't answer right away, but her hand squeezed mine and I thought that no matter what happened, no matter why she was there or what she decided to do, I would always be glad I'd said what I'd said. Simply speaking those three words—allowing myself to suggest what they suggested—had set me free.

When she finally did speak, I could hardly hear her. "I'm willing," she whispered, and almost before the words were out, we were up against each other again, our hands raking each other's skin, our mouths trying hungrily to suck new life from each other.

Neither Tonia nor I slept that night. We made love so many times my whole body ached the next morning. In between, we lay with only our fingers touching, talking about things we knew. We let our minds go wherever they wanted to go, not worrying about making logical connections or whether the other person understood everything, allowing for the gaps brought on by the lack of sleep. There was nothing I could say that Tonia didn't want to hear, no story too personal or obscure. Cat had never wanted to hear much about anything that didn't include her, but Tonia wanted to hear everything. She seemed to appreciate most those things that made us different. I told her about growing up alone with my mother, the loneliness I'd felt on my own in college, and moving to Munich when I was twenty-one. For once she talked less than I did, asking questions mostly, repeating things I said, making a joke or reciting poetry. Sometimes she seemed to want no more than to hear my voice or lie with her eyes closed and picture a place I'd mentioned. When I told her I'd gone to Granada, she made me describe it—the feeling of wandering the labyrinthine rooms of the Alhambra with their grotto-like ceilings and finely carved screens; the looks in the eyes of the gypsy women on Sacromonte as they lured travelers into their caves; the gaudiness of the crypt where Ferdinand and Isabella lay, encased in the silver they'd craved. She asked who the builders were and I told her everything I knew about the Moors. When I came to 1492, the end of their reign in Spain, she put her hand over my mouth. "The reign in Spain," she sang, laughing, repeating it over and over—just for the sound of it, it seemed—"the reign in Spain and the Spanish main...in fourteen hundred and ninety-two, Columbus sailed the ocean blue." I enjoyed what I thought was her child-like play, the humorous links her mind was making, the feeling she gave that with her nothing would ever be too serious or tragic to be redeemed.

"Everything is connected," she said into the night, her voice racing, "the Moors and Columbus and Lorenzo dying and the Renaissance leaving for Rome and then for Venice...all of them—all of them—related in ways I never saw before—the lure of the New World gold and Titian leaving Venice for Spain and the coins in his Danae shower...gold! My mother's beloved El Greco painting for Spain, *panting* for Spain, for the gold—going for gold—with those colors my father loved, those Venetian colors, there in that lovely glorious ruined old world...."

The more she spoke, the more the night itself seemed to take on colors—colors like those that appear behind your eyelids at times when you close your eyes. She insisted I paint for her with my words: vivid pictures, specific hues. When I said the gypsy girls wore purple, she made me be more exact—magenta? mauve? burgundy? fuchsia? Each one meant something different to her—a different feeling, a different mood. She had a visual vocabulary I could only guess at. I tried to imagine how she had seen the trees and the mountains we'd crossed. The orange larch against the green firs must have been more refined, more exact, to her—a flaming pumpkin, perhaps, framed by a dusky verdure. The world I entered with Tonia seemed a world full of color. Of *life*. A world where talk itself—even one's own—was filled with discovery. In the midst of it all, I remembered a question Cat asked me once. When all of your travels are over, she said, will you think of life with me as adventure? I told her yes, of course, but I knew even then that she had no idea what adventure was. But Tonia did—Tonia *did*—and her version was more beautiful and romantic than any I'd imagined myself.

# Chapter Twenty

When I walked outside the next morning the cold air stung my eyes. All I could think about was how warm it had been inside beside Tonia. Everything, even my bus, seemed foreign and lifeless, as gray and removed as the distant mountains. As I climbed behind the wheel, I heard the slap of the hotel door, then the harsh pitch of Felicity's voice: "Is it that difficult to drag a couple of suitcases down a stairway, Donald? Maybe you're getting too old for this." Her face looked especially sallow that morning, pinched between a bright red coat and her orange hair.

"Donald insisted on shaving before he would leave," she said when I hopped down to stow their luggage. "I see you didn't bother."

"We have plenty of time," I told her in a soothing voice. It was easier to be patient when I knew she'd soon be gone.

"Thank you for doing this, Joe," Donald said when he appeared. He looked old and weary and I wondered how much longer he could stand living with Felicity. I was glad I'd never find out, never have to see her again.

    The road from Lake Misurina to Cortina d'Ampezzo is only twelve kilometers long but it's full of twists and turns, each with a different view of the mountains. The sky was clear that morning, the sun like a matchstick touched to candles, bringing peak after peak to flame. I remembered that the Greeks built temples to their sun gods on the summits of their highest hills. Later, the Orthodox Church replaced them with chapels to Elias who rode a fiery chariot to heaven. I thought about telling Donald and Felicity this, but I was afraid Felicity would find some way to ruin the story. So I played a Mozart tape instead: *Eine Kleine Nachtmusik*. For a while we all listened to it without speaking. Then Felicity said, "I'll be sad to leave this part of the world, Donald. I would have liked to have seen Vienna at least. Maybe we'll do that someday."

    The way she said it made me sure they wouldn't be in Venice when I arrived two days later. They'd be back in the States by then, trying to track down Gerhard. I tried to picture them returning to their house in California, where Donald would drive into the city to work long after he should have retired. Maybe he'd stop at a club for a drink on his way home and gaze at the young men dancing, holding hands at the bar. I imagined Felicity growing angrier as the years went on and the two of them splitting when living together became too hard, not because they didn't have money but because the hope and the struggle that had kept them together were gone.

    The bus to Venice had already arrived when we pulled into the Cortina station. I put Donald and Felicity's bags in the luggage compartment, then turned to say goodbye. "Watch out for yourself," Donald said as he shook my hand. I could feel the bones through the flesh of his fingers and when I looked in his eyes I saw that for him the hope was gone already. I expected Felicity to leave without a goodbye, but at the last moment she reached out and hugged me awkwardly. Then she thrust an envelope into my hand. "I was going to have you play this on the bus," she said, "but given the company, I didn't have the heart." With that, she turned to mount the bus stairs. Through the glass, I watched her take the window seat and then turned away, free of her at last.

Before I drove back up to Misurina, I opened her envelope. Inside was a tape with *"Don Giovanni"* written in faded black on the label. When I slipped it into the tape deck, a voice that sounded strangely familiar filled the bus. It was Felicity's voice but younger and richer and kinder, full of the hope I'd glimpsed in Salzburg. All the way back to the lake I played it. And each time I rounded a corner, the mountains seemed higher, the views more beautiful, the future less certain than ever before.

When I reached the hotel, Tonia, Sarah and Rudy were all sitting where they'd sat the night before. Tonia was wearing a different blouse but the same short skirt. Her hair was uncombed and she looked even prettier that way. When I joined them, she put her hand on my knee and smiled. Neither Sarah nor Rudy seemed to care.

"Free at last, free at last," Rudy sang, "thank God almighty, we're free at last."

"Is she really *gone*?" Sarah asked.

I nodded. The odd thing was, a part of me missed Felicity. As with Donald the night before, I felt there was more to her than I'd discovered, something significant I'd missed.

Sun was streaming through the open windows, bringing with it the sounds of birds and a breeze so fresh and bracing it seemed the breath of life itself. Tonia seemed to feel the morning as deeply as I did. Between sips of the black espresso, she closed her eyes and breathed long breaths. Even the usual rolls and cheese tasted better than they had before. As I savored each bite I felt reluctant to speak, to alter the moment, but eventually I told them about the hike I'd planned for that day. From the dining room, we could see the Tre Cime peaks like petrified stumps above the trees, their long rock walls glowing a rusty pink. We'd drive to the base of the mountains, I told them. From there the hike would be easy and flat.

"Isn't there a trail from here?" Rudy asked. "After all this time in the bus, I'd like to get some real exercise."

"Since when?" Sarah said, staring at him. "Is this the same guy who won't take the stairs *down* from his apartment?"

"In New York I'm always in a hurry," he said. "There's no rush here. Besides, we're here to do things we wouldn't normally do, right? Isn't that what you've been telling me?"

"Since when do you ever listen to me?" she said. "My God, first you rip out an IV and now you actually want to hike *up* a mountain?"

"Amazing what getting away from work will do for you, isn't it?"

"What are you going to do next, go live in the Catskills?"

"We could do that," he said with a broad smile.

"*We?*"

They left the room, still bantering, to change their clothes and I reached over to put my arm around Tonia, who was gazing out at the lake, humming faintly. "I was thinking this morning," I told her, "about what you said. About staying here." She frowned and looked from my eyes to my mouth as if to make sure she understood me.

"I could be happy here," she said, her gaze shifting back to the lake and the grand hotel. "I could paint this place. Live in this place."

"Maybe we'll do that then," I said. "Maybe we'll come back here after Venice and I'll find something to do." It seemed strange to hear the words coming out of my mouth, to be planning a future, however short, with someone other than Cat. I tried not to think of Tonia as being tied to any place or anyone. Even me.

"We could do a book together," she said. "I could paint that castle we saw on the poster, with the towers and the turrets, and you could write about the prince and the princess who live in it."

"About Ludwig?" I said. "I suppose I could. I've told the story often enough."

"And I could help," she said. "Help you see and understand."

When I asked what she meant, she didn't answer. Keeping her gaze on the grand hotel, she seemed lost in a happy dream. Everything is a dream for us right now, I thought, a fairy tale about a prince and a princess.

We had to walk along the road for a while, but once we'd found the trailhead and were moving beneath the pines, our path became a long thin line that led us gradually upward. Katerina had given us each an old knapsack with a bottle of water, some small *panini*, and several Baci chocolates inside. At first, we had to walk single file, skirting boulders in places that had plunged through the forest, flattening trees. Rudy stayed out in front, stopping only to point out places he thought he might climb to see what the view was like.

"You go ahead, Tarzan," Sarah yelled at him.

"You watch me," he said. Eyeing the ridge as he walked, he stopped when he came to what seemed an easier route and said, "That's the one. I'm going up that on the way down." It was hard to believe this was the same man I'd met in Munich less than a week before, the one with the rumpled suit and difficult attitude. The hollow he'd chosen was covered in loose shale. It spilled down from a high saddle of rock and looked deceptively easy to climb. It was the kind of terrain an experienced climber would probably avoid, I thought, the kind where footholds would be hard to find. But I didn't say anything.

I wanted to hike with Tonia that morning, to be alone with her, but by the time the path broadened enough to walk two abreast, she'd fallen far behind. Rudy was out of sight by then, leaving Sarah and me alone together. I would have waited for Tonia to catch up but Sarah slowed to walk with me and seemed to have something on her mind.

"I haven't been out like this for a long time," she said, "not since moving to New York last year. I don't really like

Manhattan, but there's something to be said for starting fresh. Going somewhere where nobody knows you. Know what I mean?"

I almost told her about my move to Munich in college, my attempt to do exactly that, but something held me back. Something about her tone. The trail narrowed and I let her go ahead of me, glancing back to see if I could see Tonia. The sun coming through the trees made the needles and bark that littered the forest look like parts of a parquet floor. Only the trail itself was bare soil.

"It's funny," Sarah said when the way had broadened again and we were walking side by side. "There was a time in Portland when I wanted people to know me. Wanted it desperately. At least certain people. In fact, that's how Tonia and I became friends."

She paused, as if needing some response from me to go on, and I asked if she was one of the people Tonia had told me wanted to know her because they'd read her father's book.

"No," she said, her face turning serious. "I knew her long before then. I knew her when her mother...."

"Was still alive?"

"Yes, in a way."

"How can you be alive 'in a way'?" I asked.

"I mean in a way I knew her then," she said without elaborating.

"If you don't want to talk about it, don't," I told her. "Tonia didn't seem to want to talk about it either. I can imagine what happened."

"It's just something I haven't thought about for a long time," she said, "Tonia and I have never really talked about it. It's strange the way fate works."

"You believe in fate?"

"I don't know." She looked at me from the corner of her eye. "Do you?"

"Maybe once."

"Not now?" A hint of cynicism had entered her voice. Or maybe I only imagined it.

"Why?" I asked. "Has Tonia said something?"

The two of us had not talked about what was developing between Tonia and me since the night of the opera in Salzburg, a night that seemed long ago already.

"She doesn't have to say anything. I can see what's happening. It's pretty clear she thinks you're someone who might be able to save her."

"Does she need saving?" I asked.

When Sarah spoke again, any cynicism that might have been there before was gone. So was any illusion that we were having a casual conversation. "She doesn't know what she needs," she said. "She has a tendency to see a big change as an answer."

"An answer to what?"

"To anything. Especially anything painful." She seemed to consider carefully what she was going to say next. "Let me tell you a story," she said finally, "about my friendship with Tonia."

"As long as it's better than Rudy's story of his friendship with Felicity," I said.

"It is, in one way. At least Tonia and I stayed friends...but I knew Tonia for a long time before she ever really knew me, before I thought she was willing to be my friend." Sarah gazed ahead through a gap in the trees. We had reached a turn in the path and could see the refuge at the foot of the peaks ahead. "Is that where we're headed?"

"That's it."

"I wonder where Rudy is."

We could see most of the path we still had to climb, but Rudy was nowhere in sight.

"Maybe at the top of the ridge," I suggested.

"I don't know what the hell has gotten into him," she said.

"Travel does that sometimes," I told her. "I've seen it on tours before—it opens doors."

She looked at me skeptically. "Too many doors have opened on this trip already."

"What's that supposed to mean?" I asked.

"I don't know. I don't know what to tell you. Even where to begin—with me or Tonia or that first day I went to her house."

I couldn't tell if she was talking to herself or laying out a menu for me to choose from. "How about the day you went to her house," I said. "That sounds good and specific."

I meant to sound light-hearted, to keep the mood as bright as the day, but when she spoke, her tone was even more serious than before. "Okay, but you have to know a little about my background to understand what a big day it was for me—and maybe a little about her, too."

"Begin where you want then," I said, trying not to sound as wary as I felt.

"It's just that going to her house with her that day changed my life. People say that all the time, but it's true. If Tonia had never become my friend, I'd be a very different person. I'd probably be living in a trailer somewhere, trying to scrape by."

"You don't seem the type to have to scrape by," I said. It seemed she was being dramatic, speaking of scraping by as if nothing worse could happen.

"I almost don't see it myself anymore," she said, "especially dressed like this." She fingered the alligator on her shirt.

"What don't you see?" I asked.

"The dirt under my fingernails."

"I don't understand," I told her.

"I think you do." She turned and looked directly at me. "We're alike in ways, aren't we?"

"Not in any way I can see."

"But you admit, Tonia is different than you and me, don't you?"

"Different how?" I wasn't going to admit anything to her.

"I'm trying to help you here," she said.

"Help me how?"

"Help you see."

"Is that right," I said. "Exactly how do you think you and I are alike?"

"I was afraid you'd take this wrong—that's why I haven't said anything before. But now...."

"Now *what*?" I could feel my jaw tighten, the muscles in my back go rigid as they always did when Cat would plead with me to go back home, back to the States. Why would you want to go back? I'd ask her. Why would anyone want to go back?

"Listen, Joe, Tonia is wonderful. And I'm sure you are, too. Just listen for a minute to what I'm going to say. Let me tell you this story and I think you'll understand."

"What is it you think I don't understand?" I asked. I kept my eyes on the refuge ahead, wanting to think about nothing beyond the path around the peaks.

"Just listen. Will you listen?"

I didn't answer but I didn't turn away either.

"Tonia has given me everything in the world, taught me everything I know that's important. When I met her I was a scared little girl. I *do* know what it's like to scrape by, Joe. And to live in a trailer. That was my life. That was the only life I knew before I met her. I know that's not your image of a girl who went to a private school. But I was there on a scholarship. A charity case."

"So what does this have to do with me?"

"It doesn't really. It has to do with Tonia. To be honest, I don't care what you do with your life. But I care about Tonia, and what happens to her." I waited for her to go on, but she only looked away from me, glancing back down the path. "Listen, Joe..." Her voice was full of patience, even condescension. "...I grew up in a metal box sixty feet long and twelve feet wide. My father was an alcoholic who used to work for the railroad then took a job stocking shelves at night at a grocery store. The one good thing about his job was it kept him away from home at night, so he did his drinking during the day when I was at school. My mother worked every day to pay the little bit they made her pay to keep me at St. Agatha's. She thought that was the only way I'd ever have a chance. But when I was home, there was never anyone there." She stopped in the shade by a large rock and reached for her water bottle. "Do you want a drink?" she asked, holding the bottle out toward me. I shook my head.

"Listen, I'm all for you and Tonia," she said. "But you have to know how she is. I've seen how you look at her, the way you admire her—her openness. But you have to know there's a price she pays for that openness. For that kind of freedom. It was that way with her mother, too."

"And you think I can't pay the price, that I don't have the money."

"It has nothing to do with money." She took another sip of water and gazed off toward the refuge. "Let's keep walking." We had only gone a few steps when she stopped and turned toward me again. "I told you Tonia taught me everything, but she did more than that...she turned everything I ever did into something more, something special in her eyes. She showed me how to act, got me jobs, told me what to do when I went out with boys and then men. She cleaned me up, washed the trailer out of me...and all the time she never let me think she knew what she was doing. She always acted as if she was getting more from me than I was from her. In high school I spent half my nights at her house because there was no one at mine. She got me through high school and tried to teach me enough to get me to college but there wasn't enough for her to work with—or maybe there was just too much for her to overcome." She paused to glance down the trail again. "The sad thing is," she said, "I've never been able to repay her. Take care of her. There were plenty of times when I might have, but there was always someone there in front of me...first her father, then Gerhard. When her mother died...that was the one time I was there, but I didn't know her well enough yet. Didn't know what she was going through."

She stood for several seconds without moving or saying anything. The trail was leveling out, the trees thinning. Ahead of us we could clearly see the wooden walls of the refuge building. When Sarah started walking again, she kept her head down, and when she spoke, she measured her words, pausing at the end of each sentence at first, then talking more and more freely.

"I only know this because I was there, because I heard it and saw it for myself. It was the first time Tonia ever took me home. There's some kind of irony in that. Maybe that's why we've stayed friends all these years...sharing that. She lived in this huge brick house up by Washington Park—a million miles away from the trailer park I lived in. I was only thirteen but walking up the steps to the porch I was asking myself what the hell I was doing with this girl, why she would ever be my friend. By that time, we'd been going to school together for several years but she had never noticed me. Or at least I thought she hadn't. Everyone knew her, of course, the girl who could do everything—spell and do math and play every game better than anyone else. She was that kind of girl and everyone loved or hated her for it. The nuns loved her. They were always telling her she could do anything she wanted.

"It was sometime around Halloween, maybe a week or two before, when she took me home. I remember because her house was decorated—jack o' lanterns on every step, an orange bow on the lamppost, cobwebs in the arches over the porch. There was even a giant witch's hat hanging from the knocker. It was already dark when we got there. That's why Tonia took me to her house in the first place—she lived near the school and I didn't. We'd done some project after school and she told me her father would drive me home. I tried to say no—I didn't want her to see where I lived—but even then she had a way of persuading you…and, honestly, I wanted to see her house, to see how a girl like her lived.

"When we went inside, the house was dark. I remember the smell—like lilacs and roses and that waxy fragrance of candles coming from a line of pumpkins along the window. The candles gave the living room an eerie glow, their little lines of light shimmering across the white carpet as if it was water. I thought it was the most beautiful room I'd ever seen—with a white brick fireplace, antique furniture, and these huge framed paintings on the wall. It was like a museum or something you'd see in a movie. Tonia was quiet as we came in—I thought she was giving me time to take it all in, but I know now she sensed as soon as she opened the door that something was wrong. She called to her father but he didn't answer. She called again, leading me through the kitchen—a huge kitchen with a giant stove and every kind of appliance—to the dining room where there was a light on. I didn't see anything at first but the dark wood walls and the sparkle of the crystal inside a glass-doored cabinet. Then I saw him sitting there at the dining room table, a big empty table that gleamed with the light from a chandelier. His hands were folded in front of him and he had his head bowed as if praying. He was a thin man, and I remember he wore one of those sweater vests with the tie loosened above it. He didn't seem to know we were there until Tonia asked him if something was wrong. When he looked up, you could see this incredible pain in his eyes. 'What's wrong?' Tonia asked, sounding scared. He just looked away from her out the window."

  We had reached the bottom of the last incline leading up to the refuge. The trees were behind us and the ground ahead was full of rocks that poked out through eroded soil. Fields of grass and a few wildflowers stretched between the rocks, and the trail ran uphill through them, rising steeply. For several minutes we climbed without speaking, pulling ourselves up by gripping a bit of stone or digging our fingers into the dry grass. When we reached the top, the Tre Cime loomed above us, the walls jutting straight up from a skirt of abraded rock. The refuge was closed, so we found a place in the shade by a wall and waited for Rudy and Tonia to appear. When Sarah had caught her breath, she returned to her story.

  "So he was looking out this window. Her father. He looked out of it for a long time without saying anything. I just stood there watching Tonia, ready to do whatever she did, or told me to do. I felt entirely out of place and guilty for being there, for being somewhere I was sure I wasn't wanted. The window was one of those large picture windows, with a view of the backyard. Normally you wouldn't have seen anything at that time of night but your own reflection, but there was a spotlight on the back of the house—one of those safety lights—and it was shining on a huge maple tree. The tree still had most of its leaves. It was beautiful, all red and orange. And there was this swing hanging from one limb—you know, one of those perfect backyards, the kind you'd dream about when you were a kid.

"We stood there for a long time not knowing what to do. Then her father spoke. 'Did you see the bird?' he said. Tonia asked him what bird and he told her she had to see it. He didn't seem to have noticed that I was even there. 'Go see it,' he said. 'It's on the back porch. Oh, you have to see it.' He had found it under the maple tree, lying on the grass. It was alive but it couldn't fly. 'It couldn't fly,' he kept saying. 'Go see it.' So we went back through the kitchen and out the back door where there was a deck at the edge of the spotlight and we could hear this sad chirping. It took Tonia a while to find it. Her father had rigged up a nest in a planter box, and there was this sad little bird lying on a bed of torn-up paper. It looked up at us with one pitiful eye and I wanted to go home. Get out of there. It was so tiny and it seemed to have a crippled foot. One of its wings was caught on the side of the box and it was trying to free it but it didn't have the strength. I didn't know what to do. It was all so pathetic. You knew it was going to die. But Tonia didn't worry about what to do. She hardly looked at it before going back inside. 'What happened?' she said again. It seemed to me she knew already. But her father would only talk about the bird. 'I tried to feed it with an eyedropper,' he said. 'I tried to save it.' It was all so strange."

Sarah lay back against the wall with her hands behind her head. I waited, looking out at the mountains and trying again to picture the house, the privilege, Tonia grew up with.

"That bird was all her father would talk about," Sarah said to the sky. "He asked Tonia what she thought he should do. Asked her with his eyes on her now, as if the bird had something to do with his being able to go on." Sarah looked down toward the trail but neither Rudy nor Tonia had yet appeared. "Then, while we were still standing there, Tonia's uncle and aunt arrived. As soon as she saw them, Tonia got this panicked look on her face. 'What happened?' she said, turning to them, 'What happened!' I could tell it, too, by their faces. Her aunt spoke to her gently and took us both into another room while her uncle stayed in the dining room with her father. The aunt seemed to think it would be easier for Tonia to hear what she was about to tell her if I was there, if Tonia had a friend. The room she took us into was a bedroom where everything was pink—walls, bedspread, lamp shade—like a little girl's room but not Tonia's. Somehow I knew that. Her aunt turned the lamp on and sat between us on the bed. Then she told Tonia what had happened, speaking in an odd voice, without emotion, as if her news was meaningless. 'Your mother has killed herself,' she said. That was all. She didn't give details. But Tonia wanted details. She wanted to know everything. Her aunt tried to tell her it was better if she didn't know, but Tonia insisted. Then she sat there without reacting as her aunt told her her mother had wrapped a strand of picture wire around her neck. She had used Tonia's swing as a stool, stepping off it into the air."

From where we sat I could see Misurina down one valley and the town of Auronzo down another. Rising up around them in every direction were the austere Dolomites—crests and ridges of bare rock. The mountains thrust themselves toward the sky even as their brittle walls crumbled into fields and forests around them. Earlier, I had been anxious to escape the suffocating closeness of the valleys, the small places below the trees, but as I gazed at the barren heights I wanted to run back into them. To have something human-sized around me.

"I didn't see Tonia for several months after that," Sarah continued. "She returned to school for a while but sat by herself. No one spoke to her, least of all me. I didn't know what to say, what she was going through. It was only a year or so later, after she'd gone to Tibet with her father and they'd moved into a different house that she came back for good. She came looking for me then. She hadn't been well, she said, and her eyes said she thought I understood. But I didn't understand, not for a long time, not until I saw her eyes so bright one day it seemed there was some kind of fire in her, some way of seeing or feeling I couldn't imagine."

"When was that?" I asked.

"After her father's book appeared."

I could see Rudy below us now, beginning the climb up the hill of grass and rock that separated us from the trees. Tonia was with him. They walked together for a while then separated, each taking a different path. Rudy plodded straight ahead, pushing himself onto and over rocks that stood in his way, while Tonia took a trail that veered to the right, zigzagging over lower knolls, disappearing from sight at times. "Tell me about this book of his," I said as I watched them. "Tonia mentioned it the other day."

"I'm sure you've heard of it," Sarah said. "*Cassandra?*"

"No, I don't know it. Her mother's name was Cassandra?"

"No. Her mother's name was Mary."

Mary—I remembered the look on Tonia's face outside the Herreninsel gift shop when I told her the bridge above Ludwig's castle—Mary's Bridge—was named after his mother.

"Do you know who Cassandra was?" Sarah asked, her eyes on Tonia.

"Yes, of course," I said, "Apollo gave her the gift of prophecy." As Sarah nodded, I tried to recall the full story. There was a second part—Cassandra defied him and he took her powers away...no, he let her keep them but decreed that no one would ever believe what she said. I remembered a scene in *Agamemnon*, a clear summer night years before when I'd sat at an outdoor theater in Athens and watched an English actress, eyes wide with terror, shriek, 'How fierce a flame! It comes on me—it comes!' It had seemed my own death was nearing.

"It had a terrible effect on her," Sarah said, "She wasn't the same for a long time after that. But she didn't go to the hospital, not that time, not again for many years. I have to give Gerhard that much credit, at least. He kept an eye on her, if nothing else, kept her in control for a long time, right up until her father died."

Tonia's path was less direct than Rudy's and it would have taken her much longer to reach us if she hadn't moved faster than he did, running where the trail was flat, spinning around the corners like a ballerina. Sarah watched her with a somber expression. "I think you remind Tonia of her father," she said. "Her father when he was young. She used to tell me stories he had told her, about his travels—how he'd gone to Europe when he was young. His parents were immigrants from Italy. They wanted him to get a job right after college—to succeed in some American way—but he wanted to return to where they'd come from, to see where he would have lived if they had stayed at home. He traveled for a couple of years over here, starting in Italy, then going all over. That's why Tonia wanted so badly to end up here—did she tell you that?"

"No," I said, turning from Tonia to gaze at the peaks, the huge massifs that loomed over the ridge like palaces rising up from the sea. "But I could have guessed."

"His name was Marco," Sarah said. "Marco Polo, she used to call him when she told me about his stories. There was no end to them, she said. She thought that after a while he was making them up, but she didn't care. She loved them. All of them. That's why she likes your stories. They remind her of her father."

"So I still don't get the Cassandra bit," I said. "What was this book about—some prediction her mother made...about her own death?"

"I thought you knew your myths." Sarah was still watching Tonia. She was only a few hundred yards away now, still moving over the ground like a sprite. "Cassandra—Agamemnon brought her back from Troy—isn't that right? That's what her father's book said. She was his second wife."

"Tonia told me only that her *mother* had been married before."

"They both had. He had married in college but his wife didn't want to travel, so he left her—he told about it all in his book, about the guilt he felt for years for divorcing and finding happiness. He thought his guilt was what killed Tonia's mother. He couldn't leave the past behind, he wrote, couldn't give himself entirely to her, so she felt alone. He related everything to the myths, calling his first wife Clytemnestra and Tonia's mother Cassandra. She was like a Greek maiden, he wrote. There was a fire to her that came out in her art. She could see things other people couldn't. He called her paintings 'Rorschach tests for the soul.'"

"He wrote that?" I asked.

She smiled. "You think I'd make that up? I thought her paintings were bizarre—huge canvases full of disturbing images and jarring colors. They were the void, he wrote, dissecting them, reproducing them in color plates. He used Freud and Jung to explain them and used them to explain Freud and Jung. That's what made the book so popular—when people read it they thought they could understand all that psychology stuff at last. I did, too. I thought I knew how Tonia's mother had suffered and what her death had meant to Tonia. But of course I didn't. No one did. No one could. That's what Tonia hated about the book—it made everyone think they knew what had happened and why. Made them think they knew what *she* had gone through. For a long time she hated them for it. Hated her father, too. Hated everything about him—his stories, his travels, his romantic views. After her mother's death, he was the only person she trusted, and he had let her down. Instead of protecting her, he'd exposed her. Abandoned her. That's how she felt. Until he died, she could never forgive him for that. For leaving her alone."

"And that's why she married Gerhard?" I was studying the easy way Tonia was moving. The pure delight on her face.

"That's why she did everything—why she married Gerhard, why she left her painting and started designing games, why she didn't talk to her father for all those months before his death. For a long, long time all she wanted was to find a way to be normal."

"And when did her father die?" I asked, already guessing the answer.

"Last spring. Tonia didn't handle it well. She felt guilty. Felt she had done the same thing he'd done—abandoned him when he needed her. I didn't talk to her until July, two months after it happened. She was in a facility most of that time and Gerhard or the doctors or someone wouldn't let her have contact with anyone. She seemed almost fine when we talked—she was taking her pills—but Gerhard wouldn't let her go anywhere. He hired a nurse to look after her. When she called to invite us on this trip, I thought that meant she was finally free. I thought he'd realized she needed to get out. Needed to start her life again."

Tonia was running toward us now. When she reached us, she put her arms around me and gave me a kiss. Then she moved back into the sun and flopped down on her back.

"Tonia, are you okay?" Sarah asked.

"Of course I'm okay," she said with a smile, her eyes closed. "I'm as good as I can be." She pushed back her sleeves, exposing more skin. "With the sun and the mountains and all of this *room*, how could you not feel great?" Opening her eyes again, she raised herself to a sitting position and gazed down into a valley. "How could anyone not love this—these towns, these lakes, this day? You can see every rock so clearly, the way they absorb the sun. Was there ever, in all the world, a *better* day?"

# Chapter Twenty-One

"Have you noticed what's going on?" Rudy said to Sarah between breaths as he climbed the last few feet of the hill. His blue T-shirt was soaked with sweat and it seemed all he could do to point toward Tonia. Dropping onto the ground, he grabbed for the water bottle in Sarah's hand. When he'd taken several gulps, he wiped his forehead with his sleeve and said, "She's saying now that she's going to stay here. You've got to talk to her."

"I already did," Sarah said.

"Then talk to him." Rudy waved the bottle in my direction. "Tell him what's happening."

"I did that, too."

"So what the hell are you doing?" I thought he was still speaking to Sarah but he had turned to look at me.

"I'm not doing anything," I said.

"Sarah, talk to him." He wiped the sweat from his head with a handkerchief.

"I'll leave that to you two," she said, getting up and walking toward where Tonia was lying in the sun.

"Listen, Newhouse," he began, gazing past me at a hillside where hikers had placed rocks beside one another to spell out their names or make huge hearts with lovers' initials inside, "if Sarah told you what's going on, you know you're not dealing with reality, right?" He glanced at me for a reaction, his eyes hidden behind sunglasses, but I didn't answer. What I thought was none of his business. "I know about these summer-in-Rome affairs, these ideas people have about things miraculously working out. But it doesn't happen, I can tell you that." He paused again, eyeing me before continuing, "I don't really care what *you* do, Newhouse, but the last thing Tonia needs right now are changes. She doesn't know what she's doing. You represent something attractive to her, some kind of escape from how she's been living, but she can't escape it, not like that. It's the way she is."

"So what are you saying?" I asked when he paused. "Stay away from her?"

"I'm saying there aren't any happy endings here. You're not going to magically overcome some screwed-up period in the past."

"Maybe we should keep hiking," I said, trying to hold back my anger, wondering at the same time what he knew about my past. What Tonia had told him.

"I didn't mean you necessarily," he said. "I don't know anything about you. I'm thinking about Tonia—it was one thing before, but now she's this way. You don't know what you're getting into."

"I know enough," I said.

"Okay, you know enough. You know enough. Like I thought I knew enough about Germany. I knew enough to get my eye bashed in."

"I'm not saying I know her, Rudy. But I know enough to see that she needs *something* to happen to her, something different from what has happened in the past. You think she should just go home and not think about it, just accept the way things are?"

"You've got a wrong picture—" he began.

"I've got enough of a picture."

"She's sick, Newhouse."

"You're the one who's sick," I said. "Look at the way you treat people, the things you say. You think because you can't escape your past, nobody can. I didn't like Felicity much but at least she minded her own business. You act as if you were some great savior for her. But you didn't help her at all, did you? Now you think you're going to help Tonia?"

"You don't know anything about that," he said.

"What I *do* know is that what happens between me and Tonia is none of your business. If her husband wants to come over here and talk to me about it, he can. He should have been here in the first place. If she doesn't want to go back to him, that's her decision, isn't it?"

"Sometimes you're not in a position to make your own decisions, Newhouse. Sometimes you just have to accept the way things are."

"That's your philosophy, Rudy, not mine."

"What's yours, then, huh? What is it, Newhouse? *Carpe diem*? *Carpe* fucking *diem*? Act on your desires and your whole life will snap suddenly into line? It's not going to happen, Newhouse. You are what you are. And Tonia is what she is."

"You asked me before to tell you the truth about things, Rudy. I'm doing that now—I'm not going to walk away from this. I'm not going to just let her go."

"You're making a big mistake," he said.

"I've made them before," I answered.

The rest of that day I avoided Rudy. Tonia and Sarah strolled off together, so I walked alone. At lunch, when Rudy sat down beside them in the shade by a cluster of boulders, I sat by myself on a nearby knoll. By then it was almost three o'clock and we'd hiked two-thirds of the way around the Tre Cime. The trail had traversed a hillside of cascading rock that looked like a volcano slope, then snaked through a moonscape of tumbled boulders where the ground was the color of ash. Alternative paths had trickled away from the main trail, meandering down through the lower plains then disappearing over the edges of cliffs. It seemed at times that I was up on a high, wide stage and people were watching me. No matter how many times I told myself that Tonia and I were free to do what we wanted, I couldn't quite believe it.

After lunch we had to climb once more, this time up to a narrow ridge that lay between us and the path down to Misurina. It was cold in the shade as we climbed, and for the first time since we'd crossed into Italy the thought returned: winter isn't far off. This time I let both Rudy and Sarah go on ahead and waited at the top for Tonia. After talking with her through the night, I'd spent the morning away from her and I was anxious to make up for lost time. The things Sarah had told me had made me feel more protective of her than before, more convinced that I was right to rescue her. Sarah had said she was taking pills and I assumed they simply balanced her mood, allowing highs and lows but nothing extreme. It didn't bother me that she had been hospitalized before. Her mother's suicide, her father's book, her father's death—who wouldn't be traumatized by all that? At least she'd felt something.

As she neared, I realized she was singing but I couldn't make out the song. When she reached the ridge, she held out a cluster of wildflowers, her mouth forming a thin smile. "Mary's bouquet," she said, putting the flowers in my hand. "This is just like it, isn't it...even better?"

"Just like what?" I asked.

"That place with the castle...the view from the bridge—Mary's Bridge, you called it."

That day seemed long ago but I remembered again the sudden change in Tonia's face, the sudden quiet, when I told her the bridge was named after Ludwig's mother. I understood her reaction now and I wanted to talk to her about it. I wanted to let her know she could talk about anything with me.

"This is where Ludwig should have built his castle," she said, flinging her arms wide and twirling. "The Lake of Misery below—" She pointed to Misurina down in the valley, then lifted her arms toward the mountains. "—and snow for his sled rides with Sophie."

Singing again, she started skipping ahead of me and when she came to a hollow where the land dipped several feet, a hidden depression of grass and flowers away from the path, she dropped to her knees. Her hands went to her shirt and she pulled it over her head, exposing her breasts and her stomach. Then she held a hand toward me. When I reached her, she tugged me down to the grass beside her, keeping her eyes on mine. "Come to me, my Ludwig," she said. It was late in the afternoon and the few hikers we'd passed were gone. The ground was cold but the last of the sun lit our bodies as we made love as love was meant to be made, without shame in the open air. And all the time we kissed and touched, I felt wild and free.

We took our time hiking down the trail, stopping to look back at the evening sun on a rocky escarpment or up at the footpath that had taken us around the peaks. When the trail was wide enough, we held hands, helping each other over eroded patches where the loose dirt endangered our footing. For a long time we saw no one. We had come up the same path, so I didn't worry that Rudy and Sarah might lose their way. Tonia stared at me intently one moment, at the color of a hillside the next. She seemed to have completely relinquished her reserve, immersing herself in the present, taking notice of every sound, every color, every smell. When we reached the woods, the sun was just setting. It paused for a moment on the brink of disappearing, its flame consuming the distant hillside. Its gentle glow lit the last of the wildflowers, bright and sharp against the grass. "O that our dreamings all, of sleep or wake," she breathed, "would all their colors from the sunset take."

We hadn't gone far into the woods when we came across Sarah standing in the middle of the path, gazing up the hillside. "Finally," she said when she saw us. "You talk him down." I followed her gaze to where I could barely see Rudy's blue T-shirt moving up a rocky slide. He was almost to the top, climbing fast, each step setting off a tiny avalanche of tumbling rock. "Say something to him," Sarah said before shouting, "Rudy! Get down here!" But Rudy continued to climb. The woods around us were already dark and up where he was it was hard to distinguish anything.

"Let him climb if he wants to," Tonia said beside me. She was watching Rudy with her hands clenched, giving a pump of one of her arms as if to cheer him on.

"Stay out of this, Tonia," said Sarah. Just then, a shower of rocks rumbled down the hillside and the three of us watched Rudy move toward the slide's edge where there was a jutting of stone with at least one tree for him to grab onto. I might have yelled if he hadn't been so far away or so near the end of the dangerous part. He inched closer to the rise where a granite layer was exposed, its solid stone offering handholds. A moment before he reached it, though, he seemed to slip. Suddenly he was pitching backward, his body another boulder in a cascade of bigger and smaller rocks. I lost sight of him and then, when the tumbling debris had settled, spied him at the edge of the slide, close enough now to see the blood on his hands, the angle of his leg beneath him. Before I could think what to do, Sarah was scrabbling up the hill toward him, shrieking as she went. Tonia made a move to follow her, but I yelled at her to wait and hurried up the slope, quickly passing

Sarah. I tried not to think what the rocks were doing under me, how they were shifting, taking footholds away before I'd transferred my weight. Like a lifeguard, I kept my eyes on Rudy, trusting that I was moving fast enough to make choosing my handholds unnecessary. I had no idea what I'd do with him once I reached him. We were a good two miles from the bottom of the trail, almost that far from the top. I wasn't even sure he was alive—his body lay motionless, his clothes torn, his head against the rock.

The first thing I realized as I neared him was that he was breathing. "Don't come too close," he said, shifting only his eyes to look at me. His hands clung desperately to the rocks around him and I saw a fear in his face I hadn't seen before. Stopping several feet away, I surveyed the patch of rock below him. If I could move him to his right, I thought, I could ease him down a ridge of larger rocks that seemed more interlocked. "No, don't," he said when I told him what I planned to do. But I positioned myself beside him anyway, gripping a piece of granite jutting through the slide.

"Give me your hand," I told him. Just as he did, I heard another cascade of rocks and turned to see Sarah riding the chunks of loosened stone until they stopped.

"Stay there, goddamn it," Rudy yelled. He winced each time I lifted or lowered him but he never complained. His arm strained against my neck as we sidled down the slope like two halves of a cautious crab, forced to work together to make any progress at all. Sarah called out advice from the bottom but we ignored her, telling her to stay where she was. It was dark everywhere now and all I could see above Rudy's nose were hollow holes. I had never had an injury on tour, nothing more than a slight bruise from a sidewalk fall or a finger slice from a new Swiss army knife. I'd always wondered if I'd know what to do.

It took us an hour or more to work our way down to the trail. Once I'd moved him off the slide, I had to lower him rock to rock, supporting his leg, then his shoulder, checking every step, every handhold, twice. Sarah refused to leave until he was safely off the hill, so I sent Tonia down the path to ask Katerina and her husband Luca for help. I didn't realize how bad the leg was until Rudy was lying on the path and I'd sliced his pants open. A jagged edge of bone split the skin, revealing the milky tissue below.

"So much for Venice," Rudy said when I'd tucked my rain jacket under his head. He looked as if he wanted to say more but he winced instead and closed his eyes.

"You have what you wanted now, I guess," Sarah said to me.

"What do you mean?" I asked as I leaned back against a rock. There was nothing more I could do until help arrived. Sarah and I couldn't carry him the whole way and he couldn't walk on his own.

"I'll have to stay with him," she said. "At least until I get him home. I don't suppose this is exactly what you'd want, but your job just got easier, didn't it?"

Until that moment I hadn't thought what Rudy's injury would mean for the tour. It was, in effect, over. "I wouldn't call getting him out of here *easy*," I said.

"Yes, but several hours from now, with him in a hospital and me with him...."

There's a huge difference between imagining something that seems unlikely and picturing something about to come true. In the first instance, you can believe your life will be different if only you can make the imagined event happen. In the second, you have to acknowledge the possibility of failure.

"What do you think about that?" I asked.

"I can't say one way or the other," Sarah said. "Tonia was stable at the end in Portland, but she was unhappy."

"Stabled, you mean."

"She's not an animal, Joe. She's not some horse longing for pasture or dog straining to be let off a leash." Turning back toward Rudy, she stroked his hair. He was unresponsive now, and I wondered if he'd hit his head. I couldn't remember if the right thing to do was let him sleep or keep him from sleeping.

"Rudy," I called

"Shhh, let him sleep," Sarah said.

So I pushed myself to my feet and walked down the path. When I was a safe distance away, I stood as still as I could, listening. We had a long time to wait for Tonia to return with Luca but I listened for footsteps anyway. From time to time the sound of moaning came on the wind—from Rudy, I imagined at first, but it was soft and low, almost imperceptible, like the soughing of distant trees. Climbing a boulder at the edge of the path, I sat with my feet out over the valley and tried not to think what that night would be like as the light drained from the sky.

The sound of voices speaking Italian startled me. I didn't know how long I'd been sitting there. The twilight was gone and when I turned to see who was coming I could distinguish nothing but the beams of two flashlights working their way up the hill. I called to Sarah to ask about Rudy and let her know someone was coming.

"He's okay," she called through the black. "He's still asleep." Climbing down from the boulder, I groped my way back toward her. "I washed out the wound," she said when she saw me, "and covered it. It's been so long—you don't think he'll lose his leg, do you?"

"I don't think so," I said. "But he won't be walking for a while."

"So much for Rudy the Superhero," she said. "He told me this morning he was going to stop smoking and start walking everywhere back at home. 'I hate taking taxis,' he said, although that's all I've ever known him to do."

The abrupt shift to the city—to thoughts of taxis, images of people rushing from one tall building to another—made the night seem only the temporary dark of a movie theater. The pause between oddly juxtaposed films.

"Giuseppe!" I recognized Luca's voice but not a second one that followed it, calling out the same Italian version of my name. Then they turned their flashlights on themselves and I saw that the second man was Jürgen, the short wiry German who ran the restaurant across the lake. "We left the woman with Katerina," Luca said in Italian, anticipating my question. "Don't worry."

They had brought along a makeshift stretcher, two poles with a sling between them. Even when they moved Rudy's leg, he didn't wake up. Luca, with his broad back, shouldered the front two poles easily, but Jürgen struggled to lift the other end. When I tried to help, he waved me away. "When two of us try to go here together," he said, motioning toward the path, "one of us ends at the bottom."

The climb back down to the road took almost an hour. I walked in front, swinging Luca's flashlight back and forth to light my path, then his. Sarah came at the end, doing the same for Jürgen. Clouds had slipped in over us, swallowing the last of the stars. The uneven trail, the dark, and the heaviness of the load Luca and Jürgen carried kept us from talking. My thoughts ranged over the day—the argument with Rudy, walking with Tonia, Sarah's story about Tonia's mother and the dying bird. Every few minutes I looked at my watch, wondering what Tonia was doing, picturing her in the room where we'd lain together the night before, remembering the warmth of her skin on the grass below me that afternoon.

I expected to feel relief when we reached the road, but all I felt was a deeper anxiety about Rudy's condition and how I would feel that night when Tonia was the only one left on my tour. I was surprised to see my bus, but Luca told me Tonia had gone to my room to find the key. Rudy was clearly unconscious as we laid him across the seats, strapping the belts around his chest, his waist, and his one good leg to keep him from rolling onto the floor. Sarah looked at me with frightened eyes, saying nothing. On the way down the short road to Lake Misurina, Luca asked if I wanted him to go to the hospital with me. "I think he is very bad," he said. "Has he lost blood?" I hadn't seen much, I said and Luca nodded gravely. He asked Jürgen if a certain doctor was working that night but Jürgen didn't know. "The others up here..." Luca said, "...you know. If I come with you, I can ask them to call the right man." I assured him I'd be fine without his assistance but asked him to call the hospital to let them know we were coming.

When we reached the hotel, Tonia was standing under the awning waiting for us. Luca and Jürgen each put a hand on my arm as they scrambled out, Jürgen touching his thumb to his mouth to suggest a drink later. "No matter what time," he said. A light rain had begun to fall when Tonia crawled up into the seat beside me. "He'll be okay," she said, not to Sarah but to me, sounding as if she knew somehow. As I drove along, she seemed unable to sit still and I wondered if she was worried about Rudy or feeling the same anxiety I was about what might happen once we were completely alone. I kept my eyes on the wet roadway in the headlights, glad for the time at the hospital —the paperwork, the need to interpret, the waiting while Rudy was examined and treated—glad that for the next few hours nothing would be irrevocable.

As the road doubled back on itself again and again, leading us downward through the hairpin turns, I tried to remember how the mountains that cradled Cortina had looked that morning, how glad I had been to be up so early, to be driving Felicity to a bus that would take her away. For the first time, it occurred to me I'd slept very little in almost forty hours. I felt the heaviness in my eyelids, the tiredness from the hike.

"How long does it take?" Sarah asked suddenly.

"Another ten minutes or so," I told her.

"He won't die," said Tonia.

"How the hell do you know?" In the mirror I could see Sarah put her hand to her head, her body shaking with sobs.

"Hush little baby don't say a word..." Tonia sang only the first line but she continued humming even after Sarah asked her harshly what she thought she was doing. When I looked at Tonia, she smiled, ignoring my signal for her to stop. We passed out of a thicket of trees and suddenly the lights of Cortina dotted the dark valley ahead. The rain had stopped and despite the water still on the roadway I accelerated.

The hospital was a modern building on the edge of Cortina. A long driveway led to an entrance where two men in white coats were waiting. "*Ecco qua!*" one of them yelled at me when he saw the bus approach. "*Ecco qua!*" He motioned for me to pull up next to the entry. "*Dov'è il signore?*" the same man demanded when I had stopped in front of him. I led him around to the passenger door and showed him Rudy's limp form. He asked me something I didn't understand and I knew I'd been foolish not to have Luca come along. He tried the same question again, then began unbuckling Rudy while the second man rushed inside for a gurney.

"*Parle Italiano?*" the first man asked me when Rudy was strapped to the gurney. I assured him I did but not perfectly. "*La testa?*" he asked, slapping his hand against the side of his head. "*La testa?*"

"*No, la gamba—*"

"*Si, si, si,*" he said hurriedly, "*ma non e...*" He seemed to be searching for a word I would know. "*Alora,*" he said finally, "*non e importante. Viene qui.*" He motioned for Tonia and me to follow him. Sarah was already ahead of us helping the other man wheel Rudy through the large glass doors.

"*E difficile, eh?*" the man said as he led us down a long corridor. Sarah and the other man were nowhere in sight. I apologized for my imperfect Italian.

"*Nessun problema,*" he said, "No problem. *Il Dottore Benvoglio e qui. Il parle Inglese.*" I recognized the doctor's name as the one Luca had said to ask for.

"He's going to be alright," I said to Tonia.

"I know," she said, smiling and looking at me with eyes that were completely red. Set against the whiteness of her skin in the harsh hospital light, they reminded me of eyes I'd seen in Montana all those years before, on the albino Darden. They're only the eyes of someone who hasn't slept, I told myself.

We found Sarah sitting on a vinyl couch in a bare room outside a second set of doors. "*Aspetta,*" our guide said and disappeared through them.

"Is he ever going to come out of there?" Sarah asked. She sat with her elbows on her knees, her face in her hands. "Who the hell is going to tell them what happened?"

"Luca already has," I assured her. "There's a doctor who speaks English if he wakes up."

"*If?*"

We'd been waiting half an hour or more when the doors parted and a handsome white-haired man with drooping eyelids appeared. "Signore Giuseppe?" he asked me.

"*Si...*" I began.

"No," he said, "There is no need for you to speak Italian. I know English well." He tried to smile but didn't seem to have the energy for it. Even the need to speak a foreign language seemed to tire him. "Your friend, he is awake. He is going to be fine, but his break, it is very bad. We will need to do the surgery—two hour from now, maybe three, he is done. But it is better he stay here tonight."

I looked at Sarah. "Of course I'll stay with him," she said.

"You are going back to the States when?" Dr. Benvoglio asked.

"In a couple of days," said Sarah. "We were going to see Venice."

The doctor frowned.

"Shouldn't we? Should we fly home right away?"

"No," he said. "Is maybe okay...but the pain...is maybe too much. We see tomorrow."

"Anyway," he said, smiling, "he will be okay."

Sarah asked to see Rudy but the doctor told her to come back in the morning. When Sarah insisted on staying, he said he'd see if he could find somewhere for her to sleep. "Be careful," she said when I told her I'd check on her in the morning. Then she put her arms around Tonia and held her tightly. "You be careful, too," she said with tears in her eyes. Stepping back, she studied Tonia's face for a moment, until Tonia turned and reached her hand toward me.

"*Ciao*," she said as she put her arm through mine. Then she said it again, and again, repeating it over and over as she led me down the hall.

# Chapter Twenty-Two

Tonia sat behind me rather than beside me as I urged the bus up the hill toward the lake. She kept her arms around my neck, her lips on my ear or my hair. Every gesture was passionate now—a kiss or caress. Every word was a whisper about being closer. I positioned the mirror so it reflected her face, and for the half hour it took to drive the curves that lay between Cortina and Misurina, I alternated between watching her and watching the road. My ears overflowed with her voice. When I tried to say something, she put her fingers over my mouth. "Shhhh," she cooed, "just listen."

The moon I'd seen earlier in the evening flirted with clouds, drenching the land in light, then throwing it back into darkness. The road was empty, the openings below the trees ghostly and endless. When we crested the last rise, the land plateaued and the grand hotel rose before us. Its windows were dark, making it look mysterious, even majestic, but vacant and doomed. The land around it was still. In the far distance I could see the Tre Cime gleaming in the moonlight like beacons rising above the darkened land.

"Pull over," Tonia whispered, her fingers digging deeper into my chest, her tongue on my ear. I eased to a stop on the shoulder and she crawled over the seat into my lap. "Tell me about the hotel," she said. The night before, I'd promised to describe it for her—the way it looked in the distant past when the wealthy gathered there. If the two of us had come to Lake Misurina separately then, she would have stayed in the grand hotel and I in the inn down the road, I knew. On a night like this I might have gone for a walk and stopped to gaze up through the hotel's windows, catching a glimpse of her, perhaps, and wondering who she was.

"There were velvet chairs from Utrecht," I told her, trying to remember the details I'd read in a book, "chamois horns on the walls, and waiters who wore gold braid. The carriages would pull up in front and the footmen would take the arms of the women dressed in their satin gowns, with pearls or gold at their necks. The rooms had patterned walls and four-poster beds, huge and soft, with canopies and sheets of silk. Servants would come at the touch of a cord. And at night from the candlelit dining room, as you savored the taste of trout from the lake or a sauce from a Milanese restaurant, you could gaze at the moon on the peaks, just like now."

She put her fingers to my lips again, and for several minutes we sat with our arms around each other, gazing at those lighted peaks earls and countesses had gazed at almost a century before. Her head lay against my chest and I could feel her body rise and fall with her breathing. Outside the bus nothing moved. It seemed as if the world had been cleared of everything living—people, animals, even insects—as if we were fated to be the only witnesses to that moment. That view. That particular blood-pulse of feeling.

"Should we go back to the hotel?" I said when I felt her shiver, my words like a tear through the silent air. She nodded and stretched her hand toward the door. I thought for a moment that she had pictured what I'd described so vividly she thought we were back at the turn of the century and ours was the grand hotel. I turned the ignition on and tapped the accelerator gently, trying to keep the sound from breaking her illusion.

"Close your eyes and imagine you're Ludwig," she insisted when we were alone in her room. "Imagine I'm Sophie." We'd left the lights off and all I could see was the ashen glow of her flesh, ghostly in the light from the moon. But I couldn't close my eyes; I didn't want to take them off her. Even before she told me what to imagine, she seemed to have *become* Sophie, to have taken on the commingling of shyness and ardor that might have been a young countess's response to spending her wedding night with a king. I tried my best to play her game, to let it be more than a game, to shut out the memories and concerns that kept me from being completely present, assuming whatever identity I chose. Why not be a king? I thought. Why not imagine myself spending the most precious night of my life with the only woman I love?

Tonia put her hands to my face and slid them slowly down my cheeks. "My king," she whispered. "My romantic king." Her skin was paler than ever. My hands against it looked black and I had the odd impression my fingers were leaving smudges. When I slipped them inside the band of her skirt, she stiffened and sucked in air, as if a touch alone could bring her to climax. We stood for a moment just short of naked and my only thought was that I'd never been happier, never more at home with myself. I'd never wanted to become one with another person so fully or, failing that, to leave an impression so deep each of us would always feel incomplete without the other.

For a long time we lay without moving, my mouth on her skin still tasting the salt of her neck. Her eyes were closed and I thought she had fallen asleep, but when I tried to move off of her, she clung to me, rolling to hold her body tight against mine. "I dreamt a dream; what can it mean?" she murmured, her eyes still shut. I was about to answer, about to ask her to describe it, when she continued, "And that I was a maiden queen, guarded by an angel mild." Her eyelids opened and her black eyes stared at me. "You are my angel," she said softly. "My Ludwig."

I didn't ask who the poet was this time, nor did I try anymore to imagine myself the king. I kissed her lips and tucked her head against my shoulder. "Sleep," I said.

"Then am I a happy fly, if I live or if I die," she recited.

"Okay, who is it?" I asked, hoping that was what she wanted me to ask, that once she had told me the name she'd be willing to go to sleep.

"Blake."

"Now shhhh," I said. I didn't want to talk. I wanted only to hold her. Be next to her. I was too tired to prolong the day anymore. My only thought—the only thought I desired—was that she'd be there beside me when I woke up.

# Chapter Twenty-Three

But Tonia wasn't beside me when I woke up the next morning. The bed was cold and I had the feeling she'd been gone a long time. I couldn't tell from the light in the room whether it was early or late but I thought she must have gone for a walk or downstairs to breakfast. Lying back against the pillow, I stared at the ceiling and tried to relax. For the first time in a week I had absolutely nothing to do. A fly was buzzing through the room, making lazy circles over my head, and I remembered the lines Tonia had recited the night before, "Then am I a happy fly, if I live or if I die." Blake, she'd said. I knew him only as a painter of weirdly religious scenes, especially his illustrations for Dante—Cerberus, Lucifer, The Pit of Desire. Anxious as I was to find Tonia, I took my time leaving the warm bed and then decided to shower and change my clothes before looking for her. My shirt was heavy with sweat from hiking and everything down to my shoes retained a faint medicinal smell. I'd have to call Sarah at some point but that could wait. I didn't want to even think about her or Rudy just yet.

When I lifted my pants from the pile of clothes by the dresser, they were lighter than they should have been and I realized the key to my room wasn't in them. I searched the floor, checked under the bed, then remembered Luca telling me Tonia had gone to my room to get the bus key the night before. Thinking she must have left my key at the front desk, I dressed and went downstairs to check. The tiny lobby was empty and cold. Someone had left the front door open and a chilly breeze was blowing in from the lake. The key wasn't there, so I headed back upstairs to see if Tonia had left my door unlocked. As I passed the dining room, I looked for her there but it was as empty as the lobby. When I reached my room, the key was hanging from the keyhole and the door was ajar. Pushing it back, I thought for a moment that I was in the wrong room. Flowers strewn in crisscrossing chains covered the bed. Some were only dandelions but most were wildflowers: pinks and violets and yellows, all of the species we'd seen on our hike the day before. It wasn't till I looked closer that I noticed that the flowers were all arranged—petals clustered by hue, repeating patterns, color strings like Jackson Pollock drips. Scattered among them were postcards, all with their picture side up. As I followed them around the bed, they took me stop-by-stop through the tour. Near me was a Kandinsky painting I recognized from a Munich gallery. It was composed of thick patches of blue, red, green, and yellow with what looked like three triangular mountains in the center, one bare and brown, one blue and white, the last one black with what might have been a nose and a reddish eye. When I turned it over, I found a poem scribbled in child-like script below its title, *Improvisation —Reverie*:

> "Reverie, reverie, dream of luv
> Wishing for turrettes hi abuv
> Out on a lurk the woods beyond
> Watching the gentle lift of swan"

Leaning back against the door, I closed my eyes to catch my breath. I tried not to think where Tonia might be or what she might be doing. Snapshots from the day before flashed through my mind: the way she ran up the path in the morning, the way she sang on the hike down, the way she addressed me as Ludwig in bed. Sarah had tried to warn me but I hadn't wanted to listen. I knew I had to find Tonia—had to find her right away—but I couldn't move. The stench of the drying flowers made me gag and I let my body slide to the floor in search of fresh air. For a long time I lay with my cheek against the carpet, trying not to think or remember anything. Then, I reached up and pulled the last of the cards from the bed. On it was the painting of Venice Tonia had shown me in Munich, the one by Kokoschka done in broad, quick strokes. The sky in it was blue with passing clouds. The wash of verdigris sea spilled off the page. And a whitish glow spread from the golden ball that marked the entrance to the Grand Canal. Venice itself was little more than a line of vague buildings, the boats mere splotches marring a placid lagoon. It was the view of Venice I liked most, the first one I gave the groups I took there, leading them in by gondola along the route used by everyone for generations, including those on the grand tour: Goethe, Boswell, Byron, Ruskin. The gondolas were expensive but I wanted their first view of the world's most romantic city to have meaning. A connection with history.

I stared at the image on the card for a long time before I noticed the artist's initials, O and K, in one of the corners. When I turned the card over, it was clear Tonia had noticed them too, incorporating them into another poem in the same childish handwriting:

"OK the panter sez OK
and Ludwig livs anoo
to merry Sofy and tru luv
as god has meant him too"

Feeling sick to my stomach, I pushed myself to my feet and heard someone moving down the hall. The stretch of floor between my room and Tonia's seemed longer than any I'd ever crossed, and yet I wished I could keep from reaching the end of it. When I pushed back her door, she was standing in the middle of the carpet with a sheet wrapped around her, one hand tugging at her hair. "Why did you leave me?" she shouted, her eyes narrowed, darting away. "Why-why-why." She rushed toward the window but turned her eyes from the light. I thought the room looked strange because she had stripped the bed. Then I realized she'd pulled the curtains from their rods, too. As I stepped toward her, my heart was breaking and racing at the same time. Welts, like long scratches, rose from her cheeks. "You don't care," she screamed. "You don't care!" When

I tried to calm her, she turned without warning and crossed to the bathroom, shutting and locking the door behind her. Only then did the true horror of the situation hit me. I had no idea what was wrong with her or how to help her or how I'd even pay for the damage she'd done. The only thing I could think was that I had to call Sarah, had to get her to come back.

Picking up the phone, I reached for the hospital card in my pocket but it wasn't there. It took me a moment to remember that Tonia had put it in her purse. "Where's your purse?" I called to her. She was saying something beyond the door but it wasn't an answer to my question. And then I heard the popping of the shower curtain hooks. "Where's your purse?" I called again. When she didn't answer, I started searching the room, pawing through piles of clothes until I found it under her nightgown by the bed. I clawed my way down through it, deeper and deeper, but the card wasn't there. What I found instead, at the very bottom, wrapped in a handkerchief with a picture of Ludwig's face on it, was a pill dispenser. It was the kind with the days of the week on it, the kind people use for medicine they can't afford to forget. The slots were all full of small white pills.

The key to Tonia's room was in her purse, too, so I locked the door from the outside and hurried downstairs to ask Luca for the hospital number. I found Katerina in the breakfast room putting out rolls. "*C'era una messaggio para te*," she said when she saw me. "*Aspetta*." She crossed to the front desk and searched through a pile of papers until she found the right one. While she looked up the hospital number, I tried to read what she'd written down but my mind was too agitated to translate. "*La donna Sarah ha telephonata*," she said. I tried to concentrate. To understand. You were not in your room, she said in Italian. Sarah had put Benvoglio on the phone and he had told Katerina Rudy's leg was worse. It seemed Sarah had changed their flight to get him home. They were taking a taxi to Venice that morning.

"What time did she call?" I asked Katerina, but she didn't know.

"Early," she said. "Six o'clock?" By then she had found the hospital number. As she called it for me, I heard a thumping upstairs and tried not to imagine what Tonia was doing.

"*Non sono la*," Katerina said as she hung up the phone. "*Sono partito*." They were gone.

"Listen," I said, "there's a problem." I had to catch the people who left the hospital before they reached Venice, I told her. And I needed to take the woman upstairs with me. I'd be back in a day or two.

When I went back upstairs, Tonia's room was still empty. I knocked on the bathroom door and called her name, but she didn't answer. So I put my shoulder to the door and pushed until the jamb broke. Bedsheets were hanging where the shower curtain had been. Toothpaste was smeared across the mirror. And streams of toilet paper crisscrossed the floor. Tonia was cowering in a corner of the bathtub, holding a bar of soap in front of her. When I saw her naked body and the fear in her eyes, tears began to stream from my own. For a fleeting moment, a horrible thought crossed my mind: I could leave her there. Drive away. No one would know until they opened the door and found her. By then I'd be long gone. Out of Italy. Out of Europe. Free of everything that was happening and whatever was about to come.

Pushing the thought aside, I said her name, leaning down and speaking as gently as I could. Only hours before, I'd been lying beside this woman, putting myself inside her, wanting her to leave her life behind for me. "Tonia," I said again, even softer this time. She lowered the soap and looked at me, the fear still there but her eyes steady. There were scratches across her left breast and down the sides of both legs, some so deep they'd drawn blood. Her pale skin looked sickly in the bathroom light, the wounds a pattern of hives or swellings from a beating, but she was quieter than before. Less agitated. It seemed obscene to touch her, but I had to get her out of the tub. Had to get her dressed. Had to get her out to the bus and down to Venice. I needed Sarah to tell me what to do. "Tonia," I said, reaching my hand slowly in her direction. "It's time to go to Venice now."

But she shrank back from my hand. "I'm staying," she said. "We're staying." Her voice was plaintive at first, then defiant, her black eyes begging, then glaring through a hellish red.

"We can't stay," I said. "We have to go."

Her hands fell to her legs and she raked her skin with those bitten-down nails. I could smell her perfume, feel the touch of those same fingers against my back.

"We have to go," I said again, but she didn't answer. My hand dropped to the edge of the tub but I didn't know how to try to touch her. To pick her up. To lead her away. There was a ring of faint grime on the porcelain above her legs and something about it made her skin look gray. She wasn't meant to be here, I thought. To stay in this kind of place. My eyes drifted to the corner where the tub was affixed to the floor. Dust had gathered there, hairs that had never been swept away. I remembered Felicity thrusting the dirty condom toward me. There was dirt on the walls, rust from condensation on the ceiling, a crack in the toilet bowl. I'd been in that bathroom half a dozen times and never noticed any of them before.

Tonia had folded her arms over her breasts and was shivering like a child. "Stay here," I said. "I'll be right back. Will you stay here?" A moment later, I had returned with a blanket and her pill dispenser. "Take one of these," I said, holding a pill toward her. I didn't know what they were or how fast they worked but I hoped they'd calm her enough to get her going.

"No," she screamed, pushing my hand away. "Leave me alone! Leave me *ALONE*!"

"Okay. Okay, calm down," I said. "Stay here. I'm going to pack our things."

*Our* things, I thought as I rushed down the hall to my room. I had wanted them to be our things. To share everything. But the things we were going to share were all good. I didn't want her money or her privilege. All I wanted was who she was —who I thought she was—the way she looked at life, her spirit, her confidence. Different as our backgrounds were, I thought we were meant to be together because we wanted to live the same way: freely, with passion. Now, the confidence I'd loved, that beautiful spirit, had been replaced by fear and a troubling desire to hurt herself. Was that the pain her husband had seen, I wondered, the pain that had made him turn away?

As I packed my things I looked at myself in the dresser mirror. In the background I could see the flowers, the postcards, the walls the same dingy color as those in Tonia's bathroom. I wanted to run away and never return. But I knew—finally knew—that wherever I went, that face would go with me—the tired eyes, the bloated cheeks, the twisted mouth. All of my running, all of my moving from place to place, had led inevitably to this. This moment. The freedom I thought being with Tonia had brought was gone for good. The sense I'd had of letting go. It wasn't a lack of freedom that had caged me. It was the running itself. The nursed desire. It was the longing for something other than what I had. I knew in that moment that Cat's affair with the Swiss man hadn't been her fault. I was to blame for it. *My* desires.

I rushed my bag downstairs, then returned to Tonia's room and threw her things together. I could hear her talking to herself in the bathroom, reciting poems in a sing-song voice. When I had her things in the bus, I found Katerina and paid her for the group's scheduled nights. She tried to return some of my money—no one stayed here, she said—but I insisted she keep it.

I'd left a skirt and blouse out for Tonia, but she was still in the bathtub. Still naked. "No, come to bed," she pleaded when I tried to convince her to dress. "We can stay in bed all day." I realized she was mimicking me, repeating my words from the night before.

"Let's go to town first," I said, "Let's check on Rudy and Sarah."

"Fuck Rudy," she spit at me. "Fuck Sarah." Then she was pleading again, "Come back to bed."

"No," I said, "we need to go—"

"I need to pee!" she shouted. "Why can't I pee alone?" She stood and reached for the sheet on the shower rod, wrapping it around her as I backed out the door. "I want to pee alone!" she shouted, laughing an ugly laugh that thrust her head forward. Then she repeated the line in a Garbo accent, "I *vant* to pee alone!" There was nothing I could do but let her go. I told her to knock on the door when she was done, but as soon as she closed it I put my ear to it. There was silence at first, then faint humming, then the thin tinkle of urine falling into the bowl. I felt ashamed of myself, listening to her that way, but I wanted to catch her before she could get back into the tub. Now that she was up and around, I wanted to keep her moving. I tried not to picture her there, her skin scored, her privates dripping, flushing my seed from her body. As the water continued to trickle out, she continued repeating the Garbo line in different voices, different accents, punctuated with laughter. It seemed as if her mind was a large prism splitting a single thought into different colors.

When the water stopped, the voices stopped with it. Suddenly, the door opened and Tonia stood in the doorway holding the sheet out to her sides like a pair of wings, her eyes wide and focused beyond me. With her chin raised, she stepped with the stride of a dancer, coming toward me but looking beyond me, as if drawn by the light from the window. "Ludwig," she said, "listen." It seemed she was on a stage I couldn't see, her audience beyond the glass somewhere.

"Tonia—" I said, but she shushed me.

"Listen," she insisted. "The music." She continued to glide toward the window, her arms still spread. "Lohengrin," she shouted, her voice like that of an actress performing a role. "Oh folly! What is love? And where is it?" As I watched her, I couldn't imagine where her mind had gone, what oceans it was swimming through, what clouds it was pawing at. The walls inside it seemed to have disappeared, leaving her free to pass from room to room, bare feet tripping across the debris of memory.

"Tonia, let's get dressed," I said. "There are people out there." I pointed toward the curtain-less window but she didn't seem to see my gesture, and whatever she heard was filtered through the mist in her mind.

"Let's get dressed," she mimicked. She pulled the sheets together, looking down as if checking her train, and I began to see how I might coax her out to the bus.

"Your majesty forgets," I tried, feeling foolish, "there are people we need to see out there, people who expect us to look and act a certain way." I was trying desperately to imagine how her mind might be working, what cues might prompt her to pick up her skirt and put it on. "Here is your gown, laid out for the occasion." I held up her skirt and ran my hand along the hem like a tailor presenting his work.

"The gown laid down," she said, staring at me, her hand rising in front of her, finger pointed toward the floor. I knelt and held the blouse up to her.

"Made of the finest silk," I said. "From China."

"Silk?" She reached a hand toward the blouse.

"Silk, of course...and ermine on the fringe of the train." Taking the blouse from my hand, she dropped the sheets to slip it on and I reached for the skirt.

"Should I dress you then?" I asked, holding it out.

"You should undress me then," she said, stepping forward through the circle of fabric.

"Tonight," I promised. "Tonight."

"Tis the middle of the night by the castle clock," she recited, "And the owls have awakened the crowing cock."

As I tried to zip up the skirt she reached toward my crotch and I felt the heat of tears running from my eyes. Through her blouse I could see the hard tips of her nipples, the roundness of her breasts, and for one desperate moment I wanted to lie with her. Hold her against me one more time. Awful as her condition was, I wanted to let my mind go as she had. To imagine, if only for a single moment, that we *were* the fortunates of history, a pair of royal lovers looking out from a feathered bed high in the turret of a castle.

She wouldn't let me lift her feet to slip on her panties but I was able to fasten the skirt around her and lead her barefoot through the door by promising we'd take the sled for a midnight ride on the freshly fallen snow.

"Giuseppe?" Katerina called from the kitchen when she heard the bell on the outside door, but I didn't answer. Tonia danced on her toes, her fingers entwined in mine. "Tinkle, tinkle, little star," she sang when the bell rang. And in that moment all of the games lovers play—the terms of endearment, the childishness, the fantasies—seemed hideous. When I opened the bus door, I held up my hand like a footman, afraid that the air and the light would break through the fantasy I was trying to trap her in, cause her to run for the lake or the mountains. Instead, she merely took my hand and spread her skirt across the seat. The bus started on the first turn and I felt a fleeting sense of relief. Everything would be okay, I thought, if I could just reach the airport in time.

# Chapter Twenty-Four

It was almost 9 when we left Misurina. I didn't know what time the flight to New York departed that day, but the one three days later—the one the group was meant to be on—left at 1 p.m. By the most direct route, the drive to Venice took three hours. If the times were the same, I'd make it. As I eased the bus onto the highway near the grand hotel, I glanced back to see how Tonia was doing. She had her cheek pressed to the window, her eyes on a cluster of children waving at us with open mouths. Before we'd gone another kilometer, it started to rain and she began to hum, tracing the raindrops down the glass with her finger. Let her stay calm, I prayed. Let her stay calm.

    I drove as fast as I dared while remembering the way the tires had slid on the pass. As I neared the turnoff to Venice, however, I slowed down. There was an *autostrada* nearby where I could drive as fast as I wanted, but I'd never taken it and didn't know exactly where it went. The smaller road through the Veneto hills was more direct but it often narrowed to one lane and some areas were prone to flooding. If the rain grew heavy, the traffic would worsen and I'd lose valuable time. In the end, I took the road I knew and hoped the rain would stop.

Once I'd made my decision, I tried to focus on the road and the time and forget that Tonia was in the back. Forget the way she'd been that morning or the night before. Forget the time we'd spent together the past few days. In my years of guiding I'd learned to concentrate on what had to be done: the arrangements to be made, the schedule to be kept. I tried to think of Tonia not as the woman I'd been falling in love with but simply as the last person on my last tour. Looking out at the gray weather, the mottled foliage dulled by the rain, I tried to convince myself that I'd only been caught up in a fantasy. Hadn't I done that before, foolishly let my feelings take over? Hadn't I learned what every traveler learns: that feelings fade, the magic of a place wears off, and you have to move on? That was the beauty of traveling for a living, wasn't it—you were never stuck anywhere? But I couldn't forget what it felt like to hold her and talk to her and listen to her stories about her life. I couldn't forget that ride on the Königsee or that night in the rain at Zell am See or the night we'd just spent together, the night I thought was a beginning, not an end...not the illusion it seemed to be now. Was it only an illusion, I wondered, a deluded romp in the hay with a sick woman? Or could it be Tonia knew what was happening to her and was reaching out, reaching me in the only way she still could, through the sharing of our hearts and our bodies?

We were only a few kilometers beyond Cortina when the first downpour began. As the rain thickened, the traffic slowed. Construction work reduced the road to one lane even in places where it was usually two. Tonia didn't notice. It seemed, in fact, that she had little idea where she was or that anyone else was around. She moved from seat to seat, saying whatever came into her mind, mixing memorized verses with random facts I'd told the group about Munich or Berchtesgaden or the Tyrol. "In nineteen hundred and forty-two, Hitler made the world blue," she sang. It was all nonsense, but clever nonsense, nonsense with an eerie logic behind it, like a living Lewis Carroll novel. In the midst of it all, she mumbled something about Gerhard and suddenly I saw him in a new way. How many drives like this had he taken, I wondered. How many times had he realized too late that she'd neglected her medication? Was it possible no one in the group had been telling the truth about him, not even Tonia? That he had intended to come on the trip all along? Could it be that he and Tonia had fought about her illness and he had decided that traveling with her would be too much? Or that Tonia hadn't wanted him on the trip? Might she have convinced him to stay home so she could pursue some reckless dream of freedom, one that included me only because I was there?

Gerhard, I thought—why hadn't I called him? Whatever their relationship, whatever reason he hadn't come on the trip, she was his wife, not mine. I should have called him right away, should have told him what was happening.

But even as I was thinking these thoughts, I was remembering how it felt to dance with Tonia at the palace and the softness of her skin where I touched it in the rain. Through the streaks on the windshield, I saw her eyes looking at me, how they narrowed without dimming when she smiled and the depth in them when we were alone and the light was low. My body still wore her, as if she were a bodysuit or a chemical that aroused my skin, a tingling at first and then a burning, as if some essence of her had entered my blood. I turned the radio on and tried to forget that she was there in the back of the bus—the same woman in the same skin with the same eyes and smile and essence. I'd call Gerhard from the airport, I told myself. I'd tell him what had happened and that she was on her way. I'd hand her over to Sarah and Rudy...and then I'd drive away. There were boats from Venice bound for Istanbul and Alexandria. I could be on a different continent the next day. But was there anywhere I really wanted to go anymore?

The rain subsided near the small town of Vodo, just as the construction that had narrowed the roadway for several kilometers was ending. In the rearview mirror, I could see Tonia at the very back of the bus craning her neck to look at the mountains. She was as quiet as she had been the whole ride, quiet enough to make me think I could just drive on and we could be happy somewhere. All I had to do was get her to take those pills.

As we passed Lake Vodo, I noticed a man in a rowboat a short distance from shore. He was just letting go of his oars to push back the hood of what looked like an old anorak. At first, I saw only a face split by a dark mustache. Then he revealed a shock of coppery hair. Surrounded by the autumn colors and the gray of a lake on a dreary day, it looked like a crown. As I stared at him, I tried to think who he reminded me of. Had he worked for Luca perhaps? Or was he a friend of Jürgen's, someone I'd drunk with into the early morning hours? The rowboat and then the lake passed out of sight, but the man's face stayed with me. When we came to another lake, I scanned it quickly, as if expecting to see the same man there. It was empty except for the feathered ridges of white caps raised by the wind and a column of rain that pocked the surface as it rushed toward us, striking the side of the bus like buckshot. The radio sputtered and Tonia began to imitate the static. Spinning the dial, I tried to find something that might calm her again and came across a man's voice giving a weather report in English. The rain would end that evening, he said, his tone cheery and hopeful. Tomorrow would be a sunny day. "Here's something to help you get through the rain," he said, "Remember this?" The song he played was one I recognized but couldn't identify. Then Tonia began to sing along. She shouted the words, and all at once I realized whose face I'd seen in the rowboat. I could hear the drunken howls and the roars of laughter as the two men brayed their Creedence songs at the empty Montana sky. I fumbled desperately to change the station, but as soon as the song went off Tonia began to scream and pound her fists against my shoulder. "Okay, okay, my God, stop it!" I yelled, straining to hold the steering wheel steady while twisting the radio knob, trying to find the right station. When the tune returned, Tonia sat back against the seat and sang as loudly as she could about the rain coming down on a sunny day.

    The face wouldn't leave me now. It hovered in front of me like a decal affixed to the windshield, something I'd have to look through to see the road ahead. It seemed in that moment that it had always been there in front of me, the face not of my childhood hero alone but of the reality behind every fantasy. It seemed whatever dreams or romantic adventures I allowed myself, the memory of Chit in the trailer that night and the sight of my mother the next morning—the pale leg, the swollen face—would always be lurking inside them.

As we passed through Pieve, the skies opened up, unleashing torrent after torrent, each more violent than the last, a seemingly endless flood that caused the river beside the road to swell, the shoulders to stream with water. Even on the highest speed, the wipers gave little more than a glimpse through the windshield. If I didn't pull over, I knew, we might plunge into the ditch, but it was after 11 already, so I pushed on, slowing the bus and staying on the road by watching the hills to my left and right, threading the needle between them. I wasn't sure if I'd be able to see a car coming toward us but there didn't seem to be any cars on the road. Everyone had pulled over to wait out the storm.

A few kilometers beyond Pieve, the hills I'd been steering between became canyon walls, forcing the water to flow through a narrow channel. Puddles became small lakes. Water fanned into waves on either side of the wheels and surged against the engine, hissing and spitting. As we reached the bottom of a steep decline, the water came up over the grill, and when I pressed the accelerator for the uphill climb, the engine stalled. I pumped the pedal frantically, cranking the key, and then, with the last of the forward momentum, tried a compression start. All I succeeded in doing was stopping the bus sooner. Even before it had completely stopped, Tonia was opening the back door. Her voice, her singing, the Creedence song, trailed behind her as she moved away. I didn't try to stop her. I could hear her splashing through the standing water, pausing her singing to laugh before repeating the same line again and again, "Have you ever seeeen the rain?" She mimicked Fogerty's voice then morphed into others as the window's glaze distorted her features. Moving around the bus, she pounded the beat of the line on the metal panels, and when she reached the back bumper, she stopped, her drenched face framed by the fan-like opening made by the rear wiper. I was too far away to see the scratch marks on her cheeks but close enough to see that she was smiling as she lifted her face to the skies, letting the rain roll down.

    As I watched her sway back and forth, I turned the ignition key again and again. Each time it clicked, the radio blared for a moment and the wipers made a sweep of the windshield, but the engine wouldn't turn over. Every click made me more anxious, forcing me to chase away thoughts of what I would do if I didn't get Tonia to the airport in time. Eventually, I sat back to let the engine rest. I thought about looking under the hood but I didn't know what to look for. I knew nothing about cars or buses, not even how to change the oil. Tonia was still at the back but instead of singing she was reciting something. Just as I started to understand the words —"...*though I walk through the valley of the shadow of death, I fear no evil; for thou art with me....*"—she turned to look through the window toward me, her face blank, her eyes expressionless. I felt suddenly afraid of her and in a panic I cranked the ignition key once more, sending the blade slicing across her face. Her eyes continued to gaze at me, unblinking. *"Surely goodness and mercy shall follow me all the days of my life,"* she droned through the glass. And then she threw her head back and laughed—a loud cackling laugh that made me think of hyenas on nature shows, their teeth reddened with entrails.

    As I sat with my eyes on the windshield, the landscape beyond it blurred by the rain, I told myself if we didn't make the plane that day, there'd be another the next day. But I was afraid to think beyond that afternoon, to imagine what Tonia might do in a city as romantic as Venice. As late as the day before, I'd been looking forward to taking her there, to seeing what she would make of the home of Casanova. It had begun to seem we'd been traveling toward Venice not for a week but for years, destined to live a different life there. Everything would be richer in texture, brighter in color, truer in taste and smell and sound. And I would *feel* it all more intensely, as if it were made of all the moments I'd ever said, *"This* is life!"

    What I'm living now is life, I thought as I sat in the cooling bus, the rain coming down in waves around me—the life of those poor asthmatic children, the life the Buddhists seek to escape. The lure of travel, I thought, is only the lure of illusion, the mistaken belief that in a new country with different people and different ways, we can escape the confines of ourselves. The problem is, wherever we go, we take ourselves along.

    It took me a while to notice the rain was lightening. The thunder that had been breaking over our heads had softened to a distant grumbling. I reached down and tried the key again, and this time the engine caught. I pumped the accelerator several times and let the engine idle, making sure it would continue to run. Then I stepped out into the rain and made my way to the back of the bus, following the voice I'd hoped to hear for a long time. It was humming a tune, mumbling some of the words, and if I'd stopped to think about it, I might have recognized the song. But I didn't want to know what it was. I didn't want that song in my head to remind me of her in the days to come.

When I reached the rear fender, I saw her beyond a rain-filled ditch that ran along the edge of the road. She was bending and picking wildflowers. The pink of her blouse was vivid against the black canyon wall and her dampened hair hung in long, clumped strands like those that had brushed my face at Zell am See. She kept her legs straight as she reached for the flowers and just as she touched them I could see the bare flesh beneath her skirt, exposed to the drivers on the road.

"Tonia," I called to her.

She straightened and looked at me as if seeing me for the first time. "No," she said, "no, no, no."

"Yes," I told her, "It's time to go."

"No," she said, looking more concerned. "I need flowers for my bouquet. I have to have flowers."

"We'll buy them on the way," I said. "Come here."

I didn't expect her to respond, but when I told her to come, she came. She put her bare feet into the ditch, sinking almost to where the scratches began, then climbed the other side to where I stood waiting for her. The welts on her face had shrunk to thin lines and the rain had washed away the blood she'd drawn to the surface. "Come here," I said again, and when I opened my arms, she tucked her head into my shoulder. Placing my hands on her wet back, I stroked her hair and closed my eyes, not to imagine that the dream was still there but only because I'd never touch her that way again.

Though I could still hear the distant thunder and see an occasional flash of light, the clouds were less dark than they'd been before and the rain had dropped to a drizzle. Even though Tonia was calmer, the only way I could coax her into the bus was to allow her to sit up front with me. I was afraid she might do something unexpected on the narrow road, even grab the wheel, but I didn't have time to argue with her. It was after 11:30 and some of the cars that had pulled off the road were passing us already. If the flight really left at 1, there was no time to spare.

The bus sputtered and lurched but it continued to run as we snaked down the last long valley before Belluno where the *autostrada* to Venice began. The hillsides were empty, the two or three towns almost non-existent, gone before I'd seen them. The giant concrete columns we passed would one day support a highway extension, but in their incomplete state they looked both alien and sinister, like the powerful legs of some foreign being marching from valley to valley. I kept the radio on to entertain Tonia, settle her down. The station that had played the Creedence tune blared out song after song from the '60s and '70s, all of which she seemed to know. While she sang, she drummed on the dashboard, and if I tried to talk, she shushed me. So I turned my thoughts to what I remembered of the Venice airport. I could park, I knew, in the big bus lot near the check-in desks. I needed twenty minutes, at most, to change her ticket and get her through customs. If we made the *autostrada* by noon, I'd be okay.

We were no more than twenty kilometers from Belluno when I saw a sign warning of construction ahead. Tonia was singing a Boz Skaggs tune, substituting Ludwig for the title name—"*Ludwig missed the boat that day he left the shack, but that was all he missed and he ain't comin' back...*" As she sang, the cars ahead of me began to slow, then stop. The taillights converged, becoming two bright dots of red on the back of a battered Fiat. I could see the end of the foothills in the distance, a thin line of pale blue sky where I imagined Venice to be. The rain splattered the window like tiny water balloons and the traffic stalled even more. I waited anxiously through one song, then another, while Tonia seemed unaware of everything but the music. When a third song began, I turned to look at her. It was after noon already. We weren't going to make it.

It was still possible the plane that day wouldn't leave until later or I could find a flight to New York on another airline, but when I saw Tonia slumped in her seat—her head moving from side to side, her feet so high on the dashboard her skirt fell against her stomach—I knew she wouldn't leave my life so easily. Even if I were somehow able to get her on that plane, to hand her over to Sarah and Rudy and drive away, I'd never forget her. I'd always remember the ways I'd looked at her—first as a promise, then as a problem. Even if I never heard from her or saw her again, I'd always wonder which was temporary, which true.

It was ten minutes to 1 when we reached the outskirts of Treviso, where I pulled off the *autostrada* at a rest stop and found a payphone to call the airline. A recording told me the flight to New York had already left. I waited for an operator, who was kind enough to check for flights on other airlines. There was nothing available, not even first class, until the following week.

As I was taking this information in, Tonia was leaning across the seat to honk the horn—long, angry honks that made everyone in the parking lot look her direction. I hung up quickly and rushed back to the bus but she had locked all the doors. As I moved around the outside to try each one, she moved inside from one to the other, checking and rechecking each of them. I pounded on the windows and yelled at her to let me in but she shook her head and beat her hands against the backs of the seats. She was singing along to the radio I'd left on, shouting the words to a song by Kiss or Led Zeppelin or some damn band.

"Tonia, let me in, I have news," I tried, but she continued to shake her head. A smile spread across her face—a vicious, vindictive smile.

"...*gonna make you sweat, gonna make you grooove*," she hollered at me, putting her face to the glass.

A small crowd had gathered near the telephones, drawn by her screams and the strangeness of seeing a man moving around a bus talking to the windows. *"Niente, niente, non 'e niente!"* I shouted at them, but they continued to stare. I could see the cashier from the *autostrada* shop looking out through the glass. The last thing I needed was for someone to call the *carabinieri* and have to explain, in Italian, what was happening. I didn't know what to expect even if I was able to open a door. How would I keep her calm for the rest of the ride to Venice?

"Tonia—Sophie, listen to me," I said, remembering how I'd coaxed her into dressing that morning. "I'm going to call the church. Do you hear me? The church." She stared at me, the anger still in her eyes, but she quit singing and her hands stopped moving. "I tried them before but the line was busy. I'm going to try again. Maybe we can go there this afternoon. Will you wait for me?" The muscles around her eyes relaxed and she began almost imperceptibly to nod. It was frightening to look at her eyes, to see how many emotions were battling for dominance there. "You have to sit down, though," I called to her. "These people want to call the police." I waved my arm toward the gathered crowd. "They don't want us to marry. If you sit, they'll go away."

For several moments she leaned toward the window without moving, looking first at me and then at the crowd. She was mumbling something I couldn't make out, talking to herself or singing. "Sit down now," I yelled. If she didn't do it this time, I was going to try forcing the door but I was afraid the key would break in the lock or her reaction to me getting inside would send someone running to call the police. "Okay?"

She nodded and pointed to the front seat.

"That's the place," I said. "That's your seat, your throne." I hoped no one in the crowd understood English well enough to know what I was saying.

Tonia made her way to the front of the bus and sat down. Throwing her shoulders back and lifting her chin, she turned her face toward the front window and sat still except for a slight side-to-side tremor.

"I'll be right back. Wait for me," I called to her. Then I turned back toward the phone and motioned to the crowd to disperse. "Leave her in peace," I said angrily in Italian, "What's wrong with you all?" First one then another turned to go.

On the wall beside the phone, I found a listing of emergency and information numbers. I dialed the national operator and asked for the number of the *Ospedale Civile* in Venice. When I had written it down, I stood for a long time looking out at the bus I'd driven for the past four years—the worn tires, the faded paint, the dirty windows that gave a murky view of Tonia. As I punched the numbers into the grid of buttons, I imagined what they would do to her, how they'd encage her mind with their drugs, making her docile and dull. As the tune of tones became a series of rings, I pictured her as she'd been the previous day: running along the ridge of the hill, leaning to look at flowers, throwing her arms to her sides and dancing through the morning. When a woman finally answered, I asked if I could bring Tonia in. I mean, I said, my mind straining to find the right Italian words, can you legally take her? The woman assured me they could but a doctor would have to see her first. "*Lei 'e su esposa?*" she asked me then. I knew what I had to answer, but at first I could only mouth the words. It was the dream we'd spun together, the one still alive in Tonia's mind. "*Signore?*" the woman asked. "*Lei e la?*"

"*Si*," I answered. "I'm still here. And yes...I am her husband."

When I opened the door of the bus, Tonia made no move to stop me. There was a soft drink commercial on the radio and she was singing along, but faintly. Her chin was still raised and when she turned to look at me, her look was gentle. And regal. "Are we to go now?" she asked.

"Yes," I told her quietly. "Venice is waiting."

The engine started right away, and as I crossed the parking lot I noticed it was mostly empty. The gawkers had moved on.

"The crowds will be gathering in Saint Mark's Square," I said.

"You've let them know we're coming then?"

"I've let them know."

The Padan Plain spread around us now. When I looked in the mirror, the mountains were gone. The land ahead was flat and empty.

"Will he be waiting?" Tonia asked after a while. She had been sitting miraculously still, lulled perhaps by the motion and music as well as her addled image of how a future queen should be.

"Will who be waiting?" I asked.

"The gondolier, of course," she said with a trace of condescension, as if she thought I was playing games at a time not fit for games.

I'd forgotten I'd told her how I usually took my groups into Venice. My plan was to drive to the closest parking lot and take a water taxi straight to the hospital, but I saw that I couldn't do that. The night we'd lain together by the lake in Zell am See I'd described the approach to Venice by sea. It was the only way to approach the city, I'd told her, the way Marco Polo had returned from his journeys in China, the route Byron and Shelley and Keats had taken. I wasn't sure this was true at all. I'd come across the idea in a Hemingway novel, fallen in love with his description of being propelled across the lagoon by the proud strokes of a gondolier, the romantic link to an earlier time when there were no parking lots, no water taxis, no bridges. For a group the ride cost as much as a meal, but it was better than any dinner I could have provided, a feast for the senses—the eyes, the nose, the ears, the skin. It was a feast I'd have to indulge in one last time.

Tonia's restrained, almost lucid manner during that last stretch of highway—once she believed that we, as Ludwig and Sophie, were on our way to be married—made me wonder if her mania was fading already. Once we had navigated the maze of factories that still separated us from the sea and were on our way across the lagoon in our gondola, would her symptoms disappear as quickly as they had come? Would the Tonia I'd known at first re-emerge? Though she called me Ludwig and seemed to respond only when I addressed her as Sophie, it seemed possible she knew we were only playing roles.

If only I could have convinced myself that was true—that there was a chance we might live together as I had imagined—I would have played the role of Ludwig to the hilt. I would have *become* the mad king escorting his bride-to-be to the church. How much more like the city I wished it to be would Venice have looked to me then.

# Chapter Twenty-Five

Venice was never meant to have more than a tenuous tie to the shore. Until the Austrians laid their bridge across the lagoon in the 19th century, there was no physical connection between the fabled city and the drab societies it kept at bay. When your first view of Venice is from the sea, you sense the enchantment, the spell it cast over souls for centuries. You feel the sun and the wind on your skin, smell the air tinged by salt and decay. The only sounds are the sounds that can cross the water: the waves lapping at boats, the chimes of the campanile bells, the voices of merchants and buyers, guides and tourists from every part of the globe. The sultry atmosphere wraps itself around you, sealing you off from the world, and the sights you see are the sights you can't see anywhere else: opulent porches underwater, algae consuming their carved stone; faded facades bleached by the sun, their plaster and paint failing; bell towers leaning toward the sea, supported by sinking palaces; and glistening domes of forgotten churches designed by architects from the vanished east. Approaching this way, you pass the aging ferryboats, the neglected islands, the ships that navigate the narrow channels dredged in the distant past.

At least that's how I always pictured the entrance into Venice from the sea. It was a collection of images gathered during summer visits when the waters were calm, the clouds nonexistent. But it was late September now and the sky was a somber gray. As I approached the airport perched at the edge of the dead lagoon, clouds had lowered over us and a heavy wind was blowing past the terminal buildings. Tonia had been sitting quietly beside me, but when she saw the sign for the *Aeroporto Venezia-Marco Polo*, her legs and arms began to move and she began to call, "Marco...Marco," as if speaking to someone beyond the windshield.

"We're only going to park the bus," I told her. "We'll catch a water taxi to Murano and the gondola will be there."

But she continued to call out, "Marco...Marco," repeating the name again and again. As she did, she put her hand on my chin. Her fingers felt unnaturally cold and I wanted to look away but I let her turn my face toward hers. "Marco," she said softly, holding my gaze, her eyes swimming in seas of red. Sarah had told me her father's name was Marco...had I become him now? Was Ludwig forgotten? Grim thoughts swam through my mind about the relationships parents and children can form, the strangely intimate ways they sometimes relate to each other when there's only a single parent, a single child.

"No," I told her, "I'm *Ludwig*." It seemed important she see me not as her father or even myself but only the mad romantic king—the king Sophie loved. That seemed the only way I'd coax her out of the bus.

"Ludwig?" she said, frowning.

"Ludwig. Your lover. The king you're about to marry."

It occurred to me as I tried to convince her again that I was her king that she was drawn as much to the madness as the romance. She and Ludwig were alike in many ways, but he could dream for weeks at a time, neglecting his duties, without a Gerhard to bring him back. He wasn't just rich; he was the king. No one could tell him what to do—or so it seemed until they arrested him and forced him to give up his fantasy. It was clear to me now that Tonia didn't want me or anyone else to call her back to reality. She had stopped taking her pills because she wanted to slip the bonds of the world the rest of us live in.

"Come on," I said, "the royal coach awaits us."

She took the hand I offered and hopped down out of the bus. As we crossed the last few yards of asphalt that separated the parking lot from the dock, she walked as she'd walked that morning, like a queen or a princess, holding the hem of her skirt to the side, her chin in the air. There was a water taxi idling beside the pier.

"Murano," I told the driver, a short man with thick glasses and unshaved cheeks. He took the suitcases from me, frowning at them. "For the glass?" he asked, his fat face miming a smile as he produced a business card with the name of a glass-blowing factory on it.

"No," I said. "San Donato."

He gave me a withering look and hiked up his pants. Then he turned toward the wheel and off we went. As we sped along, Tonia leaned toward the green lagoon and I had to grab her blouse to keep her in the boat. The shoreline was nothing but tidal flats and swamp grass. I kept my eyes on the single tower I could see in the distance, the steeple of San Donato. My only thought was to find a gondola and get Tonia to the hospital.

The quay in Murano was empty when we arrived. The driver left us hundreds of yards from the church, insisting that was the place to catch a gondola. I didn't have the will to argue. The buildings around us were unfamiliar—dull structures with shuttered windows and tile roofs. A few delivery boats were tied to the pilings. Otherwise there was nothing: no boats, no shops, no people. Tonia had been calm during the boat ride but as soon as she was on land and my back was turned she began to skip down the quay. Afraid she'd slip and fall into the water, I ran after her. And when I caught her, she took my hand as if to dance as we'd danced at the palace days before. Clenching her elbows, I held her still, and when she tried to wriggle free, I put my arm around her. Then I kissed her—first on the neck, then on the mouth—hoping she'd respond. "Sophie," I whispered, "I love you." Her skin smelled sour and her hair was tangled, but her lips were soft and familiar. When they yielded to mine, I closed my eyes, trying to forget where we were and where we were going. She pressed her body into mine and tried to pull me down to the ground, but I held her up, held her tight, until I heard a call behind me, "*Gondola?*"

In all my years of traveling to Venice I'd grown used to seeing gondoliers in casual clothes, the youngest ones in Levis and T-shirts, without regard for tradition. But this one wore the old outfit: the black pants, the striped shirt, the wide-brimmed hat with a red ribbon around it. His boat was immaculate, the lacquer gleaming, the cushions at the back of the seating area covered in new black leather fringed with red silk threads. He stood on a Persian carpet, trailing his oar with one hand while beckoning us with the other. His face was as gray as the quay but his eyes had a piercing blue that seemed at odds with his skin and the day.

"*Gondola?*" he asked again, inching closer, but his look said he didn't really expect us to hire him, that he had done this too many times. With a flick of his wrist he'd be on his way.

"*Si, gondola,*" I shouted and the deep creases in the gondolier's face realigned, becoming kindly, benevolent. He floated over to where we were and held his hand toward Tonia. I could see that the flowers in the vase at the front of his boat weren't plastic, as they were in other boats, but real. And the brass fixtures on either side of the seating area weren't the usual horses with reins but winged lions lifting off. Tonia seemed as light as air as she took his hand and drifted down toward the seat, stepping onto the wooden bottom as if she'd been doing it all her life. When I slipped into the seat beside her, she slid up next to me and laid her head on my shoulder.

"*Dov'è?*" the old man asked.

"*San Zanipolo,*" I told him, directing him to the church beside the huge central hospital, trying to keep the illusion of an imminent marriage alive while ignoring the feeling that I was betraying the woman beside me.

I had worried that Tonia would anger the gondolier by moving suddenly, throwing him off balance, but she was almost eerily quiet as he eased the gondola away from the quay, guiding it out across the canal with strong, sure strokes. I put my hand on her head, remembering her father had calmed her that way. As we left Murano behind, emerging from the canal into the open lagoon, I ran my fingers through her hair, smoothing the tangles, caressing her scalp. I was trying to keep her calm, but trying to tell her, too, in some small way, that I was sorry for what I was doing.

How can I describe that ride into Venice, what it was like to sit with Tonia one last time and see our approach through her eyes? She didn't tell me what she was seeing but I could imagine it. She would be dressed in a purple robe with a cape of gold, the collar flared like a golden saucer. Below, she would wear a white silk gown that had never been worn and a string of pearls, each one large and perfect. Her fingers would be full of rings, the diamonds larger than the one Gerhard had given her. Above it all, she'd wear a tiara, while a gossamer veil would shield her face for the ceremony. My own robe would be royal blue, with endless folds that made me appear truly powerful. Over this I'd wear a cape with golden clasps that bore the crest of the royal dynasty. A golden chain around my neck would bear the emblem of my office and signet rings would grace my fingers. As we crossed the wide lagoon, the sea would fill with our attendants: ministers in scarlet robes and tricorne hats on ornate barques, priests in surplices on solemn boats spreading incense, and commoners in mismatched craft and mismatched clothes waving our direction.

The only island between us and Venice was San Michele, the cemetery where Stravinsky lies. I watched it near and pass, the whitened tombs rising through the cypress trees, the bodies buried above the ground so they wouldn't float away. Beyond

San Michele I could see Venice itself, a line of geometric shapes barely above the water. I'd always remembered it as gleaming stone, Gothic windows, majestic buildings rising from the sea. But that was the view from the canals, not the lagoon—from beside the quays as you were docking, with the city towering over you. From a distance, Venice seemed about to drown. I could see the green pyramid topping the campanile and two head-like domes, but everything else seemed to be settling. Dying. Sinking down. As I gazed at the distant line of hazy buildings, I remembered the only Byron I'd ever memorized. I'd used it to impress my groups as we entered the city, passing by the Doge's Palace:

> I stood in Venice on the Bridge of Sighs
> A palace and a prison on each hand;
> I saw from out the wave her structures rise
> As from the stroke of the enchanter's wand.

I was about to recite it to Tonia, thinking I'd be joining her in her vision, her dream, as we crossed the last of the sea. But just as I opened my mouth, the gondolier spoke. He hadn't said anything the entire time or made the slightest move that wasn't necessary to steer the boat. When I looked back, he was pointing at the sky. "*Piove*," he said a second time, and when I held my fingers out I felt the raindrops on my skin. Tonia put her hand out, too—mimicking me, I thought—but instead of checking for rain she took my hand in hers and lowered it into her lap as she turned my direction. For a long time, her red eyes stared into mine, her face full of what seemed anxiety or fear, what Gerhard must have meant when he spoke about her pain. Then her mouth moved and she began to recite a poem of her own, a poem she must have taken comfort from a thousand times, a poem I remembered only imperfectly until I found it later in a book by Keats in a Venice bookstore:

> But when the melancholy fit shall fall
> Sudden from heaven like a weeping cloud
> That fosters the droop-headed flowers all,
> And hides the green hill in an April shroud...

Here, she intertwined her fingers with mine and seemed to try to clear her eyes, her head, before she continued,

> ...Then glut thy sorrow on a morning rose,
> Or on the rainbow of the salt sand-wave,
> Or on the wealth of globed peonies...

She paused again, turning toward the city that was rising faster from the sea—the towers, the facades, the domes. The end of our journey racing toward us.

> ...Or if thy mistress some rich anger shows,
> Emprison her soft hand, and let her rave,
> And feed deep, deep upon her peerless eyes.

We were nearing the Fondamente Nuove, the broad stone quay beyond which I could see the back of the hospital: the sterile stone, the red cross. The rain was pocking the water, wetting our clothes. Tonia let her head fall back against my shoulder, her face as white as I had ever seen it. As we entered the canal, she glanced up at me and seemed about to speak again but only closed her eyes. Her mouth began to form a word but it remained unheard. On the quay two men in white were lounging by a sign that said, *Pronto Soccorso,* leaning against a wall, smoking cigarettes, laughing. Behind them the wooden doors that led into the hospital were open. While Tonia kept her eyes closed, I motioned for the gondolier to stop.

Who could stand a full description of the scene that followed? The horror of seeing her taken by the two attendants and lifted onto the quay, her arms reaching out toward me, her body straining, pitting her strength against theirs as she tried to return to the boat. Her face was no more than a shadow beyond a curtain of tangled hair, except for those eyes, those red eyes like doomed fires pleading with me, searing their image into mine, as she called my name—"Joe"..."Joe"..."Joe"—over and over and over again in that voice I still hear, calling to someone deep inside me, until the doors cut her off.

# Chapter Twenty-Six

The day we arrived in Venice—the day I left Tonia at the hospital—I left my bag at the *stazione* and wandered alone until long after dark. That was how these nights began. I couldn't stay where I'd booked the group. I was afraid I'd run into Donald or Felicity, afraid of the dinginess of the rooms, afraid to think about tours anymore. That night, I slept on a park bench, shivering, lonely, waiting for dawn. My plan was to check on Tonia's condition, call her husband, get out of town. At sunrise, I walked toward the hospital, stopping nearby for a cappuccino, stalling for time. I wasn't ready to leave her yet. Or talk to Gerhard. I didn't want to end the dream of what might have been. Or even the thought it still could be. The cappuccino was strong and sweet and reminded me of a time in Cortona, the year we spent October there. Cat and me. We rented a place on a hill by a garden, a faded villa with tile floors, and every morning we sat on the terrace, gazing out at the Tuscan hills. We told ourselves as we drank our coffee, day after day, that life would never be better than this.

The hospital stands at the edge of a square behind a statue by Verrocchio, who taught Leonardo da Vinci to paint. As I passed it that day, I remembered the story of Verrocchio letting his teenage pupil help him with his latest canvas. He told the boy to paint an angel. When he saw what Leonardo had done—how human and yet sublime it was—he gave up painting forever. On my way through the hospital doors I wondered how often he thought of that face his pupil had painted. Did it follow him into his room at night and wait for his eyes to re-open? Did he ever try to paint again or turn to angels he'd painted before and try to convince himself they were better? How did he manage to carry on when he couldn't go back to what he'd done?

When I asked about Tonia, they said she was stable. But I couldn't see her. When checking her in, I'd had to admit I wasn't her husband. Now I'd have to make that call. Now I'd have to leave her to him.

After so many days of imagining what Gerhard was like, his voice on the phone was a disappointment. He sounded distant and distracted, annoyed perhaps that he'd have to rescue Tonia again. "Can't you just send her home?" he said. He asked about Rudy. Then Sarah. Then wondered out loud if he could send someone to "fetch" her.

"No," I said. "She's *your* wife. The least you can do at a time like this is come and get her."

"A time like this," he repeated. "What do you know about a time like this?"

"Listen," I said, "whatever you've got going on— whatever you think your business demands—the most important thing right now is the woman lying in that hospital. She's your wife. She needs you. *You're* the only one who can help her."

He didn't respond. I wanted to tell him to fuck himself and hang up the phone, but I hadn't given him the hospital information yet, and what I'd said was true: he was the only one who could help her now. As it turned out, if I had hung up, I wouldn't have learned the answer to the question everyone had been asking all tour.

"There's no business," he said at last. "Not anymore. I just sold it to Nintendo."

I don't know if he forgot who he was talking to, or if he was just so pleased with himself he would have said those words to anyone. But now I knew: He had lured them all away to make things easier. No Donald or Felicity demanding their share. No Rudy angling for a new position. No Tonia distracting him. He wasn't toying with any of them; it was just business.

I couldn't tell at that moment if I hated him or envied him or pitied him. He must have known before making the deal that Tonia wasn't going to help him develop another game—that there would never be a better time to move on. "You're a lucky man" was all I said.

"I know," he said, but there was a sadness in his voice, a softness that hadn't been there before. "I'll call the travel agent right now. Thank you—for taking care of her. For staying with her through all of that. For being professional."

Before I hung up, I tried to think of another option, another course, another direction Tonia could go. If only I could get in to see her, I thought. But then what? Wouldn't my presence only set her off again? Then they'd sedate her worse. Keep her longer. In the end, I had to admit that Gerhard was the only one who could free her. When I'd given him the hospital number and said goodbye, I wondered if he'd ever know the truth, if she'd ever tell him all that had happened between us.

Maybe I should have left Venice that morning. I knew the place I needed to go. I knew it would take no more than a phone call, a time of healing, and we could move on. Life would be simpler after that. More secure. And the change would probably do me good, even if I wasn't happy. But it was impossible to turn my back. To leave her behind. I needed time. And so I went back to the waterfront and took a room at the Daniele Hotel, where Kokoschka had painted that view of Venice Tonia loved. The manager remembered me from my days leading corporate tours and gave me a deal on an upper room, one that had always been occupied when I was there with a group in summer. He told me it was the best they had, more than a room really, and he was right. The walls are covered in red satin. The skylight above them makes them glow. The furniture is vintage French, with *bergere* chairs, a *recamier*, and an *armoire* full of inlaid swirls and dark palmettes. Persian carpets cover the floor and windows open onto the water. The room reminds me of the final one in Tonia's game, *Fire Mountain*, occupied by those who've won.

At night now I walk. I wander the thin alleys that wind between crumbling buildings, opening out onto beautiful vistas or ending sometimes in sudden walls. I walk until I feel exhausted. Depleted. Emptied of thoughts about the world.

Returning, then, to my empty room, I order up some caviar, some *Dom Perignon*. While steeped in luxuries I've never known, I let my mind roam—not in future worlds but in the past. I return to holy days and sacred nights when, while traveling, I tasted freedom. Or privilege. Or passion. I know I can't go back in time, but I can live in memories. In dreams.

When the champagne bottle's empty—and I feel the melancholy coming on—I cross the room to the recamier and run my fingers across it. It's like the one in the famous David painting but reminds me more of Goya's work—his portraits of his precious *maja*: the clothed, the nude. As I touch the satin cushions, I think of all my travels have brought me. The places I've gone. The people I've met. The things I've known I'll know no more. Kicking back the Persian carpet, I stare down at the polished floor and picture Tonia's face in the ballroom—how happy she looked, how bright and sure. Then, with nothing in my mind except that face, that perfect smile, I let the melancholy overtake me. I reach out for a hand that isn't there, and for as long as the feeling lasts, I dance.

# Acknowledgements

This book has taken the long and winding road into the world, its journey starting years before I thought to write it. Thank you to John and Jen Baker for inspiring me to travel to Europe in the first place; Lee Cohrs for accompanying me on my first trip; Rick Steves for coaxing me into guiding; Dave Hoerlein, Gene Openshaw, and Steve Smith for being the best possible companions in those early years; and the owners, managers, desk clerks, servers, and cleaners in small hotels and pensiones everywhere for making travel the human and humanizing experience it should be.

Thank you to the people of Eastern Europe who, in their determination to be free, pulled down the Berlin Wall—and the Iron Curtain with it. Special thanks to Václav Havel for showing me that creative writing and the fight for dignity and hope are not mutually exclusive—that they, in fact, come from the same source.

Thank you to Columbia University's School of the Arts and especially my colleagues there who helped with the earliest drafts of this book: Oliver Karlin, Bill McGee, Katherine Taylor, Scott Smith, Raul Correa, Des Berry, Sophie Hawkins, and anyone I may have forgotten. Thank you to the *South Dakota Review* for publishing an early excerpt.

Thank you to Dave Hoerlein (again) for the gift of your great map, and to Olivia M. Hammerman for designing such a beautiful cover.

Thank you to Molly Simas for suggestions and editing that made the book better, to Maya Lubin for support throughout the publishing process, and to Korza Books publisher and editor Michael Schepps for being the best partner in the publishing and publicizing process I could have asked for.

Thank you to everyone who encouraged me along the way, especially my mother, Doris McGregor, who always let me know she loved and supported me, even when our paths diverged. Thank you to my nieces and nephews—Katie Bassett, Michelle Farkas, Jeremy Farkas, Nicole Farkas, and Emmett Hoelscher (Mr. Moak)—for a seemingly endless supply of love, joy, and hope.

Thank you, finally, to Sylvia, who has shared my travels all these years, both on the road and at home. Spending my life with you is the grandest adventure of all.

Author photo by Brian McDonnell

**Michael N. McGregor** is the author of *Pure Act: The Uncommon Life of Robert Lax* and *An Island to Myself: The Place of Solitude in an Active Life* (coming in May 2025 from Monkfish Publishing). *Pure Act* was a finalist for a Washington State Book Award and chosen by the Association of University Presses as a top-ten book in American Studies for libraries. McGregor's shorter writings have appeared in numerous publications, including *Tin House, Orion, StoryQuarterly, Poetry*, and *Poets & Writers*.

Before receiving his MFA in creative writing from Columbia University, McGregor worked as a writer for a relief and development magazine, specializing in Asia. Later, he spent a decade guiding Americans through Europe. After a long career as a professor of creative writing, he moved back to his hometown, Seattle, where he runs the website WritingtheNorthwest.com and hosts the Cascadia Writers-in-Conversation series.

# Other Titles from Korza Books

## Is It Just Me Or Are We Nailing This? Essays on BoJack Horseman
*Published with Antiquated Future*
Joshua James Amberson, Timothy Day, Jessica Fonvergne, Lauren Hobson, M.L. Schepps, Jourdain Searles and Molly E. Simas
Illustrations from Eileen Chavez, Ross Jackson, Naomi Marshall and Sarah Shay Mirk

## Split Aces
M.L. Schepps

## Poetry For People: Fifty Years of Writing
Dixie Lubin

## How To Forget Almost Everything
Joshua James Amberson

## Altogether Different: A Memoir About Identity, Inheritance and the Raid That Started the Civil War
Brianna Wheeler

## The Novel Killings
Kate Shelton

Visit KorzaBooks.com or
Follow us on Instagram @Korza_Books

Write to the publisher at KorzaBooks@gmail.com for wholesale orders